continued . . .

"Continuing the story begun in *Bloodring*, Hunter expands on her darkly alluring vision of a future in which the armies of good and evil wage their eternal struggle in the world of flesh and blood. Strong characters and a compelling story."
—*Library Journal*

"This thrilling dark fantasy has elements of danger, adventure, and religious fanaticism, plus sexual overtones. Hunter's impressive narrative skills vividly describe a changed world, and she artfully weaves in social commentary . . . a well-written, exciting novel." —*Romantic Times*

Host

"Hunter's world continues to expand in this highly original fantasy with lively characters where nothing can ever be taken for granted." —*Publishers Weekly*

"Hunter has created a remarkable interpretation of the aftermath of Armageddon in which angels and devils once again walk the earth and humans struggle to find a place. Stylish storytelling and gripping drama make this a good addition to most fantasy collections." —*Library Journal*

"Readers will admire [Thorn's] sacrifice [in] placing others before herself. . . Fans will enjoy reading about the continuing end of days." —*Midwest Book Review*

"With fast-paced action and the possibility of more romance, this is an enjoyable read with an alluring magical touch." —Darque Reviews

BLOOD CROSS

A Jane Yellowrock Novel

Faith Hunter

A ROC BOOK

ROC
Published by New American Library, a division of
Penguin Group (USA) Inc., 375 Hudson Street,
New York, New York 10014, USA
Penguin Group (Canada), 90 Eglinton Avenue East, Suite 700, Toronto,
Ontario M4P 2Y3, Canada (a division of Pearson Penguin Canada Inc.)
Penguin Books Ltd., 80 Strand, London WC2R 0RL, England
Penguin Ireland, 25 St. Stephen's Green, Dublin 2,
Ireland (a division of Penguin Books Ltd.)
Penguin Group (Australia), 250 Camberwell Road, Camberwell, Victoria 3124,
Australia (a division of Pearson Australia Group Pty. Ltd.)
Penguin Books India Pvt. Ltd., 11 Community Centre, Panchsheel Park,
New Delhi - 110 017, India
Penguin Group (NZ), 67 Apollo Drive, Rosedale, North Shore 0632,
New Zealand (a division of Pearson New Zealand Ltd.)
Penguin Books (South Africa) (Pty.) Ltd., 24 Sturdee Avenue,
Rosebank, Johannesburg 2196, South Africa

Penguin Books Ltd., Registered Offices:
80 Strand, London WC2R 0RL, England

First published by Roc, an imprint of New American Library,
a division of Penguin Group (USA) Inc.

First Printing, January 2010
10 9 8 7 6 5 4 3 2 1

To my Renaissance Man,
who takes the Class IIIs, lets me cry on his
shoulder, and brings me chocolate

ACKNOWLEDGMENTS

My Deepest Thanks to
(in no order whatsoever):

Mike Pruette, Web guru at www.faithhunter.net and fan.

Rod Hunter, for the right word when my tired brain was stymied.

The Guy in the Leather Jacket, for promo work and for telling me Jane needed a softer side.

Sarah Spieth, for help with New Orleans settings.

Holly McClure, for Cherokee info and for allowing me to study her novel *Lightning Creek*.

Joyce Wright, for reading everything I write, no matter how "weird."

Misty Massey, David B. Coe, C. E. Murphy, Kim Harrison, Tamar Myers, Greg Paxton, Raven Blackwell, Christina Stiles, Sarah Spieth, Melanie Otto, and all my other writer friends, for taking the journey with me.

My Yahoo fan group at www.groups.yahoo.com/group/the-enclave/.

My cowriters at www.magicalwords.net.

Lucienne Diver, for doing what an agent does best, with grace and kindness.

Last but never least—

My editor at Roc, Jessica Wade, who:

saw the multisouled Beast in Jane;

has guided this series into darker, more intense plotlines;

who had to spend waaaay too much time on this novel, pointing out all the problems;

and who helped me fix them. You are the best!

Y'all ROCK!

CHAPTER 1

I like the fire. Can I come play?

Molly and the kids and I were eating a big lunch when the lightning hit. The bolt slammed into the ground only feet from the house, throwing brilliant light through the windows, shaking the floor beneath us. I grabbed the table and looked up to see Molly questing with her senses to discern if the lightning had harmed her wards. She had deactivated them because lightning and wards don't play well with each other, but even a quiescent ward can be structurally damaged. She gave me an "it's fine" look, but I could tell she was uneasy. Without the wards, the house where I lived while I fulfilled my current contract with the New Orleans vamp council was unprotected.

Molly—a powerful earth witch and my best friend—and I are used to the summer storms in the Appalachian Mountains. Though they can be violent and intense, they had nothing on this monster. Outside, Hurricane Ada was pounding New Orleans, the category-two storm bringing with it wind and torrential rain, though none of the might and tidal surge of Katrina and Rita, and much less of the damage. Human memory is short; most of the natives had elected to ride out the storm, depend on the new levies to hold, and trust in the improvements to the city's infrastructure, courtesy of Uncle Sam. The only unanticipated aspect of the storm was the intense lightning and two tornados that had set down in the middle of the city's electric grid, resulting in the loss of power. The wind died for a moment and then slammed the house like a giant fist, the walls quaking. A fresh burst of rain drummed against the windows.

Without power for the air-conditioning units, it was growing muggy inside, but fortunately, I had gas-heated water and a gas stove, and the city's water supply hadn't been impacted. So the kids had sandwiches and hot canned soup and Mol and I had prime rib, mine huge and rare enough to still have a moo or two in it, Mol's daintier and cooked medium. I had even made spinach salads to placate health-conscious Molly.

Wind swirled against the front of the old house, and the noise went up a notch for a long moment, the house groaning. I had never been through a hurricane, and even a category two was pretty intense. I couldn't imagine a cat three or four, with a storm surge. It was no wonder Katrina and Rita had devastated the Gulf Coast, despite the efforts of New Orleans's witches to ward against landfall.

I finished off the steak, ate a spinach leaf, and took a tour to check for damage. The old house in the middle of the French Quarter wasn't mine—only on loan, as long as I was under contract—but I intended to keep it in the same pristine condition I got it in. Not that the vamps I worked for were making that easy.

I studied the twelve-foot-tall ceilings on both stories looking for leaks, made sure the towels at the doors were sopping up any rain that had blown in, and checked to see that the windows were secure. So far, so good—no leaks, no damage. I sniffed at the damp air to confirm that the lightning strike hadn't hit the house. No smell of smoke, just the strong odor of ozone. It had been close.

On the side porch on the first floor, my old, rebuilt, one-of-a-kind Harley, Bitsa, was safe and sound under a heavy tarp I'd bought to protect her. Out back, the granite boulders my vamp landlady, Katie Fonteneau, had brought in for the rock garden I'd needed installed were rain-slick and broken. Those were not going to survive my stay here. Already the stones were cracked and split, and one had been ground to sharp shards and piles of grit. I exchanged mass with stone when I shifted into an animal whose genetic structure and size were vastly different from my own. It was dangerous. And it always resulted in damage to the boulders. Quite a lot of damage.

The power came on for a moment and the lights flickered. The fountain in the back garden stuttered, sending water into the air, the naked vamp statue in its center glistening with wetness. The vamp sent up a last, single spurt as the power flickered and died again.

I walked from window to window, watching the wind and rain attack the subtropical vegetation and my rock garden, probably the only one in the entire French Quarter. It was beautiful, even in its current condition.

"You're pacing."

I looked at Molly, and then down at my feet.

"You need to shift. You've been in human form all week. The kids and I will not fall into the sinister hands of the evil vampires if you take the evening off." She curled on the sofa and wrapped her arms around her knees, her red hair falling in frizzy curls from the humidity, curls she hated. Angelina raced up and threw herself on the leather cushion with a gust of trapped air. Molly rolled her daughter over, keeping an eye on Little Evan, who had found his ball under a chair and was bent over, butt in the air, trying to get to it. "I'll set my wards. They'll keep us safe."

"Is Aunt Jane gonna turn into Big Cat tonight? Can I watch? Please, please, please?" Angie asked. She was only six, but already the little girl was coming into her gift and it was strong.

"No. That's private for Aunt Jane. And we do not talk about that, remember?"

Angie dropped her voice into a whisper and put a small finger over her lips. "It's a secret. Shhhhh." And then she giggled, a sound that always brought a smile to my face.

"Leo's not himself," I said, "not since I killed the thing that took over his son. He's still grieving, and my sources say grief can make vamps . . . not exactly rogue, but unstable. I don't trust him." Still, Mol was right. I hadn't shifted in too long. I could feel Beast's pelt rubbing under my skin, insistent. I needed the night.

Beast will guard kits, Beast thought at me. *I am strong. And fast. And have killing claws and killing teeth.* I shushed her with a calming thought.

"Leo won't violate your contract with the vampire council to find the young-rogue maker." Mol laughed up at me and added, "Of course, when you fulfill the contract, all bets are off."

"Thanks. That makes me feel oh-so-much better."

"Hunt tonight," Molly said. "Go running. End up at the Cherokee shaman's place and let her sweat you. You've been promising." She looked down and finger-combed Angie's curls. In sunlight, the baby-fine hair almost glowed with honey blond and strawberry highlights, but in the dimness of the storm, it lost its vibrancy. Angie smiled and closed her eyes, soothed by her mother's hand. It was nap time, and even a storm was powerless against the sleep compulsion Mol was thrumming through her elder child. "You might learn something new about your past," she added. "About skinwalkers."

"Yeah, like that they were all a bunch of crazed killers, and it's only a matter of time before I go nutso too." I had been trying for humor, but I could smell the tang of worry in my own words.

"You are not a killer, nor are you crazed. You are my best friend in the whole world." The faith on Molly's face when she looked up was absolute. "I'd trust with you with my life and with my children's lives any day of the week, Jane."

My heart turned over. I'd never had a best friend growing up, but I'd lucked out when I met Molly. She'd welcomed me into her small family and introduced me to the larger family of her sisters' coven without a single qualm. Her husband, Big Evan, wasn't so sanguine about me, but he was in Brazil, which was why Molly was visiting me for several weeks, despite the possible threat of trouble from Leo Pellissier, Blood Master of Clan Pellissier, the Blood Master of the City and head of the vamp council. "I'll think about shifting," I promised, knowing I was lying.

I looked over at Evan and found him asleep under the chair, his ball in his pudgy hands. I scooped up the baby and Molly gathered up Angelina, and we carried them both upstairs to their room. With the storm as protection, and the wards off, I could enter, settling the baby into his bed, placing the ball in the curve of his arms. I wasn't maternal, not at all, but I loved Molly's children.

Beast reared up in me, fierce and violent, her maternal instincts vastly different from any human ones. *Will protect kits.*

"I know," I said too softly for Molly to hear. Louder, I said, "Cards? Or a nap?"

Molly yawned. "Nap for me. See you in an hour or so, Big Cat."

I nodded, and as the storm outside died down and passed and the evening drew in, I went back to prowling the house and worrying. I didn't know much about my own heritage or my own past, except for the Cherokee stuff Aggie One Feather was teaching me, and that didn't include her knowing what I was: a skinwalker. The only other skinwalker I had ever seen was dead now, at my hand. He had killed, and taken the place of, Leo Pellissier's son Immanuel, maybe decades earlier, and then gone even further to the dark side, killing and eating humans and vamps. I still didn't know why. I worried that it was the nature of skinwalkers that we all went crazy eventually. I'd killed Immanuel's walker, and gotten myself into the predicament of being on the hate list of Leo Pellissier.

I'm Jane Yellowrock, traveling rogue-vamp hunter, skinwalker-in-hiding, and occasionally muscle-for-hire. I know how to fight, how to protect myself, and how to use the array of weapons that were currently under lock and key in my bedroom, safe from the attention of the children. I wasn't so good at understanding humans or witches or vampires, and I sucked at social situations, but this gig in New Orleans was giving me a chance to learn a lot about all that. And about myself.

My contract had been extended by the council, to hunt down and kill—true-dead—a master vamp who was turning scions and setting them free, feral, before the years they needed after the change to be "cured." The sire was releasing the young rogues on the populace with empty minds and unchecked desire for blood that made them crazy killing machines. I'd fought and killed two only a few weeks before. The council had asked me to get to the root of the problem, so I'd signed on the dotted line. And, though my beast was ready for mountain heights and rushing streams and deep valleys, I was beginning to like it here in the city that was made for partying.

Here, where vamps and other supernats had been for centuries, I might even discover another skinwalker. I was coming to understand that it wasn't likely, as not even the oldest of the vamps had ever smelled anything quite like me, but I could hope.

As I filled the kettle to make tea, I stilled, breathing deeply. Something smelled . . . wrong.

Between storms, New Orleans's air is heavy and wet, pressing odors against the ground, making them linger, but as the sky had cleared, the air had seemed fresh and salty. Until now.

Closing my eyes, I flared my nostrils, taking in the scent, sharp and biting. It was vamp, pungent and tangy. And more than one. Above the vamp-scent rode the stink of kerosene. And smoke.

Beast rose in me. *Fire!*

My heart rate bounded and my breathing sped. I looked up. Outside the kitchen window, light flickered. It all came together fast. Because of the fear of lightning, Molly hadn't woken the wards back up yet. Leo Pellissier was out to get me. The hurricane had knocked out electricity, phone, and cell towers for most of the city. I couldn't call for help.

Crap.

Flames glimmered and sparkled against the antique window glass, visible through the sheer covering. I moved with the speed of my kind, sprinting to the door overlooking the back and side yards. A chair clattered to the floor behind me. I pulled a silver cross and chain over my head and two stakes from my hair. Ripped open the door. Raced out to the covered porch. As I moved, my hair swung forward, getting in the way, and I slung my head backward, clearing my vision. I counted four torches, widely spaced. Fear shot through me. I should have gotten the guns.

I slid to a stop on the wet porch. Vamps stood in my yard. Unmoving—that dead-body immobility they do. Waiting. Holding torches. Time slowed, growing thick and viscous, the night taking on richness and depth. I absorbed the scene through my senses all at once.

There were four vamps that I could see, fangs descended, fully vamped out. At their feet were five-gallon containers, hazard signs painted on the sides. The scent of several more was carried on the fitful wind. One vamp was opening a container. The smell of kerosene rose.

The breeze was restless, the might of Ada coiled in its currents, but aimless now that the storm had passed. The sky was dark with fast-moving clouds. It was still drizzling; misty drops hit the flames and sizzled. The sound shot pulses of electricity through me. Other than that, the silence and dark of the early night were absolute. No cars, no music, no human noise at all.

I forced down my fear, knowing they could smell it, knowing their excitement would grow. Bravado was my best weapon, and I held the cross high. It glowed bright in my hand, the silver reacting to the presence of vamps. But they didn't recoil. They held their places, which meant they were old vamps, every one. The wind whipped once and went still. Shadows and torchlight flickered over them, harsh and unforgiving on their skin, pale no matter their original race. My heart rate sped. What were they waiting—

A black silhouette stepped out of the shadows, lithe and elegant. Leonard Pellissier. In evening attire. Here to ... visit. The most powerful vampire in the city had dressed to kill. A titter started in the back of my throat and I forced it down. Would not be smart to laugh right now. *Would not.*

Beast rose in me, taking over my reflexes, ready to move, ready to fight. Ready to rush away, back inside to save my guests. If I could. *Kits,* Beast murmured, protective instincts fighting to get loose. I held her down, but close to the surface. I needed her strength and speed.

A floorboard creaked from upstairs. Thank God. Molly must have seen the flames. She would be bringing up the wards, something defensive that would burn vamp flesh, maybe. I could hope. But it would take time. Maybe too much time.

Leo stepped to the front of the small group that circled my house, his eyes holding mine. His fangs were snapped down, white in the early night; his pupils bled black in blood-red sclera. The silver cross and capering flames reflected in his pupils.

"You killed my son," he said, eyes fixed on me.

"No. I killed the creature that took his body."

His lips pulled back, exposing his teeth, a killing grimace. "You," he whispered. Vamps didn't need to breathe much except to talk, but he took a breath, deep and slow. "Killed." Anger built in him. I could smell it, strong and sour. "My *son!*" he roared into the night.

Beast lifted my own lips, exposing my human teeth. *Change*, she demanded.

But it was too late. A dozen possible reactions and scenarios buffeted me. I could attack, but they'd set fire to the house. I could run inside, but they'd set fire to the house. I could—

"Hi. My name's Angelina."

The vamps froze, an unearthly stillness in the fluttering flames. The stillness of death. His head moving slowly, Leo looked up, from me to the veranda above.

"I like the fire. Can I come play?"

Leo breathed in, scenting her. Scenting child and witch. His body tensed. Held.

The eyes of Leo's scions flickered to their blood-master, then to me. I saw uncertainty, worry. Clearly they hadn't signed on for killing a child. Two vamps retracted their fangs with little *snick*s. The one with the open kerosene container looked at it, then back up at the little girl, deliberate and measured. His pupils contracted and he swiveled his head to Leo. Waiting.

"What's your name?" she said, her footsteps pattering out to the edge of the veranda, directly above my head. "Are you Aunt Jane's new friends?"

"Angie, go inside," I said, striving for calm and not succeeding. My heart raced like a doe in flight. Like prey. I knew they could smell my terror.

Leo pulled in another breath, his chest rising, then falling, the sound of the breath whispering through his fangs. We were balanced on the blade of a knife. Leo could go either way: kill his son's murderer and the witches he now smelled in my home, or withdraw and save the child. The Vampira Carta prohibited the killing of children, even witch children, and killing a witch could revoke the unstable peace between the races. But his grief was out of control. Had been for days now. And witches were the sworn enemies of vampires, though I didn't yet know why.

"Are you a vampire?" Angelina asked, for once ignoring me.

The torches flickered in a sudden gust, bringing her scent down from the upper porch. Bubble bath and the warmth of her skin caught in the humid night breezes, swirling down to the ground to mix with vamp pheromones and smoke. The vamps with Leo each took a step back. "Mama says you eat people."

Leo swallowed. "We do not eat people," he said, his voice carefully neutral, laced with his refined, formal French accent. "And you may not play with fire. It is dangerous. We . . . we will return to visit at a later time," he said.

He looked at me, his hatred so bright it burned in his black eyes. "This is not finished. My son will be avenged."

"I already avenged your son," I said. "I killed his murderer. I paid his blood debt and left you the body of your enemy." I had said the words before—the last time he'd visited me, insane with grief. They had worked then. I could hope they worked now.

Leo blinked. The fire in his eyes seemed to flicker and die. Something else filled the void, a hint of some softer emotion—confusion, uncertainty, perhaps—swimming through the grief. He met my eyes, held my gaze with that hypnotic focus the very old ones have.

And he was gone. Just . . . gone. Air currents swirled hard after his passage. The vamps stared up at the child on the porch above.

"Come inside, Angie," Molly said from overhead, her voice rough with fear. "You too," she said to me, though she couldn't see me from her position. I heard boards creak, and the door to the veranda closed.

"He would have led us to murder a child," a female vamp said.

"He didn't know," another said, closing the kerosene container he had opened.

"He is the master. He should have known," the female vamp insisted. "He should not have led us here."

"Dolore," a third vamp said. I didn't know the word, but there was a hushed reverence in her voice that lent it importance. "We must decide."

"I will not chain my master," the fourth vamp said. "I will not. I warn you now. There will be war."

The four vamps looked from one to another. Then, as a unit, they turned to me. And stared. I felt the weight of their eyes, holding me in place, my cross held high.

"We will uphold the Vampira Carta," the woman said. "It is law."

The pressure in the small yard drained away fast, as if a stopper had been pulled and the tension and anger sucked down. Much more slowly than Leo, but still faster than any human, the vamps left. Their scents weakened, dissipating on the erratic winds. Down the street, I heard a car start, the sound low, like a powerful growl. Headlights cut the misty dark as it passed my freebie house, and vanished into the night.

I swiveled on a bare foot and went inside, pulling the door shut behind me. I leaned against it and remembered how to breathe, hearing my heart pound in my ears, an uneven pain in my chest. I dropped the cross around my neck, swept my hair out of the way, twisting it up high, and shoved the stakes into a makeshift bun. My fingers were quivering in the aftermath of near battle.

A moment later, I felt the wards snap on over the house, the feel of magic a soft buzz on my skin. I knew Molly would be beating herself up for not activating them sooner tonight.

I hadn't been ready for attack. I would never have thought that Leo would make such a public, violent move. Which was pretty stupid in my twenty-twenty hindsight.

I went to my room and weaponed up, putting blades through their respective loops in my jeans and strapping on wrist and calf sheaths, checking and adding a new handgun in its shoulder holster, laying the shotgun across the foot of the bed. It wasn't overkill. It was necessary to cool my fear. Though the wards were back up on the house, and Molly and the kids were safe, I couldn't banish the vision of Leo, vamped out.

If I'd been properly weaponed earlier, I might have had a fighting chance against the vamps in my yard. Well, I'd still likely have died, but I'd have taken a few of them with me. I'm good. Real good. Arguably, the best in the business. Just not good enough to take on a whole blood-family of vamped-out master monsters alone. Monsters with fire. Hands shaking with the aftershock, I made the decision that I would go rogue hunting that night. If it wasn't too muggy, I'd wear a skintight skullcap, but that wasn't gonna happen. I used the hair as a weapon holder instead, shoving in stakes that looked like hair sticks, making sure I grabbed silver-tipped ones for maximum damage. I felt better with each weapon, calmer, more secure.

The kettle on the gas stove emitted a soft, steamy whistle, the precursor to the piercing one that would push through soon. It seemed like aeons since I had put it on. I stopped a moment, bracing a hand on the closet door. I closed my eyes and half prayed a single word of thanks. That had been close. I returned to the kitchen and turned off the gas, pouring the water over the tea leaves in the strainer, into the white enamel pot beneath. I stared at the steam rising from the tiny hole in the whistler spout as shock boiled up in me like the steam in the kettle.

Leo Pellissier had come to burn down my house. He had brought gallons of kerosene, torches, and his undead scions to carry out the burning. He had wanted me to die in the fire. He had been prepared to break windows, pour in accelerant, and torch the place. Literally. I shivered in the night air and put down the kettle. It was almost never cold in the Vieux Carre, the French Quarter of the old town, but the hurricane had brought cooler, wet air from the gulf. At least that was what I told myself. Uncertain, I pulled the elk-horn hilt of my favorite vamp-killer, its silvered blade shining blue in the light of the hurricane lamp. I resheathed the weapon, making sure it was loose and easy to draw.

Knowing tea would help calm me, I poured two cups of hot chai, added sugar and a generous dollop of room-temp whipped cream to each, and placed them on a tray with a stack of cookies and the lit lantern. Moving in a cone of light, I carried them to the front of the house. Another hurricane lamp flickered at the top of the stairs. I set the lamp from the kitchen on the ground floor near the staircase, the flames tossing amber light into the rooms, peaceful and safe, a bright counterpoint to the conflagration that nearly was.

Carefully, carrying the tray, I walked up the shadowy

steps. The children's room was over my own, to the left of the stairs. Tonight it was dark, the wide space unlit by the lion-shaped night-light. Yet, even dark, the room fairly crackled with wards and witch power. In addition to her warning and protective wards over the property to deflect intruders, Molly had set wards over the children for health and healing.

There was a third type of ward Mol called a *hedge of thorns* around the rocks in my garden. It was quiescent; the trigger to activate it was my blood, poured over the ground. Pretty macabre, but she wanted to protect me even after she was back home in the mountains, and the *hedge* was a last-ditch shielding, one that would seal me in over the rocks where I could shift into Beast form and heal, if I found myself in life-threatening danger. Beast was the only animal I could shift into without effort, and without having genetic material from which to take the pattern. She was something outside my skinwalker magic—something I thought a typical skinwalker wouldn't carry within her. Beast was another soul living inside me, revenant of a mountain lion whose skin I had hidden in for far, far too long, and she had her own goals, memories, needs, and secrets. She wasn't always easy to live with, but she did help keep me alive.

The inside ward over Angie's and Little Evan's room was shaped so that even I couldn't enter without setting off an alarm. But I could check in, making sure the kids were okay. I'm not the motherly sort, so it felt strange to have children in my home, and even stranger to feel protective. Fiercely, violently protective, as Beast's maternal instincts, so different from my own, spilled over into my human consciousness.

With my exceptional night vision, I could see well enough into the dim room. Little Evan was stretched out, covers thrown off, his fists tightly balled, arms to either side, his cheeks puffing with each breath. On the bed closer to the door, Angelina was curled into a ball beneath the covers, her face as angelic as her name. Both were, amazingly, already asleep. Kids.

"They won't disappear in a wisp of smoke," a soft voice said behind me.

I smiled, feeling rueful, wondering if Molly had set a ward I had never detected, one that notified her when someone even approached the children's doorway. Probably.

"Just checking," I said. Holding the tray in front of me, I turned, finding Molly in the shadows of the wide hallway. Her long, thin nightgown fluttered in the air from the open windows; her red ringlets hung down her back. She looked like something from the nineteen hundreds, except for the iPod around her neck. I set the tray on a little spindled table in the hall and offered her one of the mugs. Molly crossed the wide hallway on bare feet and took it.

"No one can get in," she said, sipping. "Not through my ward. Or at least not without fireworks going off. You don't have to prowl the house with butcher knives."

I pulled and flipped a knife. The blade caught the lamp, bright and glittering, the narrow, deep flukes along the blade appearing almost ornamental with their silvering, making the weapon strong, flexible, lightweight, beautiful, the blade's silver plating poisonous to vampires. A work of art. It was a new blade. I really liked it. "Not a butcher knife. It's a vamp-killer."

"It's a claw, is what it is," she said, the wry tone becoming drier, sharper. "I counted. You're wearing ten. Just like your Beast's front paw claws."

I shrugged. It was true; I had ten. As a skinwalker, I had a preference for big cats—puma, African lion, leopards, but mostly for the mountain lion form. It was easiest to be Beast. If I ever discover a skinwalker psychiatrist, I'm sure he'll apply some Jungian or Freudian school of thought to me, and the weapons I choose will be a big part of the analysis.

"Are you going hunting in *human* form?" she asked, her voice now carefully emotionless. When I nodded, she said, quietly, "Be careful, Big Cat. He's not finished grieving. If he has laid a trap, you might slip past him as Beast, but not as Jane."

"I know," I said. "But I have a job to do. And the sooner I get it done, the better." I slid the vamp-killer into its loop. "I still wish you and the kids would go back home."

She hesitated for an instant, clearly remembering Leo Pellissier and his vamp goons. She shook her head. "Not until Big Evan gets back from Brazil and the contractor has the new room closed in. A house with no walls means I can't ward it properly." She held up a hand to stop my protests. "We're in less danger here than we are in the hills without Big Evan. And you know we've had ... trouble lately. My kind aren't exactly popular. I'll go back in two weeks like we planned. Besides"—her tone had turned ironic, and she sipped her tea—"*you* actually need *us* now. Angie's the reason why Leo didn't burn the house down around you. He won't be back, at least until he can make sure of killing only you and not a houseful of children. And the wards will *never* be down again."

I flinched just the tiniest bit. She had a point. "Okay," I said. "I'll be careful." I took my own mug in hand, the stoneware warm and oddly comforting. "See you in the morning. Night, Molly."

"Night, Big Cat."

Downstairs, while I sipped hot tea, I put on my silvered chain-mail collar over the gold-nugget and chain necklace I never took off, added a couple more crosses, tied and strapped on my new steel-toed boots, and put on a thick denim jacket I'd picked up in a shop catering to farmers to replace the leather jacket lost in my last vamp fight. Another was on order, but until it arrived, denim would have to do. I holstered my big-ass shotgun across my back. I tugged on my hair to make sure it was difficult to grab. Long hair made a handy-dandy handle to pull in a fight, and once an opponent had it, the fight was over. Rapists and vamps liked victims with long hair. Made them easy to control. I could cut it, but I'd never shifted with short hair and didn't know if that would alter the process.

Dressed for hunting, I left the house, feeling the wards sizzle across my skin, heatless and bright, like holiday sparklers in the hands of Molly's children. I helmeted up, fired up Bitsa—my bastard Harley, put together from bits of this and bits of that—and opened the side gate. I relocked the new padlock with my new key—which hadn't kept out the vamps—and pulled into the street. Note to self: *Find out how high vamps can jump. Build brick walls and gate higher.*

I guided Bitsa through the streets, heading vaguely north.

Streetlights were out in most of the city, the few hanging traffic lights swinging slowly on their supports. Trash was piled in corners, fluttering or soaked. Signs were down. Water gurgled down gutters from roofs, raced along street gutters, and in some low-lying places flowed along the streets, hiding the pavement. I watched the curbs when I traversed these, keeping Bitsa out of deeper water. I didn't want to drown her out.

Though most everything was closed—bars, restaurants, shops, and dance clubs—cars were parked all over, along the streets, in the tiny, privately owned parking lots scattered through the Quarter. Lanterns, lamps, and candles lit windows. People sat at tables on second-story balconies, by lamplight, and the smell of food wafted down. Tinny music came from open windows; battery-powered boom boxes perched on ledges shared a soft dissonance of musical tastes. Live music, a guitar, saxophone, and drum came through an open bar door. Tables inside were lit with candles, a generator roaring in back. Small businesses that depended on the tourist trade twenty-four/seven, just to make the rent, were opening, despite the lack of city power. More generators began to hum. As power was restored in some areas, neon lights appeared here and there, advertising food, liquor, and entertainment. I motored out of the Quarter, past the church I attended most Sundays—though not today, no thanks to Ada—and quickly into less fashionable areas.

I had been in New Orleans's version of the projects before, when I was taking down two young-rogue vamps who were feeding indiscriminately and killing their prey. Rogues came in two varieties: the very, very young, and the very, very old. But both were whacked-out, hungry, and deadly. These young rogues were feral for a different reason from the old ones. Vamps spent the first decade of life chained in a basement—figuratively speaking as Louisiana had few basements because of the high water table—nutty as fruitcakes and dangerously wild. A good master cared for his young until they cured properly—regained sanity and memories—or staked them if they didn't.

My contract said I was supposed to find the vamp breaking vampire law and tradition and take him out. Or her. I would be paid a bounty for every young rogue I staked and beheaded, and the vamp council had a cleanup crew on standby to dispose of bodies and scrub kill sites, should I need their services. The council wanted to avoid any police involvement, so I wasn't supposed to call in the cops unless there was just no help for it.

Since I had taken down this sire's progeny—a young male and his even younger mate—only recently, I had an old trail to follow, but that meant I needed to find safe passage through the projects while I hunted. Which meant I had to talk to some men. Dangerous men.

The half-familiar streets had been dark enough when I last came through here. That time I had been overdressed for the locale, underdressed for the job of hunting vamps. It was a lot darker now, the night lit only by the twinkle of lanterns, flashlights, and candles as I advertised my arrival with Bitsa's guttural snarl.

The place smelled better than last time, the hurricane having washed away the odors of urine, garbage, cooked cabbage, rats, roaches, and deep-fried foods. The smells of poverty and a food-stamp diet. I passed a heavily graffitied sign that might have said Iberville Housing at one time.

I couldn't see anyone, but I *felt* eyes on me as I motored past, looking tough, well armed, and full of moxie. All of that wouldn't keep me alive, but it might make the locals pause just to see what kind of fool came into their territory at night and alone. When I was pretty sure I had the right housing unit, or at least close to it, I slowed to a stop and killed the motor. Knees knocking, a fine tremor in my hands, I unhelmeted, secured the helmet to the bike, and pulled a vamp-killer and shotgun. It was loaded for vamp, but the hand-packed silver fléchette rounds would kill humans too.

Shouting, I called into the darkness, "I'm looking for Derek Lee, ex-marine, if a marine can ever be called ex. Did two tours in Afghanistan, one in Iraq."

My voice echoed in the night. From a house behind me, I heard the distinctive *sh-thunk* of a bolt-action rifle being readied for firing.

CHAPTER 2

Have stakes, will travel

In one of Bitsa's tiny rearview mirrors, I saw a slice of light followed by a pinpoint of red. A laser-targeting sight. *Crap*. The killing spot between my shoulder blades began to itch. So I got louder, raised my voice as thunderously as I could. "Derek told me he thought he'd be safe when he came home to the United States. Instead, he found his neighborhood was full of blood-sucking vamps. He had to go back to war just to keep his family out of harm's way. So I'm looking for Derek. He knows me as Injun Princess." I didn't necessarily love the nickname, but it seemed to amuse Derek.

My voice fell away. If Derek didn't find me now and give me safe passage, I figured I'd be in a lot of trouble. For the second time tonight. Beast rose in me as the seconds dragged by. Minutes passed, feeling like hours. I started to sweat in the humid air, a betraying trickle lazing its way down my side. My heart beat a bit too fast, fear leaching into my bloodstream. I hated being passive. And I hated standing there with weapons drawn, awaiting my fate.

Finally I heard a door open. A voice called out, "Last time you hunted vamp in a dress and party shoes. Looks like you learned something, princess. Yo' mama mus' be proud."

My heart jumped into my throat and did a little tap dance before I swallowed it down and found my voice again. "If I'd ever had a mama, maybe so," I called back.

"Thought you was a Injun princess," he said, walking toward me with that measured step grunts learn early.

"Princess of my very own nook in a children's home," I said, softer. "Age twelve to eighteen. Now I'm still princess of my domain, but it's a bit far from here. You in charge of this one?"

He chuckled. "This *domain*? This lovely, sweet-smelling, clean, and pretty little patch of turf? Nominally speaking. Watchu want, Princess?"

"Safe passage. To hunt for the sire of the rogues we killed."

He laughed again, this one lower, knowing, and just a bit brutal. "Thanks for the money you sent our way, for the dead-vamp heads. It came in handy to buy more ammo. To kill the ones who came after."

"There've been more?"

"Six." He flicked a lighter and held it away from his body, using it to see me by before touching it to a cigarette—half tobacco, half weed by the smell—as he drew air through the paper and herbs. His face was lit in the flame, his black skin moist with perspiration, black shirt and dark clothes nearly invisible. The steel butt of a handgun rested in the waistband of his pants. I waited as he evaluated me in the light of the flame. "We got the heads in a cooler, kept that way with dry ice, since Ada came through. Crips are moving in too, some say with backing from a breakaway clan. We're getting low on supplies and ammo, but Leo ain't answering his cell. And we ain't getting paid no bounty."

"Ah," I said. He was making a deal. I felt Beast show teeth at the idea of negotiation. She believed in fighting first and talking after—over the blood and guts of her enemies. "Leo's grieving the death of his son."

Derek snorted at the term "death." I acknowledged, "As much as the dead can die. But he's not himself exactly."

"Rogue?"

I thought about the face and form standing in my small yard, vamped out. Thought about the dissension in his ranks. "Not yet. But something's funky. One of his scions used the word or the name 'Dolore.' You know it? Or her?" Derek shook his head no. I said, "Yeah. Me neither.

"I can send word of your kills to the vamp council. Get permission for you to talk to them. I'd even go with you to tell them they owe you. Sort of an emissary."

Derek blew smoke away from me in a long pale streamer. "Now, that would take some balls." He looked me over. "You got any?"

I grinned and let Beast shine in my eyes for a moment. I didn't know what he saw in the poor lighting, but he nodded.

"Okay. I'm not interested in talking with any fang-heads except Leo, and I'm not wild 'bout talkin' to him these days. How 'bout this? You talk, you get a deal, you keep twenty percent for the negotiation. And you leave our names out of it."

Now, that was interesting—the marine wanted to remain anonymous. "How 'bout I turn in the heads for you on my own bounty, which is twenty thousand a head, keep nothing, but you guarantee me safe passage through here while I hunt? And you back me up if I need help while I hunt for more. Deal?"

Derek thought about it a moment. "We'll need guns. Like the one you got pointed to the ground."

"You got six heads at twenty K a pop," I said. "Get your own."

Derek laughed. "Yeah, you got balls. May be crazy as hell, but you got balls. Okay. Deal. You get the best you can from the fang-heads, and me and my boys will assure you safe passage and act as backup for your hunt. Course, you cheat us and my boys will carve you up like a jack-o'-lantern." His teeth showed white in an ugly smile. "I'm accessible by cell. My card."

His card? I swallowed down a half-hysterical twitter as he pulled a card two-fingered from his chest pocket. I accepted it and tucked it into my own without trying to see the number in the dark. I handed him one of mine; he held it to the lighter and chuckled at the line. 'Have Stakes, Will Travel,' huh?" The lighter went out. "You are one crazy chick."

I just smiled, feeling the lessening of tension in the air.

"If the council puts a bounty on Leo," he added, "I want in on the gig. Got me?"

Surprise burrowed through me. "I thought Leo was your friend."

"Is. But if the man's going rogue, he'd want to be brought down. Told me so once, a long time ago. Deal, Injun Princess?"

"Deal, Derek Lee. Now, how about telling your boy to lower the rifle he has pointed at my back? Being in night sights and lasered up on makes me all itchy."

Derek laughed. "Juwan," he called. "Twizzlers."

I hoped "Twizzlers" was a code word for "A-OK," and relaxed slightly when Beast's intuition said the sharpshooter's interest had moved away from my spine. I wasn't sure how I knew when I was no longer in the sights of a gun, but it was something to do with Beast's hunting instincts.

"Nice doing business, Princess."

"Ditto, Derek." I kick-started Bitsa, sat, and walked her in a circle before giving her gas. Over my shoulder, I called to him, "I'll be starting at the place we killed the young rouges. I won't get shot there, will I?"

Derek shook his head and gave me an uplifted thumb in reply. I took that to mean that I would not get shot and that the place was safe to reconnoiter. I hoped I was reading him right.

The bike at a full-throated roar, sweat drying on my spine, I made my way down the dark, wet streets.

I did my best hunting in Beast form, but didn't want to take time to go back to the house and shift. It wasn't something I did easily away from home base, not even when that home was only on loan to me for the duration of my contract. But in human form I still had a few better-than-human senses—thanks to a century, give or take, spent in beast form—and could chase scents fairly well from Bitsa's back. Having a starting point helped.

I motored to the abandoned housing unit where I had taken down a female young-rogue vamp only a few days past. The place had acquired inhabitants; whether they were bona fide, deed-holding owners, renters, or squatters, I didn't know or care. I just hoped Derek was right about my safety and I wouldn't get shot as a trespasser.

Engine thrumming, I eased my bike down the narrow street and around to the side of the unit, cut the motor, and stalked around back. The smell of blood was faint, well washed by Ada, but under the scents of fertilizer, grass seed, and the mixed odors of kids and a small dog, I could still pick up the faint tang of vamp blood. I scouted around until I was satisfied I had the scent in my memory, then tracked to the place where Derek and his pals had taken down the female's sire, a teenaged kid, turned, and left to run wild—the rogue who had attacked a friend of mine and left her for dead. The smell was stronger here, as some vamp blood had splattered onto a brick wall, up high in a spot protected from rain. Standing against the wall, under the eaves, I breathed in the smell, my mouth open, so I drew it in through both nose and mouth, the way a cat takes scent.

And I caught the faint under-tang of another vamp. The teen male rogue's sire. I hadn't been looking for it last time I was here, too busy trying to stay alive. And the scent was familiar in an I-may-have-sniffed-it-before kinda way, or a sniffed-its-kid-sister kinda way.

After several long, deep breaths, cementing the disparate scents of chemicals and pheromones in my scent-memory, I walked back to Bitsa and kicked her to life. And I began to backtrack. The scent was pretty well washed away by the rain and I figured I'd have a hard time following it anyway, but the young male rogue had come and gone this way several times, and his scent was on trees and up under porches, places where the rain had missed. It was slow going, but I made my way out of the projects, heading toward Lake Pontchartrain.

It took me more than two hours to track the male rogue's path, off Filmore Avenue in a wooded area near a bayou, in a park in the middle of New Orleans. As I rode around it, I realized that the park wasn't that far from where I started out in the projects, yet the acreage was so large that Beast felt at home. I hadn't known it was here, and from the smell of trees, water, and a multitude of human scents, the park was huge. The storm had dropped limbs onto the paths leading in and torn down signs, but I finally found one that identified it, unimaginatively, as New Orleans City Park.

I parked Bitsa and went searching, following my nose along a path, over saturated ground, into an area marked as Couturié Forest. Here the trees grew bigger, older, limbs overarching the paths like sentinels, protective and watchful, though that was sheer fancy on my part.

Following the old scent, I skirted fallen limbs and windblown brush on the paths. The few sounds of a city crawling back to life after the storm vanished as I made my way through the trees. There was only the plop of heavy raindrops, the wet whisper of the wind in the limbs overhead, and the crunch and squish of leaves, twigs, and wet earth under my boots. A sense of tranquility and serenity pervaded the ground and the air, the way an old-growth forest feels, the loamy soil rich and fecund with life. But beneath it all was a trace of something feral. And dead. I left the path, pushing through the night.

Until I came to a vamp grave site. The stink of vamp, dead meat, and old blood had been well washed by Ada but was still potent enough for my Beast-enhanced senses.

The grave site was in a natural open area, a ten-foot circular space surrounded by old trees, rank with a miasma of overlapping scent patterns. I caught the strong recent tang of a lightning strike and charred wood, so much like the scent of burned magical wards that I was undecided on what I was smelling until I spotted the tree against the night sky, blackened and burned, its top half blasted away. The trail of lightning ran across the ground where it had cooked the earth.

I stood at the edge of the site, boots to the ankle in mud and last year's leaves, letting Beast have full rein of my sensory organs. She rose and peered through my eyes, taking in the world. My night vision expanded. My hearing took on the better-than-human enhancement. I drew in air through my nostrils and over my tongue—Flehmen behavior—seeing, feeling, hearing, smelling, tasting the place. To Beast it was sensory overload, overlapping into one multisense whole.

Nothing moved but the breeze. The dark was absolute. The wind whipped up for a moment, sending a soft sigh of sound and the patter of rain splattering down. Thunder rumbled in the distance. Beneath the scent of drenched earth, oak, maple, swamp hickory, and cypress, there was the reek of dead, decaying flesh. The herbal scent of vamps.

A hint of blood, old and thinned and washed away by the rains of Ada. And a trace of magic, both old and recently discharged. Witch magic. In a vamp graveyard. Okay, that was weird. Vamps and witches did *not* get along.

I stepped closer and something crunched beneath my boot. Squatting, I lifted a broken white shell from the muddy soil. Carefully, I brushed Ada-blown leaves and detritus away, exposing more shells around the periphery of the open area. Now that I knew they were here, I was able to make out a ring, perfectly circular, made of the small white shells. In the center of the circle was more white, and though I couldn't be sure without getting on my hands and knees, I thought it might form a pentagram.

Beast's reaction made the skin across my shoulders and along my neck prickle like hackles rising. I did not like this. Whatever it was, it was giving me the willies.

The antipathy between vamps and witches was rancorous and long-standing, like a cold war linking and dividing the races, a war that had lasted for hundreds of years, according to Molly, its origins lost in time. Yet, here in this dank and isolated place, encircled on all sides by city and bayou, the air tingled with magic, the ground was saturated with it, and the blood that soaked the soil was charged with it. Minute blue sparkles of magic tasted of nutmeg and sang a note of electric power. The witch power had been coiled, snarled, twisted into a heart of foulness. Dark magic had been done here. Blood magic. I paused and breathed deeply, hoping to find what kind of blood had been spilled—goat, chicken . . . or human? But the blood was too old and the site too exposed to hurricane rain for me to tell specifics.

I stood and dusted my hands off on my jeans, looking into the trees that surrounded this place. I saw a cross, nailed to a tree, about six feet off the ground. Another cross was several feet to the side. There were five crosses in all, nailed to trees at the points of the pentagram, and I wasn't sure, but the crosses might have been silver. Weird. The points of the pentagram on the ground lined up with the crosses on the trees. None of this made sense, not for a vamp grave, not for witch involvement, not for anything. I controlled my breathing, pushed down my fear response.

Across the ground, something moved.

A tiny patch of earth in the middle of the small clearing lifted and fell. A little triangle of soil. The bit of dirt dropped, stilled a moment, and lifted again. Something white poked out. The smell of death roiled out into the night, musty and foul. And the white thing resolved itself into fingers.

The hair rose on the back of my neck. Beast growled low in my throat and gathered herself tight. My body tightened, tension thrumming through me. I pulled my favorite vamp-killer and felt better with the elk-horn hilt of the weapon in my hand.

More soil fell away, the patch of earth rolling as something shuffled the surface leaves and scattered the shells. As something tried to rise from the center of the pentagram. The silver crosses at head height began to gleam softly.

Crap, I was witnessing the rising of a newborn vamp. A young rogue. A blood-sucking killing machine. I pulled a stake, making sure it was silver tipped. But Beast held mc motionless, watching, curious.

"Curiosity killed the cat," I murmured, adjusting my grip on the weapons.

Beast hacked with dire amusement.

The thing was skeletal, white-skinned and filthy, arms like sticks as it dragged itself out of the ground, hands and arms, knobby elbows. The head. Clods of dirt fell away. Long hair, tangled and muddy, dragged the grave. I had never seen a first rising, and it was much like *Night of the Living Dead* in 3-D, but stinkier. The rogue was female. She wore a party dress, a floral print, once pale with big flowers in bright colors, now foul with death fluids, blood, and the mud of the grave. She pulled her hips from the ground, shook her legs and feet free, and took a breath. Whipped her head to me. And found me in the night.

Her eyes almost glowed, bloodshot. Her neck was ravaged with knotted scar tissue. She hissed, snakelike, hungry. *Starving*. And coming for me. I started toward her, to finish her off.

No, Beast whispered. *Not here. Sire will scent her death. Will know you, be able to track you. Run. Like wounded bird.* I had a quick image of a bird darting from a nest, one wing held at an angle, drawing predators away. Spinning, I ran through the trees, deeper into Couturié Forest, watching over my shoulder. Behind me, the rogue grunted, sniffed the air like a feral dog, and pulled herself to her knees. I concentrated on getting away from the grave site, far enough to please Beast, who explored the world through my inadequate senses, her urgency pushing me to speed. Moments later, I heard the rogue start to follow, her balance off, her footsteps uneven.

She whimpered, mewling like a kitten. The kit sounds should have brought out the protective instincts in Beast. Instead, she hacked with displeasure and dug her claws into my psyche. I jumped a downed tree and a rill of water, leftover from Ada's deluge. Beast studied the world as I moved, looking for an ambush site in the dark.

The youngest vamp I had hunted was a year undead. Even then, their entire pasts—memories, sanity, and humanity—were still gone. It took years for a vamp to cure enough to find self-control and not kill any human it found. It took up to a decade to find its own memories lost beneath the hunger. All that was left to a newly risen vamp was the need to eat, drink, and kill for sustenance. The movements and sounds were pretty gross, and I totally got where the myth of zombies came from. Just-risen, young-rogue vamps equaled zombies. Almost literally.

The vamp behind me had lost everything that had made her human, and now she had to start from scratch, relearning how to walk, how to maneuver. Vamp speed, grace, and strength would begin to grow following her first blood meal, after she tracked and drained a victim to death. Or would have followed it, had I not found her first, and prevented that.

Then again, this was my first newly risen vamp. Hearsay among the small community of vamp hunters might be just that. The vamp on my trail might not need blood to be able to draw on vamp gifts and move faster than I could.

In a small clearing strewn with storm debris, I found a huge downed tree, its roots ten feet in the air, its limbs pointing to the sky on one side, and crushed by the wind and ground on the other. I leaped up to the horizontal trunk and walked along it to the first branch. Perched on the limb, I hefted my weapons into a better grip and waited. In my mind, Beast went still.

The rogue vamp wasn't far behind, her scent swirling along the night breezes, her footsteps faltering and noisy in the brush. I didn't think she had her vamp eyesight yet. Maybe vamp vision was part of the benefits of that first meal. Maybe it took longer. What did I know?

Crap. I was so not ready for this tonight. But at least the fear had settled with the movement and an ambush plan. I spotted her on my trail.

She stopped at the edge of the clearing, her nostrils flaring, her eyes staring and wild with that dull smolder they all had. Skin white, almost glowing in the dark, she didn't look up in the low branches, but at the ground. She sniffed loudly, air moving through clogged sinuses. She mewled piteously and wiped her face, smearing filth over her skin like accidental camouflage. Tears trickled through the mess. She was crying.

My heart twisted. Stupid to pity the crazed and dead, but I did. On some level, I sympathized. I remembered what it had felt like to be empty of memories, lost and alone, stuck in a body I didn't remember, among humans. Of course, I'd still been alive. I strangled a sigh, but the vamp must have heard. Her eyes darted up, into the limbs. She hissed. And dashed toward me.

Instead of taking the trunk as I had, she scrambled through the branches directly below me, huffing in hunger, her fetid stink rising. Almost lazily, I dropped from the branches, landing behind her, vamp-killer blade up, stake ready.

She whirled, snarled, reached for me. I stepped into her putrid embrace and touched her chest with the stake. Jaws wide, she rushed into the point. I rammed it home. It was so easy to kill the young. Too easy. The vamp paused as if frozen, her eyes on mine in the night. Humanity bled back into her gaze, puzzled and afraid. "No," she whispered on her last breath. "No . . ." She crumpled at my feet, landing between two tree limbs, her legs splayed.

I knelt beside her and pulled a miniflashlight. The beam caught her full in the face. Under the filth, snot, tears, and dried blood, she was pretty, or had been. Curly brown hair, greenish brown eyes, short, needle-thin vamp canines, traces of makeup over very white skin. They always took the beautiful ones. I had never seen an ugly vamp. Like pedophiles, they liked them young and charming and pretty.

I set the flash on a limb, the light falling over the girl, and sheathed the vamp-killer, pulling a camera. I took photos from several angles, including a close-up of her face showing her new little fangs, and another of the stake through her heart. Photos were nice, but I needed more. I never trusted stakes. Lore says that a stake to the heart is fatal unless the sire is close by; he can sometimes heal a scion if he gets there in time. I pulled a knife with a slightly curved blade, and lay the edge against the girl's neck, and put my back into it, cutting. Cold blood gushed over my gloves. A beheading was both final and proof for bounty. Newly risen, newly dead again.

When I was done, I set the head and the flashlight aside and grabbed the rogue by the heels. I pulled her far from the paths, and even farther from her burial site, and left her body for the vamp council's cleanup crew to dispose of her. If humans got to her first, she'd be hard to identify unless she had prints on file. Besides, the vamps would make sure she disappeared before an autopsy was performed. Since vamps came out of the closet, there had been no reports of vamp postmortems. The bloodsuckers liked it that way.

Until recently this vamp had been human—a daughter, mother, wife, girlfriend, coworker, somebody important to other humans. Now she was dead and gone. Hundreds of people simply disappear each year in the U.S. because they walk away and find another life, or because they're killed and their bodies never found. I had often wondered how many of the disappeared were vamp kills—wondered and never asked. The humans she left behind deserved closure of some kind, but I was betting that the vamp council wouldn't give them that. Another dead rogue so soon after the brouhaha of the last one would be bad press. This girl would become one of the state's missing and never found.

When the body was hidden, I scuffed away the drag marks with a leafy branch, and carried the head to Bitsa. I stuffed it into an oversized Ziplock bag and dropped it into a watertight carryall, which I slung over my shoulder.

I didn't have far to go, but if I was stopped by a cop, the head would be hard—though not impossible—to explain. I carried a copy of my contract with the vamp council in a pocket, and the vamp fangs were a dead giveaway (vamp humor) that I hadn't murdered a human. Plus, there was a certain cop I knew who would back up my story. Rick LaFleur owed me a favor—a big one. I had saved his sorry butt two times.

I powered Bitsa up and tooled out of the park. Parts of the city—those close to city service buildings, hospitals, and other needed locales—were already back on the power grid, windows bright, doorways spilling light into the streets, and the party that never stopped in the city that was built for partying was back on go. Music and the rich scents of cooking food filled the air. Sirens wailed in the distance, with the sharp *pop-crack* of gunshots. Cars slid through the half-dark streets, slowing at the streetlights that were functioning, ignoring the rest. Other parts of the city were still pitch-dark, and would take a lot longer to return to life as usual.

Though the windows were all dark, the vamp council headquarters's white-stucco exterior was lit with lights hidden in the vegetation, the rumble of generators in the background. I braked my bike as I turned into the circular drive, moving slowly, though there were no obstructions, limos, or armored cars, no one to look me over as I rode past, eyes following me the way professional muscle would, with a look that was half assessment, half threat. Of course, there had to be cameras. The place might look empty, but I knew it wasn't. There was always someone on duty in case of emergency, a contact vamp, with access to all the clan masters.

Parking for the servants and hired help was hidden in back, but I pulled to the front door and cut the engine, lowered the kickstand, and unhelmeted. I was wearing bloody, muddy jeans and boots, was carrying weapons, crosses, and stakes, and I knew I'd have to ditch them all when I was searched, not that I'd even necessarily see a vamp tonight. I'd probably be reporting to a blood-servant flunky. *What fun.*

Though vamp citizenship was being considered in Congress, at the moment they were treated as aliens, and carrying a weapon beyond the foyer of the council house was tantamount to taking a weapon into a foreign embassy or a federal courtroom, a good way to get jumped on and locked away. I climbed the stairs; the door opened before I knocked. A blood-servant I didn't recognize let me in—male, tall, well muscled, and bald, he looked like an escapee from the World Wrestling Federation. The guy was seriously big.

He didn't speak. He didn't have to. He pointed to a table, where I set down my head bag and removed my weapons. This was my third visit to council headquarters, so I knew the score. When I was done, he motioned me aside and opened the bag. His brows rose when he looked in, but he made no other reaction, just resealed the bag. He patted me down thoroughly, not wasting any effort on being gentle. Handing me the bag, he pointed me to the small waiting room. The big silent type.

I'd been stuck here before on my previous visits, and knew there was food. I opened the refrigerator, taking a can of Coke back to the couch. The TV, set high on the wall, was displaying the weather with Ada's northward progress mapped out in livid reds, greens, and yellows. I plopped down, popped the Coke, and drank. There were no windows. But at least this time no blood-servant stood guard at the door. Maybe they were starting to trust me. Or maybe there was just no one on duty important enough to guard, what with Ada just passing. Or maybe I was locked in. Whatever. I was too tired to care.

I waited an hour, which was no surprise. I'd waited longer on a previous visit. I drank two more Cokes and raided the kitchen for food, putting a hurting on a plastic container filled with cookies and crackers. It was near two a.m. when the door opened. The WWF-looking security guy nodded me out and took off down a hallway. I figured he wanted me to follow, and grinned at the mental picture of his expression should I start opening doors and peeking inside instead. He glanced back and frowned as if he could read my mind and didn't like what he saw. Meekly, I caught up, my head bag on a strap over my shoulder.

WWF Guy took me to the second floor, knocked, and

opened a door; the herbal scent of vamp wafted out. WWF stood back for me to enter. Inside was a library, books on shelves and piled all around, and leather chairs with small side tables. Because it was a vamp room, there were no windows. A fire burned in the fireplace with the snap and scent of real wood. An air-conditioned breeze cooled the room. Ambience achieved at the cost of the vamp carbon footprint. Vamps weren't into being green.

In a chair near the fire, a book open on her lap, sat a vamp I knew, the second in command at Clan Arceneau, Dominique—blond, pale-eyed, and at least two hundred years old. The last time I saw her, Dominique was chained, tortured, and suffering from excessive bloodletting and silver poisoning. I had threatened her and then saved the life of her clan blood-master. I had no idea if she would want to thank me or suck me dry in revenge. After all, I *had* left her chained. In silver. But she just looked me over as if I were a horse she might buy, or a slave. Dominique's family had owned a plantation before the Civil War—I had done my homework and knew a lot about the most important and powerful New Orleans vamps.

Her nostrils widened, and I knew she smelled blood. And dead vamp. She went deeply and utterly still. Before I spoke, I too took a careful breath, to see if I recognized the scent of the vamp who had made the young rogue. Dominique wasn't the sire. The tension went out of me. Not certain of protocol, I said, "You look . . . well."

"Your boots are dirty," she said, her voice as smooth as watered silk.

"Yeah," I said, handing her the bag. "The head of the vamp I just killed." Her eyes tightened, an infinitesimal flicker. "A young rogue," I said. "I'll collect the bounty later, but I need the cleanup crew sent to the New Orleans City Park to dispose of what's left of her."

Dominique opened the bag and stared at the face in the baggie. "She was young. Her fangs are not yet full sized."

I had thought her fangs were just small, not that they'd get bigger. Interesting. "I watched her rise from her grave," I said. Dominique lifted her gaze to me. "Her first rising," I said, to clarify.

Dominique closed the flap. She pressed a button on the

small table beside her. WWF opened the door fast. "Take this. Tell Ernestine that a bounty check should be drawn up for Ms. Yellowrock. Retrieve the head and return the satchel before she leaves. Ms. Yellowrock will also provide you with a locale. Send a sanitation team in to dispose of the body before morning." Dominique looked at me. "Is that all?"

I thought about Derek Lee and the heads he was keeping. For some reason he didn't want me to negotiate with the council in his name. "I have six more heads in a cooler. Young rogues."

This time Dominique's eyes did widen, surprise on her face. WWF shifted on his feet and looked at me, his gaze traveling up and down me, reassessing. A different expression raised his brows. Amusement and maybe respect. Which I didn't deserve since I hadn't killed the vamps, but now I was stuck in the sort-of-lie.

"Six more?" Dominique asked. When I nodded, she said to WWF, "See that a retrieval car is sent for the heads at a place and time of Ms. Yellowrock's choosing. Once the fangs are verified as young, instruct Ernestine to write an additional check to Ms. Yellowrock."

To me, she said, "Will there be anything else, Ms. Yellowrock?"

"Nothing at the moment," I said. Remembering manners, I added, "Um, thank you."

Dominique inclined her head, very regally. "You may go."

I hated that about vamps, especially the old ones. Everyone was an inferior, a servant. They always kept you waiting and then dismissed you, which ticked me off. But then, I was on their territory, not my own. Holding my tongue, I followed WWF out of the room.

In the hallway, he again studied me, this time as if looking for proof of my vamp-killing prowess. He gestured with his hand for me to follow him. "Six more?" he asked as we walked to an intersecting hallway.

Since he didn't ask if I had actually killed the six, I nodded.

"Damn. George said you were good."

"George Dumas?" I murmured. WWF nodded and I allowed myself a smile. George was Leo's blood-servant, first in command of Leo's household security. The guy was seriously cool. And he had a nice butt, which I might not mind seeing out of his jeans, someday.

"He says you call him by a nickname, him and Tom, Katie's blood-servant, but won't tell us what they are." Katie was the vamp who had done my employment interview, owned Katie's Ladies, the house of ill repute that backed up to mine, and was the title owner of the house where I was living. She was currently in an honest-to-Bella-Lugosi coffin, drowned in mixed vamp blood, healing from a near-true-death experience. And her bodyguard, Troll, was talking about me? I wasn't sure I liked that, but I wasn't about to tick off the security of the vamp council. I shrugged and didn't enlighten him.

"Do you give us all nicknames?" When I shrugged again, the tiniest bit, he said, "What's mine?"

I looked him over, feeling mildly self-conscious.

"No. Really. What's mine?"

I sighed. "WWF."

After a moment he said, "World Wrestling Federation?" I nodded and he laughed, the tone appreciating. He ran a hand over his bald dome, considering. "WWF. I like." He stopped at a doorway and knocked before opening it. Inside was a small room, an even smaller desk, a huge safe, its thick black door open to reveal stacks of money and papers. Sitting in a leather desk chair was a shriveled, wrinkled crone of a human, whom I instantly and tritely nicknamed Raisin, for obvious reasons.

"Ernestine, this is Jane Yellowrock," WWF said.

The woman stared at my boots and lied. "Charmed, I'm sure." Her accent was British, maybe Welsh, and I put her age at over one-fifty. Blood-servants lasted a long time, extended longevity being one benefit of letting vamps drink your blood and use you as they wanted.

WWF said, "Ms. Dominique said to cut her a check for twenty thou, and make funds available for a hundred twenty more, bounty money, to be paid on proof of death of six young rogues."

Raisin's eyebrows went up nearly to her hairline, pulling lines out of her eyelids and depositing them onto her forehead. "Six? Well." She looked me over and for some reason I couldn't explain even to myself, I felt the way I had as a teen, when I was called to Mr. Rawls's office for a discipline breach. Discipline in a children's home is swift and unyielding, especially for fighting, and while not corporal punishment, it was unpleasant. For a variety of reasons I used to get into a lot of fights, and clearly, if I had taken down seven vamps, I had been fighting, hence my discomfort. "Six," she repeated, sounding mildly surprised. She pulled a book of checks to her and lifted a pen. "Quite remarkable."

I didn't quite know what to say to that, so I stood mute, looking over the office, memorizing vamp party dates on Ernestine's calendar, categorizing everything I could identify in the safe, and staring at the electronic brain of a security system as she wrote a check, making a lot of curlicues and flourishes with the antique-looking pen. She blew on the check as if the ink took a while to dry and scooted it across the desk to me, along with a card. Her name with the initials CPA was centered on it, a phone number beneath. "There you are, my dear. Next time, please call ahead. I'll have a check ready, and will leave it at the front desk."

So I wouldn't have to bring my muddy-booted, bad ol' fighting self inside. Got it. "Thank you," I said, taking the check and folding it into a pocket. WWF backed from the room and I followed. At the front door, I weaponed up and gave a two-fingered salute to WWF as I left.

Out on the street, the muggy wind in my teeth, I shuddered hard. When I went into vamp headquarters and came out alive, I felt as if I had fought a battle and survived. Not won it. Just survived it. And for some reason that I couldn't name, this trip had been worse than the last.

CHAPTER 3

Golden eyes, my daughter

Back at home, I slipped through the ward, which was keyed to me in some arcane way that Molly had tried to explain one time and which I had totally not understood. After locking away the weapons so the kids couldn't find them, I stripped, showered, and fell into bed. Beast had wanted me to shift so she could roam until sunrise, but I needed sleep. Once on the mattress, however, I couldn't relax, seeing again and again the tiny fangs hinge down, like baby teeth in a human. Most of the time it was easy dispatching a rogue, but watching this young rogue rise in her stained party dress, and then seeing her eyes bleeding back to humanity as she died, had left a bad taste in my mouth; I felt shaken by the experiences of the night, dirty almost. I needed . . . cleansing. I rolled over on the mattress, knowing it was time to do something I'd been putting off for a long while.

At five thirty I crawled from the bed, bleary eyed and groggy, stumbled into jeans, T-shirt, and Western boots. As ready as I could be for this experience, I left the house again without eating or waking Molly or the kids.

Bitsa sputtered when I started her, but pulled into the dark street and went up to speed quickly enough. On the far side of the river (all directions in New Orleans are in relation to Lake Pontchartrain or the Mississippi River, upstream or down), I took the necessary turns and straightaways, and finally veered into a white-shell, dead-end road and the tiny house at the end. The smell of wood smoke was sharp on the air, the scent denser as I pulled into the drive.

The air was graying with light when I pushed the bell, and I started when it opened instantly. The slender, black-haired woman inside was dressed in jeans and a long-sleeved shirt. She smiled at me as if she had known I was coming—which was impossible, wasn't it?—and when she spoke, her voice was soft and breathy, in the way of the speech of the People. "*Gi yv ha*," she said, and held open the door. "*Gi yv ha*" was Cherokee for "Come in."

I nodded formally, almost a bow, and said, "Thank you, *Egini Agayvlge i*—Aggie One Feather." I wished that there was more of the People's tongue in my memory, wished that I was a *speaker*, as the People said of the few who still could converse in Cherokee. But the words were scattered and broken, mostly lost, in my damaged mind. I had spent too long in Beast form and had forgotten the ways and tongue of the People.

"Are you ready, Jane *Dalonige'i*, Jane Yellowrock, or Jane Gold, in the speech of the white man?" Aggie asked. Her voice was soft, melodious, the gentle voice of dreams and nightmares both. When I nodded, she asked, "Did you fast today?"

"I did." Beast was hyperalert, but hunkered down, deep inside me, watchful and silent.

"Then I will take you to sweat. And afterward, if you are ready, I will take you to water." The words were similar to the traditional words of the shaman, the tribal helpers. Shamans and elders would assist, free of charge, any who asked, even the white man, for healing ceremonies, council, or more practical help.

Today, Aggie One Feather was hoping to bring me into contact with my true self, my spirit self, to steer me on the road to spiritual healing. And though I had not told her what I was, she knew bits and pieces of my story; perhaps she had guessed much more. I was hoping she could help me find the child that I once had been, so very long ago. Before Beast. Before I lost my memories. Before the hunger times, which I remembered only vaguely. Before I was found wandering in the Appalachian Mountains, scared, scarred, naked, and with almost no memory of human language. Finding her here in New Orleans shouldn't have been a surprise—the People lived all over the States—but it still felt like one of the weird coincidences the universe tossed my way occasionally. Since it brought me closer to learning about my past, this time it was a welcome one.

Aggie lifted a stoneware pitcher of water and a long wooden ladle, which were ready on a table by the door. Both items looked like traditional Cherokee ware, and though I tended to have very few possessions, I suddenly wanted to own a pitcher and ladle like them. I curled my fingers in, to keep from stroking the pitcher, as she led the way outside and around back.

The sweat lodge was a low wood hut with a metal roof, located at the back of the property, hidden in the drooping limbs of trees. The smell of wood smoke was strong here, and wisps of smoke, nearly invisible in the pale half-light, wafted from a circular opening in the very center of the roof. I stood beside the doorway, watching as Aggie stripped off her jeans and T and draped them over a wood hook on the outside wall. Naked, she wrapped a coarsely woven cotton cloth around her and tied the overlapped ends above her breasts. Covered from underarms to knees, she entered the lodge. Heat blasted out. The door swung silently shut.

There were a dozen such hooks, each with its white covering, similar to Aggie's, some long, some shorter. Feeling oddly uncomfortable, I stripped and tied a makeshift robe around me, leaving my clothes on a second peg and my boots against the wall. The covering was dry, and must have been hung since Ada passed. My hair was still in a fighting queue, tight to my head. I left it that way. Barefoot, I stared at the door. I had been all around the lodge in cat and human form, but this was the first time I would go inside.

I put a palm on the rough plank door and pushed gently. The darkness inside reached out to me, warm and solid. Holding the door open with one hand, I stepped in, ducking my head to avoid hitting it on the low door header and roof supports. My bare feet stepped on a hard-packed clay floor, level with the outside ground.

A memory came, unbidden, of another sweat lodge, this one with a long step down into the dark, the floor scooped out, flat and smooth inside, but a foot deeper in the ground. A single snapshot-type memory. Then it was gone. But the vision left me with a calmness that settled against my skin like the scented dark of the lodge.

Without asking, I knew that the floor of this sweat lodge had not been dug out because the water table was so high here. Water would have collected in any depression.

I released the door and it closed behind me. Warm, wet heat and darkness surrounded me, steam rising from red coals and heated rocks piled in the center of the small hut.

Beast yawned deep inside and settled herself in my mind. She liked the warmth.

I stood hunched over, my head brushing the roof supports, letting my eyes adjust. The fire was built on a low bed of rocks, other rocks ringing it. It had been burning a long time, long enough for the heat to feel alive and powerful, as if she had known I would come today. Around the fire were low seats made from logs that had been shaped and rounded for sitting. Aggie was on a log on the far side of the fire, her eyes on the coals, her hands busy in a basket beside her. There were other baskets woven from grasses, each with a woven lid hiding its contents. The pitcher was on the ground beside her, the ladle inside.

I lowered myself to the seat closest to the door, my knees rising, and I squirmed to find a comfortable position. Aggie seemed fine with the seat, and I copied the pose of her legs, but she was much shorter than my six feet and it wasn't working for me. I stretched out my feet to the fire and waited, palms flat on my thighs, not knowing what was going to happen. No more memories came to enlighten me. I had lost so much of myself, of my past.

Neither of us spoke. Aggie, moving slowly, as if everything she did were choreographed, put a blackened length of wood on the fire, using it to shuffle the coals. Brighter red light seeped out. From a basket, she pulled something tied with twine. It was too dark in the lodge to identify, but it was a foot long, about an inch and a half in diameter, and she held it to the coals. Instantly it lit, throwing bright white light for a few seconds, the flames a greedy whisper as they ate into it. I drew in the scent. Sweetgrass. Sage. Something tart, like lemon camphor. Herbs used in making a smudge stick. *I remembered.* . . .

I closed my eyes and breathed. Time passed. Aggie added more herbs as the first of them smoldered into ash. My legs seemed to settle and relax. Sweat rose to my skin, beading, puddling, and ran in sluggish rivulets on my hands, along my arms and legs. Thick drops rolled down and plopped against the smooth clay floor beneath me. I sighed, the breath long and slow.

From somewhere came the soft sound of a drum beating a measured, rhythmic four-beat. I chuckled softly, little more than a breath. "A CD? In a sweat lodge, *Lisi*?"

From some part of my deeper mind, I knew the word *li si*. Grandmother. Though Aggie wasn't my grandmother, it was a term of respect for an elder. "Yes. *Lisi*," I said again. "*Lisi*."

Aggie smiled in the dark. I knew it, though my eyes were closed, my head back, neck stretched out. I breathed in the scented smoke. Her voice like a whisper of a dawn breeze, Aggie said, "It is music from a Cherokee musician. With only the two of us, it would be difficult to call the drums."

"Drums," I said. "I had forgotten about the drums." She lifted my hand and guided it to a handle, pressing it toward my lips. A ladle full of water. I drank. She took the ladle away.

I heard a sizzle, and knew Aggie had spilled water over the hot stones, like an offering. A gift. Steam sputtered into the scented air. As the music and the heat and the cleansing steam surrounded me, I relaxed, letting my body find the shape of the wood beneath me. Beast slept. Perhaps I did too.

Long hours later, I heard a voice in my dreams, softer than the quiet drums. *"Aquetsi, ageyutsa." Granddaughter.* "Tell me what you remember."

The drums pulled at me, calling, calling. The herbs and the heat pressed down on me. *"Aquetsi, ageyutsa*, tell me what you remember."

"E lisi." My grandmother. An old, old, *old* woman, her skin pulled into drooping wrinkles, her hair black and streaked with silver, parted and braided to either side of

her head, the plaits hanging down, tied at the ends with leather thongs and the bones and feathers of her beasts. Fire danced over her skin, down her cotton dress, to the drum in her thin hand. The drum she beat, so slowly. Four beats: one firm and three sliding, softer beats.

"*E lisi,*" I said again. "*E lisi, e tsi, e doda.*" *My grandmother, my mother, my father.* Words that had lost meaning, newly found. "*E lisi* had eyes like mine. Like my father's. *Dalonige i digadoli.* Yellow eyes."

From somewhere a flute began to play, the notes rich with sadness. I opened my eyes. Cave walls surrounded me, the roof melting down in drops and spirals, like the white man's candles, the rock magical, soft and puddling, like the sweat from my skin. The cave roof was crying the tears of the world in soft plinks, the sound of tears merging with the drum and flute.

Elisi was speaking, measured and slow. But though I could see her lips move in the flicker of firelight, her words were lost, whispered echoes. Then my father spoke, and his words I could hear. In low, breathy tones he spoke animal names. "*We sa. Gvhe. Unodena. Usdia soquili. Gvli. Ugugu. Uwohali.* When you are older, bigger, *tlvdatsi. Tlvdatsi,* like me. *Dalonige i Digadoli, aquetsi ageyutsa.*" *Bobcat. Wild cat. Sheep. Pony foal. Raccoon. Owl. Eagle. When you are older, bigger, mountain lion. Panther, like me. Golden Eyes, my daughter.*

My father's voice went on, speaking the names of animals I could choose. But I knew already, though my body was too small to find them, that I would call *we sa* and *tlvdatsi.* Bobcat and panther. Like my father. Because he had told me so.

Dalonige i Digadoli. Golden Eyes. My name.

"Wake up, Jane. Wake up," a voice murmured. "It's time to go."

I opened my eyes. I was lying on my back, looking up. I was at peace, so calm it was like being a feather on the breeze, floating. Above me, a shaft of sunlight pierced the roof, shining down through swirling smoke. Particles shifted and eddied in the bright light. I turned my head. I was in a dark room. Shadows crouched in the corners. The air was warm and dry, my skin crusted with salt. My hair, which had started out tightly braided, was loose on the clay floor beneath me and across my shoulders. I smiled. "I remember my name."

A soft chuckle came to me through the dark. "*Dalonige i Digadoli*. Golden Eyes. It is a very pretty name."

I sat up. Across the sweat lodge, Aggie One Feather sat on a carved log, her legs outstretched. She was smiling but there was a shadow in her eyes, hidden and private, closed and weighted, that she didn't want me to see. Trepidation stirred in the calm center of me, like a whirlpool opening in a pond. "What?" I asked.

She stared at me, as if trying to read my soul through my eyes. "*Dalonige i Digadoli*, Golden Eyes, is not a traditional name for one of the People." I shrugged, not knowing what to say. "And the animals you named. So many. So strange. Your parents were Speakers of the language of the People. Both of them."

I understood what she was saying. The number of Speakers left among the People was less than a hundred, even counting both Eastern Cherokee and Western Cherokee. If my parents had been Speakers, then their names would have been known. Aggie would have heard of them and know they had lost a daughter. But she had never heard of such people, and therefore, I couldn't have Speakers as parents. Yet I had memories of them speaking the language. It wasn't possible.

But then, Aggie didn't know how old I thought I might be. That was one of the secrets I had to keep, along with my skinwalker magic. I could tell her neither truth as my safety lay in my anonymity, though I had a feeling that Aggie had guessed I hadn't been entirely honest with her.

"Do you remember their names?" Aggie One Feather asked, her voice carefully neutral.

I shook my head. "*Edoda*, my father, was *ani gilogi*, Panther Clan. *Etsi*, my mother, was *ani sahoni*, Blue Holly Clan. *Elisi*, my grandmother, was Panther Clan, like my father. I don't remember anything more." *Liar, liar, pants on fire! Can she see the lie?* "My name . . . I don't know. It was just my name." I hesitated. I didn't want to lie to this woman. The People did not lie, even to the white man, who never spoke the truth. And one never lied, not ever, to an elder, even now, when most young had so little respect for the aged. So I asked a question instead. "The animals . . . What do you think the names meant?"

Aggie stood, lithe and fluid, her body belying her age, which was somewhere past fifty, if I guessed right. "I don't know," she said. "I will ask my mother. Come. It is time to go. And it is too late for me to take you to water today."

There was something in her voice that led me to think she skirted the truth with careful words, either to keep truth from me because she feared it, or because she feared me. Or perhaps because she didn't know what she wanted to say. But she didn't look at me. Not once.

I followed her into the sunlight, which was blinding, the air after the hurricane clear, the sky almost as blue as home, in the mountains of the Appalachians, the mountains of the People.

Aggie stripped and turned on a spigot I hadn't noticed, high on the wall. Water shot out and she rinsed, her skin pebbling from the cold. I kept my head turned, and when she was done and stepped away, Aggie kept her head turned as well, each of us offering the other privacy in a very public bathing. There were no towels, and we blotted off on the sweat-soaked robes before pulling our clothes on over wet bodies. Aggie gathered up our dirty robes in a bundle under one arm and gestured to the lawn, away from the sweat lodge. I plaited my hair in a single long braid as we walked, and let it hang, wet and dripping, down my back.

Silent, we crossed the yard to Bitsa. I stopped at my bike. Aggie came around to the other side and paused, her eyes on the bike. "*Lisi*," I said, searching for formal words, proper words, to bring the truth from her. "Your heart is heavy. May I . . . share your burden?" That felt right.

She shook her head, eyes on the bike. "I am not burdened, daughter. I will call when I have a clearer understanding."

And I would have to be satisfied with that. "Thank you, *Egini Agayvlge i*. I will wait to hear your counsel."

Aggie nodded, and a slight smile crossed her face. "I wish my own children would be half so respectful." She turned and went to the small house, opened the door, and went inside, closing the door behind her.

I helmeted up and took the long road back to the house I lived in until my contract was over.

When I got home, a car was idling at the front door. A man stood on the front porch, his jeans tight, the long sleeves of a button-down shirt rolled up to reveal tanned, fit arms. It was Bruiser, aka George Dumas, Leo's first human blood-servant, and his second in command, his muscle and security. My heart rate sped up just a bit. Six-four, weightlifter but not to bulging excess, brown eyes and hair. Clean-looking with a primo sculpted nose, long and sort of bony. I had a thing about noses and really liked his. In fact I liked almost every thing abut Bruiser, and so did my Beast. He hadn't been around when Leo came visiting last night. Had he known about the attack?

Bruiser swiveled like a dancer at the sound of Bitsa. His expression was solemn and he didn't smile when he saw me. That couldn't be good. I nodded stiffly, glad my face was hidden behind the face shield. Pulling Bitsa to the side and through the gate, out of sight, I locked the gate behind me. The ward was still on, and when I entered the house, a tingle buzzed against my skin, rough, like sandpaper, if sandpaper could hold an electric charge.

Molly met me at the bottom of the stairs, wearing wide-legged capris, a tee, and sandals. Energy fairly radiated off her body. "Do we let him in?" she asked, waiting for me to make the decision on security.

"Hi, Aunt Jane," Angelina said, half hidden behind her mother.

I picked Angie up and hugged her, saying, "Hi, Angie Baby." I handed her to her mother. "You two go upstairs, okay? Just for a few minutes. I have a visitor."

"A bad man?" Angie asked, more in curiosity than fear.

"Not a bad man," I said. "Just not a good one." *A white man*, I thought. *Someone I can't trust.* The thinking was left over from a childhood I could remember only in snitches and snatches, but it was powerful nonetheless.

Molly quick-stepped up the stairs, shushing Angie's protests. The ward snapped off and a knock sounded instantly on the door, as if he had been waiting for it to flick off. Bet it had burned his knuckles the first time he tried. I opened the door and leaned negligently against the jamb, not asking him in, blocking the way, my body language aggressive and challenging. I might think he was gorgeous but I wasn't ready to cede him that knowledge.

"Bruiser. To what do I own the honor of this visit?" My tone said it was *not* an honor, and George's brows rose, the gesture elegant and refined and annoyingly superior. The gesture was oddly similar to Leo's, reminding me that he had been with the Blood Master of the City for a long time. A very long time. It helped to settle my hormones.

"My master sends you greetings and a missive." The words had an old-fashioned ring, a sure sign of a powerful vamp's official notice.

I had a feeling that this formal visit might be only marginally better than Leo's kerosene and fire visit of the night before, and that brought out a belligerence I usually controlled better. I narrowed my eyes at him. "No shit?"

George didn't laugh, his eyes serious. He extended a roll of paper, a little smaller than standard eight-by-eleven notepaper. No, not paper; by the smell it was heavy vellum, rolled and secured with a scarlet ribbon. It was also sealed with bloodred wax.

"My execution order? A warning that I'm about to be burned out? If so, it's a day late."

Bruiser frowned, his brown eyes sincere. Not that sincere was anything to trust in a blood-servant. "I heard about it, Jane. If I had known what he planned, I'd have tried to stop him. Or at least I'd have called and warned you."

"Big words. Nice plan. A day late and a dollar short. So, what is it?" I pointed at the roll.

Bruiser looked at the vellum, his frown deepening. "I don't know."

"Nothing good, then." I took the vellum, slid the ribbon off, and gave it to George. I broke the seal with a fingernail. The note was short and pointed, handwritten in a slashing, cursive scrawl that screamed it was by Leo's own hand. I read it aloud.

"'To Jane Yellowrock, Rogue Hunter. The instant that your current contract with the Council of the Mithrans is completed, you will vacate the City of New Orleans. Should you decline to comply, you will be brought to me. You will not leave again.' It's signed, 'Leonard Pellissier. Blood Master of the City of New Orleans.'

"Well, that was short and bitter," I said. "I'm guessing the line 'You will not leave again' means that he'll turn me, chain me in his basement, and let me starve. Not a pretty image. Your boss is certifiable, Dumas."

"I like Bruiser better."

"Tough." I shut the door in his face.

Molly's chuckle sounded down the stairway. I felt the ward come on, the whole house seeming to buzz for a moment until it settled. "You think that was smart?" she asked me.

"Not really." Beast hacked in the deep parts of my mind. She had enjoyed it all very much, even still half asleep.

"You like him, don't you?" When I didn't answer, she sang out, paraphrasing Rod Stewart lyrics, "I know you think he's sexy, and you want his body. Come on, Big Cat, say it's so-o-o-o."

"That is not right on so many levels." I stopped at the bottom of the staircase, noting that the lamps of the night before were gone. I had forgotten to put them away, out of the kids' reach, until we needed them tonight, but Molly-the-mom wasn't forgetful. She was grinning down at me, one hand on the newel post, the other on the banister, her children on either side of her, Little Evan sitting, a thumb in his mouth, Angie wrapped around the spindles of the monkey-tail newel like a monkey herself.

The house was hot and the air was sticky, still, and dead. The widows were open, but there was no breeze. My T-shirt stuck to me and my jeans felt like a damp second skin. I started to sweat in earnest and rubbed my palms on my jeans. I needed Molly's help. "Molly, I need a favor. A witch favor." The smile slid from Mol's face, but I bulled on. "I smelled witch magic at a vamp's first rising. I need you to ask around with the local covens, see what you can find out. If there's any rumors that someone is working with the vamps."

A long silence settled on us then, Molly's face, usually so full of expression, telling me nothing. Finally she sighed, and I felt a weight roll off me. "Okay. I'll try. But the local covens aren't real agreeable since Katrina and the fluff-up about witches not doing a good enough job to ward off the storm. The press hounded them. Is still hounding them. I'll put out a few feelers and see what I get. But don't expect much."

"Thanks." Beast stared at my friend and the children through slit eyes, feeling protective and tender, feelings I echoed. *Kits. Cubs. Safe*, she thought at me.

"I'm hungry," I said.

"Big Cat's always hungry," Angelina said.

Molly swiveled her head to her daughter fast. "Why did you call her that?" she asked, her voice sharp.

"*You* call her Big Cat." Angelina looked up at her mother, her face taking on an unexpected eagerness. "Is it *bad* words?"

I snickered and Molly shook her head, scooping up Evan and taking Angie's hand. Together they started down the steps. "No, Angie Baby, it isn't bad words. But it is a grown-up name for Aunt Jane. Like when Aunt Jane calls me Molly, but you call me Mama. Big Cat isn't a name for little girls to use."

Angie's face scrunched up and tears glistened at the corners of her eyes. My heart melted. I had a flash of a cave roof, melting down, stalactites dripping down to stalagmites. Then it was gone and the trio reached the bottom of the steps. I took Angelina up in my arms. "I have a secret," I whispered, "just for you. Not for your mama."

"No fair," Molly said.

Angie opened her eyes, the tears miraculously stopped. "Just for me?" she stage-whispered back.

"Yep." I took Angie into the living room, away from the kitchen where Molly was going, Evan under her arm like a sack of potatoes. "A name, a secret name, for me. The name my mommy and daddy gave me when I was a baby."

"Not Aunt Jane?"

"Not Aunt Jane."

"Does Mommy know it?"

"Nope." I sat her on the couch and knelt in front of her. "You want to know what it is?" When Angie nodded, I said, "It's a very special name. You can tell your mama if you want to, but other than her, we have to keep it a secret for now. Okay?" Angie nodded again, her eyes wider. "And it's in a different language, which makes it hard to say, so we'll have to practice to get it just right."

Angie looked around me to the doorway of the kitchen, making sure her mother wasn't in range of the big secret. "Okay, Aunt Jane," she whispered. "We can tell Mama the secret after snack time. But right now I'm the only one, right?"

"Right. My Cherokee name is Dalonige i Digadoli. It means Golden Eyes."

"Biscause your eyes are yellow?" she asked, mispronouncing the word, as she often did.

"Exactly. Dalonige i Digadoli. Can you say it?"

Angie stumbled over the name several times before she got the syllables right. "Good," I said. "But say it very softly. The Cherokee people speak very quietly."

"Like everything is a secret?" she whispered.

"Yeah. Like everything is a secret and everything is special."

"Dalonige i Digadoli. Golden Eyes," she whispered.

"Perfect. Let's go eat. I'm starving."

"Me too. Mama says we can have Oreos and tea, biscause the milk is being bad biscause of the 'lectricy went off, biscause of the nasty storm." She tilted her head, her long hair falling to one side. "Mama says all your meat is getting icky too. She says you need to jerk it. Why do you have to jerk the meat, Dalonige i Digadoli?"

I took Angelina's hand and led her to the kitchen, where my best friend looked up from laying out cookies and pouring hot tea. "Jerk meat? That's a very good idea, Molly. I like it."

I oven-broiled and ate a steak so rare it ran blood when I cut it, while the kids and Molly feasted on tea and cookies and sliced fruit. Then Molly, Angelina, and I spent the rest of the morning slicing and seasoning the ten pounds of Beast's steak I had tucked into the freezer when Ada knocked off the power. I had hoped the electricity would be back on before the freezer warmed up, but that hadn't happened. When I left the house a little after noon, it was with a belly full of rare steak, pasta, and salad. The pungent aroma of cooking seasoned meat scented the house.

CHAPTER 4

We invade her territory

After first making sure no one was watching, I grabbed a handhold and jumped the fifteen-foot-tall brick fence to my landlady's and rang the bell at the back door. Katie's Ladies was the oldest continuously operating whorehouse in New Orleans, and her ladies' primary clients were vamps. Even with vamps, there was pillow talk afterward. Or maybe during—what did I know? But I'd learned something of value to an investigation before, when I went to visit.

Troll appeared after only a moment, yawning, a meaty fist covering his mouth, his bald pate shining as if freshly waxed in the dim sconce lights in the hallway. "Morn-awn," he said through the yawn, his big teeth seeming to reach for air. "You must be psychic.".

"Why's that?"

"Some of the girls are up. Having a snack in the dining room. Help yourself." He slung a thumb haphazardly toward the dining room. Seemingly offhand, as he headed left toward Katie's business office, he added, "Bliss is with them."

Guilt stabbed me, as I'm pretty sure Troll intended. I hadn't seen Bliss since I ditched the little witch in a ladies' room in a French Quarter club, bleeding profusely from a vamp bite, while I went tearing off after her attacker. I'd not even thought about leaving her bleeding—maybe to death—at the time, so intent was I on catching the young rogue. Since Molly came to visit, I hadn't been over here much, compounding my inattention. "Yeah. Thanks," I said. I stuck my hands into my jeans pockets and meandered right.

I heard their voices and caught their scents from three feet outside the door, and stopped, listening, quickly determining that four of the "ladies" were having a midmorning snack of coffee, tea, chilled boiled shrimp, and pastries. I picked out the voices and scents of Bliss, Najla, Christie, and Tia, who was rhapsodizing about her latest vamp conquest. My mouth turned up with real amusement at what she'd taught him to do. I hadn't even known sex was possible in that position, especially while a vamp had his fangs buried in her femoral artery. She finished with "Mr. Tom says Carlos is ready to make an offer for me, and I'll be his blood-servant for, like, a hundred years, which is way better than a human man who might dump me when I get old, and I won't get old anyway with Carlos. Well, I will but not for, like, forever."

"Come on in, Jane," Bliss said, when Tia paused to draw breath.

"Why come you thinking she out there, girl?" a strangely accented voice asked. "What? You smelling them again?"

It had been years since I'd been teased and bullied by the girls in the children's home where I was raised, but it still got to me, even if I wasn't the actual recipient of the persecution. "Bliss has a real good sense of smell," I said from the hallway. Hands still in my pockets, I stepped into the room. Giving the bully a look with just a hint of Beast peeking out, I added, "No need to be mean."

"You eavesdropping, Janie?" Christie asked, her irritation a sharp tang on the air. "No need for *you* to stand in the cold like a lost child looking in. There's room at the table for one more, even if you are an inhibited and stuffy little churchgoer."

"Christie!" Bliss said.

"She's right," I said, as I pulled a chair out with my foot and sat. "I am Christian and I guess I'm pretty inhibited— by your standards." I looked at Tia and smiled gently. "For instance, I'm not flexible enough to hang from the ceiling while a vamp is feeding on me, especially not *there*." Tia giggled, the sound childlike and innocent, which, thanks to the parents who sold their daughter out of the trunk of their car for drug money, she would never be. To Bliss, I said, "But I'm also a Cherokee, and I'm learning about the spiritual practices of the People, hoping to study their magic."

Bliss looked quickly away, her face shutting down. Bliss was still in the witch closet (or maybe she didn't know she was a witch?) and any mention of magic use made her uncomfortable.

I poured myself a mug of hot green tea from a carafe on the table, and a warm lemony scent wafted out. I was pretty sure it was a sencha green, with lemon grass, ginger, and chamomile for flavor. I added two spoonfuls of sugar and stirred, tilting my head to look at Christie. Today her hair was braided into two plaits like a schoolgirl's and her face was bare of her usual harsh makeup. She wore no rings or chains through her multiple piercings, and for once she was mostly covered, if you counted a sheer robe over baby doll silk nightclothes as covered. I'd seen her at the dinner table dressed for an evening out with more exposed, pale skin than this. But even covered and without the steel through her flesh, her expression was worldly and jaded and watchful. Christie had always been just a bit cruel to me, as if I might want to steal what was hers.

We invade her territory, Beast thought at me, sleepily. *We are Big Cat. She is we sa.*

We sa. Little cat, or bobcat. Oh, crap. I am so stupid. I didn't let the expression reach my face, but I suddenly understood what Beast was thinking, and it made total sense in a predator/prey way. Christie had been the biggest, baddest thing around, with her chains and whips and studded collars, until I showed up. And though she had no idea why, now she was not quite so big and bad.

"But you?" I lied. "You scare me spitless."

Christie laughed, a startled bark of sound. The look she sent me was considering, measuring, maybe a hint hopeful. "Yeah?"

"Yeah. I'd love to watch you practice with that whip you carry sometimes." It was Beast's desire, not mine, but why not?

"Christie is amazing," Tia said, nodding, her full lips in a little bow. "She can whip a vamp until he almost bleeds. Only almost. She never breaks the skin. She's *talented*."

I didn't know how to handle that, but the image made Beast purr. "You each have a gift, you know," I said, trying to find a way to bring up Bliss's witch gift and her unknown parentage, "something special that sets you apart."

"You mean like Christie and her whip?" Tia asked, excited. When I nodded, her eyes widened in her coffee-and-milk-hued face. "What's mine?"

Okay, maybe I could have found a better way to broach the subject, but I was into it now, and I had to answer her. I floundered a moment and finally settled on the truth, even if it might not lead where I wanted it to lead. Slowly, feeling my way, I said, "You are gentle and kind and caring, and so forgiving. And ready to offer your clients not just your body, but your love and your affection. And they notice. They can tell you care."

Tia's hazel green eyes had widened as I spoke, her mouth forming an O of surprised pleasure. "Do you read palms too?" She stuck out her hand, palm up, face eager.

"No." I shook my head. "No palms."

"Do Christie," she said.

I slouched back in my chair and fiddled with the tea mug, taking a sip of the sweet lemony tea, not quite sure how I had gotten myself into this. "Christie . . . is bold and adventurous. And controlled. She has to be to keep from hurting the wounded people who come to her for . . . um . . ." *For wild, domination-based, bloody sex? No.* " . . . for help to meet their . . . special needs. And she's brave and smart. And I think she's observant and reads people real well." When I stole a glance at Christie, she seemed taken aback, but not displeased. Thoughtful, she bit into a pastry, red jelly squeezing out the end, and she nodded as she chewed.

"Do Najla," Tia said.

I looked at Najla, her skin so black it looked bluish in the dim light. "Najla is harder. She's a survivor. She keeps secrets close to her heart. But if I was looking for a friend, I'd pick her in a heartbeat, because I don't think she'd ever betray me if she finally gave her friendship."

Najla's eyes narrowed as if she were picking through my

words for something to pounce on. Finding nothing, she canted her head and stared at me, hard. Tia clapped her hands, excited. "That's Najla. When the rogue vampire attacked Katie that time, she grabbed all the girls upstairs and barricaded the door to her room and broke up a chair and gave out stakes. She was gonna kill it if it got in. Do Bliss! Do Bliss!"

This was my chance in, but I knew I could screw it up big-time if I said the wrong words. I chose a Krispy Kreme donut and bit in. It was cream filled and chocolate iced, my very favorite, and was perfect with the lemon-drop tea. As I chewed and thought, I took in the room. This was the first time I'd been in it since the rogue attacked. The blackwood, antique dining room furniture he'd destroyed had been replaced with more modern pieces of burled pecan wood, with Spanish wrought-iron curlicues on the pedestal legs and chair backs. The walls had been repaired and repainted a warm milk chocolate, and the damaged paintings of Katie that had lined the walls and the heavy draperies had been cleaned and rehung. I swallowed the donut and licked my fingers. Drank my tea. And became aware that the four girls were watching me, silent. And they were never silent.

"Bliss," I said. They leaned in closer. "Bliss has gifts far beyond most people. She can smell things other people can't, hear things they can't. And I bet she can see things other people can't, or see things in a different way from most people."

"Like the old ladies. Remember?" Tia looked at the girls, one hand making a fast circle as if speeding them up. "Three times now. We all saw five old women, but Bliss said they were really younger, and had blue and black sequins all over." Tia shrugged as if to say, "See, like that."

"Yeah," I said, carefully. "Blue and black sequins" was a way that power signatures might be described if one didn't know what they were. "Bliss would see things differently because she can see through magical glamours. She has what the Irish might call 'the sight.' "

Bliss stood abruptly, so fast her chair rocked and spun halfway around. Silent, her blue-black hair swinging, she left the room. Tia's mouth opened and tears gathered in her

eyes. "She's mad. But the sight sounds like a good thing."
She looked at Najla and Christie, pleading. "It's a good
thing, right?"

Christie looked at me, her eyes cold. "Not if you want to
keep it secret, it isn't."

Tia looked from Christie to me, tears dropping over her
lids and spilling down her cheeks. "Bliss?" she called, and
trailed her friend out of the room. Najla gave me a look
that could have cured meat and followed them. I could
hear their footsteps as they raced the stairs to their rooms
on the second story.

"Real smooth, Yellowrock," Christie said. "How you
gonna tell her she's witch-blooded when she don't want to
know?"

"You knew?" I asked.

"Pretty sure. She's got the sight, like you said. But she
doesn't want to talk about her parents or her life before
here. Katie said to give her room to deal with it in her own
way."

Which would have been nice to know. "You've all seen
five glamoured women a few times?" When she nodded, it
was stiffly, as if she wanted to lie and say no, but couldn't
see how to pull it off. "Where? And it was always the same
women?" I asked because I had seen something like that
once before but couldn't quite bring it to mind.

"In the Quarter a couple times. In the Warehouse District once. Bliss has a regular, a vamp client who sends a car
for her and brings her to an upscale apartment in the district, so she's there pretty often. Tia has a regular on Royal
Street she sees twice a week. Don't know about it being
the same women, but it was the same glamour each time.
Middle aged, dowdy, a little plump. Why?"

"Not sure. But would you pass the word? Next time
someone sees them, call me? I'd like to get a look."

Christie rolled her eyes. "Sure. What*ever*." She slid a
punk-pink cell phone across to me. "It isn't working yet,
but you can input your number. Then get outta here. I need
my beauty sleep."

I parked Bitsa in public parking near the front door of
the NOPD on South Broad Street. The power was back

on here, traffic lights working, air conditioners humming, marked units whizzing out to answer calls. I wasn't armed, but I did have my cell phone, change for vending machines if I got hungry, a spiral notebook, and a camera. And here, the cell towers were up and running. Sweet.

I was hoping to find info and evidence about witches and vamps and the problems between them, as well as info on vamp history that might lead me to the young-rogue maker. It wasn't kosher to bring a camera into NOPD, but unless they searched me, I wasn't going to mention it. I wanted evidence, and if I was left alone with it, I was going to take copious photos and e-mail them to myself. I could take pics with the cell, but I didn't know its memory capacity, and I might need a lot. I tucked the camera and cell phone into my boot.

Inside, it was a madhouse; a couple dozen manacled malcontents reeking of vodka, beer, malt liquor, wine, cheep perfume, and reefer were waiting to be processed. Officers were darting here and there—okay, were meandering here and there—and computer keys were clacking, radios, phones both cellular and landline, were ringing, PCs were beeping, printers were clattering, and the law enforcement 911 radios were chattering. It was oddly cozy, yet I was as nervous as a cat in a room full of wolves.

Beast perked up and paid attention to the organized confusion. Her claws were doing that milking thing they did to my psyche when she was interested in something, claws out, a sharp dig into my mind, claws retracted. It wasn't comfortable, but it did keep me alert.

Breathing just a bit too fast, starting a nervous sweat, I signed in and waited for the armed guard to look over my credentials and make a phone call. While waiting, I checked my cell phone and saw I still had bars. Cool. Now, if the bars extended further into the walls of NOPD, and if I could get the camera and cell inside, I'd be set to go.

When the armed officer finally waved me through, he had to shout directions over a loud confrontation at the front door. A multipierced cross-dresser in a skintight purple-sequined evening gown—and nothing else—had started screaming about his right to go to the ladies' room, despite the clear evidence of male dangly bits jiggling against the purple dress. Thanks to her—his?—histrionics, I was able to hand off my cell and camera to myself and not set off the metal detector as I scooted through.

Moving fast, feeling a trickle of sweat slide down my backbone, I tucked both items back into my boot, accepted my visitor's badge, and took the stairs to the third floor, as per the shouted directions. I meandered my way to the back of the room, which was done in office boring and smelled of Starbucks; someone had made a run and the paper cups were scattered among the desks. By the time I saw Rick LaFleur, I was cool and relaxed—or at least I looked that way. Rick was sitting in an uncomfortable-looking desk chair, his feet on the desk, crossed at the ankle. The cop had black eyes and black hair, what the locals called a Frenchy look. And he was gorgeous, by far the prettiest man I'd ever known. He also had intricate tattoos of a bobcat and a mountain lion—my animals—hidden beneath his shirt, on one shoulder, and a ring of big-cat claws on the other. And likely a lot of scars since the attack by a sabertooth lion's claws.

We hadn't seen each other since the attack, hadn't even chatted over the phone, except for the one time when I told him what I could about the violent confrontation he'd barely lived through. Now Rick watched me as I crossed the room. He wasn't smiling. He looked cold, aloof, and not particularly friendly.

What was it about my male acquaintances and dour faces? Whatever it was, I wasn't taking it sitting down. That way led to being sidelined and one-upped. Beast had other ideas too, and I could feel her peering through my eyes. Provocative was Beast's middle name. Following her lead, I slapped Rick's feet off the desk and took their place. "Long time no see, Ricky-Bo. You look remarkably healthy for cat food."

He narrowed his eyes and set his feet on the floor. Not that he'd had much choice. His Frye Western boots and ratty jeans had been hanging unsupported in midair until he lowered them. Rick wasn't happy. Until recently, he had been undercover. I had followed him in beast form, and listened in on a conversation or two, including pillow talk. I had also saved his life, though his memories of that event were confused and befuddled. If he remembered the attack clearly, he'd be more appreciative, I assured myself. Of course, he *was* still on administrative duty. According to Troll, the majordomo at Katie's Ladies and Rick's uncle, he was permanently out of the undercover business now that the vamps in town knew he was a cop. So maybe he wasn't appreciative after all.

I leaned in to him and spoke softly. "Ricky-Bo, I need access to any files or reports about young rogues roaming free, say, in the last few years. NOPD got any vamp files?"

His eyes sharpened and I could see things taking place behind them. I was pretty sure I wouldn't like whatever he came up with. "Maybe. What do you have to trade?"

A negotiation. I should have known. "How about your life? Remember that one? And how about the rogue who killed the cops, your friends and fellow officers. You saw the photographs. You owe me."

Rick's expression closed down, into that mask they all do, cop-face. "Maybe, maybe not. How 'bout you share what you're working on for the vamps? If I like it, we'll see if NOPD has anything you can use."

I let a bit of Beast shine through my eyes and leaned in. Rick didn't run, but his body went still and I smelled adrenaline creep from his pores. I spoke low, so only he would hear, and Beast watched his eyes, evaluating him like a predator. "My contract is to bring down a vamp who's making young rogues and setting them free, uncured, to feast on the populace. I got nothing yet, so sharing is out for now, but the quid pro quo was already satisfied."

I let my eyes drop to his chest and the sabertooth claw scars hidden beneath his shirt. I had a flash of memory. An image of Rick in a pool of blood in the middle of a ruined room. It was as fresh and cutting as that night.

His eyes darkened, as if he was seeing that night too, the memory of the attack. He swore but the words were without heat, his gaze turned inward, a hand on his scarred chest. I wasn't sure what he was thinking, but I didn't like the lost look growing in his eyes. I nudged his knee with mine. "So. You gonna tell me what I need to know? About the vamps?"

With a visible effort, he pulled himself back into the

present and his gaze met mine, searching and oddly vulnerable. For a moment, I thought he might reach up and touch my face, but he sighed instead, and the sound had an "I give up" quality about it. "Yeah. I guess you got the QPQ right. I don't know what it is about you, Yellowrock." As I had no idea what he was talking about, I said nothing and after a moment he blew out another breath, this one sounding irritable again but without the resigned note. "Come on." And with that, I was in. Rick LaFleur, former undercover cop, now on administrative duty, led me down several flights of stairs to a room with no name, only a number: 666.

"Cute," I said of the numbers.

"Yeah, cop humor. We keep the weird-shit cases and the woo-woo files in here." He sounded like his old self again, lighthearted and carefree, no trace of that night in his voice. He opened the door and preceded me in. And I heard a metal drawer slide open. Over Rick's shoulder I saw Jodi Richoux. She was sliding a slim red folder into a metal file cabinet and the look she shot me was full of meaning, if I'd only been smart enough to know what the meaning was. But whatever it was, Jodi wasn't surprised to see me here. In fact, I had a feeling she had been expecting me, had seen me arrive, and beaten me to the room. I sniffed the air, smelling her apprehension as she closed and locked the cabinet drawer.

I'd had beers with Jodi before Mol arrived. We weren't exactly bosom buddies, but we had ended up on the dance floor, half drunk and whooping it up. It had been nice having a gal pal of sorts, as I had been kinda lonely until Molly came. "LaFleur, Yellowrock," she said.

"Richoux," we both said back, in offbeat unison. She nodded and left the room, giving me that look again, and glanced back to the drawer she had opened. And then she was gone.

The room was walled in metal file cabinets painted gray and military green, surrounding a long table and six metal folding chairs. No windows. Just two bare bulbs lighting the room in a harsh blaze. Rick patted the file drawer that Jodi had just closed, saying, "Everything we've gathered on the vamps since they came out of the closet is right here." He jingled a ring of keys, selected one, and unlocked the file cabinet.

Everything was a two-drawer file cabinet labeled 666-0V. On top of the cabinet were stacked three cardboard boxes. I opened a cabinet drawer to find folders divided into sections with little tabs—Clans, History, Miscellaneous, that kind of thing. My fingers itched with impatience, and I pulled a thick one on history and opened it. Loose pages shifted with a dry, raspy sound like snakes slithering on rock. On top was a police report from 1978.

"Ahhh," I said, not looking up from the folder, excitement rising. "I may be a while."

"I'm locking you in."

"What? No." I wasn't crazy about being stuck in a locked room anywhere and Beast didn't like it at all. I felt her staring out of my sockets, a growl low in her throat that I caught before it erupted out of mine.

"This hallway is full of sensitive information on paranormal investigations, a lot of it old files that are still only in hard copy format. If I had time to babysit you or had a uniform to put down here, it'd be different. For now, the lock has to do. Call my desk when you're done."

I looked back at the file in my hand, knowing I needed to stay. Okay, yeah. I could do this.

CHAPTER 5

I was living in a former whorehouse

According to police records, vamps hadn't been totally in the closet in certain cities across the globe, even before the famous staking of Marilyn Monroe by the Secret Service in the Oval Office while she was trying to turn President Kennedy. That event had revealed the existence of vampires, and shortly thereafter, witches, to the public, but prior to that, vamps had an undeniable—if shadowed and veiled—presence in such cities as Paris, London, Mumbai, Tokyo, and New Orleans. In and around the French Quarter they had attained a clandestine notoriety in the early nineteen hundreds living in Storyville, the section of the city once set aside for houses of ill repute, saloons, gambling houses, honky-tonks, music halls, and similar such places catering to the baser side of human desires.

Vamps had owned and managed at least three houses of prostitution in the district set aside by Sidney Story from 1897 to 1917, houses licensed and operated within the law. According to the Blue Book, which listed the names, descriptions, and addresses of more than seven hundred prostitutes, the vamp houses had been dedicated to "lusty lasses, a bit of blood, and the nick of a delicate whip," as well as "the finest professors in the land," professors being the musicians who played in the houses. The names of the three vamp houses were kind of corny: Countess Simone's

Pleasure House, Le Salon du Tigre, and Katie's Ladies. That last one I knew well.

I looked up to see the empty room, scanned the corners for cameras or listening devices, saw that it was clean, and blew out a relieved breath. I hadn't realized how tense I was until I let my shoulders slump. Beast might be provocative, but I was a wimp when it came to cops. I blew out another breath and forced myself to relax fully.

I glanced over the photographs of the bawdy houses, pausing at Katie's. In front of the house a blond woman posed, standing against a light pole, back arched, her skirts and petticoats tossed high to reveal long, slender legs, garters and stockings, and low boots. Her dress was open, displaying a lot of cleavage. It was Katie, her fangs displayed as carnally as her body.

The house she stood in front of was French with lots of black wrought iron in a fleur-de-lis pattern, and had a second-story balcony over the front. Gaslights burned in the early evening, reflecting on window glass. The narrow door had a leaded glass window in the upper half, and was very familiar to me. The house in the photo was where I currently lived. Great. I was living in a former whorehouse.

But a vamp on film? I hadn't known it was possible, yet, as I thumbed through the pages, I found several vamp photographs, bodies and fangs on exhibition, each one signed by the well-known Storyville photographer Ernest J. Bellocq. Bellocq had managed to photograph a number of famous vamps of the time, despite the inability of vampires to reflect on the silver used in both daguerreotypes and the later wet collodion-process photographs. I wondered how he had done it. Most people thought vamps had been photo-proof until digital cameras had appeared. And yet, here was the proof that someone had figured out how to do it.

Katie might have answered my questions about vamp history, but she was unavailable, sent to earth to heal the wounds that would have led to her final death. My first few days in New Orleans had resulted in pretty major changes in some of my employers' lives.

I stopped at one erotic photo of two vamps posed together. Katie was sitting on a bar, bottles of liquor lining the wall behind her, her head thrown back in what looked like pure carnal ecstasy. Her breasts were exposed, her skirts hitched around her waist. Her bare legs were spread. A man knelt between them, clearly servicing her with his mouth. The man looked like a fashion plate, even involved in the intimate activity. He was wearing a short-waist coat, trendy in the day, slim pants and boots, and a top hat. The top hat was still in place, as was the long black hair he wore combed back and tied in a queue. Leo Pellissier.

A strange heat pulsed through me. Remembering when Leo healed me of a wound that would have left a human facing surgery, maimed, and in serious rehab. That had been erotic too, and he had only been licking my arm. Chill bumps rose on the back of my neck.

I shook my head and pushed away the memory and the sensations that warmed my skin. I removed the camera from my boot and took photos of the photos. Thank God for digital cameras. I was honest enough to admit that I might not need *all* of these for my investigation, but an investigator can never know too much backstory.

I drew another file from the history folder. This one was marked *Vampira Carta*, which was the vamp's code of law. According to the lawyer who had done the paperwork for my license, in it was the legal justification for hiring rogue hunters, which made my livelihood dependent on it. A notation on the front cover indicated the papers had been found during the construction of the Iberville Housing Projects, on the site of the old Storyville. Iberville was the housing project where I'd killed a vamp, where Derek Lee lived. Curious, I opened the file.

It was set up a lot like the Magna Carta, with a preamble and numbered paragraphs of importance. If I remembered right from high school, the Magna Carta had thirty-seven paragraphs. The Vampira Carta had twenty-two. I wondered which document was actually older. It was written in an old form of English, or maybe Latin; fortunately, a translation started at the bottom.

The first paragraph read:

Preamble: Jules, Blood Master by the shame of sin, Master of the Guilty of England, Ireland, and Aquitaine, sends solemn greetings to all to whom the present letters come. Concerning the liberties of the dead and living, we submit this great charter to the Blood Master of Europe, the lord Lucius, our father of the Mithrans.

I turned the page. There wasn't another. The translation stopped, or the next page had been removed. I searched through the history folder, but the rest of the translation was gone, or had never existed. I set the pages on the table and quickly snapped off six shots, folded the history info back up, and went to work on other stuff. I wondered if the vamp council would let me have a translated copy of the carta, and what kind of story I'd have to use to get them to hand it over.

At the back of the file was a handwritten list in pencil on lined paper, of names and words titled Anomalies. When I read them, my skin went all prickly.

Anomalies
　　Sabina Delgado y Aguilera—shaman, Vampire, out-clan (meaning?), Cross? Second gen?
　　Bethany NLN—shaman, Vampire, out-clan (meaning? related to Sabina?), Cross? Third gen? War?
　　Sons of Darkness? What the hell are they?

There was no sig line. At some point, some cop had done a supernat investigation, and he'd clearly been left with some loose vamp ends. I wondered if he'd survived being nosy. The words were too faint to photograph. I didn't recognize the blocky handwriting and when I sniffed the page, the scent signature was unfamiliar, almost obscured by lingering tobacco smoke, as if the writer had been a two-pack-a-dayer. But something about the list felt important, so I copied it into my little spiral notebook, then texted it to myself, just in case I wasn't allowed to leave with notes, and went back to the files.

The cops had done a history on each of the clans, and rather than read the info here, I took more photos, hoping the picture clarity would be good enough for later reading. I continued searching the cabinets and came upon a stack of old MPRs—missing persons reports—with a reference to file number 666-0W. I checked the other cabinets but all of them were locked. I remembered the ring of keys Rick had carried. Shrugging, I settled to the one I had. And I spotted a red folder. A quick search told me there weren't many of them in the drawer, and when I sniffed it, it smelled strongly of Jodi Richoux. It was the file she'd been putting in the drawer while she looked meaningfully at me. Inside were more MPRs.

All the missing in Jodi's file were children and teens, all within the last twenty-five years, ten of them from recently. They had all vanished at night, all were under eighteen, all were witch children. The chill I'd been feeling off and on settled across my shoulders as I stared at the photographs and the reports.

All of them vanished at night. It was circumstantial, but could vampires be involved? I couldn't see what they had to gain.

The last witch child had vanished three months ago.

The reports were scanty and didn't go beyond interviews and I wondered how much the cops were doing to find the little witches. NOPD had a well-publicized antipathy to witches that deepened following the witch debacle of Katrina, when a lone witch coven tried to turn a category-five hurricane away from land. They got it down to a cat three, but they couldn't turn it. Their efforts and power weren't enough; the old, poorly built levees failed; thousands died in New Orleans and across the Gulf Coast from wind and storm surge. But would human anger be enough to make some cops ignore the continuing kidnapping of witch children for decades? I hoped not. But I had a bad feeling about it.

The MPRs weren't up to date, but they indicated the direction of the investigation—back into the witch community itself, which I figured was a smart place to start. Over the last decade, it looked as if every known witch above twelve years of age had been questioned, and some fifty vamps. I checked the name of the lead investigator. Elizabeth Caldwell. It meant nothing to me, but I could pump Rick later. And then I remembered the look on Leo's face, torchlight flickering across his features. His eyes on Angelina above me, his nostrils wide as he took her scent. Leo couldn't be involved with the disappearing kids. Yet the thought iced across my shoulders and down my spine like sleet, sharp as frozen knives.

I spent the next hour photographing police files. I didn't know what I was looking for until I found a folder with twenty-seven police reports in it. The reports were cases of attempted and successful rogue vamp attacks. They too went back some twenty years.

A heated frisson of certainty sizzled over my skin. This was it.

The reports were in no particular order, so I spread them out over the table. Making educated guesses, I pushed any reports that might be about old rogues into one stack, while young rogue attacks went into another. Once I got them separated, I had twenty-one that fit my profile—small fangs, unclaimed by any clan. I wanted the addresses of the attacks so I could situate them on a map and see if any particular locales stood out. Wishing for a map application on my cell phone, I jotted notes, texted them to myself, and added anything that looked interesting. Then I photographed the pages. Info in triplicate. I was *so* not losing this.

On a hunch, I did a quick comparison to see if any witch disappearances correlated with the young-rogue attacks and was disappointed to discover that none correlated exactly; they were weeks apart in some cases. But it was close enough to make me curious.

Before I put them away, I sniffed the reports. Three of the oldest reports smelled like the same cigarette tobacco on the anomaly list. All of them had been handled by Jodi. Satisfied, I put them away, making sure I was leaving nothing behind.

I looked at the locked door. And around the room. No landline phone. Hadn't Rick told me to call his desk when I was done? I checked my cell. No bars. I had texted a lot of stuff to myself and the info would be in my sent texts, but still . . . I was locked in. Beast woke and snarled. She did not like cages.

Holding her down, I knocked on the door, and before the second tap, it opened. A wrinkled patrol officer stood there, poorly shaven and overweight. I could have sworn that was powdered sugar on his shirt, like from donuts, or the New Orleans version, beignets, but I figured it was impolitic to ask or stare, and maybe something like racial profiling. Could you do employment profiling? And would it be politically incorrect? Not feeling my usual cop-induced nervousness, I smiled. Beast settled down, tail twitching. Annoyed.

"What?" he said roughly, seeing something in my eyes he didn't like. "You done?"

"Um . . . almost. I need to use the ladies' room."

He shook his head, turned away, and waved me to follow. He took me up two flights of stairs and waited outside while I went in. I pulled the phone and the camera's memory chips, discovered that I had two bars, and uploaded all the photographs to a secure Web site I'd had created last year. It was a fail-safe in case my camera and my notes were confiscated on the way out.

I started to sweat halfway through. It was taking too long. After twelve minutes, the officer opened the door to inquire after my health. That wasn't quite what he said, but it was kinder than his "Hey, lady. I'm not rushing you or nothing, but shit or get off the pot. I got work to do."

New Orleans's finest and best.

I finished, forced myself to relax again, flushed to make things sound right, and walked out. "Not feeling too good," I told the guard, holding my stomach. "Must be the unrefrigerated dinner."

"Yeah," he said. "We got a lot a' pukers in the hospital. You need to go?"

"No. I'm good," I said, doing a mental head shake. I saw the metal detector just ahead and put my hand out for a shake. "Thanks. I can find my way out from here."

The cop looked at my hand, held his to the side, and backed away saying, "No offense, lady, but you just finished being sick in the toilet."

I nodded and dropped my hand. "So I did."

He moved away, leaving me with no witnesses. I didn't see Rick on the way out, but I did set off the metal detector. I pulled my cell out of my boot, held it up to justify the alarm to a cop walking in the door, who shook his head. Feeling a spurt of relieved adrenaline, I jogged out of NOPD and slapped the rain off the bike seat. That was one problem with bikes, even totally cool ones like Bitsa. No protection from the elements. I sat on the wet leather, helmeted up, and started her, heading out into the day. I hadn't had much sleep and I needed a nap.

Back home, the house smelled divine, the scent of slow-cooking beef permeating the whole place. The smell made Beast even more eager to change and hunt. It had been days and she was getting antsy, which made her more likely to try to take control, to play me as she played with her dinner when it was still alive. "Not yet," I said to her. She huffed and milked her claws into me. I ignored the discomfort and she rolled over in a snit.

From my closet, I ferreted out a map of the city and surrounding parishes. Louisiana wasn't divided into counties, but parishes, which amounted to the same thing. With no regard to the smooth purity of the paint job, I tacked it to my bedroom wall. Onto the map, I tacked the young-rogue vamp attacks over the last twenty years. There were three major clusters and, oddly, I had been to two of them. Hot exhilaration shot through me. I downloaded my woo-woo cop photos to my laptop and spent time arranging them into proper files for printing when we had reliable power.

I had cell bars, made a few calls, left messages, and fell into bed as a secondary storm chasing the tail of Ada hit the city. Through half-closed eyes, I watched as the light through the windows darkened and rain lashed the glass like liquid fingers, seeking a way inside. Thunder and lightning rattled through the floor and up through the mattress, sending bright flashes into the room. The lights flickered on and off several times, settling again on off.

Upstairs, I knew Molly was putting the kids down for naps. Nap time in the middle of the day wasn't something new, as I often slept in the daytime after a night spent prowling in cat form. But this formal napping, of an entire household settling in for a snooze, was new and oddly comforting. I closed my eyes and sleep pulled at me, seductive and peaceful.

Also sleepy, Beast rolled over inside me, the sensation so real I could feel her pelt scraping inside my skin. My last thought was of Beast, curled in the dark, her/my tail wrapped tightly around my body. Small furry forms were curled against my belly, between my four paws, sleeping. Kits, breathing, snuffling, smelling of milk and exhaustion.

I woke to the smell of sweetgrass smoke, the sound of drums in a slow four beat, and the beeping of my cell. The dream slid away like silk sheets being pulled slowly from my mind. I opened my eyes. The storm was over, rain plinking and gurgling outside, the world brighter than two hours past. I fumbled in my boots beside my bed and answered. "What," I grated out, my voice full of sleep. Okay, so I wasn't at my best upon first waking.

"George Dumas here. You left a message"—a trace of humor crept into his tone—"before your . . . *nap*?"

A curious heat rolled over me, settling in my lower belly. That man had a great voice. Clearing my throat, I rolled to my back and stared at the ceiling twelve feet above me. Well, ten, as I wasn't lying on the floor. I mentally shook myself. I needed to be sharp when I talked to Bruiser, not a melted puddle of hormones. But I could hear the warmth in my tone when I said, "I'm that transparent?" *Crap.* I sounded flirty. I did not need to be flirty with this man. I needed to keep it professional. At that thought, I remembered the photo of Leo and Katie. Being professional.

"You sound like a child just waking up," he said, his voice soft.

I will not flirt with this man. But it seemed I couldn't help myself. "Yeah, Bruiser. I'm cute that way." I rolled into a sitting position and dropped my feet to the floor. My braid had come half undone in my sleep and hair cascaded around my thighs. I needed caffeine. A lot of it.

Beast reared up. *We need to mate.*

That stopped whatever I meant to say. After an awkward pause, I managed to Bruiser, "I need some help."

Now he hesitated. "My boss may not be interested in my helping you."

"You said *may* not. Meaning that he didn't specifically prohibit you from helping me."

"No. Not specifically."

"There are four vamp parties this week. All I need is this—to know which parties Leo won't be at, and then an invitation to attend at least one of them."

The silence after I spoke was sharp and pointed, like a bayonet held to the heart. "And how do you know there are four parties this week?" he asked. Any hint of flirtation was gone from his tone, which helped me focus, remembering that this man was Leo's security expert and would likely kill me without a thought if his boss said to.

I recalled the calendar hanging in Raisin/Ernestine's office, every date of the vamp council's social life marked in Ernestine's lovely penmanship. Not that I was about to give away anything I might need later. Flirting with Bruiser was out, now, so I settled on flippant. "I have connections here and there. Is Leo still in mourning? Well, except to leave his coffin while trying to burn me alive in my own den."

Everyone knew that vamps didn't sleep in coffins. Just very secure, hidden, underground rooms that they called lairs. *Coffins* was mildly insulting, and Bruiser said, "I understand that you were on the side *porch*, not the den, when you faced down Leo and his top scions."

Oops. Den was Beast talk. I was more sleepy than I thought. Or Beast's comment about mating had taken me seriously off guard. Maybe I should hold off baiting the blood-servant of the city's most powerful vamp until I was more awake and thinking less about Bruiser's butt in tight jeans when he delivered Leo's invitation to vacate the city, I said, carefully, "Figure of speech. You boys gossiping about me?"

"When you killed the creature who had taken Immanuel's place, you saved most of Clan Arceneau's blood-servants; Brandon and Brian are alive and breathing because of you. But you left their blood-masters chained with silver when you found them, which works against you, and despite proof that the creature wasn't Immanuel, Leo feels the loss of his son." I could hear the distaste in his voice. "For good or ill, most of the clans' security has a more-than-passing interest in you, Jane."

That woke me up better than a whole pot of tea. "Well, that makes me feel all warm and cozy."

"It shouldn't. Why do you want to attend a vampire party?"

Not so I could boogie with the rich and fangy. I thought it but I didn't say it. What actually came out of my mouth was worse. "I need to sniff them." Bruiser barked with disbelieving laughter and I could have socked myself. Thinking fast, I said, "Just after the hurricane passed, I found where the sire making the young rogues had been. He, or she, wears a striking, distinctive perfume."

Bruiser wasn't going for it. "You aren't human," he said. "I saw evidence of that myself. So, does that mean that whatever form of supernat you are has an enhanced sense of smell?"

In lieu of a formal introduction when we first met, I had taken Bruiser down and then burned his boss with a silver cross. Not something any human would likely succeed at. I was screwing this up. I lifted my nose in a self-conscious gesture that felt very Beast-like. "That invitation? The sooner, the better."

But Bruiser wasn't being pushed. "Last time you went to a vampire party, you were under the protection of Leo himself. There won't be anyone to protect you this time."

"*You* could take me." The words were out of my mouth before I could stop them. The silence lasted longer this time. A lot longer. I broke out into a hot sweat and wanted to babble to cover the silence, but I bit my lips and waited.

"I would need to inform Leo and obtain his permission," Bruiser said very carefully.

Just as carefully, thinking of the way he looked, standing on my porch, I said, "That would be nice."

"I would tell him that taking you to the soiree would be an acceptable way to keep an eye on you, and whatever you were doing."

Taking you to the soiree sounded like a date. I wondered if he meant that. A flush spread over me, hot and needy. "Um . . . yeah. Okay."

After another long pause, during which I heard pages turning and computer keys clacking, he said, "Clan Rousseau is having an event tonight in the Old Nunnery in the Warehouse District."

"Tonight?" I squeaked, lifting a snarl of my hair and getting a good look at my unshaven legs. "After a hurricane?"

"The Warehouse District is quite upscale and power has been restored there."

"I . . . um . . . I have a dress," I said, thinking of my one little black dress.

"Clan Rousseau requires formal attire."

"More formal than my dress?"

"Much," he said dryly. "If Leo approves, I'll send someone over with a selection."

Of dresses? *Oh, crap*. "I look good in black."

His voice heated. "Yes, you do. I'll call after sunset." The line went dead.

I closed the cell, staring at the floor. "Okay," I said, not sure exactly what had happened.

"Well, well, well," Molly drawled. I looked up from contemplating the floor to see her leaning against the door-jamb. "Big Cat has a daa-aate," she sang out. Smugly she said, "And Big Cat might get lucky."

I dropped back into the covers and banged my head on a pillow repeatedly as Molly laughed at me. I remembered my body's reactions to the sight of Bruiser's butt, and the tattoos of my beasts on Rick's shoulder. I hadn't kept track of the phases of the moon. If tonight was a full moon, Beast's and Molly's hope that I'd get lucky was more probable than I wanted to imagine. During the full moon, Beast was more in control than usual. And Beast hadn't mated in a long, *long* time. For that matter, neither had I.

CHAPTER 6

I'd rather be shot, stabbed, or chewed on

I grabbed the laptop, stalked to the master bath, and shut the door. Lighting candles so I could see in the dark room, I sat on the toilet seat, thinking. What had I gotten myself into? *Crap*. Online, I searched calendar sites for one that listed the phases of the moon. The full moon was two days away. Relief poured through me. I was safe.

Mate, Beast demanded.

"No," I said. "Not Bruiser."

Beast sent a rush of sexual energy through my brain and suddenly I had a mental image of Rick, naked, spread out on a bed like dessert. There were claw scars across his chest, pale against his golden skin, and his tattoos almost glowed—a mountain lion and a bobcat on one shoulder and big bloody cat claws on the other. "Not him, either," I muttered.

Thanks to the natural gas, I had a long hot shower, during which I washed my hair and did all the fun things a girl did before a formal party . . . and a date. . . . I followed it with a long cold shower, during which I argued with Beast about my sex life. The conversation ended in a draw, and when I left the bathroom, the walls still steamy because the exhaust fan didn't work, I looked more presentable, nails polished, legs and pits shaved, skin all slathered with good-smelling cream, and brows plucked. As soon as I shifted again, I'd lose all the results of the effort, so I didn't get gussied up often. But it felt really good when I did. As I primped, the smell of slow-cooking steak wafted in under the door, making my stomach rumble with hunger.

I braided my hip-length black hair and left it hanging down my back, wet and still dripping. Throwing on jeans and a tee, I made my way through the house. The sound of a man's laughter stopped me in the entry. Bruiser? No. Rick LaFleur. And Angelina.

Molly, murmuring baby talk, was upstairs and I wondered why she had left Rick with Angie. Then I smelled dirty diaper, and I knew exactly what had happened.

Moving with the silence of my kind, I stopped outside the open kitchen doorway. Rick was turned to the side, so he couldn't see me, and I paused, studying him. Rick hadn't been to the house since he was mauled. Though pale, he looked good sitting in the kitchen, holding one of Angelina's dolls as she leaned against the arm of his chair.

"And I have a redheaded Martha, and a blond Rachael who wears a long dress like a princess, and two brown-headed dolls, Sally and Mary, but *Ka Nvsita* is my favorite biscause Aunt Jane gived her to me, and biscause she gots black hair like Aunt Jane and is a Indian."

"She kinda looks like your aunt Jane too," Rick said.

"Nuh-uh. The real Aunt Jane is Chur'kee and her skin is browner, but she has scars and yellow eyes, and *Ka Nvsita* doesn't. I'm gonna ask Santa Claus for another Chur'kee doll this winter, except that Santa Claus isn't real. Did you know that?" she whispered, looking from the doll to the cop. "It's a secret. I know lots of secrets."

"Like what?" Rick asked, his gaze focusing down on the little girl.

"Like names and stuff. And how to make oatmeal. And how to start the war—"

"Just like a cop to ask personal questions of a child, grilling her away from her parent, and doing it while sounding all innocent," I said.

Rick looked up, caught in the act and not even trying to look ashamed. "Oops," he said, not sounding at all contrite. His eyes traveled at a slow, leisurely pace from my feet to my gold nugget necklace dangling over my shirt, to my face.

"But no need to be envious. I'd like to hear your secrets too. All of them."

I wasn't completely certain that it was a sexual come-on; it could have been just a cop crack, but combined with the look, I had a feeling it was more. *Fresh meat*, Beast thought at me. I laughed at her comment and Rick thought I was laughing at his. Angie smiled at us grown-ups, laughing for no reason she could see, and trotted out of the room.

"Why are you here, Rick?" I crossed my arms and leaned against the door frame.

"No power at my house. No TV. The batteries in my iPod are dead. No lights. No electricity for the stove. I knew you had gas for cooking. So I brought an early dinner." He smiled slowly, showing very white teeth. "Steak that was going bad in my fridge. With fresh greens from the farmer's market, and flowers"—he pointed to the bunch of daisies and sunflowers in a milk pitcher—"and double-baked potatoes I picked up at Mario's." He pointed at a foam cooler near the fridge. "Molly already seasoned and wrapped the steaks in foil and tucked them in the oven with your ... beef jerky." The last two words were said with a clear distaste. Seemed Rick didn't care much for jerky.

"Cozy," I said, hiding a grin.

"Nice toes," he said back.

I looked down and tapped my toes on the floor in a riffling motion. The nails were painted bloodred with gold flecks in the polish. My fingernails were painted with clear, and filed short. My stomach rumbled with hunger. Looked as though we had company for dinner.

"I also thought we might pick a day to work on our bikes," he said. "Yours sounded a bit rough last time I heard it."

"You ride a Kow-bike. I ride a Harley. Different tools—metric versus standard."

"Sometimes different tools make for a lot of fun."

Okay. Definitely sexual innuendo that time. I grinned at him and shook my head. For a gal who had been out of circulation for a few years, I was getting a lot of attention. Too bad they were cop, blood-servant, and angry vamp. I'd be lucky to survive. "Better make it later in the week. I got to get all girlied up for a party tonight. I'm guessing that grease under my pretty nails would clash with my dress."

"Party?"

"Yeah. Down in the Warehouse District at the Old Nunnery?" I made it a question, because I didn't know where the Warehouse District was or what the Nunnery was, but neither sounded like someplace I should dress up for. "Given by Clan Rousseau."

Rick's brows went up a fraction. "Oh yeah?" At my nod, he said, "You need a date? Or maybe backup?"

"I have an escort," I said, "but thanks."

"Okay. Keep my cell number handy. If you need backup, call. And if you don't need me for backup, call anyway. I'd love to debrief you on that."

"I'm not interested in being debriefed. But I might be persuaded to share some things."

Just then Angie pattered back in and climbed straight up into Rick's lap. "Uncle Ricky, what's debeefing?"

"Angie Baby," Rick said, adopting one of Angelina's nicknames. I wondered when he had heard us use it. "A debriefing is when nosy cops ask nosy questions about things most people think they got no business knowing."

Angie dropped her hands and looked at me. "Like Uncle Ricky asking me about you?"

I looked at Rick, who had the grace to give me an embarrassed half grin and a small shrug. A lock of black hair fell over his brow, vaguely Elvis-like. My heart did a little pitter-patter. The man was too good looking for my own good.

"Yes, Angie, like that," I said. I handed Angelina her doll, took her up in my arms, and carried her to the stairs. "Scoot upstairs. Help your mama with Little Evan. I need to talk to Ricky-Bo."

"Okay, Aunt Jane."

Angelina's feet tapped up the stairs. When she was out of earshot, I turned to Rick. Sweetly, I said, "If you chat up my godchild again without either her mother or me present, I'll hurt you."

Amused, Rick sat back and spread one arm out over the back of the chair beside him in an expansive posture. "You threatening a cop?" Black eyes glinting, his other hand unconsciously curled in to touch his chest, tracing the scars that had to be there.

I let my smile go, not hiding under the pretense of geniality. "Yep. I dropped you in one move the last time you needed a lesson. Angie is off-limits and you know it. That was low."

He nodded slowly. "Yeah. It was. I took advantage of a situation that fell into my lap, and I shouldn't have. I'm sorry. I won't do it again."

I wasn't expecting an apology. My estimation of the man went up a notch. Men who had the capacity to apologize—and who knew the right words with which to do it—were few and far between. I'm not a whiz at social situations, and an apology wasn't something I was emotionally prepared to deal with. "Okay," I said, sounding far less gracious than he. Voices and the sound of footsteps coming down the stairs were about to put a stop to our conversation, thankfully.

Rick glanced at the empty doorway. "So, who's your escort tonight?" he asked quickly.

"George Dumas."

Rick's eyes went wide just as Molly and the kids entered the room, effectively ending the chat. But I could see the sharpened interest in his gaze and I knew the subject would come up again. Soon. Rick was professionally interested in George. And I had to wonder why.

The rest of the day went by fast and I found myself enjoying it, even knowing that Rick was hanging around to see what would happen when my "date" arrived. The temps heated up in the un-air-conditioned house, the world all muggy and sweaty, despite the windows Molly threw open. The smell of slow-cooked beef built and poured out into the steamy day. The four of us played kiddie board games and Go Fish with Angie until she fell asleep, exhausted from the heat, and then we played Hearts until our supper of slow-cooked steaks and double-stuffed potatoes.

The lights went on and off a dozen times as city utility workers tried to get the system back up and running, but before dusk they went off. And stayed off. Again. We made do with candles and lamps, but were running low on supplies. If the electricity didn't come on and stay that way, I'd have to motor around soon for lamp oil and more candles if such could be found. Five minutes after the sun set behind the cloud bank left over from Ada, my cell rang. The number in the display was Bruiser's.

Rick watched as I took the call on the side porch. He'd been chatting happily to Molly about eighties bands, but now he had an ear half-cocked my way, trying to listen in.

Speaking softly, I said, "What's up, Bruiser?"

"Yellowrock. A woman will be there with a gown in half an hour. I'll pick you up at ten. Be ready. Be unarmed."

"You're such a charmer."

"You, on the other hand, are a bloody, sodding pain in the ass," he said equably. I often forgot that Bruiser wasn't American by birth, and then his accent would peek out, he'd use a term or phrase that sounded so very British, and I'd remember. The call clicked off and I chuckled as I returned to the kitchen.

I looked at Rick. "This is going to get seriously girlie. Maybe you should take a hike."

"I have sisters, and they always need a man's perspective when it comes to formals. You gals tend to get all froufrou, with ruffles and flowers and lace and stuff, instead of calves and cleavage—the important parts. I'll stay."

He said the last two words in such a way that I thought it might take monumental rudeness or a lot more muscles than I was supposed to have to cart him bodily from the house. I shrugged. "Suit yourself. But *ruffles*? Do I *look* like a ruffles kinda gal?"

Rick just grinned. I spent the time cleaning up the dirty kitchen and washing dishes. Rick picked up a drying towel and put things back where they had been, which told me something about the cop or raised new questions—either he was observant, with total recall, or he had been in my kitchen before.

The woman with the dress showed up in a panel van thirty-two minutes after Bruiser's call, knocked once, imperiously, and when I opened the door, strode into the house as if she were here to take over my life.

"Madame Melisende," she said, as if the name was vastly important, popped a card into my hand, and looked over the ground floor of the house. "This will do," she said of the living room. To Molly, she said, "You. Bring lamps." And strode back into the night, leaving behind the scent of numerous vamps. Which was weird.

Molly looked at me, grinned with some secret amusement, and went to gather and light more hurricane lamps. Rick tossed the damp dishtowel over his shoulder, sat back in a wing chair, and crossed his legs as if for a great entertainment. His expression just missed being teasing, which set my hackles up. Rick and Molly seemed to have an idea what was about to happen.

When Madame Melisende came back in, she was trailed by a little human assistant with a clipboard, glasses, and stringy hair. Mousey would have been the simplest description of the assistant, but Madame Melisende herself defied simple words. I looked at the card she had given me, which assured me that she was *Madame Melisende, Modiste du les Mithrans*. She was mostly human, about five feet tall, white-haired, and steely-eyed. She looked seventy, had to be at least a hundred, had the energy of a twenty-year-old, and carried that smell of multiple vamps, like a blood-junkie. Which brought out all my curious instincts, though I couldn't think of a way to ask why she smelled as she did. Humans can't smell vamps, or at least not the way I can.

Most blood-servants carry the scent of only one vamp, the result of the bonding that takes place over time. A blood-servant and vamp stay together for decades, the servant providing a safe and constant supply of blood, emotional stability, and other services—those which might, in a human household, be fulfilled by lovers, employees, and paid servants—services that the pair mutually agree upon, in return for a living wage and tiny sips of vamp blood. The sips keep the servants younger, healthier, and assure a long and vigorous life, assuming that they survive any rages, grieving, or other mental snaps by the vamp.

A blood-slave has a similar, but more casual, arrangement and may be passed around within a clan, therefore smelling like multiple vamps, but usually only one clan. Blood-junkies were a big step below, making themselves available at parties for most anything the vamps wanted, from a quick meal to a quick lay. They were the blood addicts of the vamp world, and a growing, call girl–type business in cities that catered to vamp travelers. Only a blood-junkie smelled like multiple vamps from multiple clans. Madame Melisende smelled like a blood-junkie minus the lingering smell of sex. So, weird, but not really worth worrying about.

The woman pushed me into position in the middle of the room, looking me over. She made little humming noises as she walked around me, repositioning me as she moved, arms outstretched, then down, feet together, then apart. Satisfied, she took measurements at waist, bust, midriff, above my bust, hips, butt, shoulders, arm length, and inseam, calling them out as the assistant took notes.

When she was done, Madame Melisende took the clipboard, studied it a moment, then looked at me as if passing judgment. She said in an outraged French accent, "Hmmph. You are Amazon. However shall I accouter you in the designated time?" she demanded.

A hot, embarrassed flush shot through me. Rick whooped. Molly tittered.

Though I was brought up in a Christian children's home and was raised to know better, I glared at Melisende when I said, "It's okay, lady. I'm pretty sure I can't afford you anyway. So you can just take a hike. Besides, I have a dress."

"Let me see this *dress* you claim to have," she said with an acerbic sniff.

She followed when I marched into my room and took the dress out of my hand even before I got it out of the closet. I followed her back into the light. She held it up and gaped. "*Mon Dieu.* This is dreadful, more dreadful than I can speak." And then she let out a stream of French and threw the dress across the room.

Beast leaped into my eyes. Molly's eyes bugged out; Rick's amusement faded to be replaced by something very still and thoughtful. My voice dropped an octave. "That's my only dress."

Unperturbed by whatever the others saw in my eyes, Madame Melisende drew herself up to her full nearly five feet in height. "Good! *Du chiffon. Des déchetes!*" And she spat a bunch of words to her assistant, who scurried outside.

"That. Is. My only. Dress," I said again, hearing the growl in my voice.

"No. It is not." She sniffed again. "Now you will have three proper dresses, and I will take the rag away with me, never to be seen again. And when les Mithrans ask you tonight who accouter you as a queen on the throne, you will tell them Madame Melisende. And the elders and old ones will, at last, return to me as they should."

The last statements brought me up short. The assistant came back in through the front door and piled dresses up on the couch, and went back out and came back in again with more dresses while I interpreted her comments. The woman, imperious and demanding, needed . . . help? She had lost some of her clientele? I was about to ask for clarification when Madame Melisende raised her eyes to mine and commanded, "Strip."

Rick howled with laughter. Molly giggled.

"Get out," I told Rick. Still laughing, throwing the dressmaker and me amused, delighted looks, he left, boots clomping. I closed the blinds, locked the door, and stripped. And became a dressmaker's dummy. The next half hour was pure torment as I tried on dress after dress, looked over each one in the bedroom mirror, and started to like it, only to hear the dragon queen disparage it totally. I actually quit looking in the mirror to see if I had an opinion. My preferences didn't count. Madame Melisende finally chose three dresses, brought in a portable sewing machine, and started altering.

I slipped into a robe, fell on the sofa, draped myself across the long seat, and accepted a cup of hot tea from a laughing Molly. I closed my eyes. "I'd rather be shot, stabbed, or chewed on by a rogue vamp," I whispered to her, "than go through being fitted for a formal gown again."

Molly just chortled as she settled near me on the wing chair Rick had vacated. "It does you good to be a girl once in a while," she said. "Besides, now you need a new hairdo."

I groaned. Molly laughed again, but this time I was sure I heard the timbre of a torturer in the tone. Minutes later, I was sitting on a stool while Molly brushed my hair and braided it with tiny gold beads before gathering it all up and wrapping the braids around my head in an elegant do that caught the light. Then she started in on the makeup.

It was worse than I ever expected. I hated it. It was torture, no matter how good Molly said I looked. Molly made my eyes stand out like Cleopatra's, dusted something on my skin that made it glisten like gold dust, and put enough mascara on me to weigh down my lids. And she wouldn't let me look over the work—kept turning me away from the mirror with a firm hand. I could have muscled her for my own way, but Molly is my friend and she was having too much fun for me to simply stomp out.

It was late when Madame Melisende and her nameless assistant were done stitching, hemming, letting out, and taking in. They stuffed me into a dress, brought in all the lamps, and led me, my eyes closed, to the full-length mirror. Molly, the madame, the mouse who had no name I'd heard, and a sleepy-eyed Angelina, woken just for the final show, gathered around. In total silence. And I opened my eyes. I stood there in my one good pair of black dancing heels, wearing only my gold nugget as jewelry, the dress slithering around me like, like, like nothing I had ever felt before, I stared at myself in the bedroom mirror.

I gaped. Turned. "Holy . . . uh . . . moly," I whispered, in deference to Angie. I looked like a million bucks. A stylish, high-maintenance, girly, sophisticated million bucks.

The heels added three inches to my six feet in height. The silk knit dress started at my instep and rose in a loose sheath to my hips, which were banded by satin to my midriff in a tight cummerbund look. Above that wide band was a plunging neckline, the deep V crisscrossed with satin strips, the halter top strap a satin band about an inch thick. Oh—and the slash up my left leg, which made me look totally hot, was perfect for dancing. I did a little dance step, which showed an unseemly amount of thigh. "Perfect," I said, thrilled despite myself.

Beast nudged herself into my thoughts. *Prey clothes.* She sent me an image of two cats reflected in a pool of still, black water in a clearly amorous position, the full moon over their shoulders, the male scent-marking the female by rubbing his jaw over her head and ears. Instantly I recalled the photograph of Leo and Katie, in their own clearly amorous position. Beast purred happily.

I sighed quietly so that Madame Melisende couldn't hear. A nameless feeling tremored along my skin, lifting the fine hairs. I smoothed the dress along my body. I wasn't wearing my own underwear. The madame had cut mine from me and tossed them into the garbage with a "One does not ruin the lines of a creation *avec les culottes*. Foolish girl." And she had tossed me a body smoother that looked like a torture device. I had cussed under my breath while pulling on the nearly invisible wisp of discomfort. But the dressmaker was right. The smoother was perfect, and the dress would have been ruined by panty lines.

I smoothed my hands along my sides again, feeling the prickly sensation of Beast rolling over and stretching in my mind. Sex. It was the feeling of sex.

This full moon was going to be difficult.

A single knock sounded at the door and I looked at a clock. Which was totally wrong, thanks to Ada. Molly checked through the windowed door, chuckled evilly, threw me a look, and opened the door. Rick walked in, boots loud in the quiet room. He searched the space and found me. And stopped dead.

"Good Lord Almighty," he breathed.

Molly laughed delightedly, Madame Melisende chortled with pride, and Angie clapped her hands together. "Aunt Jane is a beautemous princess," she said.

I smelled his reaction. Rick thought I looked hot. For some reason, that made me feel confident and shy all at the same time, and my palms started to sweat. I brazened it out. "Not bad, eh? For a vamp killer?" I glanced at the madame and added, "No offense to your clients."

She sniffed, glanced at her watch, and said, "Monsieur Pellissier's servant will arrive in eight minutes." She made a little hand-sweeping motion to the mouse, who jumped up from her perch at the sewing machine, began gathering all the discarded dresses, and carting them outside. The madame hung my two other new dresses in my empty closet and turned to leave, giving me the once-over, and tucking a handful of her cards into my palm. "For the inquiries. By appointment only." She sniffed one last time and went back out the door the way she had entered, as if she owned the place, the mouse scurrying behind her.

I whirled, showing a lot of leg and nearly as much cleavage. Rick sat down. As much to conceal his reaction as to keep out of the way. Molly took Angie by the hand and closed the door on the last of the fashion show. The van roared off into the very dark night.

Before Rick had a chance to say anything more about me in my dress, new headlights pulled in front of the house, the sound of an engine idling through the open windows. I had left a thigh sheath on the toilet, and while Molly went to the door, I strapped the weapon Bruiser had denied me to the back of my thigh, making sure that neither the knife hilt nor the sheath showed. Then I eased a slender blade into my hair and tucked several wooden stakes into my braids like hair sticks. A small cross I sheathed in a lead-lined packet and shoved it into the bottom of the V of the neckline. The dress held it nicely in place, and the lead would keep it from glowing by accident.

I had gone unarmed into the presence of multiple vamps once before. Not gonna happen again. With a final twirl to make sure the knife sheath didn't show beneath the fabric, I took a deep breath and listened.

CHAPTER 7

Scent-marking me

Molly opened the door before the knock sounded and let Bruiser inside with a murmured "George. Come in." His scent, clean and crisp and slightly citrusy, blew in on the night breeze.

The last time Bruiser had picked me up for a party, I didn't have an audience. I looked down at myself, all gussied up, and discomfort shot through me like an electric pulse. I flushed and took a breath to force the embarrassment back down. There was no place for blood flushes where I was going. Or for sexual arousal either. Standing in the shadows, I breathed deeply, getting myself under control. My fingers rested on the thigh strap and I felt a measure of assurance return. One slender vamp-killer, one silvered knife, one cross, and stakes. The uneasiness blew out on a breath and I turned to the door.

Bruiser was in a tux. I had seen him in a tux before, but hadn't taken the time to really study him. The suit was fitted to him, tailored to his form and cupping the curve of his butt like two smooth, happy hands. The coat sat on his broad shoulders and wisped down his chest as if it loved to touch him and couldn't let go. The blood-servant of Leo Pellissier looked like sex on a stick. Something low down in my belly tightened and heated.

Bruiser offered a cordial, businesslike hello to Rick, masking any curiosity he might be feeling. He spotted me in the doorway. It was too dark for a human to see me, but he did. His eyes followed the dress from the floor to my breasts and on to my face. "Jane Yellowrock. You look lovely."

I stepped into the front room and couldn't think what to do with my hands. So I just stood there, fighting a blush, as the two men stared at me. Molly handed me a tiny black purse on a short, looped cord and said, "From the dressmaker. Your ID and a hundred dollars are inside. Try to be home before you turn into a pumpkin."

"Miss Jane," Bruiser said, holding the door for me. I stepped out into the humid night and into the chilled, leather seated limo.

The slightly stretched Lincoln could hold six passengers on two bench seats, but just as the last time Bruiser took me to a vamp party, there were only the two of us, the privacy partition up between the driver and the back. He slid in beside me and sat close, his thigh touching mine.

The car pulled from the curb and into the dark streets, its armoring making it ride low and heavy, like a highly polished tank. I wondered if there were weapons in the body of the vehicle, like a James Bond or Batman car, but didn't think I'd get a straight answer if I asked. Behind the limo, I heard Rick's Kow-bike start up, and knew he was leaving. I glanced back just in time to see him speed away, and the wards' formidable bluish sparkle encase the house.

We moved through the blacker-than-usual night and the unlit city. The last time I was escorted to a soiree, George played tour guide, pointing out landmarks and offering bits of history. This time, he settled back at an angle, arms bent at the elbows, hands laced across his stomach, and studied me, paying close attention to the slit in the dress and the wedge of leg I had left peeking out from thigh to toes. When he had taken in the long length of leg, he lifted his eyes to my cleavage and the gold necklace there. Not that I thought he was looking at the nugget. I didn't have a lot of cleavage, but what I had was nicely plumped by the dress.

He stared. I lifted my brows at his blatant regard, and though he didn't lift his eyes, a smile twitched across his face and was gone. He dropped his eyes back down. "You have stupendous legs," he said.

"And you have a great-looking butt." The words were

out of my mouth before I could think them through and I bit down on anything else that might come out. *Careful*, I thought. Beast panted with amusement and kneaded my mind with her claws, pad-pricking back and forth from paw to paw. It was sharply painful, which was her intent.

Bruiser chuckled and finally met my eyes. "You're a walking advertisement as a blood donor," he said baldly. "Every male vamp and half the female ones will want a sample taste."

Beast went still. *Beast is not prey.* I narrowed my eyes but Bruiser went on.

"I can protect you as long as you're with me, but if you wander off on your own, all bets are off. It's not too late to change your mind." I didn't reply. He sighed softly. "Of course, there are other methods we can employ to assure your safety."

"Methods?"

Bruiser unfolded his hands and reached into his breast coat pocket. He removed a bit of white cloth and extended it to me. My nostrils flared. *Vamp!* Beast warned, recoiling.

The scent wafted out of the cloth, the peppery smell of fresh vamp blood. I drew in the air through my parted lips. It was the particular blood scent of Leo mixed with the personal scent of Bruiser. I put two and two together and scowled. "What? He offered you a taste tonight and you spat it into a hankie? How sweet of you. Sloppy seconds from a blood feeding."

Bruiser sighed. "It'll keep you safe."

"And it'll mark me as his. And yours. No, thanks."

Bruiser sighed again and set the hankie close to his side, on the leather. And launched across the seat. At me. Over me. His body on top of mine. I slid down, landing hard.

I had a weird, time-warped moment to think, *He's attacking. He's going to mark me whether I like it or not.*

Beast hissed. Time slowed further, to the consistency of melting wax.

He landed on me, hands on the limo floor to either side of my head. His mouth inches away. One thigh between mine. Intimate, close, his flesh searing against me. Flashing like brown flame, his eyes captured mine. I could smell his anger.

And something changed, charging the air between us. Fury became desire. And I was pinned. For a long moment, he did nothing. Then his mouth landed on mine. And time halted.

I sucked in a stunned breath, pulling it from his lungs. Hot mouth, lips punishing. He gripped the back of my neck. Holding me still. Holding me close.

Beast took over. Wrapped my hands behind his neck and kissed him back. *Good mate. Strong. Fast.*

Bruiser's tongue raked my lips. Heat flamed through me, scorching, burning, my skin on fire. Breasts tightened into hard buds. I opened my mouth, positioned more firmly against his. Arched up at him. Heard my moan and was helpless against it. Wrapped my arms around him. Clasped him to me. Nails digging into the jacket. He shifted his hips into me, tight into my center, hard and ready. Swollen with need.

He rested his weight on an elbow and slid a hand into the fabric of my dress. Cupped a breast and teased my nipple into a tight hard peak.

"Yes," I whispered. "Now." Need drenched me. I lifted my hips toward him.

He shoved the dress strap to the side, freeing my right breast. Twirled his tongue around the nipple. Cupped the aching tip into his mouth and sucked so hard I nearly screamed.

His free hand slid down my body and along my thigh. And stopped at the knife hilt. He froze, his body so still he could have been a vamp. He eased away. Met my eyes, pushed the skirt aside, and took the knife hilt. Pulled it from its sheath with a smooth, tight shush of sound.

Our breathing was rough, unsteady, needy. I held his eyes. Thoughts raced through his, too fast to read.

He was holding the knife over me. Pointed at my neck. So close to my carotid I wouldn't have time to react should he decide to bring it down. Beast, however, wasn't concerned. She watched Bruiser through my eyes. Despite the scent of vamp he carried, she liked what she saw.

Bruiser reversed the knife and set it on the leather seat. When he brought his hand down again, it held a bit of white. Before I could react, he wiped the blood scent along my neck and down across my exposed breast.

Scent-marking me. With the smell of a different mate. I
hissed again. Caught his hand. But it was too late. I could
see the angry amusement glinting in his eyes. "Son of a
bitch," I whispered fiercely, holding the offending cloth off
me.

He chuckled softly but there was no humor in it. The
sound was cold and rigid and full of self-mockery. "Actually, Mama was an impoverished English lady." He tossed
the cloth and slowly pushed up from the floor to the seat,
accidentally—or maybe not so accidentally—dragging
himself against my center, a cruel reminder of what had
just nearly happened. He held out a hand to lift me back
to the seat.

I fought embarrassment and a need to refuse the gesture. It would have been childish and would only make
things worse. I slid my dress back over my breast and took
his hand, allowing him to lift me back to the seat, leather
cold through my dress. I smoothed the skirt into place over
my legs.

Bruiser took the blade and held out his other hand,
patient but demanding. I flipped back the skirt again and
undid the knife sheath. He stared at my legs and the shadowed V above them, his eyes like a heated caress from ankles to the top of the dress split, only inches from where he
had been planning to go. And where I had been planning to
let him go. I shifted, dragging the skirt open wider. Okay, it
was mean, but Beast wasn't happy at being thwarted or declawed. And neither was I. I placed the sheath in his hand.

"Any other weapons?" he asked, desire making his voice
rough.

His question made me want to raise a hand to my hair
and the hidden implements there, but that would have been
stupid. "Yeah," I said. "Killer legs."

Bruiser met my eyes. Unexpectedly he grinned and the
fight went out of him. He leaned across, slid an arm behind
me, and pulled me close, one hand finding my inner thigh.
I rested both hands on his shoulders, lips parted. Holding
my gaze, he slid his hand up along my leg until the tip of his
finger touched the body smoother. "Damn," he whispered.

I stuttered a laugh and he kissed me thoroughly. And I

responded, not sure where this was going now, but pretty sure it wasn't heading to any kind of sexual satisfaction. I was right. But when he pulled away, it was with obvious reluctance. His thumb feathered over my sensitive flesh and I fought a shiver. "Killer legs, eh? You do indeed." He skimmed his hand down my leg and back up, to pause just out of reach of any kind of satisfaction. "When this is over, I'm taking you to my place and keeping you there for a week."

I flushed hotly and Beast purred happily deep inside me. I wasn't sure what "this" was, but I nodded and said, "Two."

His eyes went hot and dark. His voice dropped to a burr. "Two."

I sat, his hand on my thigh, and tried to figure out what to do next. The silence stretched, and I was pretty sure he was waiting for me say something else. Desperate, choosing a subject at random, I said, "Why did Madame Melisende lose her clientele?"

One side of Bruiser's mouth quirked and he eased me away. I wasn't sure the extra space made me happy, but I wasn't sure it made me unhappy either. "Melisende picked the wrong party in the last vampire war, and her more wealthy clients went elsewhere."

My instincts perked up. Leo's scions had mentioned war, as had the list of anomalies. "Vampire war?" I was suddenly aware that the limo was icy cold from the AC and my skin pebbled. I pulled my dress over my legs.

Bruiser glanced away from me and outside the limo. "We're almost there. No time for a history lesson." He looked at a brass—or maybe gold—bucket attached to the limo wall, filled with ice and an open bottle of champagne. Glasses were in holders to the side. I hadn't noticed it until now. "No time for champagne either, not with the time we spent . . . frolicking."

"Why did you agree to take me to this party? I figured I'd have to break your arm."

"Twist my arm?"

"No." I smiled and looked at him under my lashes. "Break. Definitely break."

Bruiser laughed but his face quickly reset itself into serious lines. "My master has a favor to ask of the Rogue Hunter."

"Crap." I dragged out the word, not liking the sound of this at all. "A favor? Last time I checked, the only thing he wanted was for me to get the hell out of town, under threat of a death by slow roasting or getting turned. Has something changed?"

"Yes. Well. There have been rumors of a realignment in the clans. Such a realignment is what began the last vampire war. Leo is asking—I am asking—for your help to stop it. Please."

I laughed once, a harsh bark of sound. "Leo came to burn me out, to burn me alive." Bruiser flinched slightly. "And now he wants me to help solidify Clan Pellissier's power base? You gotta be kidding."

"Leo is not the most dangerous creature in this city." His voice was low and certain, the tone of a man who has seen and survived too much. "It is his power that has kept the peace for so long, between beings that have few morals, and often no compunction about killing humans. He is simply not himself, lost in his grief." Bruiser's face went intense, his eyes holding mine. "I know that solving the internal conflicts between Mithran clans isn't within the parameters of your contract, but keeping humans alive is. And if there is war, it won't be contained to the vampires."

I pursed my lips, not looking at him. "I lived through the last war in 1915. It was bloody horrific," he said softly. "The violence was as undercover as they could keep it, but believe me, if you'd known where to look . . ."

I blinked. Blood-servants lived a long time, but it was still a shocker whenever I heard confirmation of that. *Nineteen fifteen. Criminy.* But still . . . I drew down my brows and crossed my arms, knowing it made me look defensive. I so did not want to help Leo Pellissier. Not in any way. "I did not kill Leo's son," I said, hearing the mulish tone in my voice. "I killed his son's killer. His son had been dead for decades."

"I accept that. Leo will eventually accept it as truth. Until then I'll . . . do what I can to keep him away from you. Will you help? For the city's safety?"

I shook my head, but it wasn't a no, it was frustration. "What do you want me to do?"

"Simply listen at the party, and if you hear anything unusual, tell me." That wry smile twisted his features again, this time seeming contrite. "Because of Leo's scent, you'll be free and safe to go anywhere you wish." I glared at him and he had the grace to grin in apology, which transformed his face, making him look younger. "And because you aren't me, and because you smell like dessert underneath Leo's scent, they may speak freely. You might hear something that could avert this war." When I didn't reply, he insisted, "If there is war, humans, many humans, will die."

Crap. He played the human card. I sighed. "Yeah, sure. If I hear anything, I'll share. Why not?" I glared at Bruiser. "But you keep that blood-sucking vamp away from my house."

"Katie's house," Bruiser said softly.

I blew out a breath. "Well, that put me in my place, didn't it?"

The Warehouse District was just what it sounded like, the place where, once upon a time, boat captains off-loaded merchandise and took on fresh wares for the next port, and where masters of industry and commerce stored it, sold it, and made their fortunes. But the formerly utilitarian buildings had been redone into artsy and expensive apartments, lofts, restaurants, and galleries.

The street in front of the Old Nunnery was packed on both sides with parked cars, each with a driver waiting inside, in the dark, or standing beside it, watching the night. Each man had the look of ex-military, wore an earpiece, and had well-toned and deadly brawn. I was betting they wore enough weapons to start Bruiser's war too. We pulled through the narrow roadway between the vehicles and up to the old building.

I leaned toward the blackened limo window and stared. The Nunnery was a three-story, old-brick warehouse with Spanish-style windows, a wraparound porch on the bottom floor with wide-arched openings big enough to drive a wagon and draft horses through. Wrought iron protected the porch above it on the second floor, and sculpted grounds were planted with magnolias, palms, blooming flowers and shrubs, and heavy-limbed live oaks old enough to have seen Jean Lafitte himself saunter through. The entire property was ablaze with light that flickered like real flame through the warehouse windows; the images within seemed to waver, blown glass giving a surreal aspect to it.

The grounds and building were packed full of formally attired and coiffed blood-servants, blood-slaves, and the rich and fangy. It swarmed like a fire-ant mound, deadly to anything that stayed nearby for too long, lethal to an enemy. And just by walking in, I was getting ready to stir it with a metaphorical stick. My palms started to sweat. "This doesn't look like a convent."

"The Nunnery is named after Samuel Nunnery, a businessman and ship owner from the seventeen hundreds. This was one of his warehouses."

The car pulled to a stop at the apex of a circular drive and Bruiser lowered the privacy window an inch. "I'll take care of us from here, Simon." The driver, silhouetted by the outside lights through the darkly tinted, bulletproof glass, gave a small two-finger salute. Bruiser helped me out into the muggy air, his hand on mine firm. I used the moment to smooth my hair, retucking the ends of several braids and checking the position of the weapons in them. The wrestling-match-slash-almost-sex on the floor hadn't dislodged anything. He shut the door, placed my hand in the crook of his arm, and started up the walk to the door. He leaned in, placed his lips at my ear, murmuring, "Play nice."

I adjusted my little purse on its extra-long strap and let one corner of my mouth curl up. "I'd like to keep my skin intact and my blood in my veins. I promise not to do anything really stupid."

"I promise to do nothing stupid," he corrected, a glint in his eye.

"Bully for you." He chuckled as we took five steps up to the massive front door, and I added, "Good English and grammar are easy for old geezers." He harrumphed, adjusted his jacket, and squeezed my arm. Glancing down, I was happy to see that neither his tux nor my dress was overly wrinkled, despite the tussle on the floor.

I also spotted long, narrow, horizontal windows below

the entry porch, running along the length of the building, behind low shrubbery—windows dark but clean. Each had bars over it. This building was one of a very few in this part of the world with a basement or root cellar. Or maybe coal cellar. Maybe dungeon. With the high water table, most such depressions filled in with water and contributed to black mold. If the space was well kept and dry, then it was likely witch-spelled to keep out water.

Witches and vamps. Working together. It wasn't supposed to happen. The two species were supposed to hate each other. My nosy instincts went into overdrive. Why did a huge warehouse need a basement? Had it once been a holding cell for contraband? Or far worse, imported slaves?

Inside the door, cold, dry air flooded from overhead vents. And the smell of vamp hit me like a closed fist. *Son of a sea lion*, there must be hundreds of them here. I closed down around myself fast, erecting barriers in my mind, barriers that Molly was helping me to strengthen, using meditation techniques. It was working, but not as well as she wanted. The vamp stink was potent, aggressive, as if they had been fighting among themselves, and it made my hackles rise. Beast peeled back her lips and showed me her teeth, hissing softly; I held her off with a mental command. Beast didn't like walking onto another predator's territory. She also didn't like it when I barricaded her off, so she sat back, allowing me the alpha position. For now.

Bruiser paused and removed two white envelopes from his jacket pocket, handing them to a security type, a tuxedoed guy with an ear wire and a tiny mouthpiece, a significant bulge beneath one arm. But he wasn't muscled and burly; he was slight, black, and had very hard, very cold eyes. He studied, memorized, categorized, and set me aside as unimportant. I could have been insulted, but being discounted might keep me safe. "George Dumas and guest," Security Dude said, checking off the name on a clipboard.

George nodded and said, "Jane Yellowrock, Rogue Hunter." I saw the man's eyes flick my way, and I was pretty sure I was being recategorized from date to dangerous. I sighed. I'd have security watching me all evening.

"Armed?" SD asked.

"She was," Bruiser drawled, giving the impression that he had declawed me himself. Which he had, actually. I frowned. SD glanced back at me and nodded as if amused at the little lady. I narrowed my eyes at Bruiser and moved inside, into a reception line.

CHAPTER 8

I am not prey!

I studied our hostess, Bettina, Blood Master of Clan Rousseau. Rousseau was a beautiful woman of mixed race heritage, mostly African and European, and I had learned early on that she had entered this country as a slave. Perhaps through this warehouse, where she now was hostess. It seemed the kind of ironic situation that would appeal to a vamp.

Vamp lore said that Bettina had pleased her master, who had later turned her, freed her, and made her his second in command. When he died in 1915—crap. Wasn't that the year Bruiser mentioned being the last vamp war?—Bettina had moved into his position of power. Of course, I'd heard other stories too, but I hadn't found anything in the woo-woo files to verify any of them.

Bettina stood five-four or five-five in heels, had more curves and cleavage than a *Playboy* bunny, and oozed seduction. She had tried it on me once, asking me to her bed. I was so not going there. Clan Rousseau's blood-master took Bruiser's hand as if to shake, but pulled him close. "George," she said, pressing her cheek to his, her accent exquisite even in the single word.

"Lovely lady," he murmured, pressing his cheeks to both of hers in a manner that seemed Old World and LA current at the same time.

Bettina turned to me. "Our brave hunter," she said.

When I offered her my hand, Bettina gathered up both of mine instead, holding them between us as she stepped close, way inside my personal space, her hands and mine bumping our bodies. Unlike most vamps, who wore minimal perfume, Bettina was drenched in it. Beast retreated from the stench and I tried not to breathe. There was no avoiding her gaze, however, when she looked up.

Liquid dark eyes pulled at me. Vamp pheromones, hunting pheromones, *crap*, *seduction* pheromones spiked on the air. I could smell them even buried beneath the bottled fragrance. She leaned in closer, up and against me, our hands trapped and brushing our chests, her mouth at my dress's low neckline. *Ick*. Bettina leaned in, pulling me down for a little cheek dusting the way she had given Bruiser. Or a blood kiss.

I am not prey! Beast warned. I tensed. No way was Beast letting me back away. She bared her teeth and claws. Flooded my system with adrenaline. Prepared to attack.

But Bettina didn't try to bite me, nor did she do the cheek-to-cheek thing; she sniffed me. As if I were *food*. I held my two selves still and fought down anger and insult. Bettina blew out a breath that went down my dress front, cold, dead air, and stepped back. She said, "The Rogue Hunter is welcome tonight, as a guest of Pellissier's blood-servant, and as one claimed by the Blood Master of the City. My home is honored."

Claimed? I blushed hotly. Leo's blood scent claimed me for him, and I had a feeling it would be stupid and dangerous to deny that status. Could others try to claim me if I declared myself free? Was there something I was missing here? Maybe I should be less ticked off with Bruiser. Or maybe I should hurt him in retaliation.

Bettina stepped back and I figured we were done, but she smiled and squeezed my fingers. She had *dimples*. How creepy was that? "I asked that the Rogue Hunter call upon me when the unpleasantness of the old rogue hunting my kind had been settled." She held my gaze, and when she spoke again, it was haltingly, choosing her words with care. "Yet, though you defeated him, I have not received such a call. I am disappointed. You *will* call upon me?"

I had a feeling she was trying to convey something more

than her words themselves, but I had no idea what. As if she sensed that, her grip loosened and her tone returned to coy persuasion.

"I still wish to know you better, who you are, *what* you are. Should you tire of Leo and desire ... employment ... when your current contract is concluded, you will call upon me. An accommodation can be agreed upon, I am certain."

Accommodation in her bed and as her dinner. As a fangy toy. Not gonna happen. Before I could say it, she stepped back again, into her place in the one-vamp receiving line, and released my hands. Bruiser retook my arm and we moved on. "Well, well," he murmured. "Leo did say you smell like dessert."

Beast is not food! "That was seriously freaky," I murmured back.

"So what are you?" he asked. "Why do you smell so tasty to them?"

"A blood meal with killer legs?" I said, hoping to deflect his curiosity.

"Yes, but you smell like sex, blood, violence, and challenge, according to Leo. Which, for a vampire, would be dessert with killer legs."

"Mmmm." I wasn't going to respond to that one. I smoothed my hair back again and stopped, my hand at my face. Beneath the reek of Bettina's perfume, I caught a whiff of the rogue maker from her palm. I looked back at Bettina. She had shaken his hand. He? Yes. I was pretty sure. And that meant he was here. I whirled back to Bettina. She was staring at me. And she inclined her head as if to agree with something, but what? I sniffed. The odors were rich and intermingled, the smell of gaslight and smoke riding over it all. No scent of the rogue maker lingered on the air.

I scanned the central area of the warehouse and breathed in the mingled scents. The front half of the building was one huge open area with three-feet-thick, old-brick walls, a slate floor, and thirty-inch-diameter brick pillars holding up the second floor, which was fifteen feet overhead. Gas flames lit the area, flickering in the air-conditioned, artificial breeze. Whatever its use in the past, the entry floor was now set up for entertaining, with a serving area to the right big enough to seat a hundred at the long table, which was currently pushed against the wall. Scores of chairs lined the room's walls. I could see no one who might match the faint scent on my hand.

However, the air was redolent with meat and spices. *Food!* Beast thought. "Later," I murmured, as if to myself. Bruiser looked my way, but I pretended not to notice. The table was laden with food for humans, and humans were gathered along it, spearing smoked salmon, ribs, something that looked like lollipops but smelled like lamb, kabobs, shrimp, fried seafood in bite-sized pieces, and boudin, a Louisiana favorite, onto plates. There were veggies and a multitude of breads and cheeses too, not that I cared.

To the left was a place set up like a parlor, with couches, chairs, tables, and a fireplace scaled to fit the warehouse, burning huge logs that looked custom cut. Bruiser led me left, to pause partially behind one of the round pillars. The seating area was decorated with French and Spanish antiques, lots of burled wood on cases holding paintings and priceless objets d'art. The upholstered furniture had sweeping lines, tufts, tassels, skirts, and gewgaws—art deco and art nouveau maybe, fancy, like something that might be seen in an old black-and-white movie. Yet everything was dwarfed by the scale of the room.

Midway to the back half of the warehouse was another area, marked off by rugs tossed on the slate floor, and here vamps and humans sat on large pillows, talking and smoking, bohemian-style. The scents were overpowering here too, pepper, parchment, fresh mint and camphor, dried herbs, subtle perfumes, and a hint of mold, though that might have been from the old building. Underlying the vamp smell were traces of fresh blood from recent feedings. Beast didn't like that stench, and hissed deep in my mind.

There were eight clan blood-families in New Orleans and it was dizzyingly difficult to keep their political and social divisions straight, but it was something I needed to know as rogue-vamp hunter in their territory. Pellissier, Laurent, Bouvier, and St. Martin were in one political alliance, with Mearkanis, Arceneau, Rousseau, and Desmarais in the other. The clan homes of the latter four blood-masters were in the Garden District, and once upon a time, they had all been thick as thieves. But from the social groupings tonight, it was clear that the alliances were changing, the vamps gathering in odd clusters. All was not right in the world of the blood-sucking predators.

I spotted Rafael Torrez, the small, black-eyed scion and master of Clan Mearkanis, and self-proclaimed enemy of Leo, in intense conversation with two unknown vamps— an overdressed guy in a red costume and a vamp with a scarred face, the wound recent and still healing.

I heard the word "Leo" from the little group across the room. And "clan," and "true-death." From the way his body tensed, Bruiser heard too. I asked, "What do they get if Leo suddenly dies or is defeated in war?"

"I'm not sure." His eyes crinkled at the corners as he scanned the room. "If Leo names a new heir and solidifies his political base, then at his true-death his power would move to his successor, who would become master of the city. Of course, the new master would then have to hold it by his own wits and might. But if Leo holds off naming an heir, if something shifts in the political alignment, if we go to war and vampires start dying, it all becomes . . . difficult."

I had a feeling that "difficult" was an understatement. I tugged him away, to the table with human food, as in food for humans, not a table full of humans to feed vamps. Having vamps around tended to make such distinctions tricky. The sexual tension between Bruiser and me and the atmosphere in the room had left me starved. "I need to eat and then mingle," I said, "to see if any of them smell like the young-rogue maker—wear that perfume I noticed," I amended. I'd never been good keeping lies straight.

I handed Bruiser a crystal plate and filled mine with smoked pink salmon. Beast panted within me. *Better raw*, she said, and sent me a vision of a mountain lion's claws grabbing a dappled trout from a stream. I hadn't known Beast fished, but it did seem like something all cats liked, whether a tabby from an aquarium in a New York City apartment or a mountain lion from a cold mountain stream.

Bruiser looked at the heap of salmon on my plate and

tilted his head in surprise, amusement, and vague conde-
scension. The expression was uncannily like Leo's, and I
wondered how many decades one had to live with a vamp
to pick up his mannerisms. It could be seriously disturbing.
"I like fish," I said, defensive. "And I'm hungry."

"Of course," he murmured. He handed me a square of
folded linen and two pieces of gold-plated utensils and
said, "Fish service."

I looked at the short, stout fork and the butter knife as
I followed him to the back of the warehouse. "Yeah?" I
turned the heavy utensils over, mentally comparing them to
the pressed metal stuff we had used in the children's home.
I was still looking at them when Bruiser placed a flute of
white wine in my hand. I looked up, surprised. The back
half of the Old Nunnery warehouse had probably once
been offices, large cubicles open to each other at floor and
ceiling for airflow. The first cubicle had a bar set up. I took
a sip and even I knew this was the good stuff. No wine in a
box for the vamps. I tasted the salmon and it melted in my
mouth. Well, not really, but I didn't have to chew much.

As I ate—wolfing down the fish, Bruiser watching me
with a slightly superior attitude, and me ignoring him—we
moved into a short, wide hallway. A group of vamps in formal wear paused and stepped to the side as if to let us pass.
As we drew even, two vamps dressed in almost-but-not-
quite matching red silk gowns started toward me; the others followed their actions as if one brain controlled them.
In unison, they sniffed the air.

Beyond them, in the shadows, Rafael Torrez stood. He
was smiling slightly, but he didn't come closer. He was
watching, his posture expectant. *Crap*.

My hackles rose and I stopped, turned to face the vamps
closest, my back to the brick wall. Their eyes began bleeding black. Fangs snapped down. Beast flared through me
and I sniffed back at them, scent-searching. For a single
moment we faced each other. Me with a plate half-full of
food. Hands full. Adrenaline shot through me as I analyzed
my defenses in an instant. The plate was glass, easily shattered, and vamps bled well. Stakes close, in my hair. Wall at
my back. I breathed out, muscles going loose and ready.

The female vamps in the scarlet silk sheaths looked

me up and down, slowly, as if committing me to memory. I didn't think they were looking over my dress to gauge the quality and cost. One of the male vamps moved toward us, flowing slowly in that inhuman balletic glide the old ones can do. He looked predatory and graceful and dangerous as hell, despite his green and red plaid cummerbund and little matching pocket hankie, the colors clashing jauntily with his fangs.

I tightened my fingers on the plate, ready to toss it in distraction or shatter it into a quick blade. Ready to reach up and pull the stakes in my hair. My hands itched with the need to *do something, now*. Bruiser stepped to my side. Placed a proprietary hand on my spine. "The Rogue Hunter," he said, not the first time it had been phrased like a title. The vamps, six altogether, fanned out, making a semicircle, boxing us in. Everything went cold and sterile. I realized they had been watching for me.

Offense is the best defense, I thought. Beast snarled deep inside me.

With a spinning motion, I slung my dinner plate to the brick floor. It shattered at their feet. Three of them jumped, startled or to miss being splattered with salmon, marking them as untrained and easily ignored. I focused on the remaining vamps. Beast leaped into my eyes and I growled, hands in my hair. Gripping stakes.

"Jane. No," Bruiser said softly, his voice carefully expressionless.

My hands stopped, nested in my braids. My heart beat like a broken drum.

From the corner of my eye, I saw the shadow move, the shadow that was Rafael Torrez, Blood Master of Mearkanis. Without lifting my gaze away, I took in this new threat. *Great. Now what?*

Rafe placed a hand on the shoulder of Plaid Guy. "No," he said.

Plaid Guy paused. His eyes were emerald, his pupils widening to black, snuffing out the green. His mouth opened in a little snarl as the new master of Clan Mearkanis came even with him and looked me over, a small smile on his pretty face. Dark, delicate, he walked the way a fencer or dancer might, feet placed with precise balance. "Not now."

Rafe stepped in front of the small group, hands clasped behind his back, and looked me over as though he might make an offer. "George, your master keeps such intriguing pets."

My eyebrows reached my hairline. "Pets?" I spat.

Rafael laughed and nodded to Bruiser. "George."

"Sir," Bruiser said, tone neutral.

Rafe turned and moved through the six vamps. They swiveled on their heels and followed him. And were gone, leaving Bruiser and me alone in the hallway.

"That was seriously freaky," I said.

"Yes. More than you know," Bruiser said, musing. "The Mithrans facing you were from two different alliances. I think this was . . . indicative. Those two in the red dresses—Lanah and Hope—belong to Adrianna of St. Martin, who is allied with Leo. Nasty pieces of work, they are, but with the scent-marking, they should have protected you. A game is being played here, but I don't know what it is." He glanced at me, that small smile hovering on his lips. "You do create interesting situations, Jane Yellowrock. How many stakes do you have in your hair?"

"Not one," I said, lying and telling the truth all at once. I had more than one, so "not one" was the truth. Sorta. I was going to have to get down on my knees and confess a whole lotta half sins, nearly sins, and wanted-to sins. Guilt wriggled under my skin.

"And crosses?" he asked dryly.

Not willing to lie outright, I said, "One tiny one you nearly dislodged in the limo."

Bruiser glanced at the plunging neckline of my new dress and his mouth did that little twitch of a quirk. "It's well secured, then. Keep it that way."

I looked at the shattered plate and salmon at our feet. "Sorry about that."

"It let us see who flinched."

I grinned. "It did, didn't it?"

CHAPTER 9

Fast cars and money lead back to dames

"George Dumas, first blood-servant to Pellissier." The soft words floated from down the hallway, bouncing off the old brick, a female vamped-out voice, the inflection asking Bruiser to join her. I glanced at him and without a word we swiveled, our bodies moving as if we had trained together for years.

A little vamp stood just inside an open cubicle with a door, the space lit with bright electric lights. She beckoned; we moved toward her. The room behind her was a big pantry, three shelf-lined walls organized with cans and boxes, with household appliances on a side wall, including a washer and dryer. We were at the back of the warehouse; I could smell the Mississippi River strong on the air. I hesitated in the dim hallway, scent-searching on a quick breath, taking her in.

She was short, model-slender, with streaked blond hair and the bluest eyes I'd seen on anyone, human or not. A diamond necklace big enough to qualify as a collar circled her neck, and diamond and blue topaz drops the size of walnuts dangled from her ears. "In here," she whispered. I didn't know her and wasn't inclined to follow. Bruiser, however, stepped closer, which brought us even. Vamp-fast, she snatched my right arm and Bruiser's left, her tiny hand like a steel cuff, cold and cutting. And strong.

Faster than thought, I reached for a stake. She yanked.

Hurled me off my feet. Tossed me inside. I hit the back shelves. Stake in hand, I pushed off. Looked back. Without effort, she threw Bruiser at me. With him in midair, the pantry door slammed. I got a quick look at it—three inches of hardwood reinforced with iron straps. A trap.

I caught Bruiser one handed. We impacted with pained grunts, the shelves ramming into my unprotected back. The lock clicked home. Using his own momentum, I shoved Bruiser aside. He hit the floor in a controlled roll on hands and knees, and got up to his feet at nearly vamp speed.

A stake in each hand, I rushed her. She was fast. The vamp caught me again and whirled me into a corner in a dance-step-smooth martial art move. She scuttled away from us. Her back against the door, hands out, placating. "I'm not here to hurt you," she said as I found my footing.

Not caring what she claimed, I pulled my tiny blade and reversed it in my grip, street fighting position. Beast hissed but stayed down, watching, her claws in my mind like steel points, her energy pouring into me. My breath was hard and swift and I flashed the blade in the too-bright lights so she would see it was silver-plated—poisonous to her kind if I cut her. I wished the blade was bigger but I felt better with weapons drawn.

Bruiser was on his feet, his hands out in a mimic of vamp grace as we evaluated the female vamp. She didn't look at the blade, but watched us, eyes darting back and forth, her feet balanced and her body posture claiming she was familiar with fighting and willing to demonstrate. And she was blocking the door.

She was also hungry, her skin pallid, but her eyes weren't vamp-black and bloody; instead, they were controlled and collected. From the remembered strength of her grip, she was an old one, powerful, and despite her small frame, I might have a hard time beating her with just the two weapons and no protective gear.

Yet she'd said she wouldn't hurt us. And she wasn't dressed for wet work. Her dress had the dragon-lady-seamstress's signature lines, looking long, lean, and elegant, even on her tiny form, midnight blue shot with silver thread, which had to be a vamp joke. And she wore spike heels in blue-black ostrich leather, little feathers on the buckles. She looked totally out of place standing in the pantry. "I won't hurt you. At least not right now. Truce."

I lowered my hands a fraction to show I'd listen. Bruiser dropped his and said, "Innara of Clan Bouvier. How may I serve you?"

"I have a message from my master."

Bruiser blinked. With that careful blandness I was coming to appreciate, he said, "You could have called." I laughed through my nose.

"I could not. My master has determined that many of the Mithrans' cellular communications are being monitored." Innara's tiny hands opened in the universal gesture of peace, fingers splayed. "Servant of the Blood Master of New Orleans and the one they call the Rogue Hunter, hear me."

I could tell I was added on only because I happened to be near, but what the heck, I'd stay to listen. Especially as a thick door stood between me and freedom.

Her voice took on a cant that said she was repeating a memorized statement. "The alliance of Mithrans is in grave danger, as is the safety of this city. Mearkanis and Rousseau have formed a new coalition, leaving the weaker clans Arceneau and Desmarais unprotected. They have allied with St. Martin, who has broken faith with Pellissier."

Bruiser cursed and went pale. I tried to figure out what it all meant. And then Innara told me. "There are now three leagues of Mithrans rather than the former two, and the new association leaves Pellissier's alliance with Bouvier and Laurent no longer in a position of strength. Pellissier's enemies plot war. Rafael has come clandestinely to Clan Bouvier to propose we join him in revolt against Pellissier. My master has agreed to formal talks, to consider this, as a ruse to gain his trust. It is said that Rafael has contacted one of the Sons of Darkness for his blessing, though this is only rumor."

Bruiser went nearly vamp-still in shock. I wondered what the sons were and why they made the blood slowly drain from his face. The Sons of Darkness . . . They had been part of something I had read recently.

Innara stepped close and took Bruiser's hands in hers. "The new union believes in the old ways. The Naturaleza has been reintroduced to the newly fledged and many yearn for a way of life the old ones among us have renounced. Rafael of Mearkanis feeds this desire with fiery rhetoric and hopes the change in balance of power will allow him to challenge for master of the city. Be assured. To protect against the new alliance, my master will again blood-oath Clan Bouvier to Leo."

I felt Bruiser's relief like a blow to my side. He'd been braced for something else. "Pellissier is honored."

"Naturaleza?" I asked, picking out that nugget for clarification.

Bruiser ignored my question. "There have been indications that Rafael was seeking power."

"Traditionally," Innara said to me, "the strength of Pellissier held us in balance and allowed us to blend harmoniously with humans. Now that is changing." She pressed Bruiser's hands. "Leo must act."

Leo was whacked-out with grief and might not be able to act. But I didn't say it.

Bruiser said, "The recent alignment between Pellissier and Arceneau is advantageous to restoring that peace."

"Arceneau has sworn itself to Leo?" Innara asked, her face taking on a fierce joy.

Bruiser nodded. It was news to me. I asked them, "Will Arceneau give Leo enough power to defeat the new coalition?"

"No," Innara said, "but if Desmarais swears to Leo, and if Leo acts quickly, then we have a chance."

I redrew the balance of power in my mind, the new alliance of vamp clans. On the one hand was Rafael of Mearkanis, with Rousseau and St. Martin pledged to him. And maybe these sons, whatever they were. Then there was Leo of Pellissier, with Laurent, Bouvier, and now Arceneau. Desmarais lingered by its lonesome. So if a new vamp war started, it would be a battle between Rafael and Leo. I didn't know enough about clan strengths to know if it would be a fair match.

Satisfied that the Bouvier vamp didn't mean us harm, I lowered my weapons. Tension I hadn't noted in her slight frame relaxed. Instantly, she looked like a child playing dress-up in her mommy's clothes and jewels, innocent and sweet and fully human, not like the killer she was. I hated how they could do that. "Leo must put aside the Dolore and take up the reins of his power," she said.

Bruiser took a step back, his face closing in. Before I could ask what a dolore was, she went on, her tone fierce, her hands fisting, trying to convince Bruiser. "You must tell Leo that if he hopes to keep the peace, he must break the new alliance quickly or there will be war—violent, bloody, and decisive. Our masters will die. We will not be able to protect our young in devoveo while they regain themselves—they will be left to run mad. Our humans will not survive. The city will be torn asunder." To me she said, "Rafael believes in the Naturaleza, the old ways, that humans are here only for our pleasure and to feed us—and that all other supernatural beings must be wiped from the earth."

The words "supernatural beings must be wiped from the earth" reverberated in the small room. That meant Molly and her kids. And every other witch in the city. And me. *Crap. Crap, crap, crap.* And then I heard the word "devoveo." What the heck was that? I'd never heard the term before, but it sounded as though it was related to the madness of young rogues. Maybe worth investigating.

"*Make Leo listen,*" she demanded of Bruiser. Her head cocked, rocking on the stem of her neck into an angle not common to humans, like a bird with a broken neck. It was just . . . so weird. She seemed to be listening to something or someone I couldn't hear. Her pupils widened, vamping out.

"My anamchara tells me that Rafael is coming. I must . . ." Her eyes landed on me, and the sclera bled scarlet. Fear pheromones skittered into the small room, brittle and prickly, and all hers. Innara took a breath, the sound loud with panic. "He will catch me. With you. He will know that my master has accepted his offer to parley, in deception."

And if Leo loses the vamp war, then a victorious Rafael will kill his enemies, I thought. *Gotcha.* Innara was self-serving, playing both sides just like her master. The vamp could tear a human apart with her bare hands, but she looked so helpless, even with the bloody eyes. I sooo did not want to get involved in this, but I was already neck deep and sinking. Tucking the stake and knife back in their hidey spots, I let

the words drag out of me. "No, he won't." Her face split
with joy. If there was also a lot of cunning behind the purer
emotion, well, she *was* a vamp.

Motioning her away from the door, I held my hand out
to Bruiser and snapped the lock. The door cracked open
and we stepped through the slit. A shadow darkened the
hallway entrance as someone approached. There wasn't
time to explain. I stepped into Bruiser, pulling the door
shut behind us, and yanked him close. And picked up
where we'd left off in the limo. He grunted once, hesitated a fraction of a second as if analyzing, and seemed
to understand.

His arms went around me, his mouth hard, and one hand
slid down my side to cup my bottom. The other slid up,
brushing the side of my breast before wrapping around my
nape. I had a moment to note that he tasted of champagne
and smelled of Leo, which I hadn't paid attention to on
the floor of the limo. He lifted me and pressed me against
the closed door, took my thigh, and wrapped it around his
waist.

In only a moment, lust pheromones wafted from him, his
mouth softened, and I repositioned my mouth under his,
glancing up the hallway. Through slit lids, I saw Rafael, heir
to Mearkanis, stop in the far end. And watch. He sniffed,
and I knew he'd detect no lust from me. *Crap. Crap, crap,
crap, and more freaking crap!* I closed my eyes and tried to
relax. But I couldn't. Not with Rafael watching. And from
the faint scuffle of shoes on the floor, others as well.

With a low growl in my mind, Beast took over. And I
let her. *Mate,* she thought at me. *Soon.* My limbs softened.
Flesh heated. *This one is strong. Worthy of us.*

Responding to the not-so-subtle signals, Bruiser slid
his tongue between my lips in a delicate brush and swirl.
I/Beast sighed into his mouth and he chuckled under his
breath, masculine and possessive. He pulled me closer. His
arousal pressed into the center of me, demanding. He'd
been holding back, waiting on me, and now he leaned me
hard into the door, the iron bands cutting into my spine.
The pain was sharp and I arched into him. His lips left my
mouth and trailed down my neck. Licking.

Oh . . . my. My breath deepened. "Yes," I whispered.

"Like that." I rolled my head back, giving him access. Letting Beast take over. My body responded, breasts aching, wanting. My hands clenched, bunching his tux coat tightly. A moment later, the shuffling at the hallway end disappeared. A long moment after that, Bruiser paused, his lips buried in the deep V of my neckline. "Are they gone?" he murmured, his mouth brushing against delicate flesh, his voice vibrating between us.

I didn't want to answer, and my own hesitation brought a titter of laughter to my lips, my chest bones bumping his mouth. I pushed Beast back down and she went, but with a catty, satisfied purr. "Yes. They're gone." I felt his smile against my skin.

"Well, damn. I guess we have to stop, then."

I laughed again, louder this time, and eased him away, my hands on his arms, my leg dropping from his waist. "Maybe later," I said before I could stop myself.

"Count on it," he said, and set me down, his hands sliding slowly along my bottom.

The door opened behind us and little Innara peeked out, looking up and down the hallway. Finding Rafael gone, she turned her attention to us and breathed deeply, taking in the pheromones and responding to them. A little smile gave her a gamine look, a bit teasing. "My anamchara says I can return now. If you two would care to join us? We would be pleased to leave this party and find a more private place. To share blood and body with you both."

I started to say, "No freaking way," but Bruiser spoke first, smoothly. "A gracious invitation. Another time, perhaps, lovely lady." He bowed over her hand and kissed it. It didn't even look weird when he did it, which was weird in itself. I shut my mouth with a click of teeth.

"We certainly hope so." Holding on to his hand, effectively pulling the three of us together, Innara leaned in to me, showing fang when she said, "This one smells . . . tasty." She was looking at me as if she was both hungry and aroused. Double ick.

"She is the Rogue Hunter, contracted by the council," Bruiser said. There was that phrase and tone again, that title. I needed to ask about that sometime.

Innara said, "We hope she lives long enough to fulfill her

contract." She dropped our hands and slithered down the hallway and out of sight. Leaving us alone.

Suddenly reticent, I adjusted my dress, watching Bruiser from the corner of my eye. He leaned against the brick, still clearly happy to see me, amusement playing across his features, the expression saying that he knew what I was looking at. His hair had fallen forward and a quick glance showed me red lipstick on his mouth. I wondered if he'd smeared it on Innara's hand. "Wipe your mouth?" I suggested.

One handed, he pulled a hanky and wiped his lips, passing it to me. "Yours too."

"Oh." I took the handkerchief. It was the same one with Leo's blood on it, but it was a little late to worry about scent-marking. I dabbed my mouth on a clean corner and held out the soiled cloth. Bruiser took my hand instead of the handkerchief. Slowly, he pulled me to him. I felt stupid jerking away or holding back, seeing a mental image of me stretched across the hallway, balanced on one foot. I smiled at it and when my chest once again touched his, he wrapped a steely arm around me and said, "We *are* going to do this. Soon."

I gulped. Beast purred. And Bruiser leaned in. Paused with his lips only a fraction of an inch from mine. "We *are*." His smile was teasing, a flash of very white teeth. He whispered, "Say it. We are."

"Oh. Um. Well. I may be dead tomorrow, you know?" When his arm loosened in surprise, I ducked away with a little dance step and said, "What's an anamchara?"

Bruiser held his position a moment longer. When he stood straight, the amused smile was still in place, reminding me a bit of Beast when she played with her dinner. While it was still alive. I thought for a moment that Bruiser would push the issue, but he didn't. Instead, he took my arm and curled it through his, leading me down the hallway toward the party.

"Anamchara has had many meanings throughout history, but for Mithrans, anamchara are soul bonded. Or mind bonded, if you prefer. It's a state sometimes entered into by vampires, an everlasting joining, an eternal mating. They share thoughts, emotions, everything in their lives, from moment to moment. It is a difficult arrangement, and one not sought by most, even after long years together." He tilted his eyes at me, his amusement growing, his words dropping lower, provocative. "They share ... *everything*. The relationship is said to be best experienced by them in sexual and feeding encounters. At the same time if possible."

I couldn't help looking down at the proof of his interest in me, and blushed furiously. *Well, hell.* Bruiser laughed again, a low sound that had Beast rolling over, her pelt rubbing against my skin. But we stepped into the open area and it took his attention as it did mine, our security training automatic. We had worked our way back to the front of the warehouse, the area with pillows and rugs. There were groups of vamps and groups of humans, but separate groups, with almost no intermixing. Soft music played from hidden speakers.

"It does have drawbacks, of course," he said, and I brought my attention back to the subject. "There can be no lies between anamchara. And it is said that if one dies, the other goes insane."

"That would suck," I said, succinctly.

Laughter spluttered from him, untouched by the sexual teasing, and I took the moment to ask, "What is Dolore? I thought it was a name, but it isn't."

He stilled. Softly he said, "It is the state that Mithrans enter when they grieve. It can make them go rogue if their blood-family and their intimate, human blood-servants are not most careful with them."

I put a hand on his arm, urging him to quiet for a moment. I tensed, smelling the maker of the young rogues. This was why I had come. My lips parted slightly and I slowly drew a breath over my tongue and through my nose, tasting and scenting all at once. I closed my eyes to concentrate. The scent marker was faint, buried beneath the aromas of cooked meat, old warehouse, and vamps galore. But it was here. He had been here.

Most of the time Beast could help me tell by scent the carriers' gender, race, mating readiness, general health, age, what they had to eat recently, others who had been in close contact—a whole host of things. But I wasn't getting much from the traces of the rogue maker I'd found. I had yet to be in Beast's form when I scent-checked him—it. I still wasn't certain of the gender. I needed to shift and prowl. I grinned and dropped Bruiser's arm. Bet that would go over well, a mountain lion come a-calling. "Go call Leo. Tell him that the maker of the young rogues has been here. I smell it. The perfume it wore," I corrected. "It's faint but it's been here. I need to mingle."

Bruiser looked at me strangely but stepped away, pulling his cell. I almost reminded him about Innara's statement that cellular communications were being monitored, but what the heck. He was a big boy.

I moved into the open area, scent-searching. I walked through the entire place in the next few minutes, breathing shallowly, letting Beast stare through my eyes and parse the scents. But the faint reek of the rogue maker vanished. It—he? pretty sure it was a he—was gone.

Frustrated, I let Beast settle back to her rest and stared out over the throng, which had grown considerably since our arrival. I spotted a small group of blood-servant-security types, all by their lonesome. They were my kinda people, and I had met some of them, so I smoothed my dress, pasted on a smile, and approached. Two of the men—identical twins, right down to the matched tuxedoes—parted to provide me with an opening. "Hey, gorgeous," one said. "You clean up right nice."

"Brian and Brandon of Clan Arceneau," I said, accepting mirror-image cheek pecks from them. "Or is it Brandon and Brian? You look restored, rested, and healthy."

"Thanks to you," one said, sliding an arm around my waist and pulling me into the group. To the others he announced, "This is the Rogue Hunter, who saved Grégoire." That got me sharpened interest from the ones I didn't know.

The other twin said, "And incidentally, our butts too. The ugly one"—he thumbed at his twin—"was nearly dead from blood loss by the time she dispatched the rogue and sent help our way. But I'm distraught that you can't tell me apart from the ugly twin. That *is* a sympathy hug you're giving him, isn't it?" he said, sliding into my other side.

Looking back and forth between them, I grinned to show appreciation of their twin-based humor. "I try to be diplomatic to the less fortunate, and if I could figure out which is the prettier twin, I would ignore him, I promise."

"That ugly mole marring the perfection of Brandon's face is how you can tell us apart."

I spotted the tiny mole at Brandon's hairline, and said, "That lovely little beauty mark?"

"Nicely said. For a killer in a vamp-whore dress," a small woman interrupted.

Shock went through me in a jolting zing. Brandon and Brian went still. I slid out of their loose embraces and in front of them, instantly assessing. Growing up in a children's home, I'd been verbally and physically sucker punched a lot, but it never got easier to take. It hardly seemed fair that she would come at me now, when I had to fight in a dress and couldn't stake her to kill her. And Bruiser had my good knife. Before I could respond, a second woman joined in the wordplay.

"Are you saying she's a vamp whore, Sina?" the second woman asked. "Or the dress is made by a vamp-whore?"

"Adrianna says she stinks of Leo Pellissier," Sina said, "but the dress is slutty advertisement too."

"Adrianna?" I asked, through lips suddenly gone numb with an adrenaline spike.

"First Scion of Clan St. Martin," Brian said slowly. "Meet her blood-servants, Sina and Brigit." St. Martin, who had just broken with Pellissier and formed a new playground gang with Rafael of Mearkanis as head bully boy. The two vamps in red dresses had been Adrianna's as well. What was this, tag-team-Jane day? A way to stir the vamp waters? I had to assume old Rafe had sent Adrianna gunning for me, but I had no idea why.

The two women had been standing together but now separated, breaking the tight grouping of blood-servants. The circle expanded, like a fighting ring, as the nonparticipants stepped back and the two women moved in. Both were short with wiry, fat-starved bodies and frizzy brown hair, though Sina was African-American and Brigit was Caucasian. They were dressed in similar black, sleeveless dresses that showed off their well-defined arms and freed their limbs for fighting. My heart rate sped up and Beast bared her killing fangs in my mind. My arms automatically lifted away from my sides, ready for defensive moves. I couldn't help the smile that pulled back my lips as Beast thought, *Fun!*

"Yeah, she does smell of Leo. The Master of the City is sucking on his son's murderer," Sina said.

"Not just sucking, you ask me." The two women laughed, taunting.

"Actually, I'm the one who scent-marked the Hunter," Bruiser's soft voice said over my shoulder, "in the hopes it would keep her from having to kill some stupid little vampire for assaulting her or some stupid little blood-servant for living up to the designation."

"You calling us stupid, George?" Brigit asked, her eyes brightening in anticipation. "You wanting to take us both on?"

"The thought is unpleasant in the extreme," he said. "It gives me nightmares."

Several onlookers laughed and the two women looked puzzled, until Sina got the sexual insult. She snarled and reached to pull a gun, stopping when her partner placed a restraining hand on her arm. But the woman's fingers held tight to the butt of a tiny weapon in a pocket holster.

"Her dress is a creation by Madame Melisende, *Modiste du les Mithrans,* not a vamp-whore. I believe that Jane has one of the designer's cards should you, or your mistress Adrianna, *ever* wish to dress well. Jane?" he asked as he took my little purse in hand, pulling the strap across my chest. I had forgotten it was there. "Ah, here they are." He extended a handful of cards over my shoulder at the little bullies, which brought his body in contact with mine. His other arm went around my waist, pulling me close against him. "Tell Adrianna the designer could make even her long, lanky body look sexy. To someone."

The twins behind me chuckled, and the laughter this time was more widespread. The two women glared at me as if I, rather than Bruiser, were the one who told them they and Adrianna looked dowdy. Brandon and Brian stepped up to either side of me, giving me a man on each side and one hanging over my back. Which felt rather nice, truth be told.

No one said anything else for a long moment. Almost

in tandem, the two women turned on their heels and left the room.

"Sad," Bruiser said, dropping his arm to cuddle me, the cards still spread. "They really needed the fashion help."

The laughter was freer and the tension level in the group dropped dramatically. "I'll take a card," another woman said. She was only a bit shorter than I, muscular, with a wrestler's shoulders, and carried a semiautomatic holstered beneath her man-style jacket. "Jackie, with Clan Desmarais," she said to me, and shook my hand as she plucked cards from Bruiser's fingers. So she belonged to the one unaligned clan. "I could stand looking elegant. It isn't easy to look feminine with these shoulders. Thanks."

"You're welcome," I said, not quite sure what had just happened.

The twins pivoted to look at me and at Bruiser, who still hung across my shoulder. "You scent-marked her for Leo?" Brandon asked.

"Or for yourself?" Brian asked.

"Myself," Bruiser said easily. "But she's not falling into my arms as quickly I'd hoped."

I ducked out of Bruiser's arms and stepped next to Jackie, who had already shared Madame Melisende's cards with another woman. She looked at me through short bangs and said, "All they ever think about is sex. Take them to a museum and they stare at the naked statues; take them to a park and they ogle the joggers; take one to dinner and he thinks it's a prelude. Something about vampires pushes up their testosterone levels to a teenager's raging desperation."

"You trying to say you don't think about sex, Jackie?" Brandon said. "Because if you have trouble in that area, I could help you think about sex."

"Thanks for the offer, sugar, but I still prefer pure humans in the sack. It's the totality of the thing, you know? Human males think about sex only every other second. A male blood-servant wakes up thinking about sex and goes to bed thinking about sex and then dreams about it till it's time to wake up again."

"Not just sex," Brian mused. "There's fighting too."

"Hunting," Bruiser agreed. "Fishing. Fast cars. Making money."

"Fast cars and money lead back to dames, though," Brandon said.

"See what I mean?" Jackie said to me, and the small group laughed.

The laughter included me, which lent me an unexpectedly warm feeling; the emotion of inclusion wasn't familiar. And then the way she used the words "pure human" intruded into my thoughts. As if the blood-servants didn't think of themselves that way. Beast didn't either. They smelled . . . different.

"Why is Adrianna coming after me?" I asked, looking through the door where the two women had disappeared. "I have a feeling I'll be meeting her servants again soon. And it won't be for tea and crumpets." I was licensed to kill rogue vamps, not humans, or even blood-servants, no matter how annoying or dangerous they might be.

"I don't know, except that you carry Leo's scent marking, and therefore add to Leo's power base," Bruiser said. I noticed that he didn't add "I'm sorry."

A flush of anger pulsed through me. The forced scent marking, meant to protect me, had turned around and bit me, hard. My fists clenched against the urge to pull a stake and ram it into Bruiser.

Wary, the security types looked at the makeup of their own group, reassessing alignments. Three men turned and left the cluster. Silent, we watched them walk away. I pushed aside my anger for later. There were worse things to worry about right now.

"They've been listening to us chat," Brian said. "Not good."

"Taking info home to the new alliance," Brandon said.

"Lotta things keep coming back to old Rafe," I said, remembering him standing in the shadows, watching me, twice tonight. "Maybe I need to pay him a visit." And get a better sniff of him and his underlings, but I didn't add that. Nor did I miss the look Jackie shared with Bruiser, though I had no idea what it might mean.

"Rafael is a problem," a woman said. "A big problem."

The talk turned to recent changes in vamp politics and

quickly became both tedious and bewildering as I listened to gossip about personal and clan relationships that had persisted for hundreds of years. Vamp gossip could originate in the seventeen hundreds, yet still be fresh and painful, and have an impact on clans today, on people dead and alive. Vamp blood feuds could last for centuries. I learned a lot but nothing that I could use. The only thing that mattered to me was the new coalitions and how they impacted my current contract. With Leo's scent marking on me, it was going to be hard to stay out of the brewing war.

And then I remembered the strange look Bettina had given me in the midst of her invitation to visit. Something wasn't right.

CHAPTER 10

Feeding frenzy

An hour later, still early by vamp standards, I asked directions to the powder room and excused myself. The crowd had reached maximum capacity, with shoulder-to-shoulder partygoers. I saw Bruiser in intense conversation with another blood-servant; was watching when he paused, drew up short, and disappeared into the crowd. I smelled vamps from Clan Pellissier several times, Leo's scent pungent on them. Two looked familiar from the fire threat in the aftermath of the hurricane. They saw me, but ignored me with vamp disdain.

The warehouse air was permeated with the stink of vamps, humans, and blood-servants. The smell of sex and fresh blood intermingled, wafting down from the second story. The mixed stench prickled my nose, a sneeze-warning, and blunted my senses, or I'd have caught the predatory smell of a hunter. But my mind was full, mulling over the twisted skeins of vamp politics.

I slid open the pocket door to the darkened powder room, seeing myself in a slanted mirror, haloed by the hall light. Stepping in, I flicked on the light.

A blur swept toward me from the left. Across the mirror. Time dilated and slowed. Beast screamed within me. Shoved her strength and reflexes into my veins with a rush of power and heat. Teeth and claws flashed in the mirrors. Falling toward me.

I dove down and right. Pulled a stake and my knife. The impact came hard, knocking the breath from my lungs. Stunning me. Stopping Beast's raging scream. Slamming my elbow to the tile. The knife spun from my nerveless grip. Clattered away.

I crashed to the tile in a jumble of limbs. Twisted my spine. Banged my knee. My *oof* of pain was buried beneath two vamp bodies. As their weight crushed down on me, my brain caught up. Before I could consider the meaning of an attack at a vamp party, they had me immobilized. Hands gripped and held me, my left arm twisted, canted painfully against my chest. Legs secured my torso and lower limbs.

I drew a breath that stank of my own fear, realizing what had happened, but too late. Angled mirror images had confused everything. My attackers had planned on and used my momentary confusion.

Mouths bit and slashed, the cuts like blows, the pain delayed. I couldn't see for the bodies. Couldn't strike out. Vision and movements were constricted by powerful hands, locked arms, and snake-fast legs. Pinning me as I struggled. Fangs buried behind my knee with none of the painkilling gift of vamp saliva. Another set buried in my right arm, above the elbow. That arm went numb as teeth grazed the nerve. I grunted with pain. The legs constricting my chest tightened with killing force. I couldn't get a breath.

They intended to drain me dry. I saw, above me, another vamp, watching. Her eyes were wide, her lips parted with excitement.

Beast shoved her strength into me. With numb right fingers, I tugged the packet free of my dress and shook my cross out. The vamp's teeth cut deeper with my action, but Beast blunted the pain. The cross flared with silver, retina-burning light. I pressed it into the skin closest. A wrist. A vamp shrieked. Ululating into my eardrum. Deafening. The sound was like a fist, beating my head. Abruptly cut off. Her body flipped away, leaving behind the acrid smell of burned vamp skin.

Fangs pulled from my knee and the body holding my chest shifted up, clamped into my jugular, cutting like twin knives. Agony branded me. Lightning shot through my veins. The legs constricting my chest were gone, but my breath was frozen in my lungs, the pain so sharp I couldn't expand my ribs.

My vision telescoped down to a narrow image, like looking through a straw. If I went out, I was dead. Beast took me over. Undulated my lower body. Held my upper torso unmoving to avoid ripping out my throat.

I shoved the silver cross into her cheek. Her wail began, low, deep, and full of torture. She rolled away, her fangs tearing out. I sucked in a breath of precious air. My blood rolled from my wounds in rivulets and splashed on the mirrors. I had a glimpse of burned face, my blood on her fangs. I pulled my legs under me. Curled my injured arm into my chest, fingers against my bleeding jugular. I recognized the two scarlet-clad vamps from the aborted confrontation in the hallway and remembered my worry from earlier. *Another tag team?* I didn't have the breath to laugh.

In the mirror I met the third vamp's eyes. The unknown. She stood over me, where I crouched on the floor. Cold power flowed from her like icy air from a glacier. Red hair, curly and wild, fanned out around her. Resting on her collarbones was a gold torque etched with Celtic symbols, and a gold cuff shaped like a snake climbed one upper arm. Her dress was cerulean blue shot with gold threads, toga-like, knotted on one shoulder, leaving the other bare. The bare shoulder was splattered with my blood like a tattoo of my death. She looked like some ancient and feral goddess. I was pretty sure her blue eyes were not quite sane.

For a fractured second she stared at my blood running down my throat as hunger blazed into her eyes, vicious and wild. Her lips pulled back. She launched, fangs and three-inch claws striking at me.

I reversed the stake in my left hand. Pushed up from the floor with my one good leg. Levering power into my shoulder, arm, stake.

She drove herself onto it. The wood pierced just below the torque, driving in three inches before she noted it. Her scream added to the others, so high-pitched it was like an emergency beacon, decibels strong.

An arm caught mine before I could alter the angle, driving for her heart. Icy flesh yanked me back, out of the small room, away from the keening vampires. Into the dark hall-way. Whirled me around, against a cold, hard body.

I looked up into Leo Pellissier's eyes. Power crackled the air around us. Beast went silent, withdrawing her claws from me, and taking with her all the strength she had lent.

He was fully vamped out, pupils black in bloody red sclera, fangs snapped into killing position, his fingernails knives. His gaze was on my throat where my blood ran fast from the torn punctures. He growled. My death leaped into his eyes. Knowing there wasn't time, I curled my fingers into my hair for my remaining stake. But he lifted his stare away, to the woman vamp in the blue dress instead.

"Adrianna," he said, his voice silky and smooth in con-trast to the snarl and violence on his face. "You trespass on what is scent-marked as mine. You and your scions attack a guest present at another's invitation. You force a blood meal. You reach across clan alliances and sow discord, a discord that is reported to me by my blood-servant instead of brought to me in a formal challenge for power."

I remembered Bruiser disappearing into the crowd only moments before my attack. Leo had arrived then, and Bruiser had told him of the conspiracy. I was sure of it. Not that it mattered. I couldn't shift in Leo's arms. And I was bleeding to death.

Leo's heart beat once, the sound startling against my ear. He leaned to Adrianna. And he smiled, fangs fully exposed and fierce. "Do you seek to challenge me for master of this city? Or is it time for you to seek the light?"

She hissed with fury. "I am not an old rogue," she said, the words accented and strange.

"Perhaps not, but you whisper discord. It is said that your blood-master seeks to form an alliance and break his oath of blood to me. Do you follow him into disgrace?"

"I am not without honor," she said, her lips pulling back to show her fangs. Which I was pretty sure was not an an-swer to Leo's question.

I pressed a fist against my neck wound. My knuckles skidded in my blood. I whimpered. Leo heard the faint mewling and stilled for a long moment, his body unmoving as a marble gravestone. When he took a breath, the move-ment of his ribs against mine was alien and foreign, as if that gravestone decided to breathe. He was scenting me the way a predator scent-searched prey. The faintest tremor quivered through him.

He blew out and swiveled his head between the two burned vamps now cowering in fear. He whispered, his words suffused with power, dark and demanding, "Lanah and Hope. Did your clan master sanction this action?" The two vamps looked at each other and then quickly to Adrianna, who faced him, her back to the sink. "Do not seek your sire for your answers," Leo said, his voice snapping like a whip. Their eyes shot back to him.

"No," one of the cowering vamps said. And her pupils constricted, her vamped state dissipating. She hunched her shoulders and sank lower, angling her neck to expose the soft tissues of her throat, the position both protective and submissive. The other ducked away, hunched, avoiding Leo's stare.

"George," he snapped. Bruiser appeared at my shoulder, his eyes on Leo as if I weren't there. "Take Jane to Bethany. Have her wounds treated."

"Yes, sir." Bruiser scooped me up as if I were a child and I gasped with pain. Started to resist. Bruiser spun into the brightly lit hallway. Fifty pairs of vamped-out eyes zeroed in on me. On my throat. On my leg. On my flowing blood. Fangs snapped down with multiple tiny clicks. My heart rate tripled and I knew they heard it, but I couldn't control my reaction, fear sliding along my skin like icy mist in a winter storm. I started shaking, hyperventilating with shock. I needed help, and not just medical. Getting out of a warehouse full of vamps with blood in my veins didn't look likely on my own. I sank against him as Bruiser strode toward the vamps. Reluctantly they parted, allowing us a pathway. Still knuckling my throat, I looked over Bruiser's shoulder.

The two cowed vamps scuttled from the powder room, their limbs contorted and spidery in their haste. Leo lifted an arm and pointed at Adrianna. A sudden gust of power rippled the air, lifting my hair like the threat of lightning. When he spoke, his voice was full-throated, ominous as storm clouds, and so full of power that it shivered through me like blizzard winds through winter trees. "Adrianna of

Clan St. Martin, kneel." I heard him take a deep breath as power swamped through the room. He roared, "Attend me!"

I caught a flash of red hair as Adrianna fell to Leo's feet. All around me, vamps dropped to their knees, compelled by his voice and authority. Power lanced through the air, sharp as sword points, piercing as claws. The blood-master of the city had spoken. The only sound was the thump of falling bodies, the shush of fabric, and the clip of Bruiser's fancy shoes on the floor as he carried me away. Not even the sound of breathing marred the silence.

The sensation of command and might began to fade. I laid my head against Bruiser's chest. His heart beat fast and sure beneath my ear. Quickly we were through the short hallway and into the empty open area, the echo of our movement on the brick walls the only sounds. A place full of the dead. I knew I should be one of them, would have been had not vamp saliva constricted blood vessels and slowed bleeding. It was bizarre, but the very nature of a vamp attack meant a victim would live a bit longer.

I tried to speak and had to slide my tongue across dry lips to moisten them. "Why did he save me? He wants me dead for killing the thing that took the place of his son."

"If Leo wishes you dead, he will exterminate you himself, not allow others to kill for him. He may be deep within Dolore, but he is still master of this city. He is still cognizant of his duties and his power structure, and for now, you are necessary to him."

"And when he gives way to Dolore again?"

Bruiser shrugged slightly. "Then he may forget everything but grief and you may die."

"That sucks," I whispered.

Bruiser chuckled. And carried me outside, into the welcome heat of the night. All of the humans, blood-servants, blood-slaves, and the junkies, were on the lawn or standing beside cars, faces etched with fear, worry, or false ennui, depending on their natures or experience. Almost in unison, they turned to us, watching as Bruiser took the steps to the walkway. The buzz of voices fell utterly silent. A breeze had sprung up, uncertain of its direction, wet with river scent.

Brian and Brandon stepped close. "How is she?" Brian asked.

"I'm okay," I lied.

"Barely," Bruiser said dryly, his arms tightening around my thighs and chest. To the men, he said, "She's losing too much blood. The attack wasn't intended to close her wounds."

"And the masters?" a woman called from the dark of the lawn.

"In bloody deep shit," he said, his British heritage showing in the accent and phrasing. To the twins he said, "Call Bethany. I presume she's in Leo's Porsche, likely 'round the block."

Brian looked at him oddly. "You sure? Bethany?"

"Leo's orders," Bruiser said. Both twins looked at me, speculation in their expressions. Brandon punched on a cell and turned away, speaking softly. Bruiser raised his voice. "This will be a difficult night, in the few hours left before dawn. I suggest you gather the rest of your clans' servants and slaves. The Mithrans need us tonight."

"Feeding frenzy," a voice murmured from the crowd.

"Maybe not. We can hope not," another said.

Cell phones were pulled and numbers punched in. Everywhere, bodies turned for privacy, leaving Bruiser and me alone in a sea of people. Down the street, a Porsche the maroon red of old blood pulled slowly down the narrow lane of open street, headlights picking out the servants, security, and drivers, their bodies showing tense in the sharp shadows, heads swiveling, staring into the dark as if watching for attack. Most had obviously seen something like this before, vamps on the edge of violence.

There was nothing in the lore about a feeding frenzy, but sharks were well known for it. I knew from personal experience that big cats could go into killing mode and destroy anything they could catch. Vamps were predators of a particularly intelligent and gruesome variety. I started shivering, feeling cold, even in the humid heat.

Across the way, I saw a shimmer of magic, hazy blue and gray sparkles. Five indistinct forms stood in the shadows of a four-story warehouse that had been turned into condos, light spilling around them from a myriad of windows. Five witches, standing at what might have been the points of a pentagram, a glamour sparkling over them, making them appear middle-aged and dowdy. There was nothing threatening about them, but I wondered why they were there and what they wanted. I guessed they were the five witches Bliss and Tia had seen. I drew in a breath, testing the scents, and caught a whiff of witch. Familiar. It was similar to the witch scent I'd caught on the grave of the young rogue I'd seen rise. Similar, but not quite exact. And then it was gone, carried by the fitful currents following the Mississippi. It felt wrong for them to be here, watching vamps, but so much was amiss right now it was hard to tease out the differing strands of the tangled problems.

The Porsche braked to a stop and the passenger door opened. No light came on inside, leaving the interior like the mouth of a cave. Bruiser leaned in and sat me on the seat in a display of grace and sheer muscle. "Leo says to treat her."

"Yes. She is . . . weak," a soft voice said. "Injured." The accent was vaguely African and touched by French, the vowel sounds mellow and very round.

Fist still at my throat, my blood drying and sticky, wet and fresh, I turned to the driver's seat as the door closed at my side. I got my first look at Bethany. She had been a black woman when human and was now the blackest vampire I had ever seen. Unlike most vamps, whose skin paled after long years without the sun, her flesh was blue-black, her lips even darker. Her sclera were brownish and her irises blacker than any I had ever seen, blacker than the People's, blacker than the darkest night. Her hair was knotted and twisted into dreadlocks and worked with hundreds of gold and stone beads; the locks were pulled to the nape of her neck, hiding her ears except for the lobes, which dangled a multitude of gold rings.

Power surrounded her like an aura, but softer in texture than the spiked, mailed fist of Leo's vamp clout. Bethany's energies were ephemeral, questing, and carried a scent similar to witch power, but more bitter. I didn't know what she had been before she was turned, but she was old, maybe the oldest vamp I had ever seen, and full of a strange power. I thought of Sabina Delgado y Aguilera, the old vamp at the chapel, who wore the white wimple of a nun. This power was like hers, slow and roiling, building and moving as an avalanche builds and moves, but with intent and purpose.

Bethany was staring at me, her gaze so dark it was like the sky on a moonless, clouded night in the Appalachians, so deep it was like staring into an ocean trench, empty and fathomless. A primal reaction sent gooseflesh over my skin. Beast did nothing, hunched deep in my mind, watching, worried, nearly—but not quite—fearful. Without taking her eyes from me, Bethany shifted the Porsche into gear and moved along the street. She looked away from me when she turned, guiding the car right, then left. Three blocks later, we were out of the Warehouse District. My shivers worsened. I was pretty sure I was going into shock. I needed to *shift*.

She pulled the car into a twenty-four-hour gas station with bars on the windows and blinding security lights and eased around back into a garbage-strewn alley. Deep in the shadows, she cut the motor. "You are injured," she said. "Do you choose to be healed?"

There was something odd about the phrase but I didn't have much choice. I wouldn't make it home and didn't have the energy to shift without the fetishes or boulders. I licked my dry lips and said, "Sure."

She lifted her hands from the steering wheel and reached out, taking the back of my head in one iron-hard palm; her other palm pressed against my forehead. Her hands were icy cold, as if she slept in a refrigerator. With implacable strength, she bent my head back. I forced down my reaction to her touch. I had agreed to this, whatever this was.

Beast, who had been oddly silent since Leo appeared, came alert and sank her claws into my mind. *Dead meat fingers. Trap!* Beast thought, drawing up power to fight or run. *I am not prey*, Beast said. I gripped the door and pulled back. It was too late. Bethany's hands stopped me, hands cold and hard as black marble. My heart rate trebled. I sucked air to scream.

She licked my throat. As quickly as her cold tongue touched me, Bethany's fangs struck. I stiffened, stopped, one hand raised, held up in silent protest; Beast hissed. An electric cold suffused my chest, seeming to fill my lungs, my heart, and travel through my arteries like a freezing river, or like the finest rum, poured over dry ice, crackling and burning. My nerves and muscles spasmed.

I had known the damage to my body was there, but the pain had been blunted by shock. Now it hit me with a slashing charge, as if every nerve at once was scraped raw by frozen steel. It lasted one brutal moment. The pain mutated into something chilled and euphoric, like iced vodka swimming with snowflakes. The sensation flushed through me and pooled in my middle like satisfied hungers, like the sensation of falling through frigid air at the top of the world, like nothing I had ever experienced.

I drew in a slow breath, my throat and ribs moving carefully. I was held in the bite of a predator, and moving too quickly could tear out the rest of my throat. Again.

CHAPTER 11

Biting things, too small to eat

Strength poured in, filling my veins and arteries, a stunning, exhilarating, arctic force, as potent as the night sky at the top of a frozen mountain. The weakness that had drained me was gone. Power shuddered through me, cold force and might. Though it reminded me of Molly's magic, it wasn't witch power, not exactly. It was something else. Something uniquely Bethany, or uniquely shamanistic. Beast panted in my mind, her breath a frozen mist, killing teeth exposed. As if she lay in a powdery snow, she rolled over, cold, cold, cold beneath her, her rough pelt brushing inside my skin, scoring along bones and nerves. Needing to shift, she was pushed close to the change by the rising energies.

As suddenly as she struck, Bethany slipped back from me, her teeth and mouth and hands sliding away, leaving me slumped in my seat, my head rocked against the side window. Slowly, my vision cleared, the dim night sky coming into focus. The waxing moon rested in the limbs of a young oak. City lights glowed in the near distance.

My heartbeat was a wet susurration, a faint movement through me. My skin was tingling, tight and expectant, as if waiting for the next pain or the next pleasure. I took a breath and the night air was damp, muggy, though the Porsche's air conditioner hummed steadily. I placed my palms on the seat, pushed myself upright, and swallowed gingerly. I touched my neck, finding crusty blood and tight

new skin beneath my fingertips. Healed. I felt . . . pretty
good. I looked at Bethany and couldn't think of a single
thing to say.

She sat across from me, swiveled at an angle in the seat,
her back to the door, her depthless dark eyes on me. No
trace of emotion hovered on her face. She didn't breathe,
didn't move at all. She might have been a black marble
statue.

When she moved to draw breath and speak, it was a
shock. "You taste of several vampires. And violence. And
the wildness of trees and rock and rushing rivers. You are
not human and never have been." Her head cocked to one
side, more lizardlike than birdlike. "I do not think I have
tasted one such as you, and I have tasted many." When I
didn't respond except to wrap my fingers around my own
throat, she said, "I gave you a bit of my essence. You will be
energized, more powerful for a time."

I swallowed again and forced out the worrying words.
"What is essence? Hope you didn't try to turn me. I don't
want to wake up all dead and fangy."

Bethany laughed, and her eyes opened wide as if the
sound surprised her. When it passed, a small smile rested
on her mouth. "Many would choose to be one of us, even
with the ten feral years. No. I did not turn you. If I had, you
would be in the near-death sleep of the turned. I shared with
you a drop of my own essence, not my Mithran essence."

I thought about that for a moment, remembering the
cold power, then guessed, "Shaman? Were you an African
shaman?"

"Yes. You know of my world?"

She seemed almost pleased with the thought, and
though that wasn't what I had meant, I agreed. "Um. Some.
A little." I mean, I could pick it out on a map.

Bethany said, "I was shaman of the Odouranth tribe,
a peaceful, farming people." Her face fell, nearly human
pain in her expression, and her voice carried the weight of
old, dusty pain when she said, "We were destroyed by the
Masai, long before they were called Masai, in the mountains of what is now southeastern Africa."

I blinked and a picture of sere grass, burned huts, bodies
on the ground, bloody and hacked, flashed over the backs of

my lids and was gone, leaving only the memory of ancient agony and grief. She looked puzzled. "You saw this. This memory, just now. Yes?"

I nodded once, the motion jerky. Her eyes watched me, her face inert. "No one has seen inside my memories in over a century."

"I saw," I said. "But I don't know why or what it meant."

"Such a sharing was . . . not unpleasant. Shall we see if more such can be shared?"

I didn't know how to respond to that, and she took my silence as indication to go on. "I was considered a woman of great value, and so was captured alive, for my magic. I was given to the son of the conquering chief as a minor wife. And when he died at the next full moon"—her lips moved slowly into a smile, satisfied and unexpected—"I was beaten and sold to a traveling slave merchant who took me to Egypt. There I was sold again, to a Roman, and taken to a new land. The land of the Hebrew."

Something about the way she said "land of the Hebrew" made me ask, "When? When were you in the land of the Hebrew?"

Sharp bewilderment creased her forehead. "I do not know why I speak to you of this. I have done so only seldom."

She had already forgotten the shared memory. That lapse was a danger sign of a vamp going old-rogue wacky. When I didn't reply, she said, "My master was a centurion, part of a legion of soldiers in charge of the destruction of Yerushalayim. Did you know him?"

Yerushalayim, also known as Jerusalem . . . The city was destroyed by the Roman army in AD 70 or so. Did I know him? *No, and he's been dead two thousand years*. I didn't say it. The expression in her eyes made sense now. Rogue. She wasn't far from going rogue. And she'd had my throat in her fangs. . . . I licked my lips, which were suddenly dry and cracked, and a question fell from them. "Who turned you?"

A little click sounded as her fangs snapped down. Her smile was predatory, as cold and barren as the energies she had shared when she healed me. Slowly, her eyes bled black and her sclera bled scarlet as she vamped out, but the transition was slow, not the eyeblink speed of the others. She seemed in control even as she lost it. Old . . . she was *old*.

"I was among the first hundred who followed the Sons of Darkness, turned by one who was among the first ten of the Cursed."

I remembered the term Sons of Darkness mentioned at the party, and that one of them had been contacted by Rafael. I'd also seen the term on a scrap of paper in room 666. She swiveled in the seat, a motion as supple and sinuous as a snake, and put the Porsche into drive. "You are not human. You have been honored to receive my essence and live." Without another word, her fangs retracted with a soft click, and she pulled out of the alley, around the convenience store, into the street. Moments later she slowed in front of my house and said, "You may leave me."

I unbuckled, opened the door, and stepped from the car, not ticked off that I'd been dismissed, as I usually was when one of them acted all high-handed. I was satisfied to get away alive. She reached over, pulled the door shut, and the tires ground away from the curb, the car a low throb in the night.

We still didn't have power and so when I was inside, I lit a single candle, carrying it with me. Filthy, I stripped, tossed the dress into the sink, added soap and water, just in case the dress could be salvaged, and showered off fast. I was almost getting used to the sight of blood rinsing off me and down the drain. Naked, damp hair unbraided and knotted in a ponytail hanging down my back, I dialed Derek Lee. When he answered, I said, "I'm hunting rogue. Want to come?"

His answer was a succinct "Hell yeah."

"Meet you at your place," I said, and closed the cell.

When Bitsa and I motored up to his housing unit, Derek and three of his guys were waiting. From the look of them, they were all military or ex-military. Cold, expressionless, ready. They were in jungle camo, boots, and bore a single pair of night-vision goggles. I could smell the steel and gun oil from the street. I didn't bother to say hi, I just killed the engine, slung a leg over the bike, and kicked the stand down.

"You leaving that nice piece a' art here?" one of Derek's guys said.

"Witchy locks. Anyone who touches it gets a shock."

"What we doing?" Derek asked, moving into the street.

He didn't introduce his crew; I guessed he didn't intend me to know their names. Okay by me. Trust had to be earned; it worked both ways. And I was starting out with a lie but there was no help for it. So much for trust. "I want to see if I can track the rogues' hunting ground, find out if there are any more young ones feeding in the area." I held up a shard of sharp stone I'd grabbed from the rock garden. "This is spelled. I feel a sort of vibration in the presence of vamps. I can track them with this." Total lie but it was all I had. I was gonna sniff them out, but I couldn't say that.

"You leaving it with us when you're done?" Derek asked.

"Sure. It'll be nothing but a piece of rock, but you can have it."

"Onetime spell. Damn witches got no heart," guy number one said.

Derek lifted a careless one-shouldered shrug of the fighting man. "After you."

Two hours later I was done. Using the *magical rock* I had mapped the entire hunting ground of the two young rogues we had killed, and the others killed and beheaded by Derek and his crew. There were no more young feeding in the projects, which relieved my mind, but I had learned nothing new, which was a bummer.

The men followed Bitsa and me out of the projects, threading through the city to vamp headquarters, a cooler full of vamp heads in the backseat of their car. I tried to call ahead, but cell towers, or the erratic power to them, were back down. I pulled up at the front door and unloaded the cooler, surprised at the weight. Vamp heads were heavy. Derek and his soldiers took off, which was still sort of weird, as I knew they worked for Leo.

I rang the bell, and when the same security blood-servant opened it, I handed WWF the cooler. He grunted when he took it and set it on the table inside. "Can I get a check?" I asked.

"Ernestine's gone home for the night. Call tomorrow." He opened the cooler and made a face at the smell. I stepped back fast. The dry ice hadn't done a very good job and the heads were ripe. WWF pulled on latex gloves and inspected the fangs, verified them to be young rogue, and wrote out a receipt. I took it and left, feeling that I hadn't accomplished a dang thing today.

Wired, unable to sleep, I stripped again, and put the weapons under lock and key so the kids couldn't find them. Grabbing my puma concolor fetish necklace and my travel pack, I stopped by the kitchen for some warm beef jerky and went out back to the rocks I used for meditation and to shift. I had two hours till dawn and a lot of frustration to burn off.

Yesssss. Hunt, Beast thought at me. I hadn't hunted in days, and she pressed against my flesh, her pelt abrading me, her claws opening and closing, sharp tips biting into my mind.

Standing on the broken rocks, I pulled the travel pack over my head, adjusted the double chain securing the gold nugget necklace to its proper length, and snapped on the travel pack. Together, they looked like an expensive collar and tote, such as a St. Bernard rescue dog might have carried in the Swiss Alps. I bent over and scraped the gold nugget across the uppermost rock, depositing a thin streak of gold. It was like, well, like a homing beacon, among other things.

Hunt. Kill. Blood and meat. Beast, while always present in the depths of my consciousness, was talking to me as a separate entity now, as a self-aware creature with desires of her own. I looked at the jerky I'd dropped on the ground, knowing she would hate it, but there wasn't anything I could do, not with the power still off. Besides, Beast needed to roam free for a while, and I needed the more perfect healing that shifting would bring. The drop of Bethany's essence had kept me alive, and if I had no other experience to compare it to, it would have seemed nearly miraculous. But it wasn't a substitute for Beast and my own skinwalker magic.

I sat on the boulders, the rock warm beneath me. Mosquitoes swarmed, biting. Beast hissed. *Biting things. Too small to eat.*

The necklace of the mountain panther—commonly called the mountain lion—was made of the claws, teeth, and small bones of the biggest female panther I had ever seen. The cat had been killed by a rancher in Montana during a legal hunt, the pelt mounted on his living room wall, the bones and teeth sold through a taxidermist. The mountain lion was hunted throughout the Western U.S. but was extinct in the Eastern states, or it had been. Some reports said panthers were making a comeback east of the Mississippi. I could hope. I didn't *have* to use the necklace to shift into this creature—unlike other species, the memory of Beast's form was always a part of me—but it was easier.

I held the necklace and closed my eyes. Relaxed. Listened to the wind. Felt the pull of the moon, growing gravid, nesting the horizon. I listened to the beat of my own heart. Beast rose in me, silent, predatory.

I slowed the functions of my body, my breathing, my heart rate, let my blood pressure drop, my muscles relax, as if I were going to sleep. I lay on the boulder, breasts and belly draping the cool stone in the humid air.

Mind clearing, I sank deep inside, my consciousness falling away, all but the purpose of this hunt. That purpose I set into the lining of my skin, into the deepest parts of my brain, so I wouldn't lose it when I *shifted*, when I *changed*. I dropped lower. Deeper. Into the darkness inside where ancient, nebulous memories swirled in a gray world of shadow, blood, uncertainty. I heard a distant drum, smelled herbed wood smoke, and the night wind on my skin seemed to cool and freshen. As I dropped deeper, memories began to firm, memories that, at all other times, were submerged, both mine and Beast's, but had been brought closer to the surface by the time in the sweat lodge with Aggie One Feather. Had that been only this morning? It seemed forever ago.

As I had been taught by my father—so long forgotten—I sought the inner snake lying inside the bones and teeth of the necklace, the coiled, curled snake, deep in the cells, in the remains of the marrow. Science had given the snake a name. RNA. DNA. Genetic sequences, specific to each species, each creature. For my people, for skinwalkers, it had always simply been the *inner snake*, the phrase one of very few things that was certain in my past.

I sank into the marrow hidden in the bones. I took up the snake that rests in the depths of all beasts and I dropped within. Like water flowing in a stream, a whirling current. Like snow rolling down a mountainside gaining momentum, unstoppable. Grayness enveloped me, sparkling with black motes, bright and cold as the world fell away. I slid into the gray place of the change.

My breathing deepened. Heart rate sped up. And my bones . . . slid. Skin rippled. Fur, tawny and gray, brown and tipped with black, sprouted. Pain, like a knife, slid between muscle and bone. My nostrils widened, drawing deep.

Jane fell away. Night was rich with wonderful scents, dancing like trout in stream, each distinct. I panted. Listened—cars, music, the sounds of humans, and the sounds of animals. Hopped from rocks. Sniffed food. Hacked. *Old dead, cooked meat. Dead prey.* Wanted hunt, to tear flesh from bone. But stomach burned with need. *Hunger.* I ate.

Belly silent, I stepped to top of rocks, broken and sharp, and leaped to top of tall fence, brick warm and high like limb in sun. Dropped down, to yard on side of house without small dog. Good eating, but Jane says no. Only opossum, deer, nutria, rabbit. Alligator. If I can catch one. Am Big Cat, but gator is big underwater.

Long time later, near sunrise, belly was full of small deer, hooves and bones and not-eat parts on the ground, my heart happy with hunt and blood. With last lick of tongue, groomed paws and face clean, and rolled over on pine needles, paws in air, staring at night sky. Was near shaman's house. Not shaman from far away, not new shaman who was also vampire, but shaman of Jane's people. Cherokee shaman. Aggie One Feather. Jane needed to be here. Jane needed shaman, though she did not know it.

Mind of Jane rose, curious. *Why?* she thought. *Why do I need Aggie?*

Did not answer. Sometimes Jane was foolish, like when she did not mate, though her body and soul needed a mate. Three males would mate with her. All fast and strong and healthy. But she did not. Curious.

Yawned and rolled to feet, nosed carcass. No good meat left. Satisfied, padded through trees and scrub and along path to shaman's, careful to step on pine needles piled deep, not on mud, careful to hide tracks. Padded along path where liver-eater had once hidden, checking for his scent. Fading. Liver-eater was true-dead.

Circled sweat house. Shaman's dogs were asleep on back stoop, snoring. Easy prey, if I was hungry. Looked at sky, dawn not far away. Time to change. Time to let Jane be alpha.

Located good place under tree with low branches. Safe, protected. Lay down on leaves and needles, their scent fresh and strong. Thought of Jane. Human. Found her snake. And shifted. Painpainpain like knives sliding on bone, cutting deep.

In the gray dark of almost dawn, I lay on a bed of pine needles, their sharp ends pricking my bare skin. "Why do I need Aggie?" I asked my other half, my voice raspy, dry, and unused. Deep in my mind, Beast rolled over and closed her eyes. I cleared my throat, said, "Big help you are," and pushed to my knees. Unclasping the travel pack from my neck, I shook out my clothes—T-shirt, lightweight pants, and flip-flops—and dressed quickly, already smelling bacon and eggs cooking nearby.

Despite the deer Beast had brought down and gorged on, I was still ravenous, the energies used by the shift partially provided by the calories in the protein and fats of the big meal. But it was never enough and I was always hungry after. The smell of breakfast cooking made me salivate.

I pulled my long hair back and tied it in a knot as I walked toward Aggie's house, hoping she and her mother would still be asleep or looking elsewhere when I exited the woods because I had no explanation of why I was in the park property that bordered theirs. I wasn't so lucky. They were sitting on the screened porch in the dark of near dawn, the older woman drinking from a mug, and I felt the weight of their curiosity and speculation as I stepped onto the lawn. Aggie stood and opened the screened door. "Have you come to go to water?"

"Um . . . yes." It seemed safest to agree, though I didn't really remember what it meant. At the sound of my voice, dogs rose and pitched from the porch, barking. Beast hacked with amusement at the sound before going to sleep in my mind.

"Are you fasting?" Aggie asked.

"Yes. And starving." And hoping she'd ask me to breakfast. She didn't.

"Go wait on the front porch. You need to pray and center yourself, and I need to gather my things. Our breakfast can wait."

I sighed. I had a feeling I wasn't going to get nourishment any time soon. Center myself, she said. Something about that thought raised my hackles, and I didn't know why. I *was* centered. I was *always* centered. Whatever the heck that meant.

Around front, I dropped down on the porch and waited as the sky began to brighten from the darkest blue of night to the bleak charcoal of early dawn. I was hungry and tired and sleepy. And annoyed, not that I'd let Aggie see that.

Faster than I expected, Aggie opened the front door and walked out, no lights on inside, which preserved her night vision. In the dark, she placed a small black cloth bag on the step and sat beside me with a stretch and a yawn, her manner grave, until she met my eyes. Hers took on a twinkle as if she could see the orneriness squirming beneath my skin. I pressed my lips together to keep from saying something crass and she chuckled softly. I wanted to make claws of my hands, but gripped them together around my knees instead, the knuckles white.

Aggie's expression went from amusement to compassion, which somehow made me madder. And again, I didn't know why. She patted my clasped hands as if to say, "Take your medicine, little girl. It won't taste bad," which surely was a lie. She then began to explain the ritual of going to water, offering explanations on its purpose, and instructing me in my part, as if I was really going to do this.

My aggravation grew until I was grinding my back molars. And I had no idea why I was so irritated. Angry. Whatever. When she paused I said, "So, to put it simply, we throw up, talk to God, and then go for a swim. In a bayou that's full of all sorts of things. Snakes. Twenty-pound rats. And alligators."

Aggie laughed, the sound like water burbling over stones, her face creased into smile wrinkles that otherwise didn't show. "Pretty much. There are ritual prayers, but I can walk you through them."

I was used to doing my praying in church, but somehow this felt natural too.

"Usually women don't have to purge," Aggie continued, "but you are a warrior woman, and my mother and I agree that you must go to water as a man would, at least this first time. After, you will be cleansed inside and out; your spirit will be open, and restored. You will be ready for battle or pain or difficulty, and you will be without the shadows of the past that darken your soul. Come. Sun's getting ready to rise, and going to water is best done at dawn." Aggie stood and reached back to the house, opening the door. From the darkness within, an old woman tottered out, Aggie One Feather's mother. Maybe I was dense, but I hadn't realized that the older woman would be joining us.

I bowed my head to her and murmured, "*U ni lisi*, grandmother of many children." It was a term of greatest respect.

Her hair was braided down to her hips, the thin tresses black as a raven's wing brightened with rare white strands. She nodded once to me and blinked into the dark, leading the way to the car parked in the yard, a little four-wheel-drive Toyota barely seen in the unlit driveway. Chattering in Cherokee, she climbed into the backseat and buckled herself in, her actions certain and determined. I looked at Aggie, but she was too busy following her ancient mother's orders to notice my dismay. Now I had two *lisi* to deal with, and it was clear whose word held sway. Elder Grandmother's.

Unable to figure out a way to avoid the ritual, and not knowing why I was feeling so stubborn, I climbed in the front passenger seat. Aggie drove us out of the cul-de-sac and down a series of shell roads, white in the dawn light. Unpaved roads in the Delta states were often covered with crushed shell, and the farther we drove, the sparser the shells on the roadway became until we were on a two-track trail, the car bouncing into and out of potholes and over washboard ruts.

She gunned the engine like a wannabe dirt-track racer, skewing around curves between ever-closer trees, the dark world bouncing in the headlights, which didn't help the state of my nerves or the condition of my hunger. Like the woman in the backseat, who seemed familiar with Aggie's driving, I held on with both hands while my stomach growled and cramped with hunger and Beast pressed paws into my consciousness, kneading, her way of offering comfort. Why did I need comfort?

The old women laughed and chattered as Aggie drove, including me in the conversation from time to time, mostly instructions about the ritual to come, and I wasn't certain whether I was growing happier about what we were going to do or more uncomfortable.

"The old beliefs say that a Great Creator made us," Aggie said as she spun the car around a hundred-twenty-degree curve and back in a graceless swerve. "There was a split in beliefs generations ago, I think influenced by Christians, with some saying the Creator still was listening to us and some saying he had gone back to the Great One, or possibly somewhere creating other worlds, and had left three guardians to watch over us."

Interesting that they had a trinity too.

"Some talk about these three guardians and some talk about the guardians of the four directions. As for actual names to call on, the major one would be *Unelenehi*, who is the Great One. It's also the name for the sun, but according to my grandpa," she said, taking her eyes from the narrowing road to give me a look that said her grandpa had been an important, knowledgeable, and wise man, "the sun was only a reflection of the Great Light behind it, which was the One. You call on this when facing east. Many people like to call on *Selu*, who was first woman, the corn mother. Her husband, first man, was *Kenati*. There was also a great female spirit. I've never seen her name written, but it's pronounced like *Ag is see qua*."

Aggie glanced at me, and seemed to catch my discomfort. Her mouth twisted in thought and she slowed, taking a particularly deep bump that cracked my head against the car roof. While I held on and rubbed my head, she and *Lisi* chatted in Cherokee for a while; then Aggie said to me,

"Going to water is not a hard and firm ritual. It isn't about calling on a specific god or a specific spirit. It is a way of recognizing our roots, our heritage, and calling on the past to lead and direct us into the future. It is as individual as the way you pray, as the god or spirits you believe in. You may adjust it according to your need, and as your god directs."

She braked, turned off the car, and got out, helping her mother out as well, white shell dust and road dust billowing past. The two women moved into the trees, leaving me sitting there, alone, the engine pinging. We were in a small clearing about half the size of my kitchen, surrounded by thin rails of young pine trees growing so close together they would keep out most wildlife.

Wordless, I opened my door, brushing it against the scrub to the side and closing it only with difficulty. I followed the women, my flip-flops spanking the earth, along a flat trail that snaked through the trees, to the edge of a bayou where the ground became so muddy my thin shoes sucked and pulled against my toes with each step. The water in the bayou channel was brown and muddy from the recent storm, running high, overlapping its banks into the trees. It was very different from the clear streams of the Appalachians, and a sudden gust of homesickness swirled through me like a dust devil.

Chatting to her mother, Aggie hung her black cloth bag from the stub of a broken tree limb and unscrewed the lid on her Thermos. She poured the liquid inside into the plastic cup top; it was hot and black, and it smelled like boiled tree limbs and lichen and pinesap. I wrinkled my nose. Aggie gave the cup to her mother, who guzzled it down and said something that sounded unkind before moving into the trees. "Mother doesn't like purging like the men have to do. She likes the women's ritual better, but it must be done."

From the woods I heard retching and my gorge rose in sympathy. I clasped my arms around my waist. I so did not want to do this.

Aggie poured a second cup and swallowed it in a single gulp before pouring another for me. "There are good reasons why we go to water," she said, her tone gentle but not soothing me. "When we face war or trouble, or some great decision must be reached, we must be clean inside and out in order for the gods, or God, to talk to us. Drink. Then go into the woods and do what you must." And this time it was a command. Aggie handed me a small baggie and tapped it. "Native tobacco. Use it like I told you. It's hard to come by these days. Don't waste it." She hurried into the trees, leaving me alone.

. . . *War or trouble, or some great decision.* Yeah, that kinda spelled out my life right now. I looked at the liquid, black in the darkness.

Beast huffed deep inside. *Jane needs this. Beast that is I/ we needs this.*

Which is why I don't want to do it, I thought back. My mental tone sounded stubborn. Whiny. Sorta the way my housemates sounded when I was a teenager and my housemother wanted us all to clean the bathrooms or do laundry. I sighed. That was why I was feeling so antsy. It had been a long time since I had to do something against my will because it was good for me.

I sniffed again and grimaced at the earthy stench of the herbal mixture before tossing it back. I gagged getting it down. The elixir from hell didn't taste any better than it smelled and it wanted to come up faster than it went down. I held it in and ran deeper into the woods. Gorge rising with about-to-die nausea, I fell against a tree. I hated throwing up. It was a crazy way to start something that was supposed to be spiritual. In the children's home the only rituals had been daily Bible study, a required theology course during my high school years, the Lord's Supper on Sunday, and being baptized, which I'd done in a river. Oddly, that had been at dawn too.

Suddenly the emetic hit and I bent over, my empty stomach cramping. I lost liquid. I lost stomach acid. I lost bile so bitter it made my teeth hurt. It felt as if I lost everything I had eaten for the last month until I was retching only air. I was cleaned out down to my toes.

Empty, I spat, getting rid of the last of my stomach contents. This was just gross.

Hunger from the shift was riding me hard and my stomach twisted into a single vicious spasm. As quickly as it began, the spasm and nausea stopped. I stumbled to a clean spot a few feet away and held on to a thin rail of a tree until I could remember to breathe and was able to stand on my own. It had been a whole lot easier just getting baptized.

Beast rolled beneath my skin, sick and angry. *Jane let human shaman give* . . . She stopped, no words in her Beast vocabulary. *Jane ate bad meat. Kit mistake. Foolish. Sick.*

Poison. Beast was talking about poison. My skinwalker metabolism began to react again, and my body rejected the potion, this time from the other end of my digestive tract. It took forever. It was awful.

I hung against a tree, pine bark sharp and sorta crinkly under my palms, and breathed as if I had run a long race. I felt hollow and tingly, drained and bare, like an empty room, sound ringing off the barren walls of my soul. I wasn't sure *what* I was feeling.

Somewhere in the last minutes, Beast had disappeared, leaving my mind vacant and lucid. I rocked, my back against the thin tree. Mosquitoes buzzed around my ankles and along my arms. I held out a hand in the dim light, my skin looking tight and drawn, desiccated. *I'm going to water.* My housemother at the children's home would throw a hissy fit if she knew.

I bounced the tobacco baggie in my palm as if measuring it. This wasn't a worship service. It was meant to be a physical and psychological cleansing. If I did it at a therapist's office or as part of a high colonic, I wouldn't think twice.

I opened the plastic baggie and sniffed the tobacco inside, the scent unlike most tobacco I'd smelled, being richer, more raw. It was an earthy dark brown, the leaves curled and moist, perhaps a tablespoon altogether. I was supposed to salute the four directions with it.

I faced east, the sky a pale gray there, against the cerulean backdrop of the night. The air was calm and expectant, the quiet marred only by the purl of water nearby. The quiet pressed against me, steady, almost solid.

Taking a pinch of the tobacco in my right fingers, I thought about what Aggie had said. This was supposed to be a ritual to prepare me to fight, a ritual of my own making, not hers. So maybe I could use my own words but Aggie's grasp of the stories and the olden times.

I held the tobacco high, as if greeting the sun, and

paused, thinking. I drew on some old Bible studies into the ancient Hebrew names of God. "I call on the Almighty, the Elohim, who are eternal." I let the bit of tobacco fall and a cool chill brushed across me, like an unseen breeze. But nothing moved, the trees around me motionless.

I turned to my right, facing south. "I call upon my ancestors, my skinwalker grandmother, and my father. Hear me." I dropped a bit of the tobacco. A sudden morning wind skirled through, taking the leaves away before they hit the ground, and died as fast as it rose. Cold prickles lifted across my flesh. I resisted the urge to look behind me. But I knew that I wasn't alone. Not anymore.

I turned west, holding up a pinch of tobacco. Aggie had used the name *Unelenehi,* whom she referred to as the Great One. "I call upon the Great One, god who creates." Again the breeze blew through, harder, stronger, smelling of wet and mold and the soil of the earth, and the tobacco was whipped from my fingers before I could drop it. My breath went hot and noisy in my throat, like a bellows wet with steam.

I turned right again, now facing north, pinching the tobacco in my fingers, my heart rate too fast, thumping erratically. "I call upon the trinity, the sacred number of three." The skin on the back of my neck crawled as I spoke the words, and I hunched my shoulders as the wind swirled past. Beast growled low in my mind, the sound far away; the place where she usually hunched was vacant.

I wasn't sure if I was supposed to complete the circle and didn't remember the instruction from Aggie, but it felt right, so I pivoted back to the east. I gathered up the last bit of tobacco and closed my eyes, my fingertips tingling and cold. I let it fall. "I seek wisdom and strength in battle, and purity of heart and mind and soul." In the distance an owl called, loud and long, the hooting echoing. Nearby another answered, three plaintive notes. Terror like spider legs crawled down my spine, yet there was no reason for fear.

I opened my eyes and looked up into the pine tree tops for the owls. If they were there, they were hidden by the gray light. The spider legs crawled faster and I shivered. I really didn't like not seeing the owls. Not at all. I closed the baggie and dusted my hands.

My stomach was no longer hurting. My heart felt lighter. Cleaner. The tingly feeling still coursed through me, slightly breathless, but exhilarated now, with something expectant, almost like joy. I wondered for an instant what herbs had been in the herbal emetic, and if they did anything other than empty my stomach.

I snaked through the trees upstream in the general direction Aggie had taken, the earth sucking at my flip-flops as if it wanted to pull me within. The world smelled fresh and new, the clean tang of fresh fish, duck and goose and hawk, the distant reek of skunk; even the mold smelled good if that was possible.

Just as the trees opened out at a sharp curve of the bayou, I caught a whiff of burning pine. In the center of a tiny clearing, Aggie and her mother were sitting on flat stones, naked except for small beaded bags hanging on thongs around each neck. Their clothes were folded neatly beside them. *U ni lisi*, grandmother of many children, tended a tiny, smokeless fire.

I turned my gaze away, wondering why so many of the Cherokee rituals seemed to involve getting naked. Knowing I was supposed to follow suit, I stripped to the skin and folded my clothes on the far side of the fire beside a third stone that I assumed was mine.

Aggie jutted her chin to the green pine boughs in a pile to the side. Right. I was supposed to pick them up and scatter them in a circle around us. Aggie had called it a protective circle. Trying to bend so I didn't expose my backside to the two women, I picked up the sap-rich branches, the bark scratching my unprotected skin, and walked clockwise around the fire, dropping a thick layer of the branches in a circle. The sap made my hands sticky but the act of bending and lifting settled my mind. Any lingering self-consciousness was gone by the time I closed the pine bough circle. The faint morning breeze died again and the air went still, heavy with possibility. Waiting.

At a gesture from Aggie, I placed the last of the green boughs on the fire. The scent of pine smoke billowed up; Aggie had said no evil could cross the circle or enter the fragrant smoke; it acted as a ward against malevolent spirits. Finished, I sat, the stone cool beneath me. The old

woman stood and faced east. Her skin hung in folds from
her arms and thighs, and her rounded belly looked like a
half-empty balloon, her breasts heavy and pendulous. But
there was strength in her limbs and something quietly powerful about her form as she raised her hands to the rim of
sun. As they lifted, yellow light pushed through the tree
trunks and touched her face. Warming her. Pine smoke rose
and swelled, curling around her, gray in the dawn.

I shivered in the morning light as she began chanting.
The language was Cherokee, some of which I remembered,
the version older than what Aggie and she spoke, the cadence formal, whispered as much as spoken. I placed my
palms flat on the ground for balance as her words brushed
over me with the smoke, rising and falling. Rising and falling. The world seemed to undulate beneath my hands like
the tides of the ocean, though I knew it didn't move.

The chill pulled my skin so tight that it ached all over as
if I'd jumped into an icy creek. Smoke batted at me, swirling, filling the protective circle. Tears gathered fast in my
eyes to fall across my cheeks and splash on my chest. The
smoke, I told myself, just the smoke. But the deeps of my
mind knew it was something else, something more, and so
did my Beast, who hunched deep inside, far back in my
consciousness, head on paws, killing teeth hidden.

U ni lisi's words had a rhythm and life of their own, ancient and powerful and full of the memories of the past.
When the chant ended, she dropped her arms. Nothing but
the soft susurration of bayou could be heard. The skin of
my face was tight with drying salt; fresh tears ran through
it, burning.

She opened the beaded bag hanging around her neck.
From it, she pulled a tablespoon of the native tobacco and
held it in her left hand. With her right, she added other
herbs, Aggie calling out their names in English for me.
"Sage for cleansing. Sweetgrass for life and joy."

Aggie's mother added a final herb, and Aggie didn't
speak its name. Perhaps it didn't have an English equiva-
lent. Or perhaps it was part of the mysteries of going to
water, and no one knew but her. The old woman rolled the
herbs all together into a fat cigarlike cylinder and tied it
with what looked like hemp string, creating a smudge stick.

She held a burning twig from the fire to the smudge stick until the herb tube was lit and smoking. She dropped the twig back to the fire and stood. She handed the smudge stick to Aggie, who took it kneeling, almost as if making obeisance.

With unhurried, circular motions, she smudged the air around her mother. The old woman was silent, her eyes almost closed, her face serene. Slowly she turned, lifting each foot and placing it just so, like a dance or the measured and balletic martial art form of Tai Chi. Her mother held out her own braids and the smoke curled around them like a living snake, touching and spiraling up. It coiled around her legs and back and belly, up over her face, more gentle than a lover's hand. As the smoke wreathed her, the wrinkles on her face softened; a small half smile touched her lips and she sighed as if some ever-present pain was temporarily gone. When she was satisfied, *Lisi* sat, eyes closed, seeming to barely breathe.

Aggie held out the stick to me and turned her back. Feeling clumsy, I took the smudge stick and came to my knees, concentrating on the smoke rising on the still air, brushing up her body like the finger of God. She lifted her hair and I held the stick so the smoke passed through it. I turned and she turned, lifting a leg so the smoke could touch the back of her thigh and curl over her buttocks. When every part of her had been blessed by the smudging smoke, she opened her eyes and smiled, though her gaze seemed far away.

With a slow gesture, Aggie indicated her mother, and I gave the old woman the smudge stick. I turned to the side as each of them had and closed my eyes. The smoke was warm, curling up from my ankles, fragrant and rich, and I breathed it in. And turned a half step, then another. Lifting my arms. Moving into the dance of the smoke.

"Hold out your hair, *Dalonige i Digadoli*." My whole body shuddered with the words, with hearing them spoken properly, in the whispered syllables of the language of the People, the Cherokee. "Hold out your hair."

I sobbed once, hard. Tears pouring down my face, I lifted my hair. Aggie's mother walked slowly around me, the smudge stick rising and falling, the aromatic smoke touching my skin, wisping through my hair, which fell through my fingers in a long veil, over and over again. The smoke curled up my legs, across my stomach. It brushed my back, touching, so delicately, my face, as if tasting my tears. I breathed in the scented smoke, drawing it deep. My lungs trembled. The world spun and steadied. My heart tripped and slowed, finding a rhythm older than human memory. I closed my eyes and breathed. Just breathed. As the water flowed in the bayou nearby, singing a nearly silent, ancient song.

"*We sa*," a soft voice whispered. "Time to go, *we sa*." Cat. *Bobcat*. One of my beasts. I heard my name spoken by my father, his voice echoing in my memory, as it had so long ago. I opened my eyes and saw the protective circle was open, and *U ni lisi* was stepping into the bayou water, Aggie behind her. I followed them to the water's edge, across a dark, slick, claylike bank, and into the bayou, thick muck pulling at my ankles. The water was clearer here, not as muddy with hurricane runoff, and I could see my feet pressing into the black mire.

I remembered that I was supposed to pray, but the words and ritual prayers Aggie had instructed me were gone from my mind. Unbidden, other words came to my lips. "I seek wisdom and strength in battle, and purity of heart and mind and soul." With the words, I bent my knees and sank beneath the water. It closed over me, dark, moving sluggishly on my skin, cool and wet, the womb of the world.

Seven times I rose and sank into the bayou, each time asking my prayer. When I came up the last time, Aggie and *Lisi* were on the bank, dressing. The sun had risen. And I was empty and light and so . . . free.

I walked through the deep mud, out of the water, and up the muddy, black clay bank. I shook both feet. Looking down, I was amazed that I didn't seem to have any mud on me. Or maybe I shouldn't have been surprised at all.

Quickly I dressed. Still silent, we put out the fire with bayou water, stirring the coals until it was cold. Together, in a short line of three, we walked back to the car and drove away.

CHAPTER 12

Would Little Evan go crunch?

I called a part-time cabdriver I used, catching Rinaldo just before he hit the sack after his third shift at a local plant. He showed up pretty quickly; I was only a mile or so from Aggie's street, trudging along in my flip-flops, hands in the pockets of the loose pants, and already sweating in the day's heat. He pulled his bright yellow Bluebird Cab over and hung halfway out the window. "You look like something the cat dragged in."

I was pretty sure the line didn't deserve the amount of laughter it got as I climbed into the front seat, but Rinaldo thought I was a party girl, always needing a ride home after a wild night out, so he probably assumed I was on a giggly high. I slammed the door and buckled in as he tire-crunched through a three-point turn and eased his way toward a paved street in the distance. With a sly grin, he slanted a look at me. "Hungry?"

"Starving. Where's the nearest fast food joint? I could eat a buffalo."

"If I ate like you, I'd be big as a house. There's a Bojangle's near here. Chicken okay?"

"Long as it's fried protein, I'll be happy." My stomach punctuated the statement with a growl. I ate as Rinaldo drove, putting away three Cajun filet biscuits, two egg and cheese biscuits, a sausage biscuit, and three servings of Potato Rounds, all washed down with a gallon of sweet iced tea. I treated Rinaldo to a biscuit and let him watch me eat, which always seemed to give him enormous pleasure and cost me next to nothing. It paid to keep my emergency transportation happy. The meal was wonderful. Half asleep, belly rounded out against the thin fabric of my T-shirt, I lolled all the way to my front door while Rinaldo listened to zydeco music on the radio, his fingers banging out the African rhythm on his steering wheel. I handed him thirty bucks, which was my standard payment, and made it inside just as Molly and the kids came downstairs, Angelina knuckling her eyes.

"Morning, Aunt Jane." She held her arms up, and though Molly had been telling her she was too big to be picked up all the time, I hoisted her to my hip and nuzzled her hair. She smelled of sleep and pillow and safety. "Did you and the ladies have a nice swim?"

Molly met my eyes over Angie's head as we maneuvered the kids into the kitchen, and she took in my damp hair. I nodded. At this further demonstration of her daughter's rare and potent gift, a gift she was trying to keep under wraps from the human media and government, Molly's reply was carefully neutral. "Sweetheart, how did you know Aunt Jane went swimming?"

"Biscause she did. And they were all naked." Angie yawned, her mouth open wide, face scrunched. "Mama, we can't go home yet. Aunt Boadacia and Aunt Elizabeth is fighting a big bad ugly that showed up in their circle last night. It was purple and red and had big teeth and it wanted to eat them, and Aunt Boadacia says to stay gone, that it would eat Little Evan. Mama, would Little Evan go crunch? Like the deer bones Aunt Jane ate this morning?"

Molly closed her eyes and mouthed what looked a prayer, maybe for guidance and protection for her gifted children. Or maybe she was cussing silently. I couldn't help it. I laughed and squeezed Angie.

Molly's sisters, both the witch sisters and the humans ones, owned Seven Sassy Sisters' Herb Shop and Café near Asheville. Business was booming, both locally and on the Internet, selling herbal mixtures and teas by bulk and by the ounce, the shop itself serving gourmet teas, specialty coffees, breakfast, brunch, and lunch daily, and dinner on weekends. It was mostly fish and vegetarian fare, whipped up by Mol's oldest sister, water witch, professor, and three-star chef, Evangelina Everhart. Her sister Carmen, an air witch, newly widowed and newly delivered of a bouncing baby, ran the register and took care of ordering supplies. Two other witch sisters, twins Boadacia and Elizabeth, ran the herb store, while the wholly human sisters, Regan and Amelia, were waitstaff in the café.

Boadacia and Elizabeth, the youngest and most adventurous of the bunch, were always trying new incantations and spells, and had been known to get into trouble with the results. It sounded as if they had a minor demon trapped in a circle and weren't quite sure how to dispel it.

Usually, they spent quite a while trying to extricate themselves from the messes they made before calling in the big guns, their elder sisters. I could imagine the ruckus when they admitted to Evangelina that they had messed up again. The eldest often had assisted with the cleanup and her tirades were legendary and generally ignored by the twins.

"Angie, how did you know that Aunt Jane went swimming this morning?" Molly dropped Evan Junior into the highchair that had appeared at my table with my guests. "Did you dream it? Were you awake and just thought it? What?"

Angie shrugged as I sat her into her chair, the table nearly to her chin. "I want oatmeal like Aunt Jane fixes it."

"It's important, honey," Molly said. "How do you know things like that?"

"I just do. I see Aunt Jane a lot. But sometimes other people. And Aunt Elizabeth sometimes talks to me inside my head. Can I have oatmeal?"

Molly's mouth formed a thin line, and I knew what the expression meant. Visions and mind-speech were new and troubling indications of her daughter's power, which shouldn't have manifested until she was sixteen, and which should have been tightly bound beneath the magical constraints applied by Big Evan and Molly when the power came upon her too potent and far too young.

"I'll fix it," I said, meaning the oatmeal. Pans banging, I turned on the gas and began making oatmeal the way my housemother had taught me so long ago. As the water heated for oatmeal and tea, I flipped on a light switch and realized that we had power. I plugged in the refrigerator and adjusted the AC down to a bone-chilling seventy-four, making a circuit around the house to close all the windows. It was already a sweaty eighty-five degrees inside. Thank God for air-conditioning.

While my guests ate, I asked Molly, "Why would the big bad ugly eat Little Evan?"

Molly touched her ear and gave a warning glance at her kids that said she couldn't say much in front of big ears. "Some things think witchy X and Y chromosomes are tasty."

Witchy X and Y chromosomes meant the things that made Little Evan a male witch, or what some called a sorcerer. I nodded. Demons like to eat male witch babies. Ouch.

"Comosos are tasty," Angie repeated, trying on the words. "Like Aunt Jane thinks deer is tasty. Would Little Evan go crunch?" Angie wasn't going to be deterred.

I grinned and poured hot water over tea leaves, a strong gunpowder green that had a good caffeine kick. "Probably. But we love Little Evan." When she tried to interrupt, I said, "Even Beast loves Little Evan. But we don't talk about Beast or big bad uglies, right?"

"I can't even tell Uncle Ricky-Bo? Biscause he's wanting to know stuff."

"Especially not Ricky-Bo," I said dryly. "He's nosy. Speaking of Mr. Nosy, I need to go to NOPD and do some more research. You okay today here, Mol?"

"We have power, and I can wash clothes over at Katie's, including the stinky diapers piling up on the back porch. I'm fine." Molly was a firm believer that diapers were the most dangerous disposable item ever invented, to be used only in emergencies. She used cloth with old-fashioned pins. Before I could ask who would watch the kids, she smiled into her teacup without looking at me and said, "Bliss will watch them." Angie wasn't the only Trueblood who could read minds upon occasion.

After a long shower to wash off the bayou stink, I multibraided my hair with lots of beads that clicked pleasantly when I walked, dressed, and made several phone calls that required me to leave messages this hour of the morning. I kissed the kids, strapped on Beast's pack in lieu of a pocketbook, made sure my cell and camera had battery power, tied my braids back, powered up Bitsa, and roared into town.

My first stop was Audubon Park, at the Audubon Trail Golf Course, one of the sites in the city where there had been young-rogue attacks on humans in the past, and the only one I had never visited. The last attack on record had been in 2001, and I quickly discovered why. The golf course had been redesigned in that year, and there was no place suitable for a grave site. That left me only two locations to worry about, which made my life easier. Able to cross it off my list, I gunned Bitsa and headed for NOPD.

I had a lot of questions and not much info. I needed to see if there was anything in the history files about the last vamp war. And I wanted to see if I could find out what Innara had been talking about last night, the devoveo. It sounded as though it had to do with the madness of young rogues. Mad young rogues was what the city of New Orleans had on its hands. And maybe I would try to get a handle on what the Sons of Darkness were. They had come up twice now; if they had something to do with young rogues, I needed to know it. And then there were the witches I'd seen across the street, likely standing in a pentagram. What could their connection be? What had seemed like a simple contract to track down a vamp breaking vamp law was turning into a bewildering investigation into vamp history and politics.

The wind in my face was damp and heated, like a warm, wet blanket, and Bitsa purred beneath me like Beast when she slept. With the world flashing by, I was feeling peaceful, rested, and strangely calm, even without any sleep. I was pretty sure the emotion I was experiencing was serenity, though I'd never felt that before. I didn't expect it to last. Cynical, but true.

I parked at NOPD, signed in once again, and waited for the armed guard to look over my credentials and make his phone call. This time, Rick came to meet me.

Like the last time I was here, he was in street clothes, but not the jeans, T-shirt, and boots from his undercover days.

Today, Rick wore black slacks, a black jacket, and a white button-down shirt. With a tie. I started to grin. The tie had little orange kittens scampering over an aqua background.

"Yeah, I know. I've fallen so far." He propped a hand on his hip, pushing back the jacket to reveal a shoulder-holstered 9 mm, and flicked the offending tie with his fingers. "My niece gave it to me."

"It's . . . cute."

He laughed, a breathy, disgusted sound. "My captain came down on me hard yesterday about NOPD dress code. They won't let me wear jeans now that I'm not undercover, so I had to buy some stuff. The tie's revenge. He hates it." He plucked the pants and jacket. "You know how long it's been since I wore clothes like this? Catholic school, grades one through six. I had to go *shopping*." He looked pained. "But no one specified what had to be on the tie. Yanks their chains, you know?" He flashed me a grin, revealing the little crooked tooth at his lower lip. He was just too dang pretty. "I have another one with pigs on it."

The casual business look suited him. But then, I had a feeling that Rick LaFleur would look good in anything. Or nothing. "You gonna yank their chains until you hang yourself? Pardon the mixed metaphor."

"Something like that. Entering the real world sucks when it comes to wardrobe. But there's good things about it. My mom is overjoyed to discover that her degenerate son isn't a reprobate after all. When she's not being pissed that I didn't tell her."

My brows rose. "Your *mom* didn't know you were a cop?"

He lifted a shoulder in a *what can I say* gesture. "Mom can't keep a secret."

I nodded, though I had no idea what it would be like to have a mother. "So. You gonna let me in or keep me out here with the cons and the reprobates you've left behind?"

"I'm guessing you want to see the woo-woo files again. Come on in. You're not armed, are you?"

"No guns, no blades." I handed off my fanny pack to him, which wasn't heavy enough to contain a gun. He didn't bother to search it or me; I passed through the metal detector without a beep.

Beads clicking softly, I followed him. In the bowels of NOPD in room 666, he tossed the file cabinet keys onto the table, lifted one finger in good-bye, and locked me in the tiny cell. Before I could call out, he was gone, and there still wasn't a phone to call for my release. I thought about the possibility of being trapped down here if a fire broke out, or if Rick forgot about me and I was left overnight without food or water. The door wasn't steel or barred, and its hinges were within easy reach. If I could find a sturdy piece of wood or metal, I could beat or pry the pins out and use some of Beast's strength to rip the door off that way. But the next time I was down here, I was going to bring a picnic lunch.

Now familiar with the filing system, I found the key marked 666-0V, opened the vamp cabinet, and started looking for history, specifically for info on the devoveo.

Instead I spotted the bio of a certain near-rogue named Bethany. There wasn't much to go on—Bethany hadn't exactly hogged the limelight in the City of Jazz.

There were no photos of her, but someone had compiled a breakdown of vamp-clan hierarchy back in the seventies, and at the bottom, Bethany and Sabina Delgado y Aguilera, the priestess of the vamps, were listed as "outclan." That word again. Interesting. I'd have to ask a couple people what it meant, as I couldn't trust the vocabulary of just one person, not about vamp stuff.

I'd seen both Sabina and Bethany in action, and they were vastly different. Bethany was slightly unhinged, African, and full of that icy shaman magic I'd never encountered before. Sabina was Mediterranean, nunnish, and sane. The only thing they had in common was power. A lot of it.

I took photos of the file to download later, and settled a folding chair close to the file cabinet. I went through it methodically, and quickly found something I hadn't seen before, a red file folder marked *Legends*. It consisted of unverified reports about vamps, all gathered through unnamed sources, paid informants, and by debriefing bloodjunkies who had gone through rehab and tried to keep straight. The folder had been compiled by the same cigarette smoker, and handled by Jodi.

There was a lot of wacky stuff in it, things I discounted or knew had been disproved at one time or another, but there was a snippet about the Sons of Darkness, the term Bethany had used for the vamps who had turned her. The Sons were supposed to be the first vamps in their own recorded history. The very first. And according to blood-junkie scuttlebutt, they had been feral for a few days, not ten years. Somehow, they'd been able to skip the curing process. At least one of them was purported to be still alive, sane, and had visited in this country in the last decade, as guest of Clan Pellissier. It might not be true, but Bruiser had blanched at the mention of the Sons. I had no idea if any of this had anything to do with the vamp I was hunting, but he'd been raising young rouges for a long time. And almost anything could be evidence pointing to him.

I pulled my pad from my fanny pack and took notes from the Legends file, things that might help me find the rogue maker, things that caught my fancy, and things that might lead me in a new research direction. I found a mention of feeding frenzies, which had been on my mind since last night, but it was from a source the cop in question doubted. The blood-junkie had told him that "Clan Desmarais went nutso crazy and killed half their servants and all their slaves. I barely got out alive." No bodies had ever turned up, and the report had been buried. Like so many of the reports in this room.

I glanced at my phone for messages before I remembered where I was. One of my calls before I left the house had been to Bruiser, who hadn't answered. If he called back, I wouldn't know until I got out of here.

I returned to the file, deliberately hunting for red folders, and I found a slim one containing a stack of police reports written in the same distinctive handwriting as the cigarette smoker, the cop who had been investigating the vamps and the disappearances of witch children: Detective Elizabeth Caldwell.

In the red folders, I found dozens of small scraps of paper, each smelling of old smoke and containing terms, names, questions. Little made sense until I found a scrap that read: *A few sips of witch blood brought the devoveo back to sanity for nearly an hour.* On another I found one that said *devoveo: the Curse of the Mithrans.* And *young rogue: the cursed.*

I sat, holding the two scraps of paper, my gut telling me that something important was contained in them, but my brain couldn't see it. So I copied down the phrases and went on with my hunt.

I wanted to read more about Caldwell's investigations, and remembered Rick's key ring. No door keys on it. But there was a key marked 666-0W. I tried it on a file cabinet I hadn't been able to get in to last time I was here. With a metallic click, the drawers loosened and the top one eased out an inch. Every file was red. Every single one. I opened the drawer and let my fingers do the walking through the tabs. It was a file on area witches, compiled by Elizabeth Caldwell. And there was one file marked *Devoveo*. Inside were reports of young rogues who had also been witches. Which made no sense at all. Vamps would turn shamans, but not witches, yet I was pretty sure they were collaborating with witches. Nothing made any freaking sense.

Settling down with several files, I spent another hour doing research and trying to find a common thread in Elizabeth Caldwell's investigations before thirst drove me to put everything away, lock it all up, and again bang on the door. And bang and bang. And bang. Eventually I heard the lock click; the door opened to reveal Rick himself, hiding behind two drink cans. "Sorry. I forgot about there not being a phone in here. Coke truce?"

I propped a hip against the doorjamb, took an icy, sweating can, popped the top, and drank. Wryly, I said, "There isn't a bathroom either." Without a segue, I said. "Who is Elizabeth Caldwell?"

Rick's expression went instantly to cop face as he shut down his reactions. "She was a good cop, killed in action in 1990. By vamps unknown. She was also Jodi Richoux's aunt."

My mind went into overdrive. Jodi had pointed me to red files, all belonging to Elizabeth. Jodi had a reason to hang around me, other than friendship. I had a strong hunch Jodi had secretly taken over her aunt's research, an aunt who had died by vamp attack . . . I'd gotten Jodi into vamp HQ. I had contacts with the vamps. I was research.

I don't know why it hurt, to learn that she was maybe

using me for a case. It's not as though we were bosom buddies. But it did.

Rick didn't seem to notice my reaction. "Come on," he said. "I'll walk you out."

Silent, we took the stairs, and Rick let me stop off in the ladies' room, where I didn't bother to e-mail the photos; instead, I checked my voice mail. One was from Bruiser, and unexpected relief flooded me. If there had been a feeding frenzy, he had survived it, sounding bland, factual, and surprisingly helpful. I hadn't expected to get anywhere with my latest request.

Back on the main floor, Rick stuck his hands in the pockets of his black slacks and casually asked, "So. Want to get dinner on Saturday? My treat."

A frisson of uncomfortable heat roiled through me. *A date?* It sounded like a date. His treat and all. It had been years since I'd had a real date. And Saturday was just after the three days of the full moon. Beast would still be feeling . . . amorous. I swallowed and was pretty sure I blushed, hoping it wasn't easy to tell with my coppery skin. "Um. I should be finished with this contract by then. Sure. Maybe eight?"

He nodded, ducking his head and glancing up at me. "Bikes. Burgers. Okay?"

"Yeah." Actually, that sounded like a fun date. And I had houseguests, so I didn't have to worry about any awkward leave-taking or expectations. "Um. Eight, then."

Rick nodded at me, gave a little one-fingered salute-style wave, and disappeared back into the bowels of the NOPD. *Crap.* I had a date. I flipped open my phone and returned the most important call that had come in while I was trapped in the woo-woo room. It was answered on the first ring. "George Dumas."

I straddled Bitsa and helmeted up. "Jane. So, you got permission for me to visit the official vamp cemetery?" Not to be confused with the grave site where I'd killed the rogue the other night.

"Yes. When?"

"No time like the present."

"On my way."

*　　　*　　　*

When I'd marked my map with the location of all the reported young-rogue vamp attacks on humans, there had
been three clusters, and one had been in the two miles
around the vamp cemetery. I needed to look around a bit.

The call ended. A man of few words, our Bruiser. But a
man of really good kisses, especially the kind delivered on
the floor of a limo. Uncomfortable prickly warmth spread
through me. I was interested in a blood-servant. Interested
as in *interested*. And Bruiser seemed pretty interested in
me. He could have turned off the security system at the
cemetery from Leo's house. Was he just using the alarm system as an excuse to see me? The scratchy warmth spread,
barbed and maddening. Yeah. I was interested.

Yet I had a date Saturday with another man entirely. A
breathtakingly gorgeous *human* man, who would be a far
better choice for romantic entanglements than the blood-
servant of the master of the city. I'd once figured Rick for
a player, but that was back when he'd been undercover. I
didn't really know him at all.

Thinking about men was frustrating and tied up my
mind in barbed wire. Not something I had time for right
now. I switched mental gears to more pressing matters, like
the feel of Bitsa between my thighs, the heated wind beating against me, and the ripe smells of the city.

I could have searched the vamp cemetery alone once
Bruiser had disabled the alarms, but he was a careful man,
less trusting than Rick when it came to keys and security
precautions. Once inside the barred gate, he entered the
first mausoleum we came to. When he left the crypt, he nodded at me once. I figured that meant I could do whatever
I wanted, but he didn't leave. He leaned against the hood
of his car, watching me from behind mirrored sunglasses.
He looked patient. Which made me nervous. If he'd been
impatient, I could have been annoyed and recalcitrant and
deliberately taken my time. It was harder with a calm and
peaceful man.

I removed my helmet and tossed my denim jacket to
the seat. From the saddlebags, I pulled a pad and pen and
began sketching the layout of the cemetery. It didn't have
to be exact or to scale, but I wanted a map to trigger my
memories later if I needed. I drew in the eight mausoleums,

labeling them with clan names and descriptions, including the naked angel statues on top of each. The last time I'd been here, several of the mausoleums had been damaged. Now there was evidence of repair work: tire tracks crushing the grass, a ladder lying flat, a device that looked like a portable cement mixer but likely was something else, and a few cigarette butts littering the ground. Bruiser picked them up as I worked, looking disgruntled. I watched him from the corner of my eye as I sketched in the chapel from which the priestess had emerged the time I'd been here in owl form. Today the place looked deserted.

When I returned the pad to the saddlebags, Bruiser wandered over. He looked pale, as if he'd been badly fed upon and not restored enough by sips of his master's blood. Last time I saw him he'd been facing a feeding frenzy. "You look a little pale. Okay, a lot pale," I offered diffidently. "You okay?"

"I've been better. Tell me again why you have to be here?"

I explained about the clusters of young-rogue vamp attacks. "Like the rogues had risen close by, and attacked the first humans who happened to be in their path."

He looked interested. "Where else have they risen?"

I briefly detailed the map, then told him more about the rogue I'd taken down the other night. "I'd never seen a rising before, and there was something really strange about it, something I don't think is part of a normal rising. The site had a pentagram and a casting circle shaped in shells on the ground. There were crosses nailed to the trees at the points of the pentagram."

I glanced at him, catching a look of utter disbelief on his face. "What?"

He shook his head. "Not possible. The crew sent to clean up the grave site in the park would have reported on that."

Now, that was interesting. There were crosses when I'd been there. Someone had gotten to the city park pretty quickly after the rising to get them down between my visit and the visit by the sanitation crew. Or . . . maybe the lightning strike I'd smelled when I first got there had changed the timing of the rising? Was that even possible? Frankenstein had risen after his maker had channeled a lightning strike into his body—early cinematic defibrillator. I grinned and Bruiser raised his brows. I shook my head to show that my thoughts weren't important.

He went on. "Any young rogue who woke in the presence of crosses would be driven back into the grave, screaming in pain."

"Maybe the pentagram and the magics performed in the soil prevented it?" Bruiser stared off in the distance, face closed, thinking thoughts he had no desire to share with me. When he didn't reply, I insisted, "But why the crosses? Okay, I get that vamps live and breathe religion, which is pretty weird for the undead, who don't need to breathe."

That startled Bruiser out of his funk. "Religion? And vampires?" His tone added, "Are you crazy?" though he didn't say it. But there was something off about his body language.

I looked out over the graveyard, keeping him in my peripheral vision. Calmly, I said, "Vampires and religion should be like oil and water, but they aren't. Because vampires *believe*. Organized religion pervades everything they do and everything they are—the myths attached to the holy land, their reaction to crosses"—I thought of the priestess, Sabina—"all the formal Christian trappings. There's no such thing as distant history with vamps. All their grudges, alliances, even though they shift, seem to have roots in events that took place hundreds or thousands of years ago. Their history, as humans perceive it, impacts their present, and whoever the rogue maker is, he's been raising young rogues for a long time. He may be driven by something that happened yesterday, a century ago, or two thousand years ago."

Bruiser shifted on his feet, an unconscious adjustment of balance. "I suggest that you not repeat such nonsense to the Mithrans." But his scent change suggested that I was dead-on with my religion and vamp analysis.

I flipped my palm up in a hand shrug and turned away. Over my shoulder I said, "I'm going to walk the perimeter of the grounds. It won't take long." Bruiser didn't reply, and I paced away, walking sun wise—clockwise—around the ring of trees surrounding the cemetery. The sun was hot, the air muggy, sour, and unmoving. Sweat trickled down my spine as I walked, trying to get a feel for the place, something I hadn't allowed myself the previous times I was here. Of course the first time I'd been in the shape of a Eurasian hunting owl, and the other time I was with Rick, so it wasn't as though I had the right senses, time, or opportunity to let the place seep in under my skin, to get to know a patch of ground the way Beast did.

Now I mentally nudged Beast awake and let my senses loose to absorb the place through its smells, the taste of its air, the springiness of the grass beneath my boots, and the magics wafting across the ground. There was power here. Not holy ground power, not ley line power. Not power that has seeped into the earth at old churches, synagogues, mosques, temples, or other places where faith makes the ground holy. Not quite the power of belief. But power nonetheless, of an old and vital kind. Though I couldn't place it, I recognized the taste of it.

I was halfway around the large clearing when the ground became damp, giving beneath me with a squelch. The air cooled, thinned, became wetter, though how that was possible with all the humidity I couldn't have said. I breathed in and scented something peppery and astringent, the faint herbal scent of vamps on the breeze from the woods, the odor itself dry and desiccated. Beneath it was the tang of decaying blood, and a trace of magic. Witch magic. I moved into the trees. The signature of power tingled faintly along my arms. Shade from the trees above me closed out the sun and some of the heat, shadows darkening the ground.

The scent of it pulled me north, along an overgrown trail just wide enough for my feet. A rabbit trail, according to Beast. She sent me an image of a rabbit and flooded my senses with the remembered hot taste of blood. "Thanks for that," I murmured to her, "but I prefer my protein skinned, gutted, boned, cooked, and seasoned." Beast hacked in amusement.

Not far into the woods I found a patch of saplings in a circle of older trees. It looked as if it might have been a ten-foot-round space once, maybe five years ago. Kneeling, I ran my hands over the bare ground, between the roots of the young trees. I found a broken white shell. Travers-

ing the outskirts of the circle, I scuffed the ground, finding
more shells. This had been a blood rite circle involving both
witches and vamps, and I bet that it was used as the first
resting place of one or more new rogues. Whatever was going on now had been happening for a lot longer than I'd
been told. Maybe a lot longer than the vamp council knew.

I found two other old circles in the forested land around
the vamp graveyard, one younger than the first, one older,
which I had missed on my first pass and caught on my
second. Back at my bike, I marked their locations on my
map, with the approximate length of time they had been
abandoned, my guesstimate based on the age of the trees.
A city girl might not have been able to tell that part, but
I had been raised in the country, and the children's home
had used the earth for more than just a playground and
parking. We had grown a lot of our own vegetables, and
had once reclaimed a patch of land to increase the size of
the garden. I remembered the backbreaking work of tree-
clearing. I knew how long it took forest to steal back land
left fallow too long.

I stood in the edge of the woods, wondering if there
were more such sites in the trees. It wasn't impossible. But
Bruiser was waiting. Patiently. Which made me feel guilty.

He was still beside his car when I walked back, his butt
against the high gloss, his eyes hidden behind sunglasses
against the light. Unlike me, he wasn't sweating in the heat
and humidity. I wondered if his ability to withstand tem-
perature changes was a result of the blood sips he got in
return for being a blood meal to Leo, or if it was natural
to him. No way to ask and be polite, of course, though if
I hadn't needed something from him, I might have asked
anyway. I grinned at the thought and he cocked his head. I
waved it away and said, "I don't guess you'd consider giving
me access to the security around this place so I can come
back anytime I want."

His lips twitched in what might have been a smile and he
shook his head once, an abbreviated but unequivocal no.

"Okay. I ran across some things in my research into
vamp attacks that you can help me with instead." Bruiser's
brow lifted a bit, as if he was amused that I'd put him into
the role of assistant. "How about out-clan and devoveo?"

I was pretty sure I knew the answers, but in my business, "pretty sure" was worth roughly zero. I needed to know for dead certain.

The heavy-lidded look slid away. "Where did you come across this information?"

Bruiser was my best source of all things fangy and I knew I had to give to get, but not this time. I hated negotiation. "My source"—if the NOPD woo-woo files could be described that way—"is confidential. I want to know what they mean."

Thoughts flickered deep in his eyes. After a moment he cocked his head and seemed to come to a decision. "Devoveo is the state of the young rogue. The ten years of insanity when they have to be kept confined. The curse of the Mithrans is the fact that they must enter the ten years of the devoveo and may not come out of it."

"Have you ever heard of people drinking witch blood to stave it off?"

He looked confused. "No. The reason witches are seldom turned is that they suffer from devoveo far beyond the usual decade, and often must be destroyed by their sires. But I have no idea what the effects of drinking their blood would be."

"Oh." Though I'd expected no new revelations, I was still disappointed.

"The out-clan are part of their history. Before the vampires were divided into clans or families, they were all one family. When their society became too large and unwieldy to manage on their own, and when humans began hunting them, there was a diaspora and many of the oldest sired clans in new lands, others later joined existing clans, banding together for safety and defense, and some few chose to be considered out-clan. From the out-clan group came the keepers of the past. They act as historians, ambassadors, deal brokers. Peacemakers when necessary."

"So Sabina and Bethany really are among the oldest. Like, nearly two thousand years old." When he inclined his head, I added, "And the ground they inhabit is holy to the vamps."

"Not holy ground. The eldest Mithrans are respected, venerated, perhaps, not worshipped. The priestess is the oldest Mithran in this hemisphere. And Bethany was her acolyte."

"Was?"

"There have been disagreements between them several times over the past centuries; the last time was over the issue of slavery during the Civil War. The rift has never been healed."

Bethany had been a slave. I could see where discord might be possible. I had a feeling there was more to everything he'd said, but Bruiser stood straight and opened his car door, leaning inside to pick up an envelope and a box, handing them to me. "The check is for the heads you delivered to the vampire council. And Leo wants you to have the other as a gift, but he didn't want it wrapped. And no, I have no idea why it should go to you."

I tucked the envelope into a saddlebag. Taking the box, I flipped back the lid. Wedged between layers of packing material were bones and teeth. The small bones looked like paw bones, the larger long ones like foreleg bones. The teeth were encased in a lower jawbone, the canines several inches long, one with its tip broken off. I was pretty sure they all came from a sabertooth cat. A cold chill shot through me. Leo had given me his "son's" fetishes, the things Immanuel had used to become a sabertooth lion and kill. The things that might have driven him insane. My instinct was to refuse them.

I heard shells crunch beneath footsteps and looked up, but Bruiser was sliding his long, lean form under the wheel. Without another word, he closed the door and started the car, backing into a three-point turn. I took it as my cue and strapped the box to the back of my bike and powered up Bitsa. I still needed info about witch blood bringing the young rogue to sanity; I'd have to ask that one later. I followed the blood-servant of the master of the city out of the vamp cemetery, hardly noticing the passage of the road beneath my tires.

Why had Leo given me the bones? What was the purpose of the sites in the woods when vamps could be put to earth almost anywhere *except* a place with crosses on it? A couple dozen other questions piled on to the original one of who was raising young-rogue vamps. I had lots more questions, but I had proved one thing to myself. Vamps and witches, likely a small, renegade group of them, were definitely working together to raise new rogues. And if the new growth in the woods was an indication, it had been going on for decades.

CHAPTER 13

Nap time, Aunt Jane

When I got back to the house after depositing the check into Derek Lee's account, I found a note from Molly saying they were at Katie's Ladies visiting and doing laundry. She and the little witch Bliss had been visiting back and forth for days in the beginnings of a friendship that I hoped might help Bliss to accept her own power. I didn't think many mothers would let their daughters near a house of ill repute, but Molly wasn't most mothers. Open-minded, tolerant, and unprejudiced, that was Molly. She even let Angie hang around a skinwalker.

Alone on the property, I tucked the box of sabertooth bones and teeth into the back garden under a rock. It was stupid, but I didn't want them in the house. It was just too creepy. I couldn't use them; the genetic structure was male and I couldn't shift into a male animal. But what did you do with a gift from the master of the city? I couldn't toss them in the garbage.

Back inside, I discovered the dress I had damaged at the vamp party hanging, dripping, in my bathroom. I had thought it ruined, but Molly had gotten all the blood out. It maybe needed a needle and thread in a spot or two, but it looked pretty good for a blood-soaked rag.

On the bed, I found a packing box and sighed. More surprises? I slit the packing tape with a knife. No one was home to hear me whoop.

I'd lost my favorite leather jacket to the liver-eater masquerading as Immanuel, and the replacement I'd treated myself to was finally here. I'd been measured and fitted at a leather shop in town, getting to be part of the design process from the leather up. From the box I pulled out a buttery soft, armored, padded leather motorcycle jacket and the loose-fitting armored leather pants I'd thrown in for good measure, perfect for fighting vamps and for riding Bitsa. And something I'd never have thought of until living in the Deep South—they had zippered, mesh pockets that could be left open for air to move through. It wouldn't help much on foot, but on a bike, I'd be more comfortable.

Not wanting to get my sweat on them, I showered off, which I was doing a lot more than I ever had in the cool air of the mountains, and dressed in my one pair of long silk underclothes before pulling on the new leathers. The jacket had rings along the side seams threaded through with leather straps so I could adjust the fit for bulky winter layers or tighter for summer riding.

Stiff, shaped armor pads—not ballistic armor, but plasticized, high-density foam armor, wrapped in silver mesh—could be inserted into zippered pockets across my shoulders, down my back, along my forearms, legs, and thighs. At the joints of knees and elbows, more flexible armor could be fitted in. Straps had been sewn along the outer thighs for sheathed vamp-killers, and there was room in the wrists for forearm sheaths. Small leather pockets with Velcro fasteners were perfect for stakes and crosses, and one pocket was plastic lined for a vial of holy water. There were straps with snaps for securing my shotgun harness in place at my back. And all over the jacket sleeves, the high collar, at the inside of the elbow, and on the pants at my groin—the pulse points where vamps usually fed—tiny rings had been sewn. Silver. To poison any vamp who did manage to bite me. It was so cool I was drooling.

When I had it all on and cinched tight and weapons in place, I stamped my feet into my new, never-worn, black cherry Lucchese boots, let my braids fall around me with tiny clicks, smeared on my favorite bloodred lipstick, took a deep breath to prepare myself, and turned to the one full-length mirror at the closet. I didn't recognize the broad-shouldered valkyrie who stared back at me. "Holy crap," I whispered. I looked so . . . freaking fine. Ball dresses were for girly girls. This . . . this was for a warrior. For a vampire hunter. "Holy freaking crap."

I was still preening when Molly came through the side door, a huge basket of folded clothes in her arms, Little Evan strapped to her back papoose-style, and Angie leading the way. When they saw me, the two females stopped dead. Molly's jaw dropped. Silently she mouthed something and I was pretty sure it was a lot stronger than my own "holy crap."

Angie launched herself at me, squealing, and I caught her up in my arms. "Aunt Jane. You look beautiful."

"Deadly," Molly said. "Wicked. And gorgeous in a deadly, wicked, vampire killer way."

I couldn't help my cocky smile. "I do look pretty good, don't I?"

Molly set the basket on the table and I set Angie on the floor to help Mol off with the papoose tote.

"I want to play dress-up too. Miss Bliss and Miss Christie gave me some stuff. Mama, show Aunt Jane."

"You let Christie give her stuff?" Christie's personal and professional style went more to spiked collars, whips, chains, and multiple piercings.

"Just some silver rhinestone jewelry. Tame stuff."

Angie took the play-pretties from her mother and modeled a sparkly rhinestone necklace. Molly pulled an old, peach silk nightgown over her daughter's head. On a grownup the gown would have come to midthigh; it reached Angie's ankles, and with the purple T-shirt beneath, it looked precious. My heart went all mushy and my throat went tight at the sight. I snapped a few pics of Angie in her finery, and Molly took more of the both of us to e-mail to Big Evan in Brazil. I printed out the best pics and hung them on the fridge. They looked really . . . nice hanging there.

I was left with an odd feeling inside, one I couldn't name, but that felt similar to the serenity that had started out my day, though this was a lot more intense than that. A lot.

Once the pictures had been sent off to Evan, we all helped me out of the leathers and boots, which was harder than getting into them. Angie kept on her finery, but I opted for a pair of shorts and a T because, despite the AC, it was still muggy and warm and the leathers had been hot. We ate a late meal of peanut butter and jelly and iced tea. The lump that had formed in my throat at the sight of Angie in her dress-up clothes expanded as we munched, as Angie smeared jelly on her face, and Little Evan spat gobs of green baby food goo and laughed. It was so . . . homey.

Afterward, still in her peach silk finery, blue eyes sleepy, Angie curled up on my bed with her Cherokee doll, patted the mattress, and said, "Nap time, Aunt Jane."

"Molly?" My voice sounded strangled. "She wants me to take a nap. With her."

Molly hid a grin, but not very well. "Big tough vampire killer all scared of a six-year-old wanting a nap? I'll be in my own bed, thank you very much." She carried the baby upstairs. Angelina yawned hugely and patted the bed again. Gingerly, I crawled onto the mattress and lay down, stiff as a board. Angie curled into my side, yawned again, and promptly fell asleep. Happy was far too mundane a term to describe my feelings. There had to be another word better suited to this sappy, sentimental, fiercely protective sensation that thumped through my chest with my lifeblood. Had to be. And it was followed by a jolt of fear, intense and icy. I knew it couldn't last. Nothing this good ever could, which terrified me down to my toes.

I eased to my side, slid an arm around Angie, and closed my eyes. Tried to relax. I could get used to having Molly around. To having kids around. They made life so much more intense and . . . And naps were a good side benefit.

Beast, quiescent all day, rolled over in my mind and sent me one word. *Kits.*

I woke at dusk to find Angie gone, the place beside me cool to the touch, and my bedroom door shut. Molly must have wanted me to sleep in. As I stretched, my cell rang, and I dug it out of my new leathers to see the number for Katie's Ladies displayed. "Jane," I said.

"Tom, here. Is Bliss over there? She has an early caller and her room is empty."

Early caller meant early customer. "Hang on." I moved through the house, sniffing. Bliss hadn't been here. Molly was on the side porch with the kids. "Not here. No one saw her leave? Nothing on the security system?"

"Just some interference about an hour ago."

Interference? I didn't like it. A sudden pulse of fear shot through me. Bliss was a witch, a witch who looked younger than her age, a witch who had no magical, protective wards on her home. Did that put her in danger?

"I'll be right over." Not bothering to change, I pulled on flip-flops and told Molly to go inside and set the wards. Ignoring her concerned face, I vaulted the fifteen-foot brick wall between our houses. It was nearly sunset and the air had that soft, balmy, glowy heat I was coming to associate with spring evenings in New Orleans. It would be a great night for a ride, my hair loose and flowing in the wind, Bitsa growling beneath me. Maybe later.

Despite my moment of fear, I didn't expect to find Bliss really gone, as in missing gone, more like stepped-out-for-some-shopping gone. And I certainly didn't expect to sense anything in the backyard, so I wasn't fully alert until I caught a whiff of magic. Witch magic. And witch blood.

I stopped and parsed the scents, pulling my braids into a knot, out of the way. Most magic has a distinctive smell. Some is a bit peppery, maybe with a hint of spice in it; some smells like fresh-baked cookies, or freshly turned earth, or wood smoke. Though I don't have synesthesia, I have to say witch magic often smells herbal and blue, like cornflowers. And sometimes a little mellow-yellow. My own magic, the scent that erupts in the air when I shift, smells earthy, musky. Vamp magic, the smell that clings to them when they hunt, pulling on the gifts of stealth and mesmeric mind games, is peppery and desiccated, the way dried herbs smell after they've sat too long on the shelf.

Here, I smelled witch magic, witch blood, and an overlay of vamp. A very specific vamp, his scent signature as knotted and twisted as a braided rope. My heart thumped hard. The rogue maker. A vamp in daylight? Or near enough to count, anyway. And he didn't smell scorched either. He smelled well fed and as healthy as a dead thing can smell. My hackles rose and Beast hunched within me, claws out and probing. I didn't have a stake or cross handy. Stupid to have left the house without them. But it was still daylight, for pity's sake.

I drew in a breath, mouth open, seeking a more familiar scent signature, but it was missing. Bliss hadn't been out here recently. I didn't need to go all the way around the house, instead ringing the bell at the back door. Troll opened it instantly, one hand rubbing across his bald head, worry on his face. "Let me see the tapes," I said by way of greeting. "And get all the girls down here for a chat." After a moment, I added, "Please," to which Troll grunted while leading the way to the new security console hidden behind the doors of a seven-foot-tall, black-lacquered chest with gold-leaf dragons capering across its doors. A new thick oriental rug was in the entry, a matching one at the console, both done in dynamic shades of gold and maroon and black. Really nifty. Troll had been redecorating.

The console—Boeing's Visual Security Operations Console Sentential, or VSOC, the same sort of system designed for U.S. embassies around the world, but scaled down for private use—was also brand-spanking-new. The system had been installed at Leo's expense, integrating the existing cameras into new software and new sensors that gave a 3-D view of the grounds, the public rooms of Katie's Ladies, and, when the girls were working in-house, additional monitoring of their bedrooms. It was a way of keeping them safe, and they didn't seem to mind.

To me it was pretty icky, and since I knew that Leo was monitoring the security systems of most of the vamp clans, clandestinely and in contravention of the Vampira Carta, and would have access to the downloads, it got doubly icky. Free porn for him. Total lack of privacy for the girls. But I hadn't said anything about that. It was something I wanted to have in reserve for later. Troll punched a button and I could hear him throughout the intercom system, "Girls, meet in the dining room, please." With another click he said, "Deon, the girls will need drinks set out, and some of those fruit cups."

"Cocktails and fruit coming, Tom." Deon was the new cook. No one would tell me what had happened to Ms. A, the former cook who had been attacked by the liver-eater, as Beast referred to the skinwalker I'd killed. Except to say she wasn't dead, which was a comfort of some sort. Deon was new, a three-star chef from the islands, who had been offered Ms. A's position. The very newness of him set my teeth on edge at the moment. I didn't know Deon, and when something goes wrong with a security system and there's a new guy around, he becomes a likely suspect for tampering.

"How much of the system was activated?"

"All the outside cameras, public rooms, and hallways. Here, at four fourteen, we have a shot of Bliss leaving the dining room. Twenty seconds later, she enters her bedroom and closes her door. Then nothing until the interference, which isn't supposed to be possible with this system."

"It isn't possible," I agreed, "for humans. Maybe a witch could interfere with it; I don't know. Play it again, and slow it down for the last two minutes before the interference." I followed the sequences one frame at a time and saw nothing unusual. No burst of magic caught on film. And I knew that magic could be seen on film at times, especially digital film, as a scatter of light particles scarring the image. I pinpointed where each girl was and where Troll was, at the time all the screens went to snow. "Let me see the kitchen."

On the monitor, I watched Deon, who was slight of form, about five-seven, and gayer than a nineteen fifties chorus-line dancer, as he washed his hands before tackling sushi. Deon had promised me a sushi-making lesson one Sunday afternoon. Beast liked sushi too; it was one raw meat we could both enjoy. But if Deon had done something to Bliss, I'd make him pay. Deon spent ten minutes slicing veggies and raw salmon before looking up, puzzled. And the interference hit. Troll grunted, seeing the perplexed expression on Deon's face. The new guy had seen or heard something.

"Total time the system was blanked was two minutes and forty seconds." Troll hit the RESET button. "Long enough for Bliss to get out or someone to take her."

"Yeah," I said. "Bring it back up and let me see where everyone is after the interference." No one had moved except Deon, who was looking out the back window of the dining room, heavy drapery pushed free, a sushi knife in his hand, and Troll, who had been working on accounts in Katie's office before the interference and was standing in front of the console afterward. "She didn't go out the front door. And if she went out the back door, I'd have . . ." I stopped. *I'd have smelled her. Right.* "Deon might have seen her."

"I got a bad feeling about this," Troll rumbled. "Somethin's wrong."

I checked Bliss's room, which was decorated in ice blues and grays. There was nothing broken, no evidence of a struggle, and her purse was on a hook in the closet, containing her ID, credit cards, and a wad of cash. I was pretty sure she hadn't left without it, not willingly.

Her room overlooked a service alley below. I checked to see if the window would open easily, and it did. There was a shed roof below. Though it was twelve feet down and looked pretty flimsy, she could have sneaked out of the house by the window. But that just didn't feel right. A gust of air blew up, carrying a blood scent. I had smelled Bliss's blood not long ago, and this wasn't hers. Someone else had bled outside, where there were also a few indications of residual magic. Nothing important.

I spent another twenty minutes talking to the girls while they drank early cocktails, and to Deon, who was the only one who'd heard anything, though from the side of the house, not the rear. When I asked him why he had looked out the back, he'd lifted his chin. "There be no windows to the side of the house. But good ears, I got, and I heard a thump from there."

"Okay. Thanks, Deon," Troll said as the doorbell rang. "That helps." Deon gave a little wrist flick and carried his unappreciated fruit cups back to the kitchen. Indigo jumped up and raced upstairs. The blonde was taking Bliss's early customer.

"I'll look around outside," I said, my curiosity growing. I left by the back door and flip-flopped around to the side of Katie's Ladies, to the narrow, unadorned utility area. It was getting darker now, the sky a deeper blue with golden clouds on the western horizon. I paused to get my bearings, and thought I heard a sound, a brief note of . . . something. But it was gone too fast, was unimportant.

In New Orleans, every square inch of possible garden space is heavily planted, with miniature gardens springing up in places homeowners and business owners in other locales would have ignored or overlooked, so the barrenness of the place was a surprise. It was no more than five feet wide, with no entrance from the street in front. The small overhang I'd seen from above was made of plywood, brittle and warped with age, and protected a push mower and gardening supplies. There was no indication that anyone had jumped from the window to the shed roof. I didn't need to check it. I could go away.

I stopped midturn. Paced back, slowly. The compulsion hit me again. *Go away. Nothing to see, nothing to smell, nothing here.* The space had been spelled, and I hadn't noticed when I was here earlier.

Resisting the compulsion, I eased down the alley, breathing in a strong, unfamiliar witchy scent, a trace of Bliss, and the tang of blood. Someone had been casting in the narrow alley. And she had bled here. I looked around and spotted a thin spray of blood up the wall. A bit more was splattered on the ground, as if the wounds had been quickly stanched. I knelt down to get closer to the scent markers on the ground. My nose was an inch from the dirt when I heard the scream, long and broken.

"Jaaaaaaane!"

A door thumped. From my house. It was Molly.

CHAPTER 14

They should all be staked

My heart stuttered painfully as Beast poured power into my bloodstream. The dusky dimness grew brighter, as if a flash had gone off inside my head, as she bled into my vision. A growl erupted from my throat. I whirled, raced toward my house.

Beast-fast, I crossed the yard and leaped, catching the top of the brick fence with one hand and levering myself up and over, the flip-flops lost in the dash. As I was vaulting the fence, I saw a ladder leaning against the brick. It hadn't been there before. I snarled.

And took in a whiff of vamp. And of witches. The trails overlaid one another in a twisting spiral from Katie's Ladies to here. Instantly I understood the trap that had sprung. They had taken Bliss, then waited in the alley, hidden under a spell that had subtly encouraged me not to check around the entire house. When I went inside Katie's, they had simply climbed the fence and come here. Then they'd attacked.

I dropped into a defensive crouch inside the walled garden. There was no siren scream of anything trying to get through the wards. Had Molly not activated the perimeter ward? Had she forgotten after I left the house? I hadn't waited to see that she was safe.

The smell of blood hit me, rich and fresh. Molly's. I/we screamed.

I raced across the porch. A blaze of magics prickled across my skin. *The wards are still in place.* But they smelled burned, ragged. Someone had blasted a hole through them at the kitchen door. The edges fluttered, singeing the air with the smell of scorched earth and ozone.

Inside, the smell of blood was stronger. Bloody prints tracked across the floor. Beast-fast, I followed them. Molly lay in a spreading pool of blood at the foot of the stairs. Bleeding from everywhere. Her eyes wide with shock, her lips mouthing words. "My babies. He took my babies."

I wasn't sure what I did next. I know I called 911. I remember a fast vision of my hands grabbing clean towels from the folded clothes. Tying them over the wounds on her torso with clean sheets. I remember fighting to shift, Beast thrumming through me. I remember tears dripping from my nose and cheeks. I remember shouting to the 911 operator that Molly was hurt bad and the children had been kidnapped.

I remember the paramedics set off the ward at the front door. And I sent them to the side, the ward wailing. And I remember, so clearly, holding Molly's blood-slick hand in mine when she fought the paramedics who were trying to help her. And the fear on their faces when they looked into mine.

I remember knowing Mol was going to die. Knowing it. Smelling death. Screaming with grief and fear. Calling Leo's. Demanding help. Begging. But Leo wasn't home. I remember Bruiser promising to bring Bethany to the hospital. The hesitant sound in his voice; he knew he shouldn't be helping.

I remember grabbing the photos just taken of Molly and the kids. For the cops. For the AMBER Alert. Rushing with police officers into the street to follow the trail of the witches and the vamps who had invaded my home. Who had stolen the kits. The trail ended in a fading cloud of diesel and a booby-trap spell that sent me tumbling. Sitting up in the street, my palms bleeding from the fall. Jumping into the back of the ambulance.

But it was all mixed up in my head, like dozens of overlapping sound bites, like being in a foreign land, the language all jumbled, the sights alien. I couldn't save Molly, my only friend. I didn't know where her children were. Bliss was gone. I was crying and useless. Useless. While Beast screamed and clawed at my mind, trying to force the change on me.

Tulane University Hospital was the only one in New Orleans that kept paranormal medical experts on salary, medicos who dealt with the needs of the supernats and their injuries. Molly was unloaded and carted into the TUH Emergency Department. I claimed to be her sister, so they let me in back, but I had to leave her to sign papers and talk to the cops. Two uniformed cops and a plainclothes guy whose name badge read A. Ferguson.

Ferguson wanted to question me, the kinds of questions cops saved for suspects. I was covered in blood, so I understood the officers being wary, but there wasn't time to waste. And Beast was too close to the surface for me to find words for them.

I called Big Evan in Brazil, left him a voice mail. Then Molly's big sister in Asheville. I managed to call Rick. And Jodi Richoux. And Troll.

I coped enough to get my story out to the cops between calls, and Rick talked to one of them while I answered the doctor's questions and talked to a surgeon who was also an earth witch. I held it together by a thread, juggling answers, questions, information. Right up until Bruiser and Bethany waltzed into the ED.

Everything stopped at that moment. The constant incredible din of the place. The continuous movement. The ever-present sense of urgency. It all stopped. Everyone stood in place, pivoted to get a better look, and stared. Suddenly I could take a breath. A sense of icy expectancy flowed over me, her shaman essence, her healing. My skin tightened into taut peaks by the power that wafted around the vamp, power that smelled of ozone and earth, a lightning storm in the jungle. Beast settled onto her haunches, quiet.

Bruiser stood in the entrance, the glass doors to the ambulance ramp open behind him, Bethany's hand in the crook of his arm. Bruiser was wearing jeans and an openneck shirt. Bethany was wearing a full-skirted crimson tribal outfit, her head swathed in an orange turban, an orange shawl over one shoulder. Gold hoops dangled from her ears and a necklace of heavy gold links circled her neck. Her feet were bare. And she was fully vamped out.

The young cop beside me pulled his weapon, but before he could raise it to fire, his partner put out a restraining hand and looked at me. He was human, about five-ten, late forties, a sergeant by his stripes. His partner looked young, still wet behind the ears. And the plainclothes guy, Ferguson, was mid-fifties. Experienced. Canny. He looked from Bethany to me and put things together as his eyes darkened.

"The victim. She's a witch, isn't she?" the detective said. I nodded and Ferguson's mouth curled into a faint sneer. The scent of fear and hatred started to ooze from his pores. He was a closet witch hater. Maybe not so much closet. His voice dropped lower. "And you didn't think it important to tell us all that? Wasting our time with witch shit?"

"Children aren't shit," I growled. He took a step back. The younger cop struggled with his partner to draw his gun, eyes switching from Bethany in the doorway, to the closer threat, me. I curled my hands into fists to keep from clawing out. "You telling me that you wouldn't have issued an AMBER Alert for two kidnapped children if their mother was a witch? That you'd take a chance on waiting?"

"Witch politics," Ferguson spat. "Their kids aren't the concern of normal humans. And that?" He jutted his chin at Bethany, still in the doorway. "They should all be staked."

In an eyeblink Bethany had crossed the floor and taken the detective into an embrace. It looked like a lover's touch, carnal, possessive, one hand at his back, the other holding his head. Her fangs braced at his throat. He struggled for a single heartbeat and went still. I shivered in the cold, dry hospital air, sweat chilling on my skin. I had never seen a human *forced* under by a vamp. They could mesmerize, but not without eye contact. Not without time to establish control. This was fast. And freaky. And illegal. And deadly.

Bethany licked along Ferguson's throat, her tongue moving between her spiked canines. She breathed in his scent and closed her eyes in what looked like sexual ecstasy. The detective groaned in her arms, aroused, stoned to the gills. He sighed happily and slid an arm around his captor, nuzzling close.

As if she couldn't hear him, the young cop hissed, "We got to stop her, Sarge. She's gonna kill him."

I spared the older cop a glance. "Probably not. But if you can't control your partner, *he* might end up dead." I heard a brief struggle as I turned back to Bethany.

She smelled the detective the way Beast smelled a fresh kill, short snuffling sniffs and long drafts of air. She moaned softly, and the sound raised the hairs on the back of my neck. George moved slowly toward her, adjusting his angle so she would see his approach while he was several feet away. "Bethy, love. He's not a danger to you. He isn't food."

"It would let children be stolen," she said, her breath on the neck of her prey. "It would let them die, like my babies died." She lifted her head to Ferguson's eyes. "Speak the truth, human creature. You have let missing children go without searching for them, yes? You would let these children die?"

He sighed and smiled, stoned on vamp power. "Witch kids. Not human."

Bethany said, "Some would call me witch and cursed. You would let my children die?"

"Let 'em die. Ain't natural." He giggled softly. "Stake you. Gut you. Cut off your head."

Bethany smiled, then looked at the cop in her arms, her eyes claiming his will. He shuddered along the length of his body as if she shook him. "You will no longer desire to stake the cursed. You will love us. Desire us. You will work to help and to find all children. Speak to this, human."

His eyelids fluttered. "Wiiii. . . . Will help. . . ." He licked his lips. "Always." His hands rose and he stroked her face. "Please? Now . . . ? Please."

"Good." Bethany patted his face. "This is good." She struck, her fangs slicing into his carotid so fast I didn't see them penetrate. Her lips formed a seal, the suction of her mouth hard. A single drop of blood teared at the corner of her lips. Five long seconds later, she released him and Ferguson slid to the floor, his neck wounds closed and only a smear of blood to show where he had been a meal. "The human will live. It will allow no more children to die."

"Shit. Shitshitshitshit," the younger cop said. "Sarge—?"

"Shut up, Micky. Shut up and go to the unit. Don't do anything. Just sit there."

Bethany looked at me and cocked her head. "I was brought here to help a witch. I smell her. She is dying."

The older uniformed cop opened a door and Bethany flowed inside, closing the door behind her. The sergeant pursed his lips, not sure what to do next. He toed the detective on the floor. Ferguson didn't stir. The cop grinned and it was a nasty sight, as if he thought Ferguson had gotten what he deserved.

I touched his arm. "Thank you. And I'm sorry about not telling you she was a witch, but if I had, some cops might have held off, might have buried the report for a few crucial, critical seconds. So I kept it to myself."

"Not all of us are sons a' bitches," he said. "My only beef is having to write this report." His radio crackled and he listened to some code words and numbers and flipped open his cell. " 'Scuse me." He wandered off. An EMT and a nurse dropped a folding gurney to the floor and picked up Ferguson, depositing him without much care or gentleness. They rolled him aside and left him there. The EMT flicked the cop's nose as he walked away. It seemed that his confession had been heard and not everyone agreed with his politics or his prejudice.

"You're barefooted. I'm accustomed to that from Bethany, but not from you."

Bruiser stood in the corner, his arms lose, staring at my dirty, blood-crusted feet.

"I lost my flip-flops." I touched the door behind which Molly and Bethany had vanished. "She wasn't this bad the other day. Bethany. Will she hurt Mol?"

"Bethy has good days and bad. Today is a bad one. But she's a healer before anything else. Your friend will be fine."

"Leo . . ." I stopped. I didn't know what to say.

"Leo doesn't know we're here. He is at Immanuel's grave site. But when I tell him, my guess is he'll stop by your place, and he won't be happy." He offered nothing else, watching me. His unwavering gaze made me acutely aware of my lack of proper clothes. Shorts and T. No bra, no shoes. Covered in blood. He didn't look all that great himself, despite the tailored casual clothes and the air of absolute confidence he wore like a second skin. He was pale, circles beneath his eyes, lines drawing his face, looking worse than the last time I saw him—probably the lingering effects of a feeding frenzy.

"It isn't Immanuel's grave site."

He raised his brows. "So? Keep a few crosses nearby."

I nodded, now more uncomfortable than before. Great. Small talk in a hospital. Two things I hated at one time. A moment later Bethany left the room and went straight for Bruiser. She wound herself around him and he moved into her embrace, the motion familiar and tender, the gesture of a lover. Something uncomfortable turned over inside me. I didn't want to know what it was or inspect it too closely.

"George. My lovely Georgie." Bethany ran one hand through his hair and he laughed softly. "Take me home now, yes?"

He kissed her fingers when she pressed them to his lips. "Did you help the little witch, Bethy love?"

"She will life—will live," she corrected. "She will live. I shared my essence and my holy blood with her. Are you pleased with me?" Her tone was needy, the sound of a child asking a grown-up for approval.

My discomfort spread. *Holy blood. Criminy.*

"Yes. I'm proud of you."

"I may drink again tonight? I hunger."

"I will see that you are well fed. You did a good thing."

"Yes," she said happily, sounding like a child praised by a parent, "I did."

Bruiser looked at me and nodded once. Without a good-bye he led Bethany through the doors and outside. I was left looking at my reflection in the closed glass, the night black beyond. If I were foolish enough to get involved with Bruiser, that was what I'd get, a bit of his time, none of his loyalty. That belonged to the vamps. It was good to know. Good to keep in mind. But the knowledge still left cold emptiness inside.

I went in to see Molly. She was lying in a darkened room, asleep beneath a warming blanket. Bags of fluid went into each arm. A nurse printed off a paper strip and looked up at me. "She'll be fine now. It must be nice to have them come when you need them."

Them. Vamps. "Yeah. It is." I took Molly's hand, and it was cold as death beneath the warm blanket. Her face was whiter than the sheets and crusted with dried blood. The nurse took a wet rag and wiped her face. The rag came away scarlet. More blood, wet and thin, as if mixed with water or IV fluids, had soaked into the sheets. Other sheets were on the floor where the nurses had tossed them to keep from slipping in Molly's blood. Evidence that the fight to keep her alive had been intense and desperate. Until Bethany appeared on the scene.

I understood why some doctors had called for a national vamp blood bank, until it was discovered that whatever made vamps vamps didn't survive removal from their bodies, but started decomposition almost instantly. If they had a preservative to give it a shelf life, hopeless cases like Molly's would survive. I stroked her hand, the dried blood brittle on her skin. "Will she sleep long?"

"I've only seen the vampires heal someone once before. He slept until morning. And then most of the next day. You should go home. Get some rest. Be sure to leave your number with the desk and they'll call you if there's any change. And they probably have a room number for her now."

Silent, I left Molly to the care of the medical professionals and did as the nurse suggested, exchanging information with the tech behind the desk. She looked twelve, fresh and clean and cheery. There were bunnies printed on her pink scrub top.

There was nothing I could do. I went home.

I stood on the side step, taking in the smell/texture/taste of my house. Blood. Magic. Fear. Cops, now gone. The wards on the house had been ripped, a hole I could see like a tear in a wedding veil, the damage flickering on the silver-gray mesh of magic. There, where the hole had been blasted, the tattered net of energy moved lazily, like a scorched curtain in a slow breeze. The edges of the hole glowed black and red, as if they were still hot to the touch. The smell of the attack was wood ash and smoking garbage, its texture on my skin like rotten fruit. Molly's alarm hadn't gone off when the attack happened, the magical assault burning through without a sound. Whatever made the hole, it was powerful.

I moved into the darkened house, my feet silent on the wood floor, and stared at the pool of blood, black in the night, where my friend had lain. And I burst into tears. Hot, choking, smothering tears that clawed up from my lungs and closed off my throat. I caught myself on the banister and eased down to the step. My body shuddered with sobs, wracking and harsh, my pain and guilt as cutting as Beast's claws on my mind.

I had let my only friend come here, even though I was fighting vamps. And even after I'd learned that witch children were being kidnapped I'd let her stay, believing that her wards and my Beast could keep them all safe. And everything I'd believed had been burned away in the magical attack on my house.

When the crying ended, I dragged myself to my feet, went outside, and stripped. Sat on the boulders. I had to find the kits and Bliss. I forced the change on myself. Pain slammed into me, scored deep, punishment, chastisement, castigation. For losing Angelina and Little Evan, and Bliss. The three were my last thoughts as the grayness took me.

I snarled, crouching on broken rocks. Pain dug predator talons deep into my pelt. Hungry fangs bit and tore. Jane did this. Punished us for another's acts. Stupid. And human. Stretched and felt pain pull through flesh like an enemy's claws. She had left no food. Growled and spat. Settled on water from fountain. It trickled from the tiny stone vampire woman at the top.

Hunt, she whispered in my mind. *Kits.*

Belly cramped with hunger, just as in the hunger times. I snarled at her, at Jane, but remembered Angie. Evan. Bliss. Liked little witch. Must protect kits. I dropped from fountain, moved slowly to burned ward. Sniffed. Hackles rose. Smelled many humans with guns.

Cops, Jane whispered. *EMTs. Paramedics. All gone now.*

Pelt settled. Leaped up steps, across porch, into kitchen. Stopped. Smelled witches and vampire—a rotten-fruit evil smell. Delicious reek of old blood, Molly's blood, from when she lay dying. I growled low. The shaman vampire healed her. I knew this from Jane's memory. Did not have to grieve.

I pulled the scents deep, through open mouth, over scent glands. A *screeee* of breath over tongue and scent sacks in mouth. Choosing the evil ones to study, learning all parts of them. They were the young-rogue makers. Knew it. Set them in scent memory, three evil vampire witches. Two unknown witches, female, and one who was both vampire and witch, male.

Three vampire witches? Jane thought. *Bruiser said witches are seldom turned because their devoveo state is prolonged, sometimes permanent.* Her thoughts turned inward, considering three enemies.

Ignoring hunger, I walked outside, jumped to top of rocks. Launched over fence. Landed on other side with silent paws. *Beast is good hunter. Will track evil vampires and witches. And Bliss. Will kill. Will save kits. Big Cat's duty. A mother's task. To kill. To eat. To take vengeance on enemies.*

I trotted into dark street. No people out. Quiet. Many shadows to hide in. I smelled Angie. Raced down street, seeing story in smells. Vampires had run here, pulling Bliss. Carrying kits. Forcing female witches with magic. They all feared. I growled. The smell of blood was close. Much blood. And the burned-paper smell of forced magic.

I stopped. Sniffed into narrow place between buildings. Three vampire witches had fed on two other witches. Had stolen their blood and much of their power. Strong magic. I padded into street, sniffing at tar road. Scent of kits ended. Car rolled away. Taking kits and evil vampires.

Thought all vamps were evil, Jane whispered deep.

These worse. These are rank with witch blood and witch magic, like rotten meat and crawly things.

Gave Jane a glimpse of maggots as I went to side of street, to empty lot where building had burned. Witches had gone there. But without kits. I smelled where witches walked, bleeding. On next street they did magic. Car came. They left.

Hungry. Home. Jane's hunt now. I padded back to Jane's den and jumped over fence, landing on rocks. And changed.

*   *   *

I came to myself, naked on the rocks, my stomach in agony of hunger. I touched my face, feeling the flaccid skin, the hollowed cheeks. I hadn't been fair to Beast or to myself to shift without food. And the calorie loss was at a dangerous level. I gathered up my clothes and limped inside. I drank a gallon of water, my throat tissues so dry they ached with each swallow. I ate a pound of jerky and opened a box of Cheerios and spooned it all down with sour milk. My stomach ached with the amount of food.

Still naked, I turned on the lights and got a bucket, spray cleaner, and a roll of paper towels. I cleaned Molly's blood off the floor, the cleanser burning my nostrils and the skin of my hands. I let it burn, the pain another penance.

Lonely wasn't something I ever felt—not ever—but the black hole inside me was so empty, so deep, it was a caving in of my soul, imploding like a mountain falling in on itself. A separateness that might be loneliness. As I worked, tears fell from my eyes and wet the bare floor.

When the floor was clean, the paper towels bagged on the side porch, the blood scent hidden under the chemical reek, I wiped my face and answered Evan's call from Brazil, and then another from Molly's elder sister Evangeline near Asheville.

Evan had already booked a flight to the States. I'd have to find a safe place to put him. Not at my house. It wasn't safe for anyone anymore. The master of the city was gunning for me. Witches had gotten in, along with something Beast had described as a vamp-witch. I thought I'd never heard of such a thing before, but then I remembered what Bethany had said at the hospital—that she was a witch *and* one of the cursed, aka a vampire. They should have been hated enemies.

Evangeline was coming as well, her tone hard and biting. She blamed me. I couldn't disagree. She was right. It was my fault. I called the hospital and found that Molly had gone to a private room. The charge nurse said she was sleeping; her vital signs were normal. Relief fluttered through me like butterfly wings, gossamer and diaphanous in the dark core of my twinned souls.

Filthy, I stood under a scalding shower and let the blood drench off me. I was getting used to seeing scarlet-tinted water swirl around my feet.

I was standing naked, damp, and chilled in my bedroom, staring at my new leathers, when the remaining wards on the house shuddered and spat. An electric banshee wail sounded, Molly's alarm when something magical attacked.

My front door vibrated with a massive thump I could feel through the floor. Then I smelled vamp.

CHAPTER 15

Hedge of thorns

In one move, I pulled the shotgun and a vamp-killer, blade back for in-close street fighting, and advanced to the front door, planting my feet with care, balanced and ready. My heart sped, my breath went deep and fast. Beast's claws tore into my belly, ready to fight. But the front door was closed. No one had broken through Molly's ward.

Barely heard over the howl of the alarm, the side door creaked. Where the ward *was* broken. I whirled.

Leo stood inside, fully vamped out, eyes bled black in scarlet sclera, fingernails like talons. His shoulders were hunched, his clothes windblown, shirt open to the waist. Like most vamps, he was slender to the point of emaciation, his chest thinly haired, ribs stark and muscles like cords, no fat on him at all. He was staring at the place where Molly nearly died. His nostrils flared as he scented her blood.

I remembered Bruiser saying that he'd been at Immanuel's grave. He was probably deep in Dolore, on the edge of madness again. Bruiser had told me to keep crosses nearby. I had a moment to wonder which of my many sins Leo was here to kill me for. I adjusted my grip on the Benelli.

Leo sniffed, short, quick inhalations, animal-like. Cocked his head to the side, the motion not mammalian, but snake-like. It made my flesh crawl. My fingers tightened on the vamp-killer. He sniffed again and closed his eyes, holding the breath in. He let it out with a quick plosive breath and snarled. Beast reacted with a shot of adrenaline to my system and a soft growl from my own lips.

Leo's eyes flew to me, to the Benelli M4 Super 90 in my right hand. His gaze traveled from the shotgun, up my arm, and down my naked body. It wasn't the leisurely perusal of a lover, but the calculated evaluation of a predator. Of a killer studying prey.

I shouted over the wail of the alarm. "I'm assuming you're here to finish what you started when you came to burn me out."

The wail of the witch alarm went silent and I started, the thirty-second siren preset into the ward by Molly leaving a deaf hole in the fabric of the universe. *If we don't have them immobilized or dead by then, it's too late,* she'd said, with a sweet grin. My heart squeezed tight with pain. Someone had the children. Someone had stolen them. I flipped the vamp-killer, the silver catching the light.

"Someone has taken the children," I told him, though I couldn't say, for sure, why I bothered.

A hint of emotion flickered in the back of Leo's eyes, chased like leaves in a winter wind. He blinked slowly. Took a short, shallow breath. The corner of his mouth lifted, almost unwillingly. He chuckled.

With the sound, his eyes bled back to human, laughter always forcing a vamp back from the killing edge. They can't laugh and be vampy at the same time; it's two distinct parts of them, one part still human, one part predator. The red bled out of his sclera and he stood straight, instantly regaining a human aspect. He took a deep breath, the motions bizarre after the inhuman posturing.

"Why are you here?" I asked, my voice soft in the odd hush. "Is it because I co-opted Bethany to heal Molly?"

"I . . . I don't know. . . ."

"Is it the Dolore?"

Something faint crossed his face, so fast the flesh seemed to ripple, as if a fragile sanity was torn like rotten silk. Almost as quickly, reason and control reentered his eyes. I kept the Benelli trained on him, the vamp-killer ready. He blinked slowly; black eyes looked me over, this time with a cool perusal. He brushed a strand of silky black hair from his olive-skinned face, flesh paled from centuries away from the sun, and when he spoke his voice was coolly wry. "I can't be killed with shotguns."

"You can if they fire rounds hand-packed with silver fléchettes."

Leo tilted his head and let his smile widen, looking me over now like an entirely different kind of predator, making me acutely aware that I wasn't dressed for company. Wasn't, in fact, dressed at all. I flipped the knife so it was point forward. "And the knife is a silver-lined vamp-killer. Neither will kill you dead instantly, but you may not wake the morning after either."

Leo had a really good smile, charming, disarming. his lips mobile and full as he met my eyes. The hard, deep, full-on vamp power rolled over me. I could feel the desire to lower my weapons. Resisted. Hanging on to Beast-induced fight-or-flight response.

"I am master of this city. Silver will not kill me easily. You have had a Rousseau as guest?"

It took me a moment to realize he had changed the subject. "No."

"Rousseau scions who stink of witch blood attacked your home, in the company of two female witches, Rousseaus I do not recognize. One is a powerful master. Intriguing. I should know every Rousseau. I have been among them in their clan home. These do not live among the Rousseaus."

My heart raced. The Rousseau Clan. Recently allied with Mearkanis and St. Martin, I remembered. Against Leo. I knew Bettina Rousseau, the clan's blood-master. I would have recognized her scent.

He shook back his hair, which brushed his shoulders. "Bethany is fragile and such energy exchange is draining to her. You will accept that no one except me asks her for healing." He said it like a command. My brows went up. With complete disregard for the gun and knife—and me—Leo turned and went back through the dark kitchen. Closed the outer door. I could see the glitter of his eyes through the shadows. "Unless you wish me to join you in your bed, get dressed. We have much to discuss. I'll make tea." And with that, Leo, the master of the city of New Orleans, turned his back on me and went to my stove.

Feeling idiotic and not sure why, worried about this new, less stable Leo and the effects of the Dolore, I closed the door to my bedroom and set the weapons on the bed. I pulled on undies, jeans, and a long-sleeved T. Fuzzy socks. I twisted my hair back and tied the long wet length of it into a knot, remembering something I hadn't recalled until now, a sharp clicking as I shifted into Beast. I'd had beads in my hair. Now they were lying in the dust and broken rocks of my garden. Inconsequential. The brain latching on to foolishness to avoid a horror.

Uncertain of the state of Leo's mental health, I slid four stakes against my scalp like my usual hair sticks, reloaded my derringer with silver shot, and tucked it into my waistband. It wasn't much against the speed and killing power of a master vamp, but it made me feel better.

I had no idea what to do next to find the children. So I was going to have tea with a possibly whacked-out vamp? Social calls while the kits were in danger? But Leo had already given me some good info: Rousseaus, or vamps of their bloodline, had the kits and they had never lived at the Rousseau clan home. And there were more than one, which was why I'd had so much trouble analyzing the braided, woven scent signature. They all had to be related. Yeah. It all made sense.

Bettina was the Rousseau clan master. Her hands had smelled of the killers at the party. She knew something. Part of me wanted to storm the Rousseau stronghold immediately, bare my teeth, break down the gates, and beat them all for info. But when dealing with kidnappings, you had to be careful. One wrong move and . . . I breathed deeply, trying to get my thoughts under control. Not succeeding much. Beast rumbled disgust deep in my mind. Flexed her claws and cut into me. Pain cleared my head.

When I reached the kitchen, the kettle was starting a breathy whistle and Leo was measuring out tea leaves, his shirt buttoned and tucked into the black trousers, long sleeves rolled neatly to the elbows. He looked earthy and harmless, or as harmless as a gorgeous, no-longer-human, clinically deceased man can look in his shirtsleeves. Drop-dead gorgeous. If I hadn't been so scared for Angelina and Evan and Bliss, I might have smiled at my whimsy.

His feet, like mine, were bare. There was something unnerving about Leo's bare feet, long and slender with a few black hairs on the upper knuckles of his big toes. He glanced up at me standing in the doorway and back, pouring steaming water over the leaves in the teapot. "I apologize for my bit of temper."

That what they're calling it? A bit of temper? But I didn't say it, settling on "Ooookay."

"Katie and I used this very pot for tea during the war." With a quick smile he added, "That would be World War One." He set the kettle on the metal rack and covered the leaves. I put cold fingers on the derringer.

I itched to be hunting the kits but . . . where? I ground my molars and went for cups, choosing two aqua mugs. I put sugar on the counter and got Cool Whip and cream out of the fridge. "Yeah?"

Leo put a tea cozy over the pot for it to steep. Making tea. The normality of it all was creepy so soon after the vamped-out demonstration at the foot of the stairs. Had he called a truce? Or had he forgotten about going all vampy on me? The last time he was here, he'd been intent on burning down my house and me in it. It had to be the Dolore. How close to the edge was Leo?

"A third cup would be nice." His tone was mild, backed by none of the power I knew he could put into his voice. "George is outside. I imagine he would like to come in."

Without comment, I got out another mug and went to the door. When I opened it, Bruiser was standing there, still wearing the casual open-neck shirt and jeans. He looked at my neck as if inspecting me for damage. I was pretty sure it was relief I saw before he blinked it away. "The ward is still in place here," I said. "If you come around to the side, you can get in without the alarm going off again."

He nodded once and turned for the gate. No wasted words. I went back to the kitchen and got out cookies. My hands trembled when I opened them. Angie Baby had eaten two after lunch today. Now she was in the hands of a witch-vamp, and I had a bad feeling he wasn't giving her cookies. I struggled with tears, the unfamiliar riptide of emotions pulling me under a swirl of fear and worry and grief. I sucked in a breath, fighting for control.

Bruiser entered just as I put cookies on the plate and Leo poured the tea. One hand on his hip, Bruiser looked at the domestic scene; his brows beetled down in worry. I accepted a warm mug from Leo. After a hesitation, Bruiser did the same, holding it as if the tea were nitro. Leo sat and indicated we were to do the same, master in my house.

No way. Not even if it kept him from whacking out. I leaned against the counter, one foot back in case I needed leverage to leap. George sat, sipping his tea, though I knew him for a coffee man. He added a teaspoon of sugar and stirred. Taking his cue, I added sugar and whipped cream to mine. When the spoons were set aside, Leo said. "George?"

Succinct, a soldier reporting in, George said, "The Executive Vampire Council has agreed to meet with a witch delegation under diplomatic protection." A shock zinged through me at his words. Vamps never had official dealings with witches. The last known discourse between the two races was over a hundred years ago. George slid a scrap of paper to me. "My master's contact with the witch clans has assured me they are willing to address the council."

My brows went way up. I leaned in and took the small paper, tucked it into my pocket. Leo had arranged this? This took reason. I started to relax.

"My master also understands that another member of the Everheart family coven, Evangeline, will soon arrive in New Orleans, as will Evan Trueblood, an unregistered sorcerer. Their arrival constitutes a new full coven in his city. Mr. Pellissier expects them to act as any tourist and return home when their visit is done."

My heart stuttered. No one but Molly and her sisters knew about Evan. *Crap.* I sipped my tea, mind racing. Evangeline Everheart had been pulling strings, using her connections to set up talks. A full coven meant five, Evan, Molly, Evangeline, and the children. *Mr. Pellissier expects . . .* My first reaction was to tell Leo to stuff it where the sun didn't shine, but I figured with a vamp that was pretty much anywhere. His words were tantamount to a command, and probably had import in the vamp/witch chats planned. So maybe I'd better not stick my big, clawed feet into the mix. "Okay. I'll pass along his . . . request." Okay, so I couldn't let it go by without a small dig at his orders.

Leo watched, nothing in his dark eyes, or nothing human, anyway. He put down his mug with a soft tap of stoneware on wood. I felt George tighten, smelled a sudden chemical change on his skin. Not fear, not exactly, but it was close. I gathered myself, preparing for whatever was about to happen. "You have been asking about the devoveo. Why?"

Nerves that had been twined about me for hours tightened. I set my mug down to free my hands; Leo didn't look quite . . . right. "I had hoped the word might be important but it isn't. The sire of the young rogues is burying his progeny—their progeny." I shrugged. "Whatever—in secret graveyards, in the middle of a pentagram with crosses all around. And the graves stink of witch magic." Leo didn't react at all, his face unreadable.

"According to my sources he's been stealing witch children off and on for decades and killing them, I think at the graves, witch blood sacrifices. My gut's saying that it's all tied in with the vamp curse, but the only way that fits, even a little bit, is one note I found about drinking witch blood being a temporary cure for the devoveo.

"But it's only a temporary cure. Unless someone's trying to spell it permanen—" I stopped midword. It made sense. "They're trying to avoid devoveo—the curse—altogether. The only ones I've heard about who did that were the Sons of Darkness. What are they? Could they be in New Orleans?"

Leo went still, that weird shift from nearly human to dead immovability, a block of pale marble carved into human shape. Bruiser set down his mug, claiming my attention. He blinked slowly, his face going white, high spots of color on his cheeks; his eyes were full of warning and he gave an almost infinitesimal shake of his head. "Boss?" he said, his voice too gentle, too wary.

What did I say? It couldn't be a big secret about devoveo, or drinking witch blood. *Crap! What else did I say?*

Everything, even the air, went still and silent, so sharp it was almost cutting, for one awful moment. "You dare speak of the Sons of Darkness," he said, his voice the barest whisper of breath. Then Leo vanished. Phased into a blur. In the visible echo of the movement he reappeared, right in front of me, in a burst of vamp-scented air. Icy dead hands like steel bars embraced me, claws cutting into me. There wasn't time to gasp. His fangs tore into my throat. Pain ripped through me, lightning agony. I heard Bruiser shouting, "No! Leo, no!"

Beast screamed, trying to shift, shift, *shift now!* Leo shook me as a dog shakes prey, shredding my throat. Teeth buried so deep I felt tendons snap and tear. My blood spurted across the room. Adrenaline shocked through me too late; I heard something heavy fall nearby, vibrating through the house. Beast screamed again. Her strength in my veins, I somehow got my hands up. Pulled two hair sticks, my motions slow as my own death. And buried them in Leo's body. The angles were all wrong. Nowhere near his heart. He shook me so hard my teeth clacked together. I tasted blood, salty and sweet. The world tilted at an odd angle.

I was falling. My blood fountained again. Landed in a bouncing heap, my blood a cascade. Drenching over a body on the floor. Spattering two legs at eye level. My carotids were severed. Again. My heart pumping out.

Beast heaved a breath that coated my lungs with blood. Screamed and tried to shift. Got my legs up under me. Spurting blood, I/we ran toward the back of the house. Past a downed George. Crashed through the back window in a shower of antique glass and more modern storm window. Stumbled across the lawn. Beast in control.

Darkness gathered at the edges of my vision. The world telescoped into a tiny spot of color and life. My pulse was fading. Cold clutched at me.

I staggered toward the rocks. Something red and burning swooped up behind me.

I sought for the snake buried in the cells of all life. I sought for Beast. But I was too injured. There was only that new emptiness at the heart of me. I managed a breath, sucking in blood mixed with the vital air. Choking. Drowning even as I bled out. I tried to cough. I fell. Landed. The rocks caught me, a cold, hard bed.

I couldn't remember how . . . how to shift. My hand fell on something hollow.

The box, Beast thought at me. *The box*. My fingers sought inside. Touched bone. The world went dark, Beast's voice the only sound. *Mass to mass, stone to stone . . . mass to mass, stone to stone*, Beast called to me, old words. Words of power. Words she knew and understood. Words she loved. *Mass to mass, stone to stone . . . mass to mass, stone to stone. Beast will be big. Beast will be big!*

Gray lights dancing with black motes floated over me. Beneath me the stones cracked and spat brittle, sharp shards into the air. The red thing at my back grew, crackling with sparks. I sank deep into the snake of the jaw I clutched. Saw the pattern. X and Y. So different. So alien. *Wrong, wrong, wrong. I can't do this.*

Beast wrenched control away.

And I *shifted*. Became Beast. Bones popped and muscles twanged with agony. Nerves tore, flames and ice burned along my limbs. My back arched. My throat healed. Pelt sprouted, bristling. Clothes ripped and slid into tangled, twisted bonds. Claws broke the flesh of my fingertips. I threw back my head and screamed.

Tired, so tired. Huffing air. Panting breath. Hot. *Tired.* I rolled from broken stone, pulled haunches beneath me. Sitting on rocks surrounded by red light. *Danger.* Red light spilled around me. Beast was big. Sabertooth big. Colors were often grayed in my Beast eyes, but something of *her* had shifted with me.

Hedge of thorns has been sprung, Jane thought.

I looked at Molly's protecting magic. Saw Jane-blood-soaked dirt and circle of red witch light. *Hedge of thorns* sparkled with nothingness, motes black like moonless night. They swarmed like moths, never lighting. Like the magics of the gray place for shifting. I growled. Much power here.

Witch power is usually gray or blue. Why is Molly's newest magic red?

Placed paw on Jane like paw on kit. *Silent. Predator is near.* On the other side Leo howled like mad wolf, vamped out. Rogue. Screaming. Caged outside *hedge of thorns*. My stomach wrenched in hunger. Too many shifts. Not enough food. Worse than hunger times. Better too. I was Big Cat now. Very big.

What have you done? Jane whispered, prey-fear in her thoughts.

I opened mouth and long fangs parted. Sabertooth fangs. *Good for killing. Big teeth.* I roared. Lion roar, like African lion. Louder than Beast scream. Claiming territory. Claiming self. *I am Beast. I/we, together, are Beast.*

Leo, chest heaving, stopped at challenge in roar. Big predator roar. I could see him. He could not see Beast. I huffed. Roared again.

Bethany walked around side of house. She was still in skirt and turban. But now she carried spear, bones and bits of stone hanging from it, tied with twine. *Raffia*, Jane thought. *Used by a shaman.* Silly Jane thoughts. Now thinking names, words her strength. Stupid words. Words unimportant. Jane nearly died. Words did not save Jane. Only Beast saved Jane. I shoved her down, paw on her chest. *Beast is alpha.*

Bethany touched Leo. He stilled. Legs wobbled. Sat onto ground, hard. Bethany pulled hair-stick stakes out of his skin. Leo hissed. Moaned. Bethany dropped sticks. Neither was silver tipped, poison to vampires. Leo said silver would not kill him. Lie? Humans lie all the time. Big cats cannot lie, scent of lie is always known. Leo was lucky. I understood lucky. Sometimes Beast ate. Sometimes prey got free. Each was luck, good for one, bad for other.

Bethany looked at *hedge of thorns*. "I heard the roar. It was much like the lions of Africa, but . . ." She shook her head. "Different." She put a hand out to touch *hedge of thorns*. And jerked away.

Huffed in laughter. Panted. Rose and padded two steps to fountain, kicking torn human clothing away. No water poured from fountain top, not with *hedge of thorns* glowing, but water in bowl was cool. Drank. Thirst gone, I sat. Watched. Predator eyes on shaman. She opened small bag and took out packets. Poured powder into leaves and put some onto Leo's wounds. She cut her skin. Gave Leo blood to eat. Smelled sweet. Belly rumbled. Hurting.

Leo panted like Beast, needing air. When he had breath, he stood. His eyes still vamped. "She is a were. I felt the power of her change; the energies were familiar, exactly like the workings of the lupus clan." Tears leaked down his face, bloody with his pain.

Leo wiped his face, blood on his hand. But he stood

straight. His eyes looked more human. "But by her roar, she is a werebeast like the one that killed my son and took his place."

The Dolore, Jane murmured to me. *Grief*.

"Not a were." Bethany scented air in short sniffs. "Taste her scent. Not a were, she. Her smell is different from them. Different from the cursed of Artemis, our enemy." Bethany walked around *hedge of thorns*. Her feet balanced like cat, her skirt moving. She shook spear with each step, shaman dance, small bones and stones and shells crackling, rattling, like tail of snake-enemy as Bethany circled *hedge of thorns*. "I do not know what she is, but she is not our adversary."

"She asked about the Sons, and about the curse. This outsider knows about the curse."

"I have read the runes." She stood beside Leo, arms wide, feet apart, toes pointing out. Butt of spear was grounded, held at angle. "The runes warn us of change, change yet again in the world of man. Perhaps this is the change foretold."

"You would leave her alive?" Leo had human look on face. Shock.

Bruiser walked from house. I growled, though was safe behind hedge. Bruiser's feet made noises to alert his alpha. "What's that red light? What's behind it?"

Humans and vampires do not see beyond light. This is good.

Bethany sniffed air. "Jane is there. And with her may be a lion. It roared." She touched spear, face sad. "So like home."

"Or she may be an African lion were," Leo said, voice stubborn, like Jane.

"No." Bethany tone was firm. "Not a were."

Bruiser licked blood from his lips. A large bruise was purple, like flower, from temple to mouth, size of big-cat paw. Remembered Bruiser body on floor. *Leo hit him?*

Yes, Jane whispered. *Yes . . .*

"Boss, someone might call the police. The red light is enough to attract the attention of the neighbors. We need to go."

Bethany turned, walked away. Bruiser took her arm. Leo stared at glow of *hedge of thorns*. "I do not know what you are," he whispered. "But you tread on dangerous ground. Leave the curse alone. Do not ask questions about the Sons of Darkness. Do not pry into the devoveo. Our curse cannot be lifted. It has been tried and the price of failure was death to our young. You have never been forced to kill your own child when she lingers, eternally mad. You cannot know the grief it brings. Stop your research. Fulfill your contract. Then go. Do you understand me?"

Beast hacked softly. *Understand. But will not obey.*

As if he knew Beast's thoughts, Leo sighed breath he did not need. Followed blood-servant Bruiser, and woman who might be mate to both of them, away. Car started in street. Drove away. Scents faded.

Padded to edge of ward. Placed paw on it. Magic swirled up, tasting of nuts and plants, things Jane would eat, but Beast would not. Red ward fell in shower of sparks and blackness. Smell of burned plants. Strong ward. Good protection. Too small to fit over entire den. Should have been over entire den: Jane house, garden, rocks-of-shift. Then kits would be safe. Anger rose at thought of kits and Bliss. Needed to find them. Kill stealer of kits. Rend flesh and spill blood. Duty of mother.

Hunger tore into belly like predator claws. Padded to house and leaped through broken back window. Went to kitchen and found meat cooked by Molly and Jane. Tore open packs. Clear plastic holding meat. Jerky. Hard and tough. But ate it. Ate it all. Hunger is angry predator.

Went back to rocks. *Hunt for kits is Jane hunt. I will give strength. The I/we of Beast will help. But Jane will stalk.* I/we lay on rocks. Thought of Jane. *Mass to mass, stone to stone . . . mass to mass, stone to stone. Jane. . . .* Pain and gray light sparkling. Pain, pain, *pain.* Rock beneath groaned and cracked. *Mass to mass, stone to stone . . . mass to mass, stone to stone.*

I was stretched on the rocks, gasping. The pain was like being flayed alive. It *hurt* to change so often, so close together. When I could, I levered myself upright and to my feet, feeling of my face and neck and running my hands over me. My throat had new scars, the flesh ridged, the skin tender and thin. It would take a lot of shifts to regain smooth skin, but at least I seemed to be my usual size.

Whenever I changed mass, I worried that I'd keep some or lose some. I didn't know enough about physics to guess how I changed mass, or to guess if retaining or permanently losing mass was even possible, and so I avoided mass change, usually sticking to creatures my own size. Beast, on the other hand, liked big, which meant stealing mass from stones. Rock had no genetic structure, was clean material to take mass from. But mass exchange resulted in the rock cracking, shattering, and often exploding.

Stone dust and sharp rock ground beneath my feet when I stood. There wasn't much left of the boulders placed here for me by Katie of Katie's Ladies. I looked into the dust and saw paw prints. Huge. Trite but true, they were dinner-plate huge. "You're crazy," I whispered to my other half. "Stark raving."

And worse, Beast had done the impossible. She had taken a male form. I could see in memory, the X and Y chromosomes in the sabertooth's genetic makeup. I had never done that. Didn't know how, even now, after the event. Deep inside, I heard Beast hack with amusement.

A heated, burned smell rode the air. The grass was seared where *hedge of thorns* had burned through. If I dug down, I knew that I'd see burned soil as deep as six feet. My blood had triggered the ward; it had soaked into the grass and dirt all the way from the house to the boulders. I could smell it drying, already decaying. It was a lot of blood. I fingered my neck. The skin there was thin and raw, new flesh, not quite healed. The injury given me by Leo in his crazy Dolore state had been intended to kill me.

Nothing I said had been deserving of the attack, even accusing vamps of killing witch children. The Dolore had made him nutso.

He grieves his children, Beast thought at me. *His son who was taken from him, and replaced by liver-eater. His daughter who he killed long ago*.

"Oh," I said softly. "Oh . . ." I hadn't put his words together that way. "Okay. So it's what? Dolore times two and I'm a handy punching bag?" Beast didn't reply. I swallowed and the movement of muscles and tissues ached. I'd had difficulty shifting. It shouldn't have been so hard. My hand drifted down and found my necklace was gone. The gold nugget necklace that tied me to the boulders here in the yard and to the boulders where I first remembered how to shift, back in the mountains, a white quartz boulder lined through with the same gold that made up my necklace. It was the gold that made my shift easier. Without it, I'd be able to shift only when I had extensive time to meditate my way into the change. Or force it, painfully.

I gathered up the beads that had come from my hair with the previous shift, holding them cupped in my hand, and inspected my clothes. My T was ruined but the jeans had somehow survived the shift and the weight gain, pushed off me as I changed. I tossed them across my shoulder. Undies were ruined. Fuzzy socks okay. I tucked them under my arm. No gold nugget.

Surely the necklace had just been ripped off and left in the kitchen. Surely Leo hadn't taken it. A shiver that had nothing to do with the warm air on my skin gripped me. My stomach growled with the need for food. Shifting used up a lot of calories. I needed to eat.

This time I went into the house through the door. Inside, I dumped my clothes and turned on the lights to study the mess. I had bled like a stuck pig. It was all over the floor, furniture, walls. Blood smeared by fighting, sprayed by arterial pressure. It was going to be a pain in the neck—pun intended—to clean it all up. And the window was ruined, all that old hand-blown glass shattered out. So much for my plans to keep this place pristine.

I spotted the necklace under the kitchen table, the double chain wrapped around a chair leg as if it had been slung and the force of the throw had snapped the chain around and around. I peeled it free and checked the clasp, which was only a little bent. I straightened it and washed the necklace at the sink, putting it back round my neck before I did anything else.

While oatmeal cooked and a strong pot of tea brewed, I cleaned up the mess. The blood was tacky, already partly dried, but it came off the floor with hot water and a scrub brush. The dirty, bloody water went down the toilet with all the other blood from today. I sprayed the floor with Clorox cleanser and let it soak. I didn't want to leave any blood evidence should cops ever need to do a crime scene investigation in the house, but removing all traces was impossible without tearing up the floor.

While I ate, I debated shifting again, this time to a raptor so I could overfly the city, but I changed my mind. Instead, I dressed in my new vamp hunting clothes, wearing my second pair of new boots—lace-up butt stompers—and made sure I had all my weapons in place, especially my old chain-link collar to protect my neck. If I'd been wearing it, Leo wouldn't have injured me nearly so badly. I'd have had time to draw weapons on him. Leo might actually be dead. I touched the thin skin, like delicate silk, ridged where the flesh hadn't knit back smoothly. I wasn't going anywhere without full garb anytime soon.

I dialed the hospital, expecting the call to go to the nurses' desk, but it was put through to her room. Molly answered. Against all expectations, she was awake, though groggy. My heart leaped, and my traitorous eyes teared up with her hello.

"Molly?"

"Hey, Big Cat. You saved my life," Molly said, not sounding strong at all, but terribly weak and breathless. Tears thickened her voice as she broke down. "My babies . . ."

"I'll save your babies," I said, helplessness like a heavy weight pressing on my shoulders. "Evan and Evangelina are on the way. I called them. They can help you heal. And then you all can help me with the search."

"Evangelina's gonna come in and take over." She laughed through the tears, the sound forlorn. "Don't let her bully you."

"I won't," I lied. Evangelina was a take-charge kinda woman. Even Beast was scared of her.

"Do . . . do you think they're still alive? Do you think someone is hurting them?"

Her voice broke on the question and my breath stopped. When I could speak I said, "Yes. No. I mean, I think they're alive and being well cared for right now." I had to believe it. Had to.

Then Molly said, "Whatever they've been stolen for, the

rite will probably take place on or near the full moon." She was trying to think like the kidnappers. God help her. But she was right. Any magic performed during a full moon would be highly amplified. And a full moon was soon. Very soon.

Molly choked back a sob. "It's not much time. Not much time at all."

"Plenty of time. I'll have them back before the full moon." I gripped my cell so hard the plastic gave. "I promise, Mol. I promise on all that I hold holy."

She sniffed. "That austere and ungiving God you worship?"

I touched the necklace I wore as if it were an amulet or icon—or a cross—the nugget warm from my skin. "Yeah. Him. I swear it. You should have gone home, Molly. You should have gone when I told you to. I'm so sorry I didn't make you leave."

"Angie said if we left, a bad man would take us on the road."

My throat closed up tight. What did it mean, take us on the road?

"I think it was a vision, Big Cat. And because of it I didn't leave town." Molly sobbed, her voice sounding broken and torn. "If you had made us leave, I'd have holed up in a hotel. And it would have been a lot worse without you close by. I'd have . . ." She took a breath, and I heard the sob in it. "I'd have died."

"Crap," I whispered.

"Yeah. Understatement of the year. And hey, you need to know. Those feelers you asked me to put out to the local covens about them helping with vamps? Not so much as a nibble. No one's talking. I tried. I really tried." And Molly was crying again, though her tears were for her missing babies, not my missing info.

When Molly had stopped crying and fallen asleep, I hung up and dialed Troll, to tell him about the damage to the house. And that I was closer to finding the maker of the young rogues and Bliss. Not exactly a lie, but not really the truth either. Not yet. But soon. I had promised. I'd given my word to Mol. I intended to keep it.

*   *   *

I inspected my map with the sites of young-rogue vamp attacks pinned on it, remembering the lightning strike in New Orleans City Park where I had witnessed the young-rogue rising. I pulled a scrap of paper to me and began listing what I knew and guessed. I was chasing Rousseaus, one a master-vamp who was violating the Vampira Carta and—by the closely related scent signatures—possibly his siblings. They were Rousseaus who never spent time at the clan home, which meant they could be anywhere in the city. I couldn't simply bust through the Rousseau clan-home door and stake them. If I attacked before I knew exactly what was going on, I'd give them the opportunity to flee, or worse, put their plans in motion immediately. I was looking for vamps using witch magic and witch children's blood, maybe doing something to avoid the devoveo. I didn't have a clear picture of it yet, but it was here. It was right here in front of me. Whatever the heck *it* was.

I stuffed my supplies in Bitsa's saddlebags and tore off on the Harley, moist, heated air touching me through the unzipped mesh pockets, otherwise deflected by the new leathers I sweated in. I needed to see what had happened to the newest grave site in Couturié Forest in the New Orleans City Park.

It took time to build the sites where humans were killed, buried, magic was done, and young rogues were raised. Time and magic and privacy. And so far as I knew, there were only three places where that had been done, and only two were still in use. I had to bet that the young-rogue maker would go back to one of them rather than start new elsewhere. I bent over Bitsa and urged her to more speed.

The park was closed this late, but I parked Bitsa a block out and jogged in, searching, following my nose along the paths. The ground wasn't rain saturated now, but had absorbed the moisture dropped by Ada, and the detritus of hurricane winds had been cleaned up. The smell of damaged trees and rain-beaten plants was still strong, but without the waterlogged, slightly salty reek from before. I left the path and quickly found the ten-foot-diameter circle. I remembered that a cleanup crew had been sent to dispose of the body, and they had obviously been here too. The crosses had been ripped from the trees and the pentagram of shells had been scattered. I could smell the humans who had cleaned the place up, two men and a woman, sweating in the heat of day, sunscreen and deodorant and soap and shampoo scents still on the air. And above the odors of the crew, the more recent scent of a solitary vampire. One who had stolen the children and Bliss. He had stood here, within the last two nights, right where I was standing, studying the scene. And he'd been angry.

I could taste his fury, building, hot and feral, but controlled for all that. Had he come to raise the young rogue? I remembered the smell of Hurricane Ada's lightning when I first came here, my curiosity what a lightning strike in the middle of a major working would cause. He'd walked off, angry and alone. His rogue had risen without him. Had risen early. . . .

So where would he go? Where would he start another circle? Someplace where he felt safe? Would he go back to the vamp graveyard, a place where he'd worked for a long time and never been discovered? Vamp-fast, I raced back to Bitsa and fired up my bike. With a screech of wheels, I tore from the park and toward the river, the traffic lazy and slow this time of night.

I called Bruiser's cell on the way, alerting him that I'd be setting off alarms. He didn't volunteer to meet me there, didn't comment that I was alive. He sounded distracted. He promised to turn off the system and hung up. No British gallantry or etiquette in him tonight.

I reached the vamp cemetery and wove Bitsa off the old road and around the gateposts, cutting the engine when I was inside. Exhaust fumes rose around me, poisonous and rank. The silence of the dead filled the night. I unhelmeted and set the kickstand. Pulled the Benelli from its harness rig and checked the load. Again. I clipped a flex strap to it and slung it to my back, easier to pull from than the riding rig.

I set four silver crosses on chains against my chest as a twofer: they'd glow if a vamp was nearby, and they'd poison any vamp who touched them—well, except for Leo, if he was to be believed. I pulled two stakes, careful to make certain that they were both silver tipped, and held them in my right hand, one pointed out, one pointed in. My largest vamp-killer in my left hand, its eighteen-inch blade bright in the night, I stalked into the graveyard.

My night vision was better than most humans', I figured because of all the years I'd spent in Beast form, so I didn't need a flashlight. The white marble walls of the crypts were shining pristine beneath the nearly full moon. The white shell pathways glowed against the black ground. Dull reddish light flickered in the stained glass windows of the chapel, a single candle indicating that someone was present. Sabina Delgado y Aguilera, the priestess of the vamps, was home. I wondered if she was taking callers.

I checked the crypts, satisfied that they hadn't taken damage. Then I walked around the graveyard, taking in the night through nose, mouth, eyes, ears. As I walked, the skin on the back of my neck rose. A feeling of tiny claws skittered up my back. I had a feeling that I'd missed something when I was here last.

I wasn't prescient. But I was getting a bad feeling.

CHAPTER 16

They killed me already

I checked the old sites for new activity of a rising-rogue sort. There was nothing new at any of them, but at the third one, my feet touching the displaced circle of shells, I smelled something bad. The smell of death, rank and sweet and foul.

I moved upwind into the trees, away from the graveyard. Drawing on Beast's instinct, night vision, and svelte, lissome grace, I moved between the thickly growing trees, silent, not a leaf cracking beneath my boots. Sweat trickled beneath my leathers. I carried the vamp-killer in my left hand, the Benelli in my right, the butt stock collapsed so I could hold it one handed.

As I walked, the sickly sweet smell of death grew, and beneath it, an even older scent—blood left to rot, the sacrifice for whatever dark magic had been done here. Floating along under the blood and death scent was the ozonelike taint of witch magic. Magic only recently spent. Magic still fresh and potent, smelling of piney woods and mushrooms, roses and fresh-turned earth, with a hint of brine, the scent of an earth witch with strong abilities and affinities for growing things and with the soil itself. Or maybe two earth witches, working in tandem. And under it all was the scent of dark rites. Fear, blood, and sacrifice. My hands clenched on the weapons and I relaxed them only by an effort of will, focusing my attention back on the scent signatures

and what they might mean. I didn't like this. Not at all. The
musk of my own fear-sweat joined the heat-sweat trickling
down my sides. I unfolded the stock and held the Benelli at
ready, able to fire one-handed if needed for a close-range
shot, or quickly brace it with my left arm for a more distant
one.

I didn't smell the fresh odor of anyone, maybe not since
Ada. So the magic had been set on a timer or a trigger,
warded for scent so no one could find it, and was only recently initiated. Since I hadn't smelled the site or the magics
when I was here last, it had likely been under a stasis spell,
but that didn't mean that there wasn't someone coming
soon. Or someone approaching from downwind of me. The
back of my neck itched, an uneasy worry. I remembered
the smell of angry vamp at the city park rising site. He had
come back to see what rose, to inspect his scion.

Holding Beast close to the surface, I moved through the
trees with catlike grace, slowly lifting and placing each foot.
As I moved, I felt for my direction and decided I was heading vaguely north. Beast was better at knowing her bearings than I, but worse at translating and communicating
her directional sense. I was sweating heavily, the new leathers' mesh pockets not a big help without a bike-generated
breeze.

A tingle of broken magic brushed across my skin.
I stopped. I had found a new ten-foot-wide circle in the
trees, the shells still covered by debris from the hurricane.
I sniffed, parsing the various scents, analyzing. Something
was different here. Vamps rose on the third day after they
were turned and died their first death. But from the smell,
this one had been in the ground a lot longer. Long before
Ada. Something said this was important.

Both instinct and experience told me that the many kidnappings of the witch children were about these vamp risings. With the thought, fear started to rise but I crushed it.
I couldn't give in to emotion until the children were safe. I
would not. I forced my mind back to the puzzle.

Why would witches and vamps work together to steal
witch children? Why graves with crosses? And why leave
a newly turned vamp longer in the ground? It was sense-
less. It had something to do with the curse and the curing

process—but what? Stopping, I leaned against a tree, my vertebrae pressing through leather into the rough bark. I listened, sending out my senses to taste, scent, hear, feel everything on the night breeze. Traces of magic floated along the skin of my hands and face, appearing tattered, smelling scorched. In Beast-vision, the traces looked much like the broken wards on Molly's house.

Ahead, something groaned softly and breathed through thick tissue, the sound making me think of a congealed mass. I tossed the vamp-killer lightly up and down in my hand, making sure of a firm, sweat-free grip. Ever more slowly, I moved deeper into the woods, staying downwind. The four crosses on my chest began glowing palely, alerting me to the presence of a vamp.

Something coughed. The sound was human, or almost, long and retching. A glob of something gooey was spat and my stomach wanted to turn. Beast's hackles rose, the skin and fine hairs along my neck and shoulders reacting to her instincts, in a rippling of raised flesh. She pushed my nausea down and away, looking through my eyes.

I slid through the trees, silent as a predator stalking prey. I saw movement as something paler than the trees lifted. It resolved into an arm, rising to wipe a face. A male, black, wearing a once-white shirt and dark pants, stood in a little clearing just ahead. His feet were bare. Moving drunkenly, he sat on a downed tree, coughing and spitting. I was about thirty feet away, close enough to study him with my better-than-human night vision. The pants resolved into jeans, and the shirt into a long-sleeved dress shirt, sleeves rolled up and a T-shirt underneath. He was about twenty, with tats up the side of his neck and along his arms in full sleeves. The neck tat caught the moonlight, revealing a black widow, red-dotted abdomen the size of a silver dollar beneath his ear, and its legs wrapped around his neck as if it held on while pumping venom into him. I was pretty sure it was a gang tat.

He smelled of old death and decayed blood and fear. The reek of the grave. Grave dirt and a degenerated slime clung to him. I must have made a noise, because his head came up, inhumanly fast. Far faster than a new vamp should have been able to move. He vamped out, fangs like small needles snapping down and eyes going blacker than the underside of hell. Without a visible tell, he attacked. My crosses blazed with light. A delayed fear response hurtled into my throat.

I raised my left arm to block him and fired one-handed, a three burst, the barrel lifting with each shot. He dodged around the first two blasts, so fast I could see his motion in overlays of images, white shirt shifting back and forth. The blaze of firing burned out my night vision, the last shot pointing to the sky, going wild.

He took me down. Crashing into the brush. I grunted as his weight landed on me. Fear slammed through me. His hands on my wrists shoved my arms apart and down. Trapping me. His fangs tore at my throat. Hitting the silver rings on the leather. Ripping through to the silver chain-mail collar beneath. He screamed with pain. Pulled back. And met my eyes. Spat. He drove for my face with his left claws.

One hand free, I jerked away. His claws landed where my head had been. It was not the uncontrolled action of a young rogue vamp.

It was the action of a trained warrior.

I punched with the vamp-killer into his unprotected side. But he was no longer there. He was on the far side of the shell circle. Vamped out. Holding his stomach. "Hungry," he said. "Please."

I rolled upright, taking up my weapons with me. Dropped the Benelli on its strap and slung it back, out of the way. I pulled two stakes, silver tipped and wicked sharp, and started across the clearing. Beast-fast. Before I realized that he had spoken. I halted so quickly I nearly tripped. This was a newly risen vamp—I knew it by the size of his tiny, needlelike canines, by the sight of the disturbed grave in the center of the pentagram. I *knew* it. No newly risen vamp was capable of coherent speech. They were rabid, feral killing machines, gaining the memory of speech over time. They had one need, one function—to eat. And through meeting that need, they killed. But this guy talked. He had said *please*. And he wasn't attacking. The silver crosses weren't hurting his eyes. He was . . . watching me.

I could hear my breathing, strident in the awful silence. Dread crawled along my skin like slimy snakes in the darkness. I brought my breath under control, but when I spoke, my words were breathy and puny sounding. "You understand me?"

After a moment, he nodded. One quick downward jerk of his chin. He understood.

And then, suddenly, as if it had been there all along, waiting, I understood. The timing of the disappearance of witch children had never corresponded to the appearance of young rogues. Because these young ones were in the ground a lot longer than the expected three days. They were bound into the ground with a spell, like a stasis spell, to keep them there . . . in the hope that longer in the ground meant greater sanity. The vamps I was hunting had managed to raise a vamp that was sane right away. With no need for curing, no insanity. No curse. No devoveo.

All the other young-rogue risings had been failed experiments. But this time it had finally worked.

But why the crosses in the trees? Maybe the spell that kept the vamps in the ground longer was also intended to make them immune to the power of the cross. Vamps who didn't suffer from the curse, and didn't suffer from the cross. "Crap," I whispered as the implications flashed through my mind. The experimenter had wanted to make sure his creations weren't flawed.

The value of a spell to raise sane young was enough to start a war over. Rousseau, St. Martin, and Mearkanis—were all three involved? No. Just Rousseau. No other clan scent was on this.

"Hungry," he said again, the word whispered and rough.

"I know you're hungry." His throat worked with need at my words. I held up the vamp-killer, letting the moonlight through the trees catch on the silver. "But if you can wait, if you can hold off, I'll get someone here to help. Understand?"

He nodded again and closed his eyes. "Hurry. Don't know how long . . ."

My mind raced. The first young vamp I'd taken down in this city had been restored to his sanity enough to make it into a club, into the ladies' room, and attack a woman. He'd made a mate for himself. He'd claimed territory. Not normal. Not for a new rogue. They got their name from their lack of sanity. Why hadn't I thought of that until now? Because I was settled into the rut of my own expectations.

I sheathed the stakes and pulled my cell, praying for bars. There were three, and though I really didn't want to call any of Leo's people, not after the big boss tried to eat me for dinner, I didn't have a choice. I speed-dialed Bruiser. When he answered, I said, "I have a newly risen vamp in control of his faculties, behind the chapel at the vamp cemetery. He says he can wait for a blood meal if you hurry."

"Talking? Not possible," Bruiser said.

"Fine. I'll stake him and we can argue over it later." The vamp across the clearing tensed and blinked slowly. I shrugged to show I wasn't serious.

Bruiser cursed once, succinctly. "Leo is . . . not available. I'll bring one of his scions. Try to keep him alive." The connection ended and I folded the phone back into its pocket.

"You got a name?" I asked the newly risen guy.

He seemed to think, and as he did, the sclera of his eyes bled back white, as if the act of answering a question brought him back to his humanity. "LeShawn LeShawn . . . B . . . Brandt."

They didn't remember their names. Not for five years or more. "LeShawn, you think you can make it through the trees about two hundred yards?"

"I . . . try," he said. His fangs retracted and his human teeth were chattering in the heat as if he was cold. Which I imagined he was. They were always cold when they hadn't fed.

I controlled my fear and my breathing, making sure my reactions didn't push him over the edge. When I was calm, I pointed with the stakes again. "That way. You go in front."

He moved slowly, his feet shuffling in the underbrush. He shouldn't even be able to walk yet, or at least not without that zombielike lack of coordination. It took the newly risen a lot longer than this. A *lot* longer. Yet the girl who had risen in the park had been a typical young-rogue vamp and she had been under this same spell. Why not this guy?

Because of Ada and all the ambient energy she had brought ashore. The lightning had disrupted the stasis spell.

Near me, LeShawn paused and raised his head, that weirdly snakelike move they all had, and sniffed. "You smell good. Like meat and . . . sex."

"Move along or you'll smell like dead meat."

He laughed. *Crap.* He *laughed.* That totally human laughter that took most of them a decade to relearn. He looked back at me, the grin still on his face. His eyes were human, brown irises with night-wide pupils. On my chest, the crosses decreased their glow. His eyes lit on my neck just below my jaw, the sliver of unprotected skin, and he breathed deeply, closing his eyes. "You smell so . . . good."

My crosses brightened, a weird fluctuation I'd never seen before. "LeShawn. Snap out of it or I'll stake you and you'll be true-dead. *LeShawn.*"

His eyes opened and he was partly vamped out. "They killed . . . me . . . already."

"Who killed you, LeShawn?"

He shook his head and gripped his middle, whispering, "It was dark. Hungry, hungry, hungry." But he turned and went where I pointed, back south, his bare feet noisy in the underbrush. I kept fifteen feet or so between us, and my shotgun up. I hoped it was enough space for me to react if he vamped out and came at me again.

This vamp was the key to understanding the kidnappings. To finding Angelina and Little Evan. This vamp could talk. Hope soared through me, but I wrestled it down alongside the fear.

It looked as though we'd make it. I could see the chapel through the trees, glowing whitely in the rising moon. LeShawn slowed, his back to me. He put out a hand to steady himself as he stepped between two trees. His claws were out, sharpened and two inches long. They pressed into the dry white wood of a dead tree with small snaps as he tightened his grip. With his other hand, he gripped his middle. Stopped. My crosses began to glow again, making me blink against the brightness.

He was breathing hard, the reek of dead tissues stinking on the night air. I kept my voice steady, not reacting to the fight-or-flight impulse flooding my system. "LeShawn? Keep it together, man. Keep moving."

He turned, allowing me a half-profile view of his face,

and dropped his head. "Can't. Can't do it . . ." His hand on the tree made a fist. Cutting his palm. I smelled vamp blood, like dried sage on the air, sharper than the stink of death. He held out his hand, seeing the thin blood there. He put his palm to his mouth. And sank his teeth in. Sucked.

"LeShawn?" I took a single step closer.

"Hu . . ." He quivered. Fell back against the tree, facing me, pressing his jaw into his palm. Sucked hard at his own torn flesh. He sobbed with frustration. "So . . . so hungry. Hu . . . huuu . . ." In a flash he leaped at me, eyes insane with bloodlust. Vampy rogue insane. Time did that little shift and he seemed to slow, hanging in midair. Snarling. I raised the stake, gauging his arc. And he came down. At me. Onto the tip of the stake.

I watched it puncture his shirts. And knew my mistake even as I felt the silver tip slide between ribs. He crashed onto me, his claws closing reflexively on my upper arms. Time juddered and resumed its slow pace.

"No!" I hit the ground with the force of his leap, LeShawn above me. Shock on his face. Too late, I jerked at the stake, pulling it back. His eyes bled back to human. We bounced. I used the bounce to twist from beneath him. Yanking the stake. It caught on a rib and held. We were no longer at the proper angle for it to slide free. Time slowed again, flashes of reality painted across the dark of the night.

Twisting, the stake hung on the back of his sternum, trapped between ribs and the hard plate of bone in the center of his chest. His claws brushed across the metal of my jacket sleeves. Tiny clinks. The motion threw him farther to the side. Down. Hard. The landing shoved the stake into his heart with a little give. A small reduction of pressure as it entered the heart chamber. And all the way through, rubbery on the other side.

The sharpened silver tip cut through his shirt at the back. Stinging vamp blood splattered up in a thin fountain. Small droplets splashed my face. The vamp sighed. Died. Shock stabbed through me. "No. *No!*"

On my hands and knees, vamp blood burning my face, I cursed long and hard, spitting my words at the earth. Frustrated tears leaked from my eyes as I swore. I levered my body up, sitting beside LeShawn on the bed of pine needles, one hand on his body, my legs splayed. The endorphins of victory shot through my bloodstream, clashing with the knowledge that I had lost my best link to the witch kidnappings and the maker of the young rogues. For an instant my emotions whirled, more dizzying than liquor, hotter than sex. I had survived. I had lost. "Oh . . . no," I whispered. I gagged with shock, the taste acidic and burning.

I took a breath that smelled and tasted of vamp blood, heavy and rank in the air. The elation dipped and died, crushed beneath the despair. "LeShawn. Crap." Tears pooled in my eyes, making him waver in the dark.

I had to cut off his head. I knew that. It was the only way to give him true-death. If his maker were here, or if I had used the ash stakes, without silver to poison his blood, he might have been brought back. Maybe. And maybe not. I wasn't sure. I hadn't known what I'd been dealing with until too late. Until after I had staked him.

Sitting on the bed of pine needles and leaves, I pulled my cell and hit REDIAL. When Bruiser answered, I could hear the sound of a car in the background, a faint, steady hum. "Never mind. He couldn't hold it together."

"True-dead?"

"Not yet. But I hit him with a silver-tipped stake. Through and through his heart."

Bruiser put it together aloud. "If we try to bring him back, it'll spread the poison through him before he can heal. That's even assuming we could find his master to give him a meal. Bethany is not well tonight. Leo could do it. But he's . . . not himself yet."

I bet he wasn't. I sighed, the sound whistling shrilly in the phone, and spoke mostly to myself. "I'll put the silver stakes away for the rest of this hunt. Not that it does me much good now." I cursed again, but my words held no heat.

"Hold off bringing him true-death until after the priestess has a chance to check him out. If he was sane enough to talk, immediately after his first rising, she may be able to tell why."

I knew that the priestess had once spent the night in the chapel just ahead, but I didn't know for absolute certainty she was there tonight. I hadn't peeked in the windows. And

Bruiser didn't know that I knew about her lair, if that was what the chapel was.

And now the lying and half-truths start. But I'd tell any lie I knew to get the children back. "How am I going to get to her?" I temporized. "I'm on my bike. I can't be carting a body across town." All truths. Truth hiding the lie beneath it.

"I'll contact her. Take the body to the chapel porch. Wait for her there."

Yeah. Right. "Okay." I managed to keep the ironic tone out of my voice. Then hope sizzled up in me. "Will Sabina feed him back—"

"No," Bruiser interrupted. "Sabina won't revive a young rogue. Don't ask. She's out-clan."

I closed the phone without a good-bye, tucked it away, drove the bloody stake into the ground, cleaning it. I'd wash it later, otherwise the acidic vamp blood would corrode the silver. My face stung where his blood had splattered me, and I used my saliva to clean it off. When I had my breath back, I tucked my crosses out of sight and stood. Secured my weapons.

With a grunt, I hefted the body up, over my shoulder. Already it stank of new death on top of the other scents: old death, vamp blood, and the grave. He had to be permanently dispatched. Otherwise there was a slim chance he'd rise at the full moon, a rogue of a different sort; a lot more deadly than the newly risen. There had been a few accounts over the years.

Placing my booted feet with care, I carried him out of the woods and into the moonlight. He was heavy, and I was tired. Beast's offer of strength didn't extend to non-emergency situations and it certainly didn't extend to carrying a vamp out of the woods. I stumbled twice and nearly dropped LeShawn once.

Ahead, I could see the chapel, candles lit in the blood-tinted stained glass windows, the light throwing bloody shadows onto the shell walkways and the grass all around. I was approaching from the back left, and as I rounded the building, I saw Sabina Delgado y Aguilera, the priestess of the vamps, on the front porch. Just as I had expected, she had been in the chapel. And maybe not all was lost. Maybe the priestess had info she didn't know she had, which might lead me to the rogue-makers. If I asked the right questions, she might say something that would help. If I was quick with the right words. If I said all the right things and kept all the other things silent. *Might, maybe, if.* I was running out of time. I took a steadying breath. People skills weren't my strongest talent.

Once again Sabina was wearing a white skirt and an outfit that looked like a nun's habit but made of heavy white cloth. The wimple hid her hair and framed her face with white, catching the moonlight and forming pools of darker shadows. Her hands were folded into her sleeves like a mother superior's and her face was set in an austere expression, ascetic and grave. Ha-ha. Vamp humor.

I was huffing for breath as I walked toward her, making sure my boots crunched on the grass and the shells of the walkway. Making sure she heard me coming. She didn't turn to me, giving no indication that she heard me at all. She was immobile, still as the marble statues atop the crypts in the graveyard. A statue dressed in white cloth.

When I was twenty feet away I stopped, steadying the body. LeShawn's hands bumped my back and buttock. I had no idea what to call her. It didn't feel polite to call her Sabina. I said, "Bruiser—George Dumas—said he'd call the priestess."

She didn't turn to me and the angle made it hard to see her lips move as she said, "He did. You are Jane Yellowrock, the creature who is helping my people."

Creature. Okaaay. That brought me down a bit. Helped me to focus. The children. And little Bliss. That was all that mattered. "This vamp just rose, his first rising, a couple hundred yards into the woods. He knew his name, was talking and coherent, walking with balance, able to take direction. Able to hold off bloodlust for a while. We were walking here to meet George and one of Leo's scions and bloodservants to get his first blood meal. But he lost control, attacked me, and I had to stake him. I mistakenly used silver and pierced his heart."

Slowly, she turned her head to me. Her shoulders stayed perfectly still, her head moving on the stem of her neck. The motion was almost robotic. Not human. I was glad I'd

stopped so far away. Her mouth opened in her expressionless face, and she spoke with the certainty of experience,
history, and Truth. A pronouncement. "A young vampire
has no control. No speech. No memory. A young vampire
is a ravening beast."

Beast was silent at the insult. "That's what I thought, until now," I managed, LeShawn's weight pressing me into the
ground. "I think it has something to do with his rising in a
charmed witch circle and pentagram, crosses nailed to the
trees at head height, and the smell of decayed blood in the
ground. Blood magic.

"No," she whispered, the note fading in the night.

I needed her to believe me. "It's true," I said. "It's happened before, hasn't it? I've heard the Sons of Darkness
rose without devoveo. Someone has been able to replicate
that." As I was speaking, it occurred to me that maybe I was
stupid to mention the Sons again, after Leo's reaction, but
I'd thought he was just being nutso. Apparently not.

At the words "Sons of Darkness," she started, and her
eyes went half-vampy. Beast roared to the surface, and I
tensed as Sabina stared at me, her gaze the most predatory
I'd ever seen from her. But then the priestess seemed to
win some internal battle, and her eyes eased to near human. Beast snarled and settled back.

"Listen, lady, this guy's heavy," I said. "And his body fluids are dripping all over me. Mind if I put him down before
we continue this conversation?" So much for my people
skills. I am so stupid.

But the priestess didn't look as though her nose was
out of joint at my tone. She pointed at her feet. I adjusted
LeShawn's weight with a little shoulder twitch and knee
bounce and crossed to the porch. I eased him down, but his
head clunked on the cement floor anyway. Good thing he
was already dead or he'd wake up with a headache. I took a
deep breath and blew out the strain. LeShawn hadn't been
a linebacker, but he'd been a meaty, muscular guy.

The priestess was suddenly gone. Just not there, the
porch empty, leaving only a localized breeze where she had
been. I blinked in surprise, looked around to make sure
she hadn't come toward me; I had started to call out when
she returned just as fast, appearing on the porch holding

a short stubby candle in a little glass bowl, a white plastic box, and a chair. I managed not to flinch or make any move that might be construed as prey movements. Sabina didn't smell of fresh blood, and I had no idea how long since she had really fed, deeply enough to be satisfied. I had no desire to be her next meal.

Moving at more human speeds, she placed the chair near LeShawn and held out the candle and the box to me. I took them both and hitched a hip onto the porch, catching my breath and placing the candle so its light shone near the dead vamp's face. The box had a baby on the top and turned out to be baby wipes, which seemed seriously weird, but I was out of my league and I had no real idea of what was normal or not. I cleaned the blood and the grave-goo away as Sabina studied the new corpse.

Several silent minutes later, she leaned down and began to cut through LeShawn's shirt with a tiny pair of scissors no longer than her fingers. "Let me," I said as I gripped the edges of the cut shirt and tore it from neck to hem. A final snap ripped it through. When I was done, I realized the vamp could have snapped me in two as easily as I had the shirt. Despite what she looked like, she wasn't an old lady. She was an ancient vamp, which meant powerful. I could stop doing old-lady favors for her.

The tats on the guy's chest were both prison tats and the kind of fancy work only a master artist can create. The black widow on his neck perched at the top of a web spanning his entire torso and both shoulders, and the other tats were caught up in the web. There were crosses and hearts and inked initials, the word "MOM" with a red rose, a tombstone with the name Mary on it, an eagle, and a pit bull. And there were scars, one from a knife wound and two from bullets; the scars had been included in the artwork. It was a tapestry of his life, of the good moments that had made him who he was, and the bad times that had shaped him with pain. There were also arcane symbols and initials—the gang tats that claimed him forever.

Sabina sighed. "I believe you."

I looked up in surprise. "Why?"

"Those tattooed with crosses do not survive to rise. The crosses should have burned through him to the bone when he awoke." She sat back in her chair, which creaked softly in the night. "Where is this place of magic?"

I pointed in the general direction. "And there are three other sites, older and overgrown, in the woods nearby."

Her lips thinned and turned down, making wrinkles in her pale face. "How could this be? I am here. I would have known. I *should* have known."

"Not if humans prepared the ground by day and witches set it under something like a stasis spell combined with a protective ward. Not if the vamp waited until nearly sunrise to do his work," I said, thinking of the vamps that took the children, moving at dusk, sunlight still bright on the western clouds. Had witch magic given them protection from the late-day sun? Or were they practicing other magics on themselves? Yeah. That.

They're not just trying to defeat devoveo. They're trying to make an übervamp. A vamp with all the strengths and none of the weakness of regular vampires. My breath caught.

Sabina seemed to come back from a faraway place, and when she spoke it took her a moment to find the words. Or perhaps the language. How many languages and dialects did a person learn while living two thousand years? "Witch charms hid where this child rose? Powerful witch charms?"

"I'd say so, though I haven't had a witch out here to scan the place yet. Do you recognize the scent of the makers?" My heart tripped again with hope.

Sabina leaned down again and drew the air in over her mouth and through her nose, much as Beast scented. She went still, the breath dead in her lungs. "The smell is familiar," she breathed out, scenting again. "No." She sat down with a sudden thump, her white skirts on the porch floor. Sitting there, she shook her head, a weirdly human gesture, her expression dumbfounded. "Surely not . . ."

I realized that Sabina, priestess of the vamps, knew exactly what was going on. She had seen the kind of vamp burial before. When she didn't go on, I prompted, "Not what?"

"It is not possible. The maker I scent is long ago true-dead. I killed him myself." Her face cleared of the nearly human emotion. She smelled again, her nostrils fluttering.

"His heir. He made himself an heir before he died. Yes."
She sniffed again. "Yessss. His heir is now the leader, but he
does not work alone. His acolytes assist him."

My hope died. I kept the reaction off my face by an effort
of will, clenching my teeth together against the setback. If
Sabina didn't know the makers, I was back to square one.

"The makers are of the Rousseau line and are young,
only a few centuries old." She stood again, moving human slow, studying me. "I cannot help you, creature who
hunts."

I figured I was the creature who hunts, and my blood
spiked, sharp and fast, through my veins. But I shoved my
need to know of my kind deep. Not until the kits were safe.
I turned back to the body of the dead vamp.

"I did not believe that any of us could bear the power
of a cross without burning." It was said with that tone she
used when making pronouncements of ultimate Truth, like
a law of nature and physics, like: None of us can fly, none
of us can breathe underwater, and none of us can survive
without blood. But it wasn't true.

"*You* did," I said softly. "The night the"—I wanted to say
liver-eater, but changed it in time—"old rogue attacked.
You drove him off with a cross. A wooden cross. And it
blazed like pure silver."

Sabina Delgado y Aguilera's eyes raged into black pits.
Her fangs snapped down, three-inch-long spikes. She was
on me before the crosses hidden in my collar had time to
glare with light. Before I could blink. Before I could draw
breath. Her motion was so fast that I didn't have time to
reach for a weapon. Her hand slammed me against the wall
of the chapel so hard I heard the stucco crack. Icy fingers
tightened around my throat. Her breath moved against my
jaw, cold and smelling of old blood and dry herbs.

CHAPTER 17

Our sin has multiplied

Sabina was shorter than I, yet my feet dangled off the ground, my body against the chapel. Her fingers were like steel, cutting into my throat, twisting the steel chain links of the collar into my flesh, yet only the collar allowing me any breath at all. I was pinned, my neck stretched out. I couldn't reach any weapon that might be effective against her.

I forced my panic down, but there was nothing I could do about my racing heart or the fear-sweat that beaded on my skin. And the children had only me to help them right now. I forced my hands to fall to my sides. Held myself tightly against another brainless move.

She spoke, and I had no idea what she murmured, but it sounded like Latin, like a ... liturgy. And this was the priestess of the vamps. I had said that they had a religion. Maybe I was more right than I had guessed.

When she paused to draw breath, I tried to speak. "Please." My voice was whispery from my arched position and from terror building beneath my breastbone. I forced out the words. "I seek. Absolution." With the word, a faint tremor ran through Sabina. She eased her grip on my throat. My breath whistled in my newly healed tissues. Relief flooded through me.

I had been to water, had been prepared for battle. Purified. I drew on that calling. I could feel again the sluggish current flowing over me as I dropped below the surface.

The warmth of the air when I stood, my feet in the muck of the bayou bottom. The blackness when I again went under. Strange peace flowed through me, tranquility lapping at the far corners of my mind like the black bayou, dark and slow. The emotion felt as if it had been hiding, holding itself silent and still until now when I might recognize it, use it. And I understood. This fight for the kits was the reason I went to water. This was the battle Aggie One Feather had foreseen.

Serenity flowed along my skin and settled into the distant crannies of my mind and heart, sifted through my nerves and soothed my flesh. I closed my eyes. I repeated my calling. "I seek wisdom and strength in battle, and purity of heart and mind and soul."

The serenity that flowed through me seemed to move through my skin, bleeding into hers. She took a slow breath.

Her fangs clicked back in her mouth, her body trembling, her eyes bled back to human. She set me on my feet and stepped away. Blood pounded into my head. The world reeled around me and I caught myself on the edge of the porch, fingers digging into the underlip. Somehow we were on the ground beside the chapel, the dead vamp's legs near my hand. I carefully moved away as if he might stand up suddenly and attack.

"Show me the site where this rogue rose on my land." It was said in the command tones the very old ones use. Duress. Coercion. Vamp magic. It rippled over me like dry sand scattered in a smooth arc, burning and sharp. I *wanted* to go into the woods. *Wanted* to go back to the burial site marked with white shells. I turned and faced the woods, my booted feet on the crisp grass.

Beast touched the compulsion with a paw and batted its control away. I could almost *see* it unravel from me, like the fringes of a shawl pulled free from the weave. *Crap*. Sabina was strong. I took a breath, keeping it slow and steady. I didn't want her to know I was unbound from her power, not if I could help it. I still had too much to learn.

I smoothed my hands over my thighs and kept myself from drawing a weapon. She was so fast I'd not get it halfway out before I was dead. I swallowed and it hurt, reminding me of her strength. "Sure. This way." Legs shaky, palms sweating, I led the way back into the woods. I didn't hear her footsteps follow, but the starched cloth of her habit made little chuffing sounds, cloth-on-cloth. The skin on my throat rose into fresh prickles at the thought of her behind me.

Still in command mode, she said, "Tell me what you know of the cross of the curse. And how you know it."

The compulsion rippled over me, black motes of power, tinged with purple, ringing my chest, making it hard to breathe. *Cross of the curse? The one she used to chase off the liver-eater . . . ? Yeah.* But lying wasn't my strong suit and lying so close to compulsion was probably impossible. I'd have to lie with the truth. Was that any less a lie? Something else to worry about later. After the children were safe.

"A little bird told me that you used a cross to chase off the creature who was attacking you. She said that it's a . . . powerful weapon."

She was suddenly at my side, visible in my peripheral vision. "Who is this little bird," Sabina purred, "who speaks of the Blood Cross?"

I took a chance. "An owl."

There was silence between us until we neared the ring of white shells. I would have known we were close even without the direction sense and the sense of smell that was stronger and finer than any human's, known by the glowing of the crosses nailed to the trees. They reacted to Sabina's presence from forty feet away, glowing brighter until Sabina had to stop, shielding her eyes from the brilliance.

Her voice breathy with pain, she said, "I smell the sire; most certainly Rousseau." Her eyes covered, she backed away several steps. "This place reeks of the past, of evil once battled and conquered. It stinks of witch magic, burned and strong. I smell the blood of sacrifice. Of witch blood that was spilled here. The blood of our sin.

"I have failed," she moaned, "and now our sin has multiplied." Her voice rose to a wail. "Our sin has multiplied."

She presented me with her back, bent and hunched in pain. When her wail and its echo had dissipated, a silence settled on the woods. Sharp and acute, as if the forest itself listened for more. Long moments later she whispered, "I will give you answers at the chapel. Return there." In a heartbeat, with a rustling through the trees and a frail movement of wind, Sabina was gone. The crosses brightened for an instant and dimmed.

I now knew without doubt what was happening in the circles. A Rousseau was killing witch children, their blood and fear powering a working of dark magic to increase the number of days a vamp spent in the grave, in order to raise a vampire who was sane. It was the only thing that made sense.

My heart filled with rising desperation as I tramped back through the woods to the chapel.

I stopped at the edge of the vamp cemetery, surprised. I hadn't really expected Sabina to be waiting, but she sat in the chair, moonlight bright on the white of her clothes, her face in shadow. I moved slowly to her and saw that Le-Shawn had been moved in my absence. And beheaded. His body had been rolled to the bottom of the stairs at the front of the building. His head sat to the side on the stump of his neck, positioned to stare at Sabina. Which was disturbing on so many levels.

Again, I deliberately made noise when I approached from the side and rear and eased my butt onto the porch, one booted foot on the ground, sweating in my leathers. Neither of us spoke for a long time as the night air moved sluggishly across the cemetery. Night birds called. A bat fluttered close by and away. Sabina sat statue-still, breathless, pulseless, dead. When she took a breath for speech, it startled me and I jumped, but Sabina was staring at Le-Shawn's eyes, his appearing focused, as if he watched us—a trick of the moonlight.

"You talked of the Sons of Darkness. They are not oft spoken of by my kind. Their shame is all our shame."

I didn't reply and Sabina took another of the weird-sounding breaths. "There is a scrap of parchment remaining, from the first history of our kind and the first prophecy of our savior. The original parchment is oft copied, oft translated. As priestess, I retain a scrap of the original scroll as well as an early copy. It tells of the Sons of Darkness and their great sin. It tells of how they made us. The Sons shared with us their blood curse, creating a race of beings with many gifts, yet bearing great agony, great pain, the sin of the world in our blood." She paused, and I heard a barred owl call from far away, hooting in the species' four- and five-beat melody. It always sounded like "*Who cooks for you? Who cooks for you all?*" It was answered from even farther away, the notes plaintive. Owls liked it here. The silence between us had stretched and I didn't think Sabina was going to continue. When she spoke again I jumped.

"And though they sinned the darkest sin, the Sons prophesied the salvation of our kind." She cocked her head, still watching LeShawn. The blood had leaked onto the white shells and into the ground. "If it is discovered that you are the savior, the one who will bring us to peace, then I will tell you all. Only the savior of the Mithrans may yet hear the entirety of the old tale." Her eyes were suddenly on me, their weight like a lead-lined blanket, heavy and immobilizing. I was careful not to meet her gaze. She studied me. "But I think you are no savior of my kind. My wait is not yet concluded. I may not yet seek my ending." She blew out a breath that smelled of old blood. Very old. Again, I wondered when she last ate.

Sabina licked her lips and I felt as if an electric shock passed through me. I tended to forget that she had once been human, and might still be capable of human gestures. Sabina held her eyes on me. "I scented three Mithrans at the place of rising, all familiar to me but from long ago. I thought it impossible for a vampire with a lair in this city to remain unknown to me. I thought it equally impossible for a small family or even a solitary vampire to survive in Pellissier's hunting territory; they would have been dispatched long ago. But the past has returned and brought its evils with it."

She seemed to expect a comment, but I couldn't think what I should say. When I didn't reply she looked away. "A witch child was killed at the place of first rising. The child was drained of his blood and his body taken away."

I couldn't help it. I flinched. Sabina went on unperturbed. "Such is against the Vampira Carta, against our ways and customs, punishable by true-death. Will you bring the culpable ones to the day?"

I nodded. "But you have to help me," I said. "Do you know anything that could help me find the vampire who is doing this?"

"Clan Rousseau once practiced blood magic, which required them to sacrifice with the blood of human and witch children. Some of these Rousseaus denied the guilt that all Mithrans must carry, and that older Mithrans must, by law, pass on to their scions. They claimed the way of the Naturaleza—believing that they had the *right*, as predators, to hunt and kill humans. And they claimed that the sin of the fathers was not passed to the sons." She shook her head. "Their sin was discovered and these Rousseaus were wiped away in a great purge."

Excitement shot through me. I had heard of the purge. And this bit of history was tying all my information together.

"A strange form of insanity has always run in the Rousseau bloodline. Not something of which we oft speak. But it is there, nonetheless." Sabina looked back at LeShawn. I nearly trembled at the release from her gaze. His eyes were glazing over in death, milky and no longer appearing to watch the priestess. His features seemed to sag, and Sabina's mouth turned down at the corners, seeing it. She looked old, her skin like creased silk. I breathed out my relief slowly, and wondered if she could smell the pheromones of respite in my breath, in my sweat.

"Many of their line never find sanity after they are turned. Several decades pass and they still rave. Many such must be put down by the clan master." Her words took on the cadence of pronouncement and coercion, the vamp compulsion vibrating in her tones. "Look to the Rousseau Clan. Look to the long-chained. Look to the dark arts. Look to the island and the history of bloodshed. Look to any who survived the purge, who were forgiven their sin and survived the cleansing."

Beast held off the force of her compulsion with claws pricking my mind; I could think and remember her words, yet not get sucked under by her. I realized that the priestess was giving me clues in her command. Not very good clues, but better than I'd had so far. But she might also be telling me to do more than I planned.

"Sin must be judged," she continued. "Absolution, if given in error, must be rescinded. Retribution and justice must be meted out on the sinners and the guilty."

She hadn't said I had to bring them here. Had she? I was careful not to promise more than I could. And was equally cautious not to refuse. "The vampire council hired me to kill the rogue maker. When I find him, he'll be destroyed along with his scions. Their heads will be taken to the council as proof."

"'The workman is worthy of his hire.' You will be rewarded for bringing an end to this evil."

I was smart enough to note that Sabina hadn't exactly said I'd be paid. She said I'd be rewarded, which could mean anything, including my death to keep her secrets.

Sabina turned to me, a half smile on her face. "You will not find death at my hands or at my order."

All righty, then. The vamp was reading my mind or my body language. Either one meant that it was time for me to move on. "I'll say my good-bye, then." I slid off the porch and to the ground.

"You may leave the head of the newly risen. I will see to it that bounty payment is waiting for you at the council building." After a moment she smiled. "You may call upon me again." And she disappeared with that weird brush of old-blood-scented air. The door to the chapel snicked closed. And I hadn't even seen it open.

I swore softly, looking at the body and head. Sabina had pretty much told me to leave it alone. I wasn't about to disagree. No way. I crunched across the shells to my bike and helmeted up. I knew the young-rogue makers hadn't been at the Rousseau clan home. Yet Bettina had smelled of one of them at the vamp party.

I paused before kicking Bitsa on. Bettina knew. She had from the very beginning. She'd had to. She was their master. All I had to do was get Bettina, shackle her in silver, and make her tell me. I had the formal invitation to visit, and Leo had access to the security systems of all the clans. There was a good chance he'd know—and that meant Bruiser would know—where her lair was.

I looked at the sky. The sun was rising. First I'd see Molly. Then it was time for a chat with Bruiser. A long chat. About

purges and the Rousseau Clan. And the long-chained. And
security systems. I was close to finding the children and
Bliss. I knew it in my bones.

Molly was sitting up in bed brushing her long red hair. She
stared blindly out the window, her face slack and grieving,
tears trailing down her cheeks. I stood in the door, silent,
watching, and my heart clenched like a fist. Her babies
were missing and it was my fault.

"I'll get them back."

The words were brittle in the high-ceilinged room and
Molly started, the brush stopping halfway. She closed her
eyes and, with a visible effort, controlled her misery and
completed the brushstroke. When it reached the tips of
her hair, she set it aside and wiped her face. "I know you
will." She forced a smile on her mouth and held out an arm.
"Come here. I have things I need to say."

I forced my feet to cross the room and sat stiffly beside
her on the edge of the mattress. She curled an arm about
my waist and, with my own eyes prickling, I held myself
rigid against the comfort she offered. I didn't deserve it,
though Molly wasn't likely to accept any of my opinions.
She pulled me over to her, against her hip, and laid her
head on my shoulder. And she burst into tears.

My voice froze. So did my body. Inflexible as a day-old
corpse, I raised one hand and clumsily patted her shoulder.
And then Beast put a paw on my mind and took over. *Jane
is predator only. I am mother of kits. I am alpha.* The words
resonated in my mind; surprise radiated through me with
the echo. Beast took over my hand and stroked Molly's
hair. Took my other arm and encircled Molly, drawing her
closer.

I'm more than a predator—

*No. Jane is predator only. Not mother of kits. Not mate.
Jane is nothing except part of Beast. Killer only.*

The words stilled my thoughts. Pain spiraled through
me, cold and crystalline, like frozen, shattered quartz.

My mouth opened, and it was Beast's words on my
tongue, falling from my lips. Her tone was lower than mine,
raspy as a coarse sponge on stone. "We will take back kits.
We will kill predator who took them. Jane and Beast, to-

gether, will rend them. Bone from flesh, blood from veins. We will kill. Will retake kits. This I swear on my own kits."

Molly stopped breathing. Her heart beat hard twice and then smoothed to a fast cadence. Carefully, as if fearful of springing a trap, Mol pulled back and stared into my eyes. Her pupils widened. Her lips parted. I heard her heart rate speed, her breath hitch. "Son of a witch on a switch. Beast?"

I purred softly. Stroked her hair once. Then I stood and walked from the room.

It was dawn, and heavy heat was already starting. I'd never been in a place where the air had weight and pressure, like a pressure cooker forcing the air to bear down against my body. It had a sensation of urgency to it, the way that holding my breath underwater created the necessity to rise and breathe, as if each breath was possibly my last.

We were on the road out of town, wending through the traffic and the heat, before Beast let me go. My mind was still in shock mode, trying to see why Beast said I was only a predator. Only a killer. It wasn't true. It wasn't. But it was going to take a killer—and a pretty dedicated one—to bring Angelina and Little Evan back to Molly alive. And Bliss. Had to remember Bliss.

I bent over the bike and sped past a semi belching diesel fumes. The cars in front of me blurred together as I rode and thought. I took the streets by instinct and muscle memory, thoughts banging around inside my head like a heavy-metal drummer on meth.

I pulled up in front of the Rousseau clan home; its front door was hanging open in the early dawn. I pulled the Benelli even before I killed the motor. Drew my biggest vamp-killer. Moved up the walk and into the silent foyer, ready for anything. But it was a waste of effort. The clan home was empty and quiet. I prowled through deserted rooms, kicking open closets, checking under beds, in bathrooms, and in pantries. From the lingering smells, the place had been vacated during the night. And it hadn't been voluntary. Blood stained the walls and floors in several places. The air was still tainted with the heated smell of burned magic and the stench of the rogue maker and his two cronies. I was familiar enough with them now to parse the three different scent signatures, so similar that they had to be all of the same bloodline. The three siblings had attacked a vamp clan home. And won.

I returned to Bitsa and headed back out of the city. At the first gas station I came to, I pulled in and up to a pump. Ignoring the stares of the other patrons, I strapped my shotgun to the bike. Removed my leather jacket against the rising heat and stowed it in one of the sidesaddles. The mesh collar went beside it, the stakes and vamp-killers as well, leaving me still well-armed enough to fight a small war. Feeling more comfortable, though smelling of night-terror sweat, I filled Bitsa's small tank up with gas. While it gurgled into the nearly empty tank I pulled my cell and hit REDIAL, calling Bruiser. It rang through to voice mail. Fortunately, I knew where he lived. Remounting, I roared against the current of the rush-hour traffic out of the city. The farther I rode, the denser the traffic got, the madder I got. Leo and Bruiser were keeping things from me, things I needed to know to get the kids back. And Bliss. Couldn't forget her. By the time I reached the drive to the Pellissier clan home just before seven thirty a.m., I was royally ticked off.

The house was at the end of a well-paved but little-used road, no other houses within sight, plowed fields all around, horses walking from barns into the day, heads bobbing, mares with foals gamboling along. Curling-limbed live oaks arched over the long, slightly uphill drive, the house built on high ground, some twenty feet above sea level, higher than anything around it. The Pellissier clan home stood on a bend of the Mississippi River, which I could smell through the trees, the river air wet and sour and powerful even at a distance. The oaks to either side passed at speed as I roared up the drive.

It might not be smart to come here, even though this wasn't Leo's daytime lair, and likely none of the Pellissier scions used it as a lair except in emergency. But in the daylight, I didn't have to worry about vamps; I needed answers and this was the best place to get them.

I slowed as I neared the white-painted, two-story brick house. Bruiser and three others were sitting at a large, round, cloth-covered table on the front porch, eyes on me, Bruiser quickly hiding the relief he felt at seeing me. He had wondered if Sabina had killed me. Not enough to help me, of course.

I was clearly interrupting an important conversation, business talk over china and a meal. As if I cared. I came to a stop at the front steps and cut the engine, my booted feet on either side of Bitsa. I set the kickstand and dismounted, throwing a leather-clad leg high for impact.

I blinked against the bright sun, and suddenly realized that I hadn't slept—really slept, like more than a nap—in days. Something else I could deal with after I got the kits back, like my being a killer and nothing else. The smile that lit my face with the thoughts must have been pretty ugly, because one guy's hands disappeared beneath the table, going for a weapon.

I climbed the steps, my boots the only sound, loud in the morning air, my eyes holding Bruiser's. An answering smile curved his lips up on one side and his eyes slit in consideration, though he lounged back in his chair in casual unconcern. The anxiety of the three with Bruiser had a smell and it gave me a perverse pleasure to worry the little group. "I see you survived Leo's temper tantrum last night."

Bruiser nodded. "As did you."

"Barely. Can't say the same for the Rousseau clan home."

His expression hooded over. "Tyler, Louisa, Dale, we're finished for now. Give me an hour with Miss Yellowrock." Like well-trained dogs, they got up and left us alone. As if to break the tension, Bruiser leaned in and rang a little silver bell on the table. Seriously. He rang a bell. And a woman in a white and gray maid's uniform appeared from the side door.

"Tea for the lady," Bruiser said, without taking his eyes from me. "A nice, black, single estate." To me he said, "Have you breakfasted?"

I propped my hands on my hips, knowing my stance was hostile and aggressive. "Not today."

"Eggs, bacon, fruit, cereal?" he asked, the genial host, offering an informal list.

I was about to refuse, but my stomach rumbled in answer. And why not? I had to eat. I was drawing on Beast's power and that used a lot of energy. "Half dozen eggs over easy, a rasher of bacon cut thick and cooked crisp. Lots of toast, no butter," I said to her, playing as though I didn't see the general shock at the amount of food I'd requested. "And thank you." When I smiled at her, there was no half-way about it and the Latino girl smiled back, ducked her head, and returned though the side door. See? I can be nice.

Bruiser indicated a chair at his left. I didn't see any reason to be obstinate or difficult—any more than I already was—so I took it and sat, the legs of the chair scraping hollowly on the porch flooring. I smelled gun oil. Bruiser was armed on his own home turf. That seemed relevant, but I wasn't sure how or why.

The food must have been cooked and sitting on a warmer, because the little maid reappeared immediately, carrying a large tray. She served me. Bruiser poured my tea. So far, so good. I hadn't had to kill anyone. Yet.

CHAPTER 18

Three hundred years, give or take a few decades

The food was good, the yellow of the eggs sloppy, and the toast perfect for sopping it up, protein and fat in every bite. It was a meal that could be eaten fast, even with the quantity I'd ordered. I didn't waste time on conversation; I just ate.

When the food was gone, I waved my fork at my plate, set it down with a soft clink, and met Bruiser's eyes. "Okey-doke. Thanks for the breakfast. So, tell me a couple things. Tell me what happened at the Rousseau clan home. I know you got security camera feed from it. Tell me why the human cops hadn't been on scene. Tell me about the purge." Bruiser started in shock. I slouched back in my seat, my tea-cup in hand. "And tell me about the Rousseau clan's insanity. And while you're spilling your guts, tell me about the long-chained." He snapped his mouth shut, eyes hot with anger. I laughed. "Don't worry. I didn't torture it out of any-one. Sabina told me. And it's need-to-know info because she thinks it's all tied in with the maker of the young rogue."

"Sabina talked to you . . ." he breathed. When I didn't comment he said, "You have a way about you, Jane Yellow-rock." He reached for the coffeepot. I slammed his hand down, pinning it to the tabletop with mine, and said, almost in a growl, "Tell me. Now. I don't have time to play nice."

He was silent, staring at our hands, though he didn't try to pull his free. "Giving you any information without Leo's approval could be costly to me."

"Not giving it would be costlier," I said.

Bruiser looked from our hands to my face and said, "I'd like coffee." I removed my hand and he filled his cup. Set the pot aside. "The Rousseau clan home's security system went offline a little after two this morning. By the time Leo's people arrived, it was deserted. We don't know what happened." When I said nothing to that, he added cream and sugar, stirred, sipped, and went on.

"The purge took place after the events of the slave uprising on the island of Saint Domingue—called Haiti today. You know of the revolt?"

Before I could catch myself, I blinked, and was instantly sorry that I'd given my reaction away. Sabina had said something about an island. I shook my head no. He smiled ruefully, clearly not believing me. "A history lesson, then.

"Many don't know that the island was a haven for Mithrans. The clans there lived in a strict social and political society based on race and wealth, with the white vampires at the top, the vampyres du couleur libre—the free vampires of color who were landowners and slave owners in their own rights—in the middle, and the slaves at the bottom as workers, sexual toys, and blood meals. Most of the slaves were treated barbarously."

Bruiser's voice hardened. "The slaves wanted freedom. The vampyres du couleur clans had little political power due to their race, and they wanted equality with the white vampires. The whites wanted status quo. Some, both white and mixed race, had the witch gene and practiced blood magic, dark rites. Some with the witch gene never quite regained sanity, even after they passed the devoveo state and were unchained. I've read accounts of the atrocities they practiced. Their cruelty was legendary.

"Escaped slaves called maroons fled to the mountains, where they organized, collected weapons, and carried out raids against their former captors in a series of rebellions over half a century." His hand made a little flapping motion to show a give or take on the length of the revolt. "The vampyres du couleur libre eventually joined with the revolt to kill or oust the white Mithrans, led by a variety of men, both human and vampires.

"A vampire, François-Dominique Toussaint Louverture,

turned some of the discontent maroons and helped plot one of the major uprisings. He and his allies led a revolt under the Spanish flag that toppled the French colony. It was violent and brutal, with carnage on both sides. Some of the white landowners escaped to the U.S.; many more died, along with over ten thousand slaves. Three of the surviving vampire clans, including some who practiced blood magic, came to Louisiana in 1791, upsetting the political scene here."

"The Rousseau insanity? They were nuts because a lot of them had the witch gene?"

Bruiser's mouth turned down, forming deep channels on either side of his mouth. He topped off his coffee, warming it as he thought through what he wanted to tell me. "The clan has always been known for a weakness in the first sire's blood. All of his first scions took more than a decade to find sanity after they were turned. It was worse in the second generation, with nearly half still chained after two decades. On Saint Domingue, that first sire experimented on his slaves in the search for a cure, instituting a breeding program to create offspring with the witch gene, using them in ceremonies that were intended to cure his chained scions. When he was killed, his children took up his studies—"

"Studies?" I didn't try to keep the irony out of my tone.

"It was barbaric." His words were a hatchet of sound, short and cutting. "The island was liberated in the revolt and the clan came here, bringing his records and taking up the experiments. They found a partial treatment, though I couldn't say what it was, and some scions who had been chained for decades became sane."

"The long-chained ones," I said, intrigued despite myself.

"Yes. But there was war among the New Orleans clans, followed by the purge, which decimated two of the Domingue clans and put an end to the experimentation. The first Rousseau master and his records were destroyed in a fire with most of his long-chained scions. His heir built a special lair on their family grounds and even today keeps their devoveo chained for up to fifty years before destroying them. One account suggests that about forty percent find sanity, though what memories may be lost is still questioned."

"All of them are destroyed after fifty years?"

Bruiser hesitated. He looked intensely self-contained, as if he picked and chose what he wanted to tell me out of a basket of history, gossip, and myth. I'd have felt better if he had rocked back on the chair's back legs, tapped his fingers on the table. Anything. But he was as motionless as Leo, except that he still breathed and his heart still beat. "There are rumors that some scions, specially loved ones, might be kept longer. But no evidence of it has ever been uncovered."

"So if one of the long-chained ones, say, one kept around a *lot* longer than the usual fifty years, found sanity, he might have memories of the first sire's old methods. And he might have started the experiments again. That might be why Sabina didn't smell anyone she knew, except that it was an old Rousseau." At Bruiser's confused look, I explained about the burial sites and the crosses, about LeShawn and the kidnapped witch children. And the priestess's claim that a witch child had died at the burial site.

When I was done, Bruiser said, "Rumor claims that Renee Damours of Rousseau Clan found sanity before the purge, and her brother Tristan not long after. Their children weren't so lucky." Bruiser must have seen my reaction. "Yeah, Tristan was her brother *and* her husband. The breeding program wasn't just practiced on their master's slaves. Rumor persists that two of their children and another brother are still among the long-chained, alive, somewhere."

"These children. They'd be how old?"

Bruiser showed his teeth at me and saluted with his coffee cup. "Three hundred years, give or take a few decades."

Back in the city, I stopped at the house and called Jodi Richoux. "What, Yellowrock?" she said as she picked up. "I'm up to my ass in blood at the moment."

Which sounded like one of my worst days, but I didn't sympathize. I filled her in on the situation. She didn't deny when I suggested that she'd been investigating the witch children's disappearance herself after her aunt had died. "I need back into the woo-woo room, and I have pertinent info to trade for it," I said. "The Rousseau clan home is empty, open, and looks as if there's been a fight inside. George Dumas says the security was breached at two a.m. It has something to do with a vamp war brewing."

Jodi cursed. "I could have gone all year without hearing any of that. I'm working a gang murder in the Warehouse District. Crips took down a handful of MS 13 leaders and two vamps, a massacre that might be tied into your vamp war. Woo-woo room is open for you anytime, but be there at five to decompress and reorganize." She hung up.

I blew out a breath. Southerners were supposed to be polite. So far, I wasn't seeing it here. Rick returned my call and I asked to see the vamp files again. I needed to go back and find everything they had on the Rousseau clan. When he asked why, I gave him the same spiel I'd given Jodi and he said to come on in. I had free access. Lucky me. Without taking time for a shower or a nap, I grabbed a few things I might need, hopped back on Bitsa, and gunned the motor for NOPD. Sleep pulled at me as I rode. I needed rest, but I couldn't stop. Not until the kits were safe.

"How about you leave me the keys this time? Or prop the door open with a chair?" I shoved one of the little plastic chairs across the dull floor tiles with a screech.

Rick smiled and leaned a shoulder against the doorjamb, effectively blocking the only exit, crossed his arms, and gave me his best bad boy grin. If I hadn't been worried over the kits—the *children*, for pity's sake—I might have been appreciative. I blew hair out of my face and fisted my hands on my hips. "What?"

"How long since you slept? You look like sh—really tired."

"Gee, thanks. You sure do know how to make a girl feel pretty."

"Pretty you're not. Interesting, yes. Intriguing, yes. Pretty is too . . ." He scrunched up his face, thinking, looking at the faded ceiling tiles. "Too soft for you."

All of a sudden the anger that had fueled my body in place of sleep escaped in one huge irate sigh. And because there was nothing else underneath the rage, supporting it, giving me strength, I burst into tears.

When I came up for air, I was sitting on the table leaning into Rick, my face buried in his chest, my tears soaked through to his skin. Which smelled really wonderfully good. Faint shirt starch, aftershave, Ivory soap, gun oil, and man. I tightened my fingers on his jacket, not wanting to let go. It was stupid and girly and . . . But I felt safe for the first time in . . . well, a long time. His hands made wide circles on my back and shoulders, massaging me through my shirt. I settled my face on his shoulder, not wanting to look up. Not wanting him to see me. I was an ugly crier. Red nose, snot, puffy eyes, ick.

"Sorry." My voice was rough with tears. I cleared it and tried again. "Sorry I got your shirt wet." Rick eased me back. When he could see me, I realized that the bad boy image was temporarily gone and something deeper, richer, was in its place. A strange feeling, prickling like fur, danced down my spine, expectant, waiting.

His mouth came down slowly, hovering near mine. I could smell his breath, which carried coffee and something sweet, like pastry. He held my eyes, a question in his, as if asking permission. When my hands tightened on his shirt, he pulled me closer. To the edge of the table, my legs beside his. Eyes on mine, he drew a fraction nearer. I raised my face, just slightly. A delicate, slow dance of approach, warming. And he touched my lips with his.

It was a gentle brush, a delicate sweep of his lips over mine. And then a hover, questing, his mouth barely touching. Lips parted slightly. Fractionally. I sighed. Closed my eyes. And the worry and fear and tension seeped away. I let his arms hold me.

Instead of deepening the kiss, which I expected, he brushed my lips with his slowly back and forth. Murmuring, "It's okay, Janie. It's really okay." His arms firmed. Lips hardened on mine. He pulled me closer. Finally I slid my arms around his shoulders and held on, feeling Beast purr steadily in my mind. His tongue touched mine and my sigh became a thrumming hum of sound. One hand cupped my head, cradling me, his thumb on my cheek. One hand stroked slowly down my hair and back.

Long moments later, I smiled against his mouth and felt his smile follow, breaking the intensity. I eased back and met his gaze, which was warm and focused on me with tight concentration. "Thanks," I said, my voice rough.

He grinned and broke away, steadying me as I found my balance. "I've been wanting to do that for a while now. But"—he eased back and looked at his watch—"let's talk."

We did. I filled him in on everything that had happened, everything I had learned, from my impromptu history lesson, to all my guesses. I put it all together for myself and for Rick, from the smell on Bettina's hands at the vamp party, to the rising of a gangbanger tattooed with crosses. "I think the Damours—Renee, Tristan, and maybe their brother— were all witches, were all the long-chained, and all woke up. I think they might have perfected a spell to make progeny who don't ever go insane, and don't react to crosses. I think they're working on a spell to bring sanity to any rogue." I studied Rick. "If they succeed, there'll be no stopping the vamps. No way at all."

Rick was quiet, his face in cop mode—a hard, unfeeling mask. After a long moment he said, "I've heard of Renee Damours. Word is, she made a play for the master of the Rousseau Clan about thirty years ago and lost to Bettina before she disappeared into the city's underbelly. But all we got is rumor and gossip. We don't really *know* anything."

He turned to the vamp file cabinet and opened the second drawer, withdrawing two files. I hadn't gotten to this batch in my study. One thin file was a history of the purge. A thicker one was a history of the Rousseau Clan, which I took, and, at his instruction, thumbed to a section on the Damours, all five of them. I flipped to a page detailing Renee's history, to discover that most of the info was speculation and rumor gleaned from unnamed sources; it was only marginally better than nothing. According to the file, Renee Damours didn't attend parties, didn't attend gatherings— the command performances of the entire vamp assembly to deal with matters of the vampire state or the health of its members—no matter who demanded them. She didn't travel, and didn't troll for fresh meat. "She's a stay-at-home kinda gal," I said, "for decades. She's got to have cabin fever."

Rick hummed a note of amused agreement.

She seldom left her lair, which was rumored to be in the Warehouse District, the same part of the city where the most recent vamp party took place—when I saw the witch glamour and the watching witches. Not likely that the witchy happenings were an accidental concurrence; at this point, I wasn't willing to believe in coincidence.

Rick passed me another sheaf of papers, photocopies of letters and news accounts with a face sheet titled "History of the Purge." Date of occurrence: the late seventeen hundreds. Page two was a summary composed by Elizabeth Caldwell, who noted that Renee Damours had brought her chained family to New Orleans from Haiti and immediately purchased several large blocks of land, including some along the Mississippi, in the Warehouse District. Again, we were back to the Warehouse District. The entire district had smelled vampy. Renee could easily have a hidden lair there.

Rick murmured, "Want to hire me to look up the current owners of her original land?"

Without looking up I said, "Sure. Just put it on my tab." I couldn't help the wry smile that pulled on my mouth. I had hired Rick when he was undercover to look into some land ownership and purchases. So far, I hadn't paid him.

"You *are* going to pay me for my time, aren't you?"

I pulled a folded money order from my jeans pocket and held it out to him. He grunted, unfolded the paper to check the amount, and grunted again. "Nice. This is more than I was hired for. What's the rest? Tip? Or do I have to . . . work it off?"

His question had a decidedly erotic tone to it and I didn't have time for flirting, not with Angelina and Little Evan missing. "Tip. Definitely tip."

"Spoilsport."

"But you can buy the beer on your tip money on Saturday night. After the children are back home safe and sound."

"Deal." His voice was toneless again, all business, the life-or-death business of being a cop. I sometimes envied them the ability to turn that stony, cold mien off and on.

I felt a vibration and Rick pulled a cell phone from his pocket, opened the cover. His brows went up as he checked a text message. "I'm being shunted to the special cases division. I have a conference today at five in"—he checked the text again—"room 666. What kinda meeting place is this?" He closed the cell and put in back in his pocket. " 'Bout time the brass gave me something to do besides paperwork. I hate paperwork. What?"

I pulled my brows back down and stuck my eyes back on the file. "Nothing. Can I get copies of these files? It's a hassle coming all the way down here every time I need info."

"You'll miss me, but I'll see what I can do."

"I haven't slept in two days. I'm heading back to my bed."

Rick leaned in and pushed back the hair that brushed my cheek. Tucked it behind my ear. His fingertips were warm on my skin. "Alone?"

I spluttered with laughter. This guy could twist anything into innuendo. "Don't take this the wrong way, but I certainly hope so."

So tired I could barely think, I made it home and to my rumpled bed, where I stole four uninterrupted hours of sleep, waking only when someone knocked on the front door, three distinct taps, leaving the wards sizzling in reaction. It had to have hurt, telling me that it wasn't a delivery or a salesman. It was more imperative than that. I had a visitor. Or maybe a Visitor. The queen of England would knock like that, taps to announce herself, not to ask admission.

I wrapped up in the chenille robe that came with the house, tied it snuggly, and went to the door. Peeking through a clear pane in the door's new stained glass, I wasn't surprised to see Mol's oldest sister, water witch, professor, and three-star chef, Evangelina Everhart. Evangelina was a bigger, broader, more authoritative version of Molly, a three-star-general version of Molly, wearing a business suit, panty hose, and a posture so upright it looked as if she were born with a witch's stick up her backside.

She was carrying a suitcase. My heart did a nosedive. A cabdriver behind her unloaded two more cases onto the curb. Evangelina looked up and met my eye through the pane of glass. Too late to pretend I wasn't at home.

I opened the door and stood aside. Evangelina looked me over from bare toes to mussed hair. Her lips pursed, censure on her face at the evidence that I had been napping while her sister was in the hospital and her niece and nephew were missing. I grinned sourly and walked away without a word, leaving the door open. Evangelina and I weren't the best of pals. To her, I was the Hell's Angel, motorcycle-riding, bad-influence friend of her younger sister.

I put on a kettle of water for tea, listening to Evangelina pay off the cabbie and carry her luggage over the threshold. The front door closed with a restrained snap. Molly's ward was still up, but it clearly recognized family; she entered with no problem and stepped into the kitchen. Standing in the entrance, she sniffed, looking around again at what was left of the signatures of Molly's broken, ripped wards. I could still smell the burned, scorched reek of energies torn and blasted through.

"No one should have been able to break through this." She sounded surprised. And maybe a little scared. "No one. Even an entire coven would have had trouble blasting through it."

"That was my thinking. Cream and sugar? Mug or cup?" I waved at the table, an invitation to sit.

Evangelina turned her intent stare to me. "Both, please, mug, and if you have a shot of whiskey to go in it, that would be nice."

My eyes didn't bug out, but it was a near thing. I shrugged an apology. "I have beer."

Evangelina returned the shrug, saying "never mind" with hers, and sat at the table, kicked off her sensible shoes, pulled off her suit jacket, and leaned back. I could smell her feet and the odor of dried sweat and worry. She had been on the go and under stress for too many hours. She ran her fingers through her hair, scratching her scalp and yawning. It was the nearest thing to relaxed—or maybe simply exhausted—I'd ever seen her. "I think beer might clash with the tea." When I laughed tiredly, she said, "I'll get some whiskey later. For now, I apologize for waking you. How long since you slept?"

It wasn't the sarcasm I'd expected. It almost sounded

concerned, which was nearly my undoing. Again. But I would *not* cry in front of Evangelina Everhart. I put cookies on the table, on a plate, cookies Mol had baked for her kids, white chocolate macadamia nut. They were still soft, and that fact brought tears to my eyes. It hadn't been all that long since the children were taken, but it seemed like forever. Tentatively, I said, "Two days. Give or take." Evangelina took the plate and rearranged the cookies, not as if she disapproved of my arrangement, but as if she needed something to do with her hands. Her face got more pinched, holding in her emotions, her eyes on the cookies. "Can you tell me what is happening?"

For the second time today I recited the state of affairs of Molly, her kids, and the vamp/witch problem. When I finished, Evangelina said, "I heard that there was a vampire war threatening. Is that real or gossip?"

"Real. I think. The vamp clans have realigned loyalties. Even though Rafael of Mearkanis is the one who might challenge Leo for master of the city, I'm guessing that Clan Rousseau is the one pulling strings, fomenting a vamp war. I'm betting that the political dissatisfaction is just a cover so they can get this rogue-spell to work without getting caught and executed under the Vampira Carta." I put leaves into the strainer and the teapot into the sink, the familiar motions bringing me some much needed calm.

"Not an unlikely assumption."

"What I don't understand," I said, "is why witches are helping them."

"That's part of what I'm here to find out. I've put in a call to the coven suggested by your Leo to meet tonight. Do you want to join us?"

I looked at Evangelina in surprise. I had never expected her to include me in her witch business. "Um . . . he's not *my* Leo. And I have a meeting with the local cops at five. I think they've decided to launch a special investigation."

"Too little, too late." Her voice sounded weary. She ate another cookie, but I was pretty sure she wasn't tasting it.

We sat silent until the timer went off, lost in our own thoughts. I poured tea, and we drank.

Then I made a phone call. I had something brewing in my mind—something that seemed a lot like a plan.

CHAPTER 19

No good deed goes unpunished

Room 666 was just as dull and boring as ever, but this time it smelled heavenly. From the bottom of the stairs I smelled fried grease and onions and seafood. Jodi had brought takeout food with her, thank God. Despite my worry over the kits, my stomach growled as I pushed open the door.

The cops were sitting around the little table, Jodi and Rick and another guy I didn't recognize, all with colas in sweating cans in front of them. When I slid into the seat next to Rick, he gave me a look. "You coulda said you were coming too."

"I coulda. More fun this way."

Jodi said, "You two flirt on your own time." Rick snorted. I popped my Coke open so I didn't have to respond. "I've been offered this case because my boss is ticked that I have an in with vamps." She glanced at me. "Since I attended a vampire council meeting."

"No good deed goes unpunished," I said. Jodi and I had attended a council meeting together, a first for an NOPD cop at any level of authority. Her boss had been peeved not to be invited, and in a childish reaction, had clearly been giving her scut cases.

"I can't promise it will help any of our careers, especially if any more witch children are taken, but I've been offered the witch child kidnapping cases, the newest and the cold cases. Those previously investigated by my aunt Elizabeth.

We'll be under the SCD, the special cases division," she said to me. I nodded. "The current investigation—"

"There is no current investigation," the third guy growled.

"Right. Well, there is now. And I've requested that you join me, but it isn't mandatory. You want glory and promotion, you'll say no. You want to do some good, you'll stick around."

"I'm in," the third guy said. He leaned over the table and put out this hand to me. "Sloan Rosen." I took it and shook. He was human, African-American, heavily tattooed, even on his fingers, with jailhouse tats. Which was very interesting. They reminded me of LeShawn'n.

"Jane Yellowrock." I looked at Rick and back, drawing conclusions. "You were undercover too?"

"With the Crips. Until last year when I was outed by arresting four of the top local boys. Now I have a bounty on my head, some secretive vamp clan is out to get me, and the big shits can't figure out where to put me. And I figure you're here to make sure we'll all go down fighting."

I put it together with a twisted grin to show I was being ironic, not insulting. "So, as far as the brass is concerned, having you on this team puts all of us in danger. The vamps can track your scent, and the Crips are standing in line for you and would happily take us out to get you." He nodded slowly, lips pursed, and I said, "But if it makes you feel better, Leo Pellissier will probably plow through all of them to get to me for killing his son. Just being near me is a death sentence. Bet Leo wins."

"You two children can have a pissing contest about who has the biggest bounty on your heads later. For now, we have work to do. Rick, pass out the food; Jane's stomach is growling so loud I can't hear myself."

Rick stood and placed grease-stained bags in front of each of us. I smelled oysters inside mine and started salivating. The kits were missing, I might have a hard knot in my belly, but the Beast still had to be fed.

"I want you all to study the info on the stolen witch children," Jodi said. "Look for ties, connections, anything that might have been missed previously." She flipped files at us the way a cardsharp flips cards and we all set them to the side of our paper plates of food and opened both. I don't know how Jodi was able to leave her bag closed, but she did, and kept talking.

"Because there was never any proof the witch kids were killed, taken over state lines, and because no ransoms were ever demanded, neither FBI nor the state police has ever been called in. Until now, local policy has been to shunt the disappearances to inactive juvie case files thinking that the kids just ran off and will be back, or that they were taken by human family members to get them away from witch influence." She looked at me. "Thanks to an official letter from the office of the Blood Master of the City, that policy has now changed."

Office . . . Bruiser. Bruiser had done that.

Hard delight gleamed in Jodi's eyes. "I've been told you had something to do with it," she said to me. These cases might not advance her career, but she wanted them. It wasn't well-known, but Jodi's mother was a witch, and I was guessing that so was her late aunt. The relationships gave her a personal interest in discovering what had happened to the missing witch children and acquiring justice for them if possible. I tilted my head to show it was nothing. Which it had been on my part. Bruiser had done it.

"According to Jane," Jodi continued, "witch children are being killed in black magic ceremonies by vampire criminals who are raising young rogues. Clan Pellissier would like the offenders 'brought to the day.' "

I looked up at that. My current contract with the vamp council used those words, whose archaic meaning meant killed true-dead.

"George sent us a copy of your contract," she said to me. "The figures are blacked out, of course. But it gives us official permission to carry silver rounds in our weapons and stake any vampires we catch in the act of black magic."

"Sweet," Sloan said through his sandwich. It came out "Shhhwee."

"Rosen is our electronics guy. He took down the Crips mostly with electronic monitoring. He stole their books and put a stop to a lot of weapons and cocaine trafficking that had connections to a South American vamp clan. We're still hunting down three humans with the evidence he collected. If we need anything listened in on, he's our man."

"If it helps at all," I said, "I think a Rousseau is responsible for young rogues being raised all over the city and for the witch children kidnappings." I filled them in on what I knew and what I guessed. I pointed at the file cabinets. "The red folders helped."

Jodi gave me a knowing half smile. "Rick said you wanted copies of the woo-woo files sent to your house. They'll be messengered over by a marked unit ASAP."

Sloan drained his Coke can, set it on the table with an empty twang. To Jodi, he said, "We done? 'Cause I'm outta here. Dinner with the wife and kids."

"After eating all that?" Jodi said, swiveling so he could get his longer legs out.

Sloan stood beside her, wiping his mouth with a paper napkin. "Fast metabolism." He balled up all the empty papers and utensils. I shoved the last bite of bread and oyster in just in time, and salvaged a paper boat of fries and onion rings. Jodi cleaned the table with a disinfectant wipe she took from her pocket.

"I'll keep you up to date, Yellowrock," she said, "until we get the Trueblood kids back."

"And Bliss," I said. "She was taken by the same guy."

"Right. Bliss. You did know her real name is Ailis Rogan, didn't you?" When I shook my head no, she asked, "Do you know if she has any family? 'Cause Katie's bouncer has no record of any."

"No. Bliss wasn't very forthcoming about her past."

"Runaway?" Sloan asked. "I'll check old records and see if anything matches up."

"I'll e-mail you all our addys," Jodi said to me. Waving her arm to indicate room 666, she said, "Our official work area is here and next door. The brass's idea of a joke, I'm sure. I'll get some PCs, a landline phone or two, an empty file cabinet, a whiteboard, and a map.

"I'll be here and at my desk for paperwork till midnight thirty. Later."

She and Sloan Rosen walked out together. I didn't look at Rick as I got up and slid across from him to the warm seat just vacated.

Out of curiosity, I said, "What do you know about a guy named Derek Lee, former marine? Lives—"

"I know Derek Lee. Word on the streets is that he's put together his own little army and is going after gangs. We have a few unexplained bodies that might be notched into his bedpost, like the bloodbath in Crips territory Jodi came from today. How do *you* know Derek Lee?" That last was a cop question, asked in a toneless, staccato voice, with an underlying threat.

I shrugged. Cop threats don't impress me much. "I heard he's going after vamps and gangs with vamp connections. I'm thinking Derek works for Leo from time to time." When I said the words, several little things clicked in my mind. "Question: If the master of the city officially recognized that some of his species were practicing ritual black magic, and a purge became legal by the Vampira Carta, what would happen to the clans?"

"I don't have a degree in Mithran Law, They could be disbanded or reorganized by the master of the city. Why?"

An unconscious *Holy crap* sounded in my mind. At my adrenaline spike, Beast stirred and stared across the table. "Derek said something about the Crips once. If he's been fighting them, it might be with Leo's unofficial backing."

I had called Derek before I left the house. I was meeting the ex-marine and his crew soon, to raid a few warehouses in the district, looking for the lair of a vamp who kept her children chained for the safety of the public. Not something I wanted the cops to know. Not something I wanted Leo to know. Unless Leo had been pushing me in that direction all along. Had I been herded like prey? Beast snorted in affront.

"I don't know what the hell you're thinking, lady, but you're startin' to scare me again."

I looked at Rick. Who was looking at me just the way a woman wanted to be looked at. Not something I could put into words, but a look I recognized when I saw it. He reached out a hand and I placed mine into his, letting a smile soften my lips.

Knowing I was probably screwing up something that might be really good if I gave it half a chance, I said, "Did Leo tell you to seduce me?"

Rick dropped my hand, leaving it in the middle of the table. He wiped his mouth with a paper napkin as if he were

wiping beer—or the remembered taste of my mouth—
away. "No one tells me who to sleep with." And he left me
alone in room 666.

I pulled my hand back into my lap. "That went well."
Beast hacked a laugh. I stood. I had work to do, most of it
on the computer and in the files I'd photographed and sent
to myself, the files from this very room. Odd how I ended
up back here all the time, in the woo-woo room. On the
way out of the NOPD, I discovered that I had missed a call
from Derek Lee. And what he told me made me smile.

Half an hour before dusk, I roared into the Breaux Mart
grocery store where Derek had told me to meet him and
set my booted feet on the pavement. The black steel-walled
van that pulled in beside me and idled might have worried
a lesser woman. Cops call them snatch vans, among other
things, none of them nice, because the vehicles are perfect
for grabbing a woman or child and making off with her. I
reached over my shoulder and placed a hand on my shotgun, ready to pull. I wasn't frightened, just cautious. Really
cautious. A faint click sounded and the tinted window lowered with electronic smoothness. I cut the engine and set
the kickstand. Derek pushed back dark glasses. "Jane with
the funny last name."

"Derek with the marines. How long you been working
with Leo Pellissier?" Me and my smart mouth.

"Six months. Ever since the Crips decided to make my
boys into their boys and kill any who thought better of the
offer. Why? You got a problem with it?"

This wasn't the first time I'd heard mention of the Crips.
Another coincidence? Not likely. It was all starting to come
together. Not that I had any idea what the final picture
would look like. "Not really. I'm not fond of the Crips or
any other gang that allies with a practitioner of dark magic
and a few rebel vamps getting ready to start a vamp war."

"Is that what's happening?"

"I'm thinking yes."

"You ain't stupid, Injun Princess. I'm not *fond* of *any*
fang-heads. But the devil you know . . ." he said with a bitter smile.

"The story of my life. How many you got with you?"

The side door slid open, revealing six young men—three I knew from mapping the hunting territory in their neighborhood—kneeling in the back open space, all but one dressed in black combat fatigues and armed to the teeth with military or military surplus equipment. I spotted shotguns, one assault rifle, numerous knives and vamp-killers, but nothing in the way of body armor. When I commented on that, one of the men unbuttoned his black shirt to reveal a chain-mail vest and a neck choker, a T-shirt beneath to protect his skin. "Silver-plated steel works better in combat with a vamp than armor. Guns are loaded with silver shot." He nodded at the shotgun strapped to my back. "What you carrying?"

"Various weaponry. Shotgun is a Benelli M4 Super 90, loaded with silver-fléchette, hand-packed rounds."

"The model M4, designated by the military as a Joint Service Combat Shotgun? That M4?" I half smiled and he went on, the early-twentysomething man sounding as if he quoted from a military handbook, showing off. "Steel components have a matte-black, phosphated, corrosion-resistant finish. The aluminum parts are matte and hard anodized, the finish reducing the weapon's visibility during night operations."

From the back, another man took over. "The model M4 shotgun is considered by many experts to be nearly idiot-proof, and requires little or no maintenance, operates in all climates and weather conditions, can be dumped in a lake or pond and left for long periods of time and not corrode. It can fire twenty-five thousand rounds of standard ammunition without needing major parts replaced. That Benelli?"

"That Benelli," I agreed, my smile widening. "Mostly, though, I just like the fact that it's idiot-proof." The men shared a masculine chuckle for the little lady and her nice, safe weapon. "All you guys ex-military?"

"Why you asking?" the first man asked. His tone made it clear they still weren't interested in me knowing their names.

"We have a license to kill any vamps harboring the maker of the young rogues, and the young-rogue maker himself, of course. But there's no room for human collateral damage. Local law won't turn a blind eye to mistakes.

So we're looking for the best of the best, which means military, not gangbangers. Shooters have to be sure—absolutely sure—what you fire at."

"Not a problem." Guy number one tossed me a set of low-light infrared goggles. "One man wears these. He goes in alone and quiet—recon. Places all humans visible to him as warm and living. Then the rest of us go in and take out anything dead and cold."

I bumped his age up to mid-thirties as I turned over the goggles. I hadn't known for sure that vamps wouldn't register on infrared. Learn something new every day. "Sweet," I said, tossing them back.

"The gear is from bounty money. Cash you got us for the vamp heads paid for all this."

Which got me thinking. If they were working with or for Leo, why hadn't he paid for their gear? Questions for another time. "Master sergeant?" When he nodded, I said, "I'll make a run-through ahead of the van, spotting any eyes. You got ears?"

The same guy tossed me a headset. I pulled off my helmet and settled the headset on. "Now, this is what I'm talking about." I had used civilian-style headsets once before in Asheville, when I worked a dicey run to track thefts from a secure warehouse with the security firm where I did my internship. This wasn't too different. "Testing."

"Copy, Princess," a voice said into the earpieces.

"I e-mailed you the street addresses of the likely warehouses," I said.

He turned a small laptop to me, the screen showing a map. "The Warehouse District is upscale and we might have to do on-foot recon. You got too many weapons to pull it off. Hicklin here looks the part."

I finally got a name, or half of one. It was a start. I looked Hicklin over, a twenty-something with slicked-back hair and a shaped Vandyke beard. "Nice suit."

"Itches," he complained.

"I bet." I kicked Bitsa into life. Beast rose through my consciousness and stared out through my eyes. I gave the master sergeant a nod and wheeled my bike around, heading toward the Warehouse District and a war with some of the Rousseau Clan. I didn't bet on it being pretty.

*   *   *

We reached the Warehouse District, the area yuppie-crowd
trendy, many of the old warehouses remade into retail and
living space for the upwardly mobile. Museums and art
stores were everywhere, some chic, all expensive. Many of
the old warehouses had been redone into fancy condos and
apartments, homes with indoor pools, gyms, and security. I
didn't expect any less than great security from the warehouse I was looking for. I peeled away from the van following me and took side streets, rounding corners with tight
leans and a burst of speed, checking out the back ways for
the intense, varied scents of the rich and fangy.

Beast reached through me, testing the wind for vamp
scent, and just as the sun was setting caught a whiff. An old
vamp in sunglasses and loads of sunscreen out for an early
stroll turned to stare after me as I whizzed past. But he was
alone. And he was someone I recognized from the vamp
graveyard when Katie was put to earth. A Desmarais elder. Not my quarry. Not my prey. I was looking for mingled
Rousseau smell—lots of vamps in one place.

Half an hour later I was on a back alley off Iberville, near
Decatur Street, when I caught a whiff of them that quickly
grew stronger. Mixed Rousseau smells and an odor of rot
came from a ventilation shaft in a brick building that took
up half a block. The likely lair was on the back, opening to
what once had been an alley. Parking took up a goodly space
in back, enclosed utilities area on one side. There were no
windows on the lower story at back and sides, three rotating
security cameras, one secure garage-style door that looked
heavy-duty steel, and next to it, one steel entry door with a
tiny steel-mesh-reinforced window, the kind of glass used
in prisons. The door had its own keypad entry, camera, and
intercom speaker; the security was tight and up to date. Perfect. I glanced at my research. This was one of the addresses
once owned by Renee Damours, though the title had trans-
ferred to a Henry Poitier back in the nineteen fifties. "Possible target," I said into my mike. I slowed and eased around
front; gave the address to the van boys.

The front of the place had been subdivided into three
businesses, one an art store. I parked Bitsa in the next block
and unhelmeted. I was wearing too many weapons to look

like a shopper, but I could look as though I had bike problems. I knelt near Bitsa and pretended to study the back wheel.

Hicklin appeared from my left, meandering, one hand in his pants pocket, tie loose, his phone hanging from one ear. His voice came over my headset, chatting, just a guy killing time window-shopping after work, maybe waiting for a lady friend to join him for supper in one of the hip, pricey restaurants nearby. "You know it, man," he said. "Boss is banging her and his wife is clueless. She catches him and the business will go into a divorce settlement. We'll all be out of a job. . . ." He nattered on as he studied the wares in the windows, getting the lay of the land, looking for cameras and other security. Looking for back doors. He entered the business on the corner, an art store with statues in the front windows, colorful, modern swirly things that looked like clayware. "Later, man."

Inside, Hicklin chatted up the salesgirl, flirted, a natural-born player, all the byplay coming over the headset, which looked like his cell phone. I tinkered with Bitsa. Hicklin had a date with Amy later in the evening if he wanted, but he finally got to the point, asking her how long she'd worked at the store, and discovered she was the owner's daughter. "Tell me about the building. I have a sister who's a chef, relocating up from a chef school in Charlotte. I'm considering investing in a restaurant for her."

Amy filled him in, leaning across the counter, chatting with the rich customer. "It's, like, two hundred years old, with walls three feet thick. The woman who owns it is one of the old vampires, kinda creepy, you know, like *real* old? Not humanlike at all. She uses the back half, all three stories, the lower one for storage for her businesses, and the top two floors for living. If you call her living."

"I've seen vamps, but not an old one. What's she like?"

The back of the building sported a windowless lower story and wide, arched windows on the two top floors. I hadn't consciously noted it but they'd been heavily draped. Cars could be pulled into the lower level through the garage-style door using an automatic opener or the keypad. Perfect vamp lair.

"Short. Pretty, in a pale-as-death way. But not real human-normal." Amy took up a strand of shoulder-length hair and twirled it around and around her fingers as she thought. "One night she shows up here, asks me if I'm interested in being a blood meal for a friend of hers. She'd pay me, like she was a pimp or something. I was so not into that. I told her no, thank you. And she stands there, unmoving, not breathing, for over *two hours*. I had customers and we had to work around her, like she was a statue or something. It was freaky, you know? And then I looked up and she was gone. When I checked the security cameras, she just disappeared. Like she teleported out something, except the door opened real fast and closed."

"How did she get in and out? Is there a door from her part of the warehouse to here? Or to one of the other stores?"

"No way. She's real into security. She'd freak if we had a way to her side. Daddy thinks she bribed a fire marshal to keep the sections separate against local fire regulations."

While the two decided on a time to hook up for the evening, dinner and maybe more, I said, "Derek, this looks promising." More than promising. By the scents, I knew this was it. Had to be. Tension shot through me. "How do you want to do this?"

"I copy. You wait here till my boys say they're ready. We got monkey stuff."

"Monkey see, monkey do?"

"No. If you see no evil and hear no evil, you can't rat anyone out. No offense."

I smiled. "None taken. Security cameras?"

"Will go out exactly thirty seconds before the doors blow. On my mark, start around back. When you hear the blow, move fast."

"Got that."

"Copy, Injun Princess. The word is copy."

I just grinned and waited. All along the street, true night fell. New Orleans is at its best at night, balmy air like a caress, smells of the river and cooking foods, people walking leisurely, languid after a hot day at the office. I felt rising tension, mixed excitement and fear, knowing I could be on the verge of getting back Molly's kids. I checked the foot traffic. "Derek? What about foot traffic?"

"We're okay out back. On my mark, and thirty, twenty-nine ..."

I started Bitsa and motored with the countdown as I followed the lethargic after-work crowd. I was at the back parking area when a muffled *boom* took me by surprise. And took out all the lights in the block. "Go, go, go, go, go!" Derek shouted into my headset. Adrenaline shot through me. Beast reared up high in my mind, claws piercing. I gunned Bitsa and raced through the human-sized door, now hanging by one hinge, just behind a man carrying a shotgun and a sword, a black satchel over his back. *Derek? Maybe.*

I abandoned the bike just inside. Pulled the Benelli and opened out the folding stock. The smell of vamp was overpowering. Rousseaus. Lots of them. The point man moved through the darkened building, checking everything out with his goggles, giving report as he moved. By the commentary, he was twenty feet in front of Derek.

"Hallway, clear. Left, clear. Right, clear. Stairway"—a door banged open and a cool shaft of air fell into the hallway "clear on this level. No bogeys noted above. No way down."

Left meant a room to the left. *Right* was a room to the right. There was no downstairs. I understood. Over the headset came "Garage clear. Two vehicles. Both cool to the touch. Garage exterior door, one interior door for entry. Locked. Steel reinforced. Hinges on inside. Camera down."

From outside came the words "Fire escape clear. No doors or windows opening. No movement."

"Hallway door, no window," the man in front of Derek said. "Locked, reinforced, hinges inside."

"I got it," Derek said. He knelt in front of me. I didn't watch what he did, but covered us from behind. Just in case one of the rooms had a doorway we hadn't seen. Or a concealed exit. Or a hungry vamp sleeping under a table.

"Back." Derek and the point man backed up and we each entered a room, Derek with me. "Five, four"—I covered my ears to protect them from the explosion—"three, t—" The explosion took out his words. Dust blew into the hallway, along with the smell of rotten meat and old blood. It was a charnel house effluvia. Derek cursed.

The point man disappeared inside the dark opening. We'd been in about forty seconds, according to my time sense. I was expecting human servants. Armed. So far, nothing.

"No live ones," the point man said. "All dead. Lights." Derek and I rushed inside as the point man pulled off his goggles and knelt, weapon up and ready to fire. The lights flickered once and came on. The sudden illumination sent a shock of tingles through me. Followed by a shock of another sort.

The windowless room was fifty by forty, give or take, with a fifteen-foot-tall ceiling. The walls were painted a soft coral, oriental rugs were piled deep, and leather furniture, tables, lamps were scattered in small groups, as if someone had wanted the place kept appealing. Except for the far corner where the floor was concrete with a drain in its gently sloped center. Along the walls in that corner were cots made of blackened steel and chained to the cots were vamps. No humans, no witches. I counted quickly. Nine vamps on ten cots. The tenth cot was covered by rumpled, stained sheets.

"We got cameras," someone said as we entered.

At the sudden appearance of humans—of bloody meat, to the vamps—they all vamped out, screaming and wailing and fighting the restraints. Steel cut into wrists and ankles, and the smell of fresh vamp blood mixed with the reek of old, decaying vamp blood. The empty cot bothered me. A lot.

I scanned back and forth, the Benelli at ready. Behind me, the point man was letting in the others from the garage entrance. They raced to take out the inside cameras and I heard the *shhhhft* of spray cans, the chemical smell adding to the reek in the room. "We got nine vamps restrained. One missing. Seal exits," Derek said, reading my mind. The door to the garage shut firmly.

"I got the door," Point Man said, heading back to the door we had come through.

That left us with four shooters inside. I moved across the room to the concrete-floored area. It was about ten-by-ten with a showerhead hanging over the drain; a lever and a handheld sprayer on a long tube hung nearby. Soap and clean cloths were in a basket, and liquid bath soap and industrial cleaners stood on a narrow, wheeled table. Above it were butcher tools, the blades looking well used and well cared for, sharp. The narrow table was clean but blood lined the cracks. I bent and sniffed. A lot of blood. For a long time. From a lot of humans and not a few vamps. Under the table was a zippered body bag, and it wasn't empty.

Trepidation climbed up my spine on cold gluey feet. I swung the Benelli out of the way and knelt. My fingers were quivering as I opened the zipper. A vamp face appeared. Not Angelina. Not Little Evan. Not stuffed together into the body bag. The vamp's head was separated from the body. True-dead. And he'd begun to stink. Like, really stink. He'd been dead long enough for his skin to be slippery and oozing. I rezipped the bag. Sniffed again. There was no scent of the kits. No scent of Bliss. They weren't here and hadn't been here. But maybe upstairs?

I stood and repositioned the shotgun as I walked between the cots. There were little racks above each bed holding what looked like medical charts with ID and medical details on each, which included date of birth. I stopped at the two teenagers, a boy and girl on thick foam mattresses, Adora and Donatien Damours, brother and sister. The family resemblance was evident even beneath the vamped-out teeth and eyes. Both wore clean hospital gowns and bowties, both had been showered and their blond hair washed. Both had long faces, with firm chins, high foreheads. Both were hungry. Gaunt. Starving. I looked around. They all were starving. The girl was trying to lick her own wrist where she was bleeding, but her shackles kept her too far away. She was mewling with need. I checked the other ID cards.

Sick things. Kill them, Beast murmured as I read.

I agreed, but there were reasons not to, important reasons, primarily Angelina and Little Evan. Besides, killing the long-chained wasn't covered by my current contract, which made this a job for the council. "No Tristan Damours," I said. "So maybe the rumors are right and he found sanity. Or maybe that's him in the body bag."

"Company," a voice said in my headset. Over the speaker I heard the sound of feet clattering on stairs. Someone was coming down the inside stairs. "Heat signature is human. Two of them. Wait, one. There's a vamp with them." They weren't trying for stealth either. I could hear them without the headset.

"Another on the fire escape," a second voice said. "Moves like human."

"Let's have a chat with our hosts," Derek said.

The men quick-stepped toward the stairwell but positioned themselves outside. One man threw something. I closed my eyes and covered my ears just in time. The explosion shattered through my hands, against my eardrums. The flash-bang took out the humans descending the stairs. I had no idea what effect it might have on a vamp except to make him mad.

Derek and his boys raced into the confined space and brought down three forms. The humans were on the floor, incapacitated by the noise, but the vamp was fine, if by fine that meant really vampy and ticked. But he wasn't fighting, which was odd. Derek's men shackled them all, the humans in steel, the vamp in silver. I stepped into the stairwell.

The vamp hadn't fought because he had been snared with a silver mesh net formed of tiny interlocking crosses; his face and hands were burned and blistered. Derek had thrown the net, bringing down the vamp with no fight at all. I fingered the glowing mesh. "Now, this is cool. I got to get me one of these."

"I'll send you to my supplier later," Derek said. "Silent alarm went out three minutes ago. We probably got another three minutes before the cavalry shows up. Either make him true-dead or talk fast. The silver mesh will make him uncomfortable enough to maybe chat a bit."

"Good." I toed the vamp. He wasn't pretty, a recent, partially healed scar marking the left side of his face diagonally from outer brow, alongside his nose, across both lips, to the right side of his chin. He looked tough, a warrior, given vampire life for some great sacrifice, maybe. It didn't happen often, but it did happen. And I had seen him at the vamp party at the Old Nunnery. "Where are the witches?"

He spat at me. Before the spit fell, Derek landed a kick in the vamp's side. He oofed with pain. I knelt beside him so he could smell my scent. And I pulled a vamp-killer, my favorite knife, eighteen-inch blade with a hand-carved, elk-horn handle, a gift from Molly's husband. His eyes widened and he met mine, pulling a vamp glamour. "Release me." The words reverberated through me, aching with need. Beast put a paw on my mind, and pressed down, giving me control I lacked on my own. I took a breath, feeling the sticky command dissolve. He tried again. "Release me and I will give you all that you desire." English wasn't his first language, his accent vaguely Italian.

Derek shook his head. "We're Leo's. We got protection from vamp mind control."

"Tell you what, bubba," I said, "you tell me where the Damours are, and maybe I'll let you live."

His eyes bled back to half-human, the whites less bloody, the pupils less black and wide. I was pretty sure his irises would be brown when he wasn't vamped out. "You do not fall to me?"

"She's the Rogue Hunter," Derek said. "She don't fall to nobody." He was staring at the far wall, gun at the ready, not letting his eyes meet the vamp's, a weird look on his face.

"I have heard of this one. You follow her? A *woman*? She is not even human."

"She's more human than you. Now answer the nice lady or she'll blind you. I know you can heal from it, but it'll be painful. And time-consuming."

More human than you? Nice lady? And he didn't react when the vamp told him I wasn't human. . . . *Great. Can't a girl keep a secret or two?*

"What are you? You do not smell of witch, like my mistress and masters."

I was right. Renee, her brother/hubby, and currently un-named other brother were witches/vamps, no longer members of the long-chained, and no one knew how long the adults had been sane. They were witches who practiced dark magic, yet who had survived the purge. And they were killing witch children in spells. More and more, it all made sense.

I pivoted on a heel and went back to the long-chained ones. I sniffed, mouth open, along the bodies of the

Damours' three-hundred-year-old teenagers. They fought and growled, tearing at their shackles as I did so, fought to get to me, to the blood in my veins. I caught a whiff, buried under the scent of vamp. Both children carried the witch gene.

CHAPTER 20

Thief-of-kits. Die.

Ignoring the men and vamp on the stairway landing, I raced up the stairs and into the apartment. I disabled a man with a knife, a chef by the smell of his clothes, bonked him on the head with the pommel of my vamp-killer, and left him unconscious at the entry. The apartment was opulent in red and white, lots of white marble, white-painted wood, lots of red fabric. The color of blood seemed to appeal to vamps as a decorating scheme. Go figure. I breathed the place in, scenting. It reeked of human blood donors, multiple vamps, pain, and sex. I raced from room to room, some with beds, some without, one with a complicated rack hanging from the ceiling, chains and tools of a bloody trade organized on shelves. There was a drain here too. There was no indication in the apartment's scents that the kits or Bliss had ever been here. I abandoned it for the third floor.

This was a private place, one huge room, divided into sections by furniture groupings. The place reeked of the Damours, their scent patterns overlapping and intermingled. I knew what they wanted now, I knew what they were trying to do, and the knowledge made the stink stronger, darker, permeated with evil, though surely that was only my imagination.

A large dining area was to my right with a table to seat twelve; a larger living space was ahead, with lots of leather. Two sleeping areas were just beyond, each with king-sized

beds made up with fur. Lots of real fur. Vamps liked loung-
ing on dead things. By the smell, this was a major lair of
the Damours. I made sure the huge apartment was empty,
finding a small but ornate bathroom tucked away in a nook,
but no other individual rooms. Again the decor involved a
lot of marble—floors, walls, pillars holding up the roof—
but the color scheme was black and red, with black marble
and deep scarlet fabrics. I stopped and turned, scenting
with mouth open. Something was wrong. Something was
missing.

No humans, Beast murmured. *No human blood. They
do not feed here.*

"Or they don't feed on human blood here." My body
tightened, hard and sharp.

I walked to the beds and lifted a pillow to me. Bliss's
scent wafted out. Bliss and sex. The Damours were feeding
off witches. Fury-fear spiraled up in me, flaming and icy,
electric. Angelina? I climbed across the bed, mouth open,
dragging in air over tongue and nose with a *scagghing
sound. Relief shuddered through me. Angie hadn't been
savaged here. But what I did smell brought me up short.

The vamp on the landing below had been in the beds of
the Damours, recently. So had other vamps, including Bettina, Rousseau Clan master. I lifted a pillow and breathed
in her scent, the stink of her sweat. It was laced with fear.
She had not been here willingly. She had wanted to escape
them. I should have gone to visit when she asked.

"Princess?"

I twisted on one knee and saw Derek at the door.

"We're ready to take the heads of the rogues on the
cots."

"Belay that. Until we find the kids, these particular rogue
vamps get a pass. If we kill them, then there's no reason to
keep Angelina and Little Evan alive."

He nodded his head, but it was resigned. "Fine. We can
use them as bait." He looked at his watch. "Time." He
meant time to go.

"One more minute," I bargained.

"Baldy just disabled one of my men and took off. Sixty
seconds and me and my men are outta here."

Discarding any pretense of human speed, I raced from

the bed and slammed open the armoires on the back wall, the doors rocking and banging as I passed. They faced the windows, all of them dark wood, carved with curlicues and flowers and leaves, dragons and gargoyles, faces out of legend and nightmare. Vamp scent roiled out of each until the next to last. And from it witch scent rose, fresh and potent and powerful.

I paused, hands clenching on my weapons. "They were here. The children." There was a mattress on the floor of the armoire, sheets and a blanket, small shackles on long chains. And a doll. A black-haired doll with yellow eyes, like mine. *Ka Nvsita*. The doll I gave to Angie.

Icy fear sliced through me. Tears stung my eyes. I sheathed the shotgun and picked up the doll. The scent of Angie's fear and the salt of her tears were ripe in the doll's clothes. But there was no scent of blood. I thanked God for small favors as I closed the door and secured the doll inside my leather jacket. "They were here only moments ago. How did they get by us?"

I looked at the last two armoires. Maybe . . . ? The next hold paintings, stacked in tightly. I yanked one out and saw a witch circle and pentagram. And vampires. And children. And lots of blood. "Derek? Get a couple of men up here and take these"—I nodded to the paintings—"as many as you can." He started to refuse but I passed him the painting. His mouth twisted down, hard, and he spoke into his headset.

The last armoire wasn't an armoire. When I pulled the door, a black space yawed open, a narrow stair leading down into darker night. The smell of sex, witch, and vamp led down. I remembered the utility area on the side of the building. I hadn't seen a door but one could be hidden there easily enough. "Derek?" When he looked at me, his shotgun out, braced across his body, I said, "They went this way. It leads down. Look for a passageway through the garage or a door to the outside. I'm taking the stairs."

Derek cursed with a marine's efficiency and disappeared, directing two men to take the paintings and get them into the van. I started down the stairs.

Beast, already close to the surface, shoved her way into my forebrain. Pain gathered at my fingertips as if claws pushed through. Pelt roiled just under my skin, aching, wanting to be free. My eyes adjusted to the lack of light. I can see well in murky dark, but my vision is no match for vamp eyes, which can see in total dark. I found the stairs by feel, the treads deeper than normal with maybe a twelve-inch drop per riser. My steps were slow and careful, my mouth open to scent, short snuffs drawing in air.

According to the scent markers, vamps and witches had come this way only moments ago, but no echo of sound remained except for my feet on the treads. They were hollow like wood, not quite smooth, not freshly sanded and lacquered. The passageway smelled old beneath the reek of vamp and witch-fear, with a moldy undertone of tea, indigo, rice, and cotton. And lots of human women and more human fear, though most from long ago.

Maybe it was an original passageway from the eighteen hundreds, or earlier, and had been remodeled into the back of the armoire as an escape hatch. An image came to me, bright and sharp, though I'm not gifted with vision. Maybe just stuck with a too-strong imagination, mixed with the fear in the smells. But I saw black women, wearing chains and little else, the scents of melanin from their skin, and iron and blood and fear, semen and degradation. A slave ship captain had used this passageway to test out his cargo before he sold them. I knew it with certainty and an impotent fury burned in me, the fury of a people who had served in slavery, much like the imported Africans. The fury of a woman, understanding hopeless captivity. The fury of Beast, feral and untamed.

Anger burned along my nerves and tingled through my skin. I nearly missed a step deeper than the others. And then was brought up short on the next three that had lower risers, as if the stair risers had been sized to create discomfort and confusion. I walked down the narrow passage, my eyes adjusting to the blackness, my other senses expanding, reaching out, testing the air. The echoes dulled, shortened, and I knew I was at the bottom. Ahead of me was a faint line of light. I reached out and found a leverlike handle. Pushed down on it. A door opened. Three men dressed in black ringed the door. I scented Derek and raised my hands. "Just me," I said, my voiced clotted with fury and failure. "Just me."

"We never saw this door in the shadows. If they came through here, they're long gone," Derek said.

Over his head, the moon was rising, the first night of the three-day-full moon. The three days most usually associated with the dark arts, with the moon change of weres, with Beast's sex drive. If the Damours intended to sacrifice the kits and Bliss, they'd do it during the full moon for optimal results.

I walked to the curb, smelling the fading scents of vamp and witch. And an overlay of diesel exhaust. They were gone. I had no idea where their captors had gone to find safety. Once again I was back to square one. I took a breath that hurt my lungs. Tears stung my eyes. I was nearly out of time.

I walked back into my house, smelling Evangelina Everhart, the oldest of the witch sisters, and Big Evan, Molly's still-in-the-closet sorcerer husband. And smelling Molly. She raced to my arms when I came in the side door. Slammed into me, holding me tightly. Over her shoulder Evan looked at me, his gaze murderous, his red beard vibrating with contained fury, promising retribution for the loss of his children. I hadn't been very good to Evan; I had placed his wife in danger more than once, nearly gotten him killed once, and now allowed his children to be stolen. The fact that I hadn't been present when they were taken had little relevance in his mind. Or in mine either, if I was honest.

"You don't have to worry about how to kill me," I said to him. "If I don't get your children back, I'll be dead trying."

"Better be," he rumbled. "Or I'll skin you alive, pelt and flesh."

Evangelina, who didn't know I was a skinwalker, looked back and forth between us in confused consternation, then took solace in food and tea, as was her wont. She dished up a hearty stew from a pot on the stove, scooped a round of brown rice in the center, placed small salad bowls at each plate, and dumped buttery biscuits from a steel tray into a basket. Comfort foods. "Sit. Eat," she commanded. I peeled

Molly out of my arms and passed her to Evan, who looked as if he was ready to rip her away from me. I removed the shotgun harness and laid it across the kitchen cabinet, but other than that, I remained fully armed.

I sat, picked up my dinner spoon by feel, and dipped it into the stew and rice.

"Tell me," Evan said. I put down my spoon and blinked at my tears.

"No. She eats first," Mol said sharply. "Look at her. She's about to drop."

I lifted my spoon and shoveled in the stew. Intellectually, I knew it was good, but it could have been ashes for all I cared. I ate mechanically, emptying my bowl in minutes. Snubbing the salad, I took four biscuits and placed them on the bread plate, dumped honey and butter on them, and applied the spoon to them too. When I was finished, Molly brought me another bowl of stew. And then another. I was eating as tears rolled down my face, and I realized that none of the others was eating at all. They were watching me. When I finished my third bowl, I sighed and pushed away the empty dishes. Without looking at any of them, I wiped my face, took my tea mug in hand, and started talking. I told the tale. All of it except the parts about Beast; I took credit for her contributions and for once she didn't seem to mind.

As I ate, Evangelina told about the witch coven she had visited. They had claimed they knew nothing about the attack on my house, but there were inconsistencies in the story they told, and Evangelina could tell they were keeping things back. Also, only three members met with her, when there were supposed to be five adult members in the coven. So something was hinky, not that Evangelina would ever use such a term.

Before she finished, while I was still eating, a knock sounded and Rick opened the side door. I'd heard his Kowbike and knew he was coming. I introduced him around and Evangelina dished him up a bowl of stew.

He sat and dug into the food; halted with mouth full, chewed, and swallowed. "Dang, this is good." He looked at Evangelina. "You cook this?" When she nodded, he looked at me and said, "No offense, but our date's off. I have to marry her." My tears had dried and I twitched a strained smile. He was trying to lighten an impossibly dark situation, and I appreciated that. Not that it would work. He went back to the stew, dipping a biscuit into it and sopping up the juice. He also changed the subject.

"I got news from the files. I spotted something when I was photocopying the witch and vampire files." Too involved with the meal, Rick didn't notice the intense interest of the three witches at the table. I was pretty sure he knew Molly was a witch, but not the others.

"That witch vamp Renee and her husband were once—when they all were human—the owners of the clan's bloodmaster, Bettina." My mouth fell open. Rick grinned at my reaction. "Bettina was sold by Tristan Damours in 1770 to a vamp madame named Bethany who shipped her to New Orleans and put her to work as a sex slave in the Quarter. Bettina had a gift for satisfying customers and she and Bethany ran a successful business."

Bethany had owned slaves? I shook my head, wondering about the rift between Bethany and Sabina during the Civil War. If it hadn't been about slaves . . .

"Later she got sick—I talked to a nurse I know and he thinks it sounds like the clap. Bettina was turned at Bethany's request to save her life." Rick pulled papers from his leather jacket and passed them to me. I took the pages, opening them to expose a photo of Bettina, decked out in the clothes of a soiled dove, a corset, pantaloons, and a shawl.

"Bethany didn't turn her?" Evangelina asked.

"No. She's out-clan, and no out-clan can turn a human. They can't offer safety during the chained years, so they can't turn anyone. No protection. And at the time, the info of the Rousseau curse of insanity was still a secret. When he was asked, the Rousseau master agreed to turn her and adopt her into his clan."

He turned a page and pointed to a line written in a flowery cursive script. "Bettina was set free by accident, here in New Orleans—no one says what kind of accident—when she was still rogue. She went hunting for the Damours to kill them. She failed. When Bettina became blood-master of her clan, she had power over Renee and tried to kill the long-chained Damours. Renee stopped her. No record of how."

He stuffed half a flaky biscuit into his mouth and talked through it. "Bettina is our way in. We need to talk to her. If we can find her."

I felt a vibration and opened my cell. It was Derek Lee. "Yeah?"

"I'm out front. Take these pictures. They give my men the willies."

"How many did you get?"

"All of them."

"Who came when we got out of there? Cops?" I didn't look at Rick, but he was looking at me, speculation in his gaze as he ate.

"No cops. Human blood-servants and slaves. I left a man watching from across the street. They're loading the long-chained ones into an eighteen-wheeler. Cleaning out the place. My man'll get a tracking transmitter on it if at all possible. That's what you meant by using them as bait, isn't it?"

I could hear the grin in his words. "Thanks."

"Let us have the bounty on the heads of the long-chained and that'll be thanks enough."

I remembered the faces of the raving vamps. The way the girl vamp licked at her own arm, trying to taste her own blood. On one hand, it seemed wrong to give them true-death if there was any chance at a sane future, but not if that future sanity was promised at the death of children. "They're yours."

I closed the cell and stood, looking down at the witches. "I have some evidence." Rick looked up at that, his expression saying clearly that he wasn't sure he should be here. "Don't ask," I warned him. He sat back and set down his spoon.

"I have a feeling this stuff isn't pretty. It might involve the ceremonies where vamps sacrifice witch children." Molly touched her mouth, her fingers quivering. "If you can't handle it, go upstairs. And you," I said to Rick, "you stay out of sight and don't look at the deliverymen." I went to the door.

Derek Lee already had a half dozen paintings on the

porch. I grabbed two in each hand and carted them inside. They were in heavy gilt frames, each weighing about forty pounds, a lot heavier than they'd felt back at the lair, with adrenaline surging and Beast close to the surface. I propped the paintings against the couch and went back for more. The van roared off as I worked. There were fifteen paintings. Rick was lining them up on the floor, propped along the furniture.

Her mouth in a tight line, Evangelina was changing the order, separating the paintings into two groups, one group on one side of the room, facing the other. I closed the door when I brought in the last one. Molly was in Evan's arms, her face in his shoulder. I could smell her fear. Evan's fear was subsumed beneath a rising anger. Evangelina's scent was more complex, her emotions tightly controlled.

Rick was ignoring me, studying the paintings. I joined him. This wasn't the first time that I had gotten important info from vamp paintings. "Good thing vamps chronicled their every important move in oil on canvas," I muttered. "Self-obsessed bloodsuckers that they are."

Evangelina said, "That trait may have come from the fact that silvered mirrors reacted to them and didn't show their reflections well. So they sat for paintings to see how they looked." She had separated the paintings into two groups according to time period, one batch with the female participants dressed in belled skirts, big sleeves, and corsets that came to a point below the navel, and for the men, knee pants, lace and satin, ugly big-buckled shoes, with white hair piled up tall. The other batch depicted people—well, vamps and witches—in high-waisted, slender dresses that showed a lot of cleavage, delicate shoes, and natural-colored hair.

Though the participants changed through the years, all of the ones in charge of the ceremonies held knives and had fangs. Some of the vamps in the center of the witch circles and pentagrams had fangs and were clearly raving; in several paintings, they were the two teenagers I'd seen in the warehouse, the long-chained ones. The sacrificial children were dead, their throats cut, lives forfeited in the pentagram's center. In others, they were being drunk from as they died.

In the later depictions, the experiments had changed several times. One showed the long-chained ripping out the throats of the sacrifices and drinking them down. In one, the adult was, I guessed, Renee. Her husband and her two children were in the circle, savaging a human. Two younger, fangless children were being sacrificed by Renee, a silver knife held high. On the latter canvases picturing both Damours, a bearded vamp was assisting the ceremony. The brother? Wasn't he supposed to be the last of the three to find sanity? I rearranged the order of two paintings and smiled grimly. "Evangelina, you're the educated one. What time periods are we seeing?"

"I never made a study of fashion," she said dryly, "but I'd say the older batch is from the seventeen hundreds and the more recent from the early eighteen hundreds. This one"—she tapped a painting in which the participants wore modern-looking clothes—"I'd say came from the nineteen seventies."

"That's what I figured." In it, only the children were in the circle, feeding on a witch child. Adults stood outside, at points of the pentagram. They bore striking resemblance to one another. They had to be the Damours.

"You understand this?" Rick asked. "Because I sure don't."

"There *were* no notes of the Rousseau experiments from the seventeen hundreds. Nothing was destroyed in the fire." I turned one of the oils into the light better to study the face of the strange vamp. I wondered who he was. "These paintings were the records of experiments, shipped to the States, probably in the frames, but behind other, less important paintings. Some of the later ones were maybe painted here. But whenever they were painted, this *is* the Rousseau record of the experiments to rid the clan of insanity."

"They could be transported, hidden behind other paintings, but in plain sight, and no one would ever know," Evangelina said.

There were definite differences in the styles of the paintings as well as the experiments. In the older set, there was no pentagram in the witch circle. No crosses on the trees. In the more recent batch, all the elements I'd seen in the young-rogue burial sites were present. Except . . . "In the older ones, the circles and pentagrams are made by cutting into the earth, like with a spade. In the newer ones, the circles are made with other things. Something that looks like powder or flour in one, flowers in one. Feathers. And stones in two, one with pebbles, one with shaped stones, like bricks."

"And the sacrificial athames in the older depictions are steel. The most recent ones indicate silver," Evangelina said. "The vamps in charge change."

"And there's this bearded guy. He's in . . ."—Evangelina counted —"six of the later paintings. Look at his position. Almost as if he's in charge now. And I'm betting that necklace on his chest in all the paintings is an amulet that lets him draw power from the others."

I studied the amulet. I didn't know much about gems, but it looked like a pink diamond or a washed-out, pale ruby, about the size of my thumb from the last knuckle to the thumb tip, faceted all over. It was on a heavy gold chain, a thick casing holding the gem, the casing shaped of horns and claws. It looked barbaric, brutal, and powerful, an artifact from a distant time and place.

"That's what they intend for my babies?" Molly asked. She was standing where she could see all the paintings at once, her hands fisted so tightly her fingers were white, fear and grief and fierce anger on her face. I wanted to promise that I'd get to the children in time, that I'd save them. But the promises were for me, not for her. Molly knew what we were up against now. I nodded instead and went to the last painting from the eighteen hundreds. It was different from all the others. In it was an extra figure racing downhill, her white dress flying back with her speed, eyes blazing, holding a flaming, bloody cross. Sabina Delgado y Aguilera coming to the rescue, her face in a rictus scream of pain, her arms on fire, flames licking up toward her body. The vamps in the circle were running away, faces full of terror.

Sabina had known exactly what I was describing when I told her about the young rogue and the witch circle in the woods. She had known and hadn't told me.

A soft knock sounded at the door and Molly whirled, the reek of her rage and panic bitter on the air. No one had set wards. I peeked through a sliver of clear glass, glanced back once to see Rick with his weapon drawn and Evan with his hands out in a warding gesture. I opened the door. Two witches stood on the shallow stoop. I had never seen them before, but I recognized their scent.

Beast reared up fast, her pelt pressing against my skin, her claws sharp in my fingertips. *Thief-of-kits!* Beast lunged into my mind. Flamed into my eyes.

One witch, petite and blond, stepped back fast, shock on her face. Threw up her hands, palms out, power gathered there. Before she could throw the spell, I leaped. Was on her, a vamp-killer at her throat. Her thief-of-kits scent oily in my nose. "Any reason I shouldn't just kill you where you stand?" I growled.

Screaming sounded all around me. The other witch begging, Molly shouting my name. Evan roaring. But the witch's terror was so strong it was sweet in my nostrils and mouth, heady. Her blood was mine. I slid the blade across her flesh, only a fraction. The witch's skin spilt. She was crying. I inhaled, smiling, showing killing teeth. Whispered, "Thief-of-kits. Die."

It was Evangelina who placed her hands on my arms, power flowing up from her fingers like cool bayou water, drawing away my rage, her voice soothing. "Wait. Not yet. Not just yet. Jane, let her go. I have her. She will not get away."

I met her eyes, my voice hissing and guttural. "Thief-of-kits."

Amazingly, Evangelina smiled, and suddenly she was beautiful, greenish eyes sparkling, her face young. "And we have her now. She will not get away." She pushed at the vamp-killer, a gentle pressure. I blinked, Beast vision overlapping with mine. Evangelina's peace chilled my killing heat. Soothed me like a hand down my pelt. I let her press the weapon away. My fingers slowly opened, one at a time. I released the witch. Under Evangelina's hands, my rage eased, settled back, and found a resting place, like a sun-warmed rock in my mind. Unsteady, blinking in the sharp man-light, I stepped back. I was still holding the knife. It was the one Evan had carved for me and when I looked up, I saw his eyes on the hilt.

"Please come inside," Evangelina said to the two witches, her tone genial and gracious, a hostess asking guests in. "And you will tell us everything." Her lips twisted into a smile that made my heart stutter. "Or I will kill you myself."

My Beast liked this woman. She was wise and strong.

I went inside and busied myself making tea. Ignoring the stares from the others. Finding my place, myself again, inside Beast's angry heart.

The witches' story was simple, and so stupid that it was believable. A vampire sorcerer, a male witch who had been turned, had come to their small coven, five women of the same bloodline, who worked together. He'd claimed he had proof that Leo Pellissier was kidnapping and killing children who carried the witch gene, killing off the next generation of witches to cement his waning power. He had proved he was more powerful than Leo by walking in the last rays of the sun. They had believed his story. Against the wishes of the city's other covens, they had agreed to help. Working with them, he had identified several undocumented witch children and teens and staked out the perimeters of their homes.

When the attack came against Bliss, protected behind only electronic security, without wards, the vamp and the two witches were watching. Two vamps, most likely Renee and Tristan, had spelled Bliss, who had come out of her room through the window. The watching witches had attacked to save her. But the vamp who had befriended them turned on his witch helpers, joining the Damours. Both witches were injured.

The Damours had placed an amulet on each witch's chest, into her blood, and drained her power. Carrying Bliss and forcing the wounded witches, they had climbed over the fence and blasted their way through the wards on my house. They'd taken the children and gotten away, dropping off the conned, injured, magically drained witches to make their way home in the dark.

"Why didn't the vamps drain you?" Rick asked.

"One tried. The little girl who lived here hit him with

something," the smaller blonde said. "I didn't see what, but it stopped him. He looked at her, and then he let us go. It was weird."

Angelina. Angelina had caught his attention. With her strong powers bound just under the surface, Angie Baby was the perfect sacrifice. I wanted to rip the heads off the witches' shoulders for their stupidity.

"We were both pretty bad off, drained of our gifts," the other witch said, "but as soon as we could, we came straight over here to tell you." The witches looked at each other and back to me, fearfully. The women were sitting around the kitchen table, Rick leaning against the cabinet, Evan standing in the doorway, as if he couldn't be any closer to the grouping or he would kill someone. Evan was a huge man. If he lost his temper, he might be dangerous. I stood off to the side, silent, knowing that Beast was still in my eyes, the full moon holding her close to the surface. For now, she was content to let me remain alpha, but I didn't expect it to last.

The smaller blonde said, "I'm Butterfly Lily. My mom is Feather Storm." When she saw Evangelina's brows go up, she grinned. "Okay, not our real names, our coven names, and the only ones we'll give you tonight." Her smile fell away as if the tissue beneath broke apart and pulled the emotion with it.

"We thought we were doing the right thing, saving witch children, working with the vampires to heal the rift between our races. Picking the winning side." Butterfly Lily ducked her head and her voice went softer. "Mom and I are not real powerful. Mostly we're used as routing for group workings."

She said to Evangelina, "We brought him to our coven. He promised to help us catch the kidnapper. We believed him. He was convincing."

Evangelina said nothing, her expression both sad and condemning. She sighed. "Go on."

"I know. It was stupid. *We* were stupid. He had us watch the vamps for weeks. Had us track them to their parties and to their lairs. Gathering information."

There had been five witches outside of the vamp party,

under a glamour. Hiding. Watching. This coven. Doing the dirty work of the Damours.

"He got us to track down every nonaligned witch and witch child in the city so he could *protect* them. He said that once he had enough evidence to prove that Leo Pellissier was kidnapping witches, he was going up against the blood-master of the city. When he won, he'd declare peace with us and sit down to negotiate."

I was fighting an enemy I'd never met face-to-face. An enemy I'd seen only on canvas and in the young faces of his children. I wanted to weep.

Feather Storm said, "The city's covens are . . . really mad at us. We'll help any way we can."

Beast under control, I left the room, and brought back the painting that showed the ones I thought were the three Damours and their children. I shoved the painting in front of the women and they recoiled from it as if it were evil. "These are the witches who took the children?" I asked. When the witches with the silly names nodded, I looked at Rick. "If all three of the adult Damours are sane, that means the blood magic ceremonies worked at some point for adults, but didn't work on children. They're experimenting on strangers, turning them, changing the ceremony each time, trying to find what will succeed. That's what this is all about. This is the proof. It's a way to bring people over without the insanity of the devoveo, the young-rogue state, and to allow the long-chained to find sanity. It ties everything together. And it means they're close to a solution to the devoveo.

"They know if they're caught they'll be killed and there will be another purge, so they're attacking first, forging alliances with two strong clans, undermining Leo's power base, pumping up his enemy Rafael. I have a feeling they might be getting the Crips to fight other gangs too, keeping the police too busy to see what's about to happen, which is a war with Leo. Tell Jodi. See what you can put together."

My cell rang and I answered. Derek said, "No dice, Princess. My guy got a transponder onto the truck taking the long-chained, but the security found it. We lost 'em."

My heart fell. "Okay, Derek, thanks." I disconnected and looked at my guests. "I'm going out," I said. "I'll be back." They fussed and yelled and made a stink, but I reweaponed up, got back on Bitsa, and took off.

I should have slashed his tires. Now there was nothing I could do about Rick following me on his Kow-bike. Not a dang thing.

CHAPTER 21

Will not be caught in predator's stare

I had no idea how late it was and I didn't care. I called Bruiser and told him what I needed. Unlike my house-guests, he didn't argue. When I reached the vamp graveyard, I roared around the gate and up the shell drive to the chapel without setting off any alarms. I killed the bike and stalked to the steps. The Kawasaki came to a halt behind me. The night fell silent. I didn't glance back, but I could smell gun oil and knew Rick had drawn his weapon.

I raced up the steps. Banged my fist against the chapel door. It echoed within and against the crypts behind me. I heard the softer *scrunch* of shell as Rick left his bike and joined me, standing a little to my left.

There was no answer to my knock and Beast, fighting her own fierce frustration, bled strength into my blood in a raging of power. I gripped the door handle and turned. Threw my body against the painted wood. The door slammed open, banging into the inside wall. With Beast's night vision I took in the place at a glance.

The chapel was one long room, white-painted walls and backless wood benches in rows. Moonlight poured through red-paned stained glass windows, tingeing everything with the tint of watered blood. At the front was a tall table holding a candle and a low bowl of incense, smoking, filling the air with the scent of rosemary, sage, and something bitter, like camphor. A rocking chair sat beside the table, and on its other side, a low stone bier carved with a statue lying faceup, marble hands crossed on her chest. I strode to the bier and identified the carving as Sabina. It was her coffin. I had a feeling she slept in it.

I pushed the stone cover, bending and putting Beast's strength into it. The top moved with a heavy, grating sound, stone on stone. It weighed several hundred pounds. I heaved, breathed with a groan, shoving, the air painful in my lungs. I moved it a few inches. Behind me a lighter clicked and flame brightened the room as Rick lit candles. Holding one, he joined me and we looked through the narrow opening, into the crypt.

The stone bier held no coffin, but was padded and lined with tufted white silk. There were boxes inside and I pulled three of them out the narrow crack I had made. With a callous disregard for vampire history, I opened each, exposing in one a bit of parchment from a scroll. It was so old it was crumbling, bits of brown flaking away. I closed the box and lifted the next one. There was a name burned into the top, Ioudas Issachar. Which meant exactly nothing to me. Opening it, I found a velvet-lined interior, cradling the cross the priestess had used to dispel the liver-eater when it attacked her.

"That's the cross in the picture," Rick said. "The one the burning vampire was carrying."

I pulled it from its velvet bed and Rick moved the candle closer. She had called it the Blood Cross. The wood was unshaped, tightly grained, the pieces like rough stakes, the splintered ends smoothed and oiled. The wire that wrapped the two pieces, shaping them into a cross, was brass, green with verdigris. The cross was weighty, much heavier than it appeared, and it was old. Ancient. I held it to my nose and smelled no smoke, no flames, and the wood was discolored only by time, not fire.

"You would dare to steal from me?" Before I could turn, Sabina was on me. Her eyes were vamped out. Her fangs snapped down. Faster than I could draw a breath, she bent me back across her knee. Claws pierced through my leathers and chain mail, her fingertips drawing my blood. "Thief," she hissed.

Sabina's hinged fangs slowly swung down, three inches long, white in the candlelight, touching my throat above my collar. My throat was barely healed from Leo's mauling; I might not survive this one. A harsh *schnick* sounded and Rick held the barrel of his gun to her temple. She didn't react. But Rick no longer moved. The taint of fear poured from his pores. She had immobilized him with her mind. He couldn't even breathe. I knew what it felt like to be held like that. The adrenaline-spiked terror.

I swallowed. A bead of cold sweat trickled from under my arm and touched a pricked spot on my side, stinging. "No. Not steal. Borrow. Whatever this is, it works like a weapon on vampires. I just need it to save three witches, two of them children, who will be sacrificed in the next few hours or days." I felt her tighten, a near-human reaction, to my words. "I need to use it like you did, when you raised the flaming cross and chased the vampires away from the blood magic they tried." Her body reacted again, easing, softening. I heard Rick take a strangled breath. "Let me use the Blood Cross," I whispered.

Her head snake-tilted, the motion eerie. "Do you claim to be our savior, then?"

"I don't think it's likely," I said.

"Yet you dare to touch the Blood Cross. The cross of the curse. *The cross of Ioudas Issachar.*"

"*Ioudas Issachar*," Rick forced out, the *S*s sibilant with his straining. "Judas Iscariot."

The priestess and I looked at Rick. His face was grayish, his eyes fighting panic. I felt Sabina release him enough for him to draw a full breath. "Ioudas Issachar," he breathed again. "Judas Iscariot." His eyes tilted to me. "Catholic school. Latin 101."

"You know the history of sin and shame that is our birthright?"

Rick's expression said he had nothing else to offer. I took a shot and said, "The Sons of Darkness. And the Blood Cross."

Sabina's expression didn't change, but when she opened her mouth she laughed. The sound was lonely as a wolf howl, the power in it thudding into the walls and making the window glass ring. The candle flames wavered with its vibration. A desolate humor, bitter as wormwood, slicked my skin with its desperation. "The Sons of Darkness."

Just as she had taken us over, she released us. Faster than I could follow, she was gone; the candle flames fluttered, nearly guttering in the small whirlwind of her movement. She was across the chapel in an eyeblink. She stared at the cross in my hands. It was glowing faintly now, a curious phosphorescence. Rick took several gasping breaths, loud in the silence, his knuckles white on his weapon. We shared a glance, and he blinked, breathing hard, deciding. Something moved deep in his black eyes, like the trail of an alligator in dark water.

Carefully, he slid the 9 mm into his shoulder holster. His hand was shaking, a fine tremor as if an electric current flowed through him. The gun wouldn't have killed Sabina fast enough to do us any good anyway, even if it was loaded with silver shot and he emptied the clip at her. She was too old. She would have killed us both as she died. Rick controlled his breathing, and moved, standing at my side, our shoulders touching, facing the priestess.

"Who were they?" I asked. "The Sons of Darkness? What is the Blood Cross?"

Sabina stood, white in the disturbed candle flames, wavering with the shadows. Resignation and something more intense than relief flashed over her. An emotion so sharp it left a residue on her flesh like a scar, like a battle ended, and then it was gone.

She took a breath she didn't need and sighed. Her eyes bled back to near-human, her fangs clicked back into the roof of her mouth. When she spoke, it was with the formal cant of an oft-repeated quote. " 'Ioudas Issachar, son of Simeon, then one of the twelve, went to the chief priests, and said to them: What will you give me, and I will deliver him unto you? Hearing it, they were glad, and they promised they would give him money. And they gave unto him thirty pieces of silver.' You know this story?"

"The story of Judas Iscariot, the betrayer of the Christ."

"The thief," she said. "The murderer. The bringer of evil." I nodded.

" 'And the thief betrayed his master with a kiss of love.

And the great teacher and healer, he who was without sin, was killed upon a cross. And Ioudas hanged himself. His body was buried.' All know this. And though all believed that he was dead, the tomb was empty, and the teacher walked among his followers. They claimed he rose from the dead. But what the Christian scriptures do not say is what happened on the fourth day.

"When the sons of Ioudas heard that the master had risen, they went to the mount of the skull to find the cross where he died, to steal the wood bathed in his blood, to work arcane magics with the blood and the cross. But the crosses of the thief, the murderer, and the rabbi had been pulled down, broken up, and piled together, the wood confused and mixed."

A frisson of presentiment washed over me, chilling my skin, slowing my blood. My hands clenched on the Blood Cross. I looked at it, at the wood that was glowing with a strange, steady warmth.

"'They took it all. By dark of night they pulled their father's body from the grave, and with their witch power and arcane rites they laid his body on the pile of bloody, broken wood. Some say they sacrificed the life of their small sister on the wooden pile. Some say not. But whatever rite they used, they sought by their magic to raise their father from the dead. And he rose, though he was yet dead, his soul given over to the night and the dark. Soulless, he walked for two nights, a ravening beast. And he could not be killed, though he rotted and the flesh fell from his bones to writhe upon the ground. And thinking that some benefit might yet be gleaned from their sin, his sons drank the blood and ate the flesh of their father. And they were changed.'" Her eyes focused, coming back as if chased, returning to the now from the story she told, the history she recounted. Sabina looked back and forth between us. A bloody tear trailed down her pale cheek though her face was empty, hard and cold as a carved stone.

"'They rose, but not as they had hoped. Because of this abomination of evil magic, they were cursed to live only in the night, Sons of Darkness, they and their descendants. They craved blood ever after, rising each night, feeding and killing. And after a time they made others of their kind. But the progeny rose as ravening beasts, bloody murderers. The devoveo.'" Her face was almost pensive. Almost, but the difference, the . . . lack . . . was unsettling.

"As we inherited the curse, so we inherited the wood of the Blood Cross. Though it often kills the bearer, burning her unto true-death, with it we can bring much power against blood rites and evil. It is our only salvation."

I wasn't sure what she meant. Not quite. Not . . . really. "The cross." I lifted it, stared at it. The soft phosphorescent glow brightened under my gaze. Prickles moved across my shoulders like my pelt rising. Rick took a half step away, brought himself up short with a visible effort. Staring at the cross I held. "The Blood Cross. It's wood. Wood from the cross of . . ."—I took a breath that ached, cold and dry, like breathing down ashes—"Christ?"

"Or the wood from the cross of the thief or murderer," Rick said, his voice cool and dry.

Sabina didn't answer. I set the glowing cross in the box. In the velvet bed shaped for it. And pulled my hands away. As I did, the phosphorescence died, leaving only wood. I closed the box and set it behind me on the stone bier.

Had I held part of the cross of Christ? Or only bespelled wood? Could I believe anything Sabina had said? Could it possibly be true? The important thing, I realized, was that she believed it. Whatever this cross was made of, it had real power over her. A shiver raced through me. I wavered on my feet and Rick caught me one handed, steadying me. He was moving fast, faster than a normal human, still touched by vamp blood from Leo's healing, perhaps.

I pulled the parts of my scattered mind, of myself, back in, breathed deeply to cement them for this moment. I found my voice. "You stopped a blood rite with the cross once before. If I can find where it will be done, will you bring it and stop this rite?"

"No."

"Oh." Her answer shocked me. After seeing her in the painting, the cross flaming in her hands, I had expected that she would help stop the Damours. I felt the adrenaline seep out of my system. I had no place else to go now. I knew she wouldn't let me take the Blood Cross. She would kill me and Rick and a hundred others to keep it safe with her.

To Rick, she said, "The foolish human who draws a useless gun on a Mithran Elder will wait outside."

I looked at Rick, his eyes black in the night, though he didn't look at me. He was staring at the box that might hold part of the Holy Cross. Or might not. He'd been a Catholic schoolboy. The hidden relics of the true cross were part of Catholic lore for two thousand years. He swallowed, the sound loud in the silent chapel, but when he spoke it was with his usual insouciance. "If you aren't out in fifteen minutes, I'll come drag your cold dead body out and give it proper burial."

I laughed softly through my nose. Reached up and pushed the Elvis curl back across his head, letting my fingertips scrape gently over his forehead, my touch demanding his attention. He dragged his eyes to mine. Something blinked back into them.

"Thanks," I said. "But you better get help first. I have a feeling she'd be hard to kill."

"You think?" He touched his throat, straightened his shoulders, and left the chapel, his boots tapping on the stairs leading to the graveyard of the vamps.

"I cannot help you to defeat this evil," Sabina said. "I cannot lift the Blood Cross again so soon. I would not survive a second immolation in a decade." I remembered the painting of Sabina, racing downhill, her arms on fire. Had she nearly died from using it? And again when she chased away the liver-eater? She moved with that lightning speed, leaning over the open stone casket. Close to me. My body reacted, but far too late, with a small spurt of fear and power. She caught my eyes and held me, her mind strong as steel chains, standing so close I smelled the vamp scent of her, dry and heated, like wind over a desert, arid and barren, and beneath the desert scent, oddly, faintly, like dried rose petals. "But I will give you a sliver of it."

My mind went blank like a snow-blown night, no thought, no emotion, nothing. Sabina was giving me . . . what? I had a moment of disconnect. Of being lost in the snow of my own thoughts, cold and confused and disoriented. For a moment that seemed to last longer than it should.

A warning whispered deep in my mind. *Not prey. Will*

not be caught in predator's stare. A silent weight of claws against my brain, pressed down. Slicing.

Surprise flashed across Sabina's face. She broke her stare and turned away, bent and rose and pivoted again, all in one motion, her eyes again holding me in the dim light. "It is priceless. It has left my hands only once before, in all the long years it has been in my safekeeping. You will return it to me when the threat of blood rites is shattered."

I nodded like a toy doll, agreeing to anything, everything, without thought. She had rolled me. My hands went sweaty and clumsy. "With this you are invincible over anything not of the Light. It will destroy the descendants of the Sons of Darkness, even the eldest of the Mithrans. To prick the skin of a vampire with a sliver of the Blood Cross will cause him to burn, ashes to ashes, dust to dust. True-death. All others of the cursed will sicken and likely die.

"But you must use care. It is possible that your kind are cursed of the Dark as well, though from a time long before the cross. If the wood of the Blood Cross pricks your skin, you may fall violently ill. You may die."

My heart shuddered in my chest. "My kind? You know what I am?" My words were only a whisper in the dark of the vampire chapel.

"You are she who walks in the skins of the beasts." She looked down into the bier, as if she would inventory the contents. Or as if she wouldn't look me in the eye. Beast, who had withdrawn into the deeps of my mind, looked out again through my eyes. "The owl . . . It came to me, at a time of gathering and blood, when we put Katherine to earth to heal. It cried out its lonely call to me, a bird of the night, a bird of a different place and time. The owl has long been a harbinger of change, of danger, of loss. You are that beast of change and loss. That harbinger of bitter defeat. Of true-death."

Beast's pelt roiled under my skin, uneasy. I had no idea what to say to Sabina. I hadn't intended anything when I chose the Bubo bubo form to skinwalk in the first time I came here. I'd just needed to be a large bird to conceal my scent, so I could fly here and spy on the vamps, back when Katie had been put to earth to heal. I hadn't known owls meant something to vamps.

Sabina held out a small drawstring bag, destroying the moment when I should have spoken, should have asked her more. I took the bag and it was much lighter than I expected, silk velvet outside, padded within. I felt something inside it, long and slender, the length and shape of a ballpoint pen. Or a hair stick. Or a small stake.

Understanding came to me all at once, all the old lore, all the deeper meaning of the curse of the vampires. "This is why wood stakes kill vamps, isn't it? Because you were made through magic and blood and wood, from long-lost earth magic, knotted with evil." I stared at the velvet bag in my pale hands. Shadows and candlelight moved across my flesh as if searching for my twined soul. "This is why you have to drink blood to stay alive. And it has something to do with why so many of you don't survive being turned, don't survive the chained years. Right?"

"It is the curse we bear." She turned away and sat in her chair, rocking, the wood creaking quietly. She said, "Two Mithrans mind-joined tonight. I felt the joining, I felt their intent." She tilted her head in that reptilian manner, staring across the room at her broken door, hanging skewed on its twisted hinges. "It is little known that I am open for a moment to any of my flock who choose the anamchara way. As they join, they open, and I am part of them, part of their mind and their purpose. Tonight Rafael of Mearkanis and Adrianna, scion to St. Martin, banded together and killed her sire and his heir. Then they joined their minds into one, and made alliance against their enemies. In that moment, I knew their minds as I know my own.

"They intend to move against the master of the city after the full moon, taking him in personal combat. Then they will kill all the witches in the city, claiming this territory as their own. And they will kill the Rogue Hunter, she who hunts their kind, for they fear you." She smiled slightly, her head still tilted as if her neck were broken. "You do not seem so fearful to me. I hope my trust is well placed, my weapon truly given."

"I hope so too."

"The heavens move with both order and chaos," she said, as if searching for meaning, for the words to explain the unexplainable, "with light and dark, energy and matter, emptiness and fullness. This is a time of change, when many tides rush together." She raised her head to its proper position. "When the old ways return, when the old darkness fights for supremacy against that which is new, against the light of the world." She touched her lips with her tongue, and it made a dry raspy sound, inhuman and cold, like snakes slithering against one another.

Visibly, she gathered herself. "It is not within my duties or power to interfere in a legal challenge against the master of the city, but it would be dangerous for the humans should the allied challenge of St. Martin, Mearkanis, and Rousseau defeat Pellissier. Without an heir, such a challenge is a great danger to him." She looked at me. "Pellissier is like a rock in the confluence of many streams, attacked on all sides, buffeted."

The old vamp had been awfully agreeable about helping this time, when she had been so obfuscatory before. It must have been some freaky vision she saw in the midst of the vamps' mind-joining. It made me suspicious, but I had no one else to turn to. "I can let him know about the attack," I said. "Without mentioning your name."

Sabina inclined her head and I figured I had been maneuvered into doing her bidding. Before I could respond, she said, "There will be no more blood rites in the forest near this place. I have seen to it. The three Damours will not be allowed to enter this holy ground again. If they have another place for the rites, they will go there, forced there for the light of the moon."

I couldn't help the grin that split my face. I knew where the children and Bliss would be. I knew!

Sabina chuckled, her face instantly human-looking, mobile, and weirdly cheerful. "Go now. You have much work to do and little time."

I felt as if a large hand pushed me toward the outside, toward the night and the full moon. All at once, the candles were snuffed and the chapel went dark, as I left the place I had desecrated, passing beyond the door I had ruined. I stepped from the chapel to the sound of the stone lid being slid into place on her bier and the chair treads starting to rock on the wood floor. Outside, under the light of the full moon, shadows rested black across the grass, striping the white-shell walks like wounds in the skin of the netherworld, open and bleeding into the land. Rick was standing at the bottom of the stairs and when I descended, he gripped my arms, stopping me. "You okay?"

"Yeah. I think so."

He searched my face, his Frenchy black eyes holding me more securely than his hands. Finally he nodded. "Okay. That was seriously weird."

"You were listening?"

"Yeah. What next, Master Vampire Hunter?"

"I need to talk to some guys I know," I said, shooting him a look, thinking of Derek Lee, putting it all together. "I need to go to New Orleans City Park. And I need to talk to Leo."

He nodded, his face serious. "Visiting Leo sounds like a fun date. I'll bring the beer."

I spluttered with laughter, which was what he'd intended, and some of the darkness Sabina had painted on my soul dissipated. He reached up and traced the corner of my lips with a fingertip, the caress soft, making me shiver. I stepped away and he dropped his hand. "Seriously, Rick. I need to talk to Leo, tell him about the plot and the coup and murder of St. Martin's master and heir. We're gonna have a lot of dead vamps and a lot more dead humans. But I don't have *time* to do that and . . ." I looked up at the full moon. Frustration zinged through me. "I can't do it all. I can't deal with Leo *and* get the kids back *and* kill the blood-sucking Damours. And the kids are more important than anything else." I didn't have time for everything, and so someone was gonna die who shouldn't die. And it would be my fault. Again.

"As a cop, I have to warn you that even though the legal definition of a vamp as human hasn't been established in the courts, killing one without a contract might be considered illegal. Except for killing rogues. Usually. So I don't want to know about that part. But as to warning Leo, I'll do it. Well, Jodi and Rosen and I'll do it. What?" His eyes narrowed. "What's that look for? This isn't just your fight, you know. We live here. We'll be the cops cleaning up after the bloodbath."

I took a breath. It seemed to fill me for the first time

since Sabina grabbed my throat. A curious delight kicked around inside me. With one exception—a bad exception, when a cop I liked a lot was killed—I've always worked alone, so I wasn't used to having help. But Rick was right. This wasn't just my fight. "You'll go talk to the master of the city." It wasn't precisely a question, and not a statement either, but somewhere in between. "Right now," I clarified.

"Sure. Why not? Got nothing better to do than kick some master-of-the-city vamp-butt."

I chuckled, imagining that scene.

"Or just dicking around with his mind. Me and Jodi might like that. And Rosen," he added.

"Okay. Thanks."

Rick straddled his bike and called Jodi Richoux and Sloan Rosen, and both agreed to meet us on a narrow bridge a mile from the Mississippi. I had made my call while Rick made his, the beauty of modern life, instant multiple-person communication. Rick helmeted up and I followed his lead. And then, because I had to head that direction anyway, I followed him back toward the city. A mile out, just past a small bridge, he slowed and pulled under a tree. Leading me to think they had been working late, the two other cops were already waiting. They'd gotten here fast, the engine of an unmarked cop car still hot and ticking.

Jodi was sitting on the hood, dressed in what I was coming to think of as her uniform: dress slacks, little stretchy shirt, boots, and jacket. Sloan, standing beside her and leaning against the car, was wearing jeans and a dark blue Windbreaker with the word POLICE emblazoned across it in big white letters. I filled them in and they discussed how the three-man crew wanted to handle the upcoming talk—which they decided should be off the books and unreported to the high muckety-mucks of the NOPD brass. I liked these three. They thought outside the vamp box. Feeling as though the talk with Leo Pellissier was in good hands, I roared off for a quick stop at home and then a rendezvous with black magic and blood rites in the park.

CHAPTER 22

Pardon me if we don't bleed for you, babe

My arrival at the house woke everyone, the bike's roar better than an alarm. Before I entered the house, I jogged to the pile of broken boulders and scraped my gold nugget across a larger piece of stone—a lodestone of sorts to the shift I'd need soon. Moving fast, I grabbed five pounds of steak out of the fridge, shoved them into a Ziploc, and tossed them onto the porch. Tossed a bag of Snickers on top.

I made it to my bedroom and back out before Molly and Evan met me at the bottom of the stairs, following me and babbling questions I refused to answer. I just didn't have time. But Molly noticed the two zippered bags and the fetish necklace I'd come for and blocked the door back to my bike with her body. I thought about taking the ruined window, but when I looked that way, it had been boarded over with a sheet of plywood and Evan had taken up a stance in front of it, his arms crossed over his barrel chest, his red beard sleep-tangled. Sighing, I looked Molly in the eye, letting a bit of Beast rise in me. "You know better than to pen me in."

Her white gown outlined her rounded curves, making her look too soft and feminine to best me in a fight, but her expression belied her size. She looked as if she'd try to take me if I pushed past her. "Tough." When I scowled at her, she said, "Not until you tell us what's happening. Why you're going to . . ." She pointed at the necklace and didn't finish the sentence.

"It's the first night of the full moon. And I think—I hope—I can find the site of the rites tonight. But I need to go *now*."

"And you think we'll let you try to stop an act of black magic, a major working of blood rites, *alone*?" She was aghast, her tone asking me if I was out of my mind. "Jane Yellowrock. Someone *stole our children*. If you think you know where they are, then we will be there. Like it or not." Her face hardened. "And besides, the vampires who took our children are witches. You'll need us to stop the rites without making all the magic go haywire.

"What?" she demanded of the surprise on my face. "You didn't know you can't just interrupt a major working without consequences? You'll need us to fight. And you'll need us to protect the children."

"I knew," I grumbled, remembering the smell of the torn and blasted wards. "But you'll be in the way of me finding them." My eyes told her I'd be in Big Cat form. "I have some . . . guys . . . who will be close by. They'll have guns."

"Which will not stop a blood rite without a detonation big enough to take you all out."

"Crap." I hadn't planned this well enough.

"We'll be close by," she bargained, "with whoever you're working with. Out of sight. You'll have your phone. You'll call us when you find the site. Then we'll come. And we can bring your weapons."

"Why wouldn't she have her weap—"

Molly cut her sister off with a single motion, a cutting swipe of her hand. "Not important." Evangelina went silent. She had appeared at the opening to the kitchen, her presence blocking another exit, a fact Beast did not like at all. Three angry witches had her cornered. Her claws came out and cut into my mind. "Where will you be?" Molly asked.

I sighed. Beast wasn't the only one feeling trapped. Molly had just backed me into a metaphorical corner too. I knew what could happen when a spell went wrong, when magic went haywire and escaped the confines of the working that contained it. It wasn't pretty. And it had been known to interfere with my own magics in unpredictable ways. Grudgingly, I said, "I'll be at New Orleans City Park in an area called Couturié Forest. It's several hundred acres, and I'll be off the beaten paths. You won't be able to find me in time."

Without taking her eyes from me, Molly said, "Evangelina?"

Her sister, dressed for sleep in a long sleep shirt, stepped around me in the dark and handed Molly something. Molly rubbed the surface with a thumb, and brought it to me. It turned out to be a river stone painted with a black symbol. It was wrapped with silver wire and hung on a silver chain large enough to wear in either of my forms. "Put this around your neck. It works like a tracking device for maybe a half hour. Hold the rune for ten seconds between your thumb and forefinger to activate it, and we'll have a good idea where you are. We can find you." She pointed at the rune, which looked like a capital *F* with the horizontal arms broken down at an angle. "Ansuz, a rune meaning a revealing message or insight, communication."

I sighed, long and frustrated, but slipped the silver chain around my neck. "Okay. Fine. Wait for me near the soccer fields at the park. But if you get hurt or shot I'll make you regret it."

Derek Lee and his men met me at the entrance to the projects, their dark van under a rare functioning streetlight. The side door slid open when I wheeled up. The smell of exhaust mingled with the hot grease of fast food and weed from inside. The men were all decked out in the latest military and paramilitary toys. My own personal army. Even with my worry, I couldn't resist the grin when I pulled up and cut the engine. "Dude. You guys look seriously whacked."

"Dude? Whacked?" Derek laughed at me from the driver's seat, his teeth white in the moonlight. "Girl, that is so white-chick."

I chuckled, the laughter easing my tension. "Not me. I'm part of an enslaved, seriously abused, cheated, lied-to, and ripped-off minority. Two, if you count that I'm female."

"Pardon me if we don't bleed for you, babe."

I knew sarcasm when I heard it and my smile widened. I had too many people depending on me tonight. And I still wasn't sure what the heck I was doing. The snarky retorts reminded me that these guys, at least, could take care of themselves.

"What we got?" one of the men in the back asked.

"Did you get a look at the paintings you dropped by from the raid?"

"We saw."

"We're going to rescue two witch children, a witch adult named Bliss, and maybe a human or two, being sacrificed by witch vamps under the full moon. Blood magic, black magic, and secret weapons," I said, thinking of the sliver of wood in its velvet bag.

The men laughed, something appreciative and eager in the sound. "That's cool. Long as there ain't any cops around to spoil the fun."

"No cops. They're busy elsewhere." I got a thumbs-up for that and Derek tossed me a small metallic device. I caught it one-handed.

"GPS. So we can find you. Or drop it any place we need to get to and we'll be there."

"Handy." I tucked it into my jacket. My pals and their find-Jane devices. "We'll be in the New Orleans City Park. I want you guys to wait on the soccer fields for my call. And, uh, a group of witches will be joining you." At the look on the men's faces, I added, "They'll be there to provide shielding against magical attack."

"Witches are nothing but trouble."

I found his face in the cavern of the van, Hicklin, the good-looking guy they had used to flirt with the shop girl. "It's the parents of the kidnapped kits. Children," I corrected. "You want to be the one to tell them no?"

He sighed. "No. But they won't think like soldiers. Won't think like shooters."

"So tell them what you want in terms of protection. And if they disagree, invite them to stay home."

Hicklin shook his head in disgust and slid the door shut. I wasn't making a lot of fans today. I kick-started Bitsa and wheeled her into the murky streets. Exhaustion settled around my shoulders like a heavy blanket, heated and scratchy.

The moon was still high in the sky, a distant white orb that pulled at me, a tide shaping my animal self. I gunned the engine and bent forward over the bars. Dawn was still hours off.

Hurricane Ada was a distant memory, and I knew right away it wasn't going to be a piece of cake getting into the park this time. The thirteen hundred acres were gated and its keepers were patrolling. I left my bike two blocks out on Fillmore and jogged in, slipping past a guard standing in a guardhouse. Finding the shadows. Locating the forest by smell and need. Vanishing into the trees. It would have been poetic, but for the weapons and the raw meat in the Ziploc . . . and the hard stone of fear I was carrying under my breastbone.

There weren't any boulders in the park, not like my home in the mountains of the Appalachians, and I knew it was going to be hard to shift here. But I'd not find the blood site any other way. Not in time. If it wasn't already too late.

Beast stretched under my skin, eager, her pelt pressing against me. *The woods are lovely, dark, and deep. But I have promises to keep, and miles to go before I sleep*, I thought at her. Robert Frost. One of few things I remember from high school. And one of even fewer things that Beast and I agreed on totally. With the quote, I began to relax, slipped beneath a branch and off the path, deep into the woods, using Beast's senses to orient myself in the forest. It didn't take long.

Beast stopped me just short of the place where I'd beheaded the young rogue I'd watched rise from Ada-soaked ground. The wind was warm, wet, fitful, a breezy frustrated child, prevented an outlet for her anger. I smelled only growing things and fertilizer, exhaust from the surrounding streets, the sour tang of bayous that trailed around and through the park.

The tree I'd stood on to wait for the young rogue had been left in place, a convenient seat, though its branches had been cut away, leaving only piles of sawdust and the mixed smells of many humans in their tangled stead. I liked the spot and I set the steaks on the bent arch of tree, removed my weapons. And my new butt-stomper boots. Folded my clothes over the trunk.

Standing barefooted on the loamy ground, I breathed deeply, centering myself. Taking in the park and the dense, ancient trees. The scents came alive, small animal smells, individual tree scents, the tang of something blooming and oily. The sounds became a racket now that I listened: shush, slither, slide, tap, and patter of animal movements. The nearly soundless flutter of owl wings. The sounds of man faded into the background, the gift of the forest's peace sliding under my skin.

I needed to shift. Needed senses that I didn't have in human form. I needed Beast's night vision, her acute hearing, her keen sense of smell, because, like the sites around Sabina's chapel, there would be more than one grave site in this forest, and I had found only one. It meant leaving behind weapons I could wield only in human form, like guns and knives, but the trade-off would be worth it.

Holding the fetish necklace, I sat on the tree and closed my eyes, letting the forest soothe me. It wasn't my forest, but it was still earth, living things with roots pushing deep, soil rich and fecund with years and seasons and the power of the moon, animals to inhabit it. I was so tired and woozy from lack of sleep, I felt as if the ground were tilted beneath me. But Beast had slept more than I, and I'd be refreshed as soon as I shifted.

Beast rose into my eyes, pressed against my flesh. It was the full moon and she was ready to hunt. To kill. To be Big Cat.

When I was centered, my beast close to the surface, our minds mingling and twining like our souls, reveling in the coolness, I checked the zippered leather bag and made sure my stakes, derringer, cell, and lightweight clothes were there. This time, instead of hanging it on my neck, I tucked it into the larger zippered bag, and added my vamp-killers, several more stakes, and a vial of holy water to it. Pushed the GPS device and the velvet bag containing the sliver of the Blood Cross into pouches. When I closed the satchel,

I was doubly careful to make certain that it would stay closed, keeping my treasures safe.

I had never hunted with such a large bag on my Beast back, and wasn't sure how this was going to work. But I hadn't ever fought three sane witch/vamps either, and I needed all the help I could get if I found them and was forced to act alone. I adjusted the bag, the gold nugget necklace, and the new silver chain with the rune around my neck. This could get awkward. I had a mental image of Beast tripping over the bag strap and going for a tumble.

Beast snarled, miffed that I'd think she would be so clumsy.

My bare bottom on the rough bark, my feet shoved into the damp soil, I gripped the gold nugget, holding it firmly, thinking of the rocks in the garden of the freebie house. Thinking of Beast.

I held the necklace and closed my eyes. Relaxed. Listened to the wind, the pull of the full moon, high above me. I listened to the beat of my own heart. Beast rose in me, silent, predatory. Crouched, claws out, eyes staring at the world.

I slowed the functions of my body, slowed my heart rate, let my blood pressure drop, my muscles relax, as if I were going to sleep. I lay forward on the tree, breasts and belly scraping on the rough bark in the humid air.

Mind slowing, I sank deep inside, my consciousness falling away, all but the purpose of this hunt. That purpose I set into the lining of my skin, into the deepest parts of my brain, so I wouldn't lose it when I *shifted*, when I *changed*.

Kits. Find the kits. Keep them alive.

I dropped lower, deeper, into the darkness inside where ancient, nebulous memories swirled in a gray world of shadow, blood, uncertainty. I heard the memory of a distant drum, smelled herbed wood smoke, and the night wind on my skin seemed to cool and freshen and whirl about me. As I dropped deeper, memories began to firm, memories that, at all other times, were half forgotten, both mine and Beast's.

As I had been taught so long ago by my father, by Edoda,

I sought the inner snake lying inside the bones and teeth of the necklace, the coiled, curled snake, deep in the cells, in the remains of the marrow.

Vaguely, I thought it felt easier since I went to sweat, and went to water. Much easier to find the snake, even at a distance from my mountains and my natural hunting ground. The snake opened before me, thousands, millions, all alike, caught in the cells of the fetish necklace.

I took up the snake that rests in the depths of all beasts and I dropped within it, like water flowing in a stream. Like snow rolling down a mountainside. Grayness enveloped me, sparkling and cold; the world fell away. And I was in the gray place of the change.

My breathing deepened. Heart rate sped up. My bones . . . slid. Skin rippled. Fur, tawny and gray, brown and tipped with black, sprouted. Pain, like a knife, slid between muscle and bone. My nostrils widened, drawing deep.

Jane was gone. I hunched on downed tree of former hunt. Found balance. Night came alive—wonderful, new scents, heavy on air, thick and turning, like Jane dancing to drums and music. Soil, birds, prey smells, trees—many more-than-five trees—but forest was still small; not like my hunting ground in mountains. Only tiny patch of hunting ground here. Too close, I smelled humans. Rabbit. Opossum. Mold. *Blood*. I panted. Listened to sounds—cars not too distant, music closer, voices talking, muffled.

Gathered limbs beneath, *lithe* and *lissome*—always remembered her words for me. Good words. I liked.

No ugly man-made light here, no shadow-stung vision. Clear night and moon, bright. More stars above than at her den. Good place to become Beast. I stretched. Front legs and chest. Pulling back legs, spine, belly. Delicately, with killing teeth, lifted necklace she dropped. Fetish. Bones of a big cat. Set fetish on her clothes.

Hopped from tree. Landed, four-footed, stable. Studied forest in night. No predators. No thieves-of-meat. Sniffed food. Hack of disgust. *Always old meat. Dead prey. Long-cooled blood*. Tip of tail twitched, wanting chase. To taste hot blood. But stomach rumbled. Always so, after change. *Hunger*. She left this, an offering to appease Big Cat.

I ate. Long canines tearing into dead meat. Filled stomach. Cold food did not satisfy need to hunt, but more important things now than deer or rabbit, more important than blood and killing joy. Hunt kits. Save kits. Kill vampires. I ate for strength. For speed. For killing. Afterward, licked blood from whiskers and face. New pack and gold and silver chains in way, but . . . needed things. Her things.

Hunt, she called. *Hunt for kits.*

Delicate nostril membranes fluttering, expanding, relaxing. Many new smells, some with value, some without. Most important . . . smell of witches and vampire on the wind. Raised nose to dancing wind. Opened mouth. Long *screee* of sound, pulling scents in. Sought place of vampire smell.

Long moments later found trail of wind, of scent. Padded through trees, into small forest. Soil was damp and rich with living things. Birds called in small forest. Padded, silent, following scent of magics and vampire. Jane had come this way before. I found path that wasn't, winding between trees.

Smells grew stronger, humans and vampire and magic. Good smells for hunt. Good prey. Light in trees ahead. Felt thumps in earth, vibration, sound. Like heartbeats, but not. Hunched low, I cat-pawed closer, back paw into place of front paw. Saw through trees. Same place young rogue rose.

Jane looked out through Beast eyes. *They came back to the same place? I don't understand. I thought they would be nearby, but not here exactly. It shouldn't be this easy.*

Humans foolish. Prey decisions, I thought, haughty. *Stupid humans with man-light in trees. Stealing night vision. Stupid prey.*

I crouched and wc/I looked between trees into open circle. The blood-servants of Adrianna who attacked Jane at the vampire party dug into earth with narrow shovels. Jane's surprise urged: stand up tall, like cat on two legs. I stayed hunched. Smart hunter, good predator.

The women were short with frizzy brown hair, wiry, fat-starved bodies. Not good eating. Stringy. One was dark skinned, and the other was pale, smelled of onion. They dressed in black and sleeveless shirts that freed their limbs to fight. They smelled of chemicals to ward off buzzing mosquitoes, and they sweated in the night. Making the witch symbols. *Sina and Brigit*, Jane thought, *remaking the circle and pentagram.* Sacks of shells sat to the side, piled on a wheelbarrow. Crosses were nailed to the trees. Silver crosses like before. The blood-servants were nearly done making the circle and pentagram.

"If this works," Sina huffed, "I'll help Adrianna kill that bloodsucker. Dark right of kings be damned. He'll never force himself on me again. Never."

"You keep saying that. And I keep agreeing."

Leo forced a feeding, Jane thought, *at the vamp party, during the feeding frenzy.*

I sniffed, smelled Leo. *Yes.*

"Bastard blood-sucking vamp."

"Shut up and dig."

Then they talked no more. Head low, shoulders high, I turned and circled around site, searching for path in. Like rabbits, humans always take same path. Easy to track, nose to earth, huffing in scents. Found path, wide enough for buffalo. Moved fast along it, following it back, back, back through trees, to street in park, over bridge for cars, past sitting places where many humans can gather in herds like prey to watch games. Followed scent to gate and out onto street. Slinking through shadows. To car parked close. Smelling of beer and blood and sex and anger. Looked back.

They'll come through here?

Ignored Jane stupid question. Looked at street sign. Memorized it for her. Harrison Avenue. Car swept by. I crouched in night, still, noiseless. When it was past, moved on silent feet to shadow of gate.

Saw another car move along the road. Long black car, black windows. It slowed. Wind of passage raced ahead of it. Stank of vampire. Smell of kits and fear. Anger raced through my blood, fast and hot. *Kits! Found kits!*

Car pulled up behind blood-servant car. Vampire opened door. Vampire got out. *Tristan and Renee and their brother*, Jane thought. Other vampire smells. Some I knew. Two, three more. More-than-five vampire. More-than-five to kill. *Kill them now?*

No, Jane said. *Too many even for Big Cat. Shift. Get my gear. Get Derek Lee's help.*

Watched to see how many vampires there were. How

many to kill. More-than-five. Jane counted. Fear sputtered in her heart.

Padded through shadow, back to small forest. Found safe place beneath low plant and watched circle, watched blood-servants who worked.

CHAPTER 23

I had the marines. Ooh rah

Studied prey working with shells. Females. Angry. Not watching forest. Night-blind from man-light in tree. Not good hunters, but they would be fast from vampire blood. They helped to hurt kits. Will kill them to protect kits.

Not yet, Jane thought. *Not in Beast form. We have to wait until the vamps bring the kits, then attack, with help from Derek and his soldiers.*

Hacked softly. Disgust. *Beast strong. Beast kill blood-servants.*

But Jane rose, showed memory of stakes and knives, cutting into vampires. *We can fight together. I/we of Beast.*

Panted approval. Padded back into forest. Back to tree and all Jane's gear. Did not want to change. Did not want to shift and give up alpha. But Jane and Beast together were best killer. Leaped to tree. Hunched. And thought of Jane. Of snake in her bones. Gray place reached out and took me in fist with claws. Cut Beast with sharp claws, with knives. Pain. Pain, pain, pain . . .

I fell from the tree and landed hard on the bare earth, grunting. Gasped a shuddering breath that hurt on my bruised ribs. "Ohhhh," I moaned, keeping my misery quiet when I wanted to cry out. *Crap. That hurt.* Still lying on the ground, I pulled the unneeded bag from my neck and opened it with shaking fingers. Tore into the plastic bag of

Snickers candy bars and bit into the sticky sweetness. I ate four before the shakes stopped. Then I dressed fast, but not in the lightweight clothes I had expected to use. In my fighting gear, moving fast. Molly and Evan and Evangelina would be in the soccer field soon, and I didn't want to be caught naked. I wanted time to direct them away from the magic site. That many vamps working together would be a danger even three witches working together probably couldn't overcome. The vamps would mind-steal them in a heartbeat and then what good would their spells be?

Dressed, I hit Derek's GPS device and I called Molly's cell, reporting in, telling her what I had seen. "You can't get to the site, Molly. That many vamps would know you were there and take you out before you knew what was happening. You can't come."

"How many?" Her voice was strained, tight with the need to do something, anything, to save her babies.

"Renee, Tristan, and their nameless brother; the three of them are weak vamp-witches. Adrianna of St. Martin, Rafael Torrez of Mearkanis are here, and I'm pretty sure they've secretly made him clan master. He smells like a blood-master, full of mixed vamp smells. I think Sabina was wrong about the timing. I think the coup d'état will start from here, tonight, with vamps who plan to reign over humans like they did on Haiti."

"What?"

I hadn't told her about the challenge against Leo. There hadn't been time. "I also saw Bettina of Rousseau, but she smelled weak. I think they've bled her nearly dry. Adora and Donatien, the young-rogue teens who are bound, gagged, and fighting like mad things. Bliss and the kits. Bliss has been bled so much she's nearly dead. I don't think she'll survive tonight." *My fault.* The thought thudded through my veins with my blood. *My fault.* I tucked the cell under my chin and finished adjusting my boots, pulled the shotgun harness over my shoulders, and clipped it in place. Shoved the vamp-killers back into their loops on my leather pants. I stomped my new boots, settling my feet in them.

"We're coming," she grated.

"Molly, you can't get to me in time. You just find their limo on Harrison Avenue and make sure it won't run. And kill any vamp who comes out of the forest." She was crying with frustration. Her strangled sobs made my hands sweat. I wiped them down my leathers, but they didn't absorb sweat from either side. "Molly!"

"Okay." She hiccupped and swallowed hard, fighting for control. "But if you need a shield, just hold the rune again. We're putting something together that can find the amulet and give you protection."

"A 'find me' charm that works as a relay?"

"Yeah. Exactly." She sounded miserable, barely holding it together.

I breathed out, relief making me tremble. "Hang in there. And thank you, Molly." Then, "Make it ten feet in diameter? The shield? No more? And can you let bullets move out but no magics or bullets move in?"

"I don't—"

"Will do," Evan said from a distance. "Ten feet."

"Good. Stay safe and out of the way." I clicked off and hit the speed dial for Derek.

He answered with the words "We're two klicks out."

"Meet me. And, Lee? We got five sane vamps in charge, two insane ones in shackles that need to stay that way, one bled-out and starving clan master who'll drain us dry if she gets half the chance, and three hostage witches."

"Girl, you do know how to throw a party." He disconnected.

I didn't know how long it would take seven former marines to find me, but I figured it wouldn't be long. It wasn't. Watching the moon, I waited. Beast alerted me that they were close, moving in two small, parallel groups. I turned toward the south and waited. When they didn't appear when I thought they should, I said softly, "Y'all waiting for engraved invitations?"

Derek laughed just as softly and stepped through the foliage nearly as silently as Beast. I looked the other direction and waited. Hicklin stepped out and pulled off low-light-vision goggles. "Not bad, girl. Not bad." He held out a strip of wire, which turned out to be a headset. Obscurely pleased, I took it, hoping it was the same one I'd used before, because otherwise, well, that was just icky. But fear of losing my current approbation made me not ask. I checked and all the men were wearing the low-light-vision goggles. They'd be able to see as well as my Beast. Maybe better.

I knelt, found a sharp length of wood from the tree trimming, and began drawing in the dirt. One of the men aimed a narrow-beamed flashlight on the drawing. "I'll take point. We'll approach from downwind so they won't smell us coming. When we get there, we'll find a ten-foot-diameter circle with a pentagram in the middle, crosses at head height. Path the vamps will use to enter is here." I tapped the earth. "We stay south, from this location to here, and we'll be downwind of them unless the weather changes. They shouldn't smell us coming.

"The crosses will be glowing so night vision will be compromised for us. Not sure what will happen for the vamps. Under other circumstances they'd be blind and in pain, but this group is seriously different." I heard an affirmative grunt from my left. "If the paintings are correct, the hostages will be in the center of the pentagram, bound and likely unconscious."

"I guess that means we should leave behind the RPG launcher," one of them said from the dark. They laughed but I wasn't sure he was joking.

Pretty Boy Hicklin settled a fully automatic machine pistol on a strap over his shoulders. "The witch patrol?"

"Will not be joining us. But I do have a single, one-use protection spell. Ten feet in diameter."

"Impermeable?"

I wasn't sure what he was asking but I took a chance. "Bullets out, none in. Magic . . . I'm not too sure about tossing out magic, but none will make it in." I forced down the vision and remembered the scent of Molly's singed and torn ward. Bad luck to think of failure in the face of battle. "You ready?"

"Girl, we are *always* ready." The small group laughed, sexual innuendo in the tone.

Great. A bunch of macho soldiers. But then, for what I needed, nothing could be better.

"What kinda spell are they working? What are we going up against?" another guy asked. His eyebrows were shaved, with short strips of dark skin showing through. He had other bald symbols shaved into his scalp. "This a hostile spell?"

"Something to bring sanity to young rogues or the long-chained. Probably not hostile. But it might be hidden behind a ward, hard to break. We'll need to intervene before they complete the circle, but I'd like to see how they start."

"Guards?" When I shook my head, Derek said, "We find any guards, take them out without blood. The vamps'll smell it otherwise." To me he said, "We'll go in on your mark. Location?"

I knew he was referring to the GPS numbers. I sighed. "You'll just have to follow me. One column, when you see the glowing crosses, spread out to my right."

"You didn't use the GPS, did you?"

Beast didn't have fingers to carry it or the mind to understand a bunch of numbers. Not that I could say that. And I wasn't about to offer excuses. "No."

Before they could reply, I headed into the forest, drawing on Beast's senses and silence. The forest folded itself around me. The soldiers followed, quiet even to Beast's senses. I controlled an amused hack and let the forest take me.

It felt like a much faster trip back to the witch circle, perhaps because I was surrounded by more firepower than I'd ever seen. Even without the rocket-propelled grenade launcher. Or maybe because I was sure of my bearings now. Whatever. It worked. For once, I felt safe going into battle against vamps. I had the marines. Ooh rah.

The crosses glowed just ahead, pale and silvery, bright enough to steer by, alerting me that the vamps had already arrived. Derek stopped us with an upraised hand and a whisper into his mike. I smelled humans, some close to us. Moving like a wraith, Derek approached me and whispered, "Gangbangers. Crips. I count three. You?"

"I smell four." Which should have come out another way, to protect myself, but then Derek already knew I wasn't human. The Crips's presence was proof that the coup d'état would start soon, and that Leo's enemies had been using the gangs to steer NOPD attention to other matters and away from vamps. The vamp war was ready to begin.

He breathed out a laugh and sent his men out in a circle.

I heard a few faint scuffs, one breath sighing into the night, but no screams, and no scent of blood. I guessed that the Crips were goners.

I double-checked my crosses to make sure they were still covered. I felt more than saw the soldiers flow out to my right. Silent. Deadly.

They surrounded the southern side of the witch circle, downwind of the vamps, positioning themselves so they wouldn't catch cross fire. And they waited.

The blood-servants packed up the shovels, empty shell-sacks, and wheelbarrow, and trundled nosily out of the artificial glen as the vamp witches milled around, talking in low voices. In the wake of their passage, I moved closer to the witch circle, knowing their noise covered any I might make. I sensed Derek's men moving in as well, but I heard little; they were pretty good for humans. Head tilted, I followed the sounds of Sina and Brigit for long minutes. The sound of doors slamming. Then nothing from the distant humans. In the circle, the vamps took their positions at the five points of the pentagram.

I moved in until I could see Angelina, Little Evan, and Bliss, visible below the tree foliage. They were lying on the ground, tied and gagged in the middle of the circle. Bliss looked more than half dead, pasty pale, unconscious, sprawled, arms behind her back. She was naked; fang marks showed at neck, inner elbows, and groin. Angie and Evan Jr. were barefoot, in unfamiliar pajamas, and they were tied, their eyes closed. I could see the energies of a spell over them, Evan's pink-tinged, Angie's a dull gray. The surprise in the circle was Bettina, also naked, white as a ghost and half bled out, tied, her wrists behind her back. She was shackled to Bliss.

I remembered the smell of her in the Damours' bed. I wasn't sure why Bettina was there, but then these vamps were being chased and harassed. Maybe they needed more vamp blood for the ceremony. Maybe they had changed it yet again, added another factor. But it was clear that Bettina wasn't intended to last the night.

There wasn't a lot of room in the circle for all the bodies. I was glad the children were unconscious. They shouldn't have to see this kind of thing. No one should.

Kneeling to see through an opening in the leaves, I got a good view of the witch circle. The crosses were bright, shining on the trees, but the vamps seemed impervious to them. Not in any pain at all despite the close proximity. They all wore dark mirrored sunglasses, and I smelled sunscreen on their skin in addition to a protection spell. They had devised a spell to keep them safe from the crosses. If sunlight and crosses didn't stop them anymore, how long before they came up with a way to magically fend off other vamp weapons: wood to the heart, silver shot? My job was gonna get a lot harder if we didn't get these guys stopped.

The vamps weren't all witches and *none* of them appeared particularly powerful, but they all smelled like wit—

I dropped my hand to my favorite knife, gripping the hilt hard. I suddenly understood the presence of Bliss. All the vamps had fed from her, so they carried her witch blood. They might not all be able to work magic, but they could be used in spell-working, just as low-power witches could be used to rout power in a major working.

I couldn't discount the presence of Adrianna and Rafael, however, as powerless. They were mind-joined. They might have more power than I could estimate. So it all came down to the fifth guy, the nameless Damour brother, the vamp in the paintings from the Damours' lair. I'd never seen him in person. He was smooth shaven now, and lithe, a warrior. He had been bearded in five of the paintings. Without the beard, and shaved bald, I never would have recognized him. This one would be dangerous as a rabid cat to fight.

He was dressed all in black, and took his position on the north point of the pentagram. He carried an athame with a steel handle and an obsidian blade that caught the light in faceted glints. I was pretty sure that meant he was taking the point of power.

He unbuttoned his shirt, pulled it from his shoulders. He was wearing the amulet from the paintings, the pinkish stone on the heavy gold chain.

"Gather," he said, "with the moon as power and witness. Gather and join, share power and minds. Gather and become one."

Renee bent over her children and peeled off the tape

that sealed their mouths. Instantly they began to moan and squeal. The vamps and witch/vamps took their places at the points of the pentagram, Tristan with his back to me, his wife to his left, and Adrianne and Rafael to either side of Baldy. I eased two vamp-killers from their sheaths and turned them point back, along my forearms. This would be down and dirty.

Baldy removed the necklace and held the gem in his palm, the gold chain hanging, swinging back and forth. Holding out the athame, he pierced his thumb with the glass blade, hissing with pain. Three drops of his blood fell on the faceted gem and the smell filled the air, acrid and acidic. He passed the necklace to his left, or widdershins, and I was pretty sure major workings always worked sunwise, or clockwise. Was a widdershins working meant for evil?

The gem and athame left his hands and a glamour fell, showing me what was beneath. And I had been so wrong. Baldy was a powerful witch. He glowed with witch energies, so bright that the humans with me might be able to tell what he was. The composition of his circle changed everything. I was facing big magic by three witches against knives and bullets. I needed Molly, Evan, and Evangelina to deal with the magic attack. And I had told them to stay away. I was batting zero tonight. And my failures might kill everyone who was depending on me.

Thirty feet from the witch circle, I stood and adjusted my weapons, my breath coming short through my nose, working to keep my breathing silent. I tucked a hand into a pocket and felt for the velvet bag. I had no idea how to use the sliver of wood. But I had it if I needed it.

Adrianna took the gem and athame from Baldy. She added her own three drops of blood to the gem and passed it to Tristan. I got a good look at the gem and it had changed color, the tint deepening, as if the blood stuck to it. Or somehow was being sucked inside it. It now had a mist of magics around it, a dark light of oily color and black sparks. When Tristan passed the gem to his wife, it was bloodred, glowing like a ruby, the light swirling around it blackly.

With a long downward stroke, Renee sliced the pad of

her thumb and rested the gem in the open wound, bathing it in the pooling blood. Power shot from the gem like a small tornado. The white shells of the pentagram and the circle began to glow, a sickly white light that brightened the trees and leaves.

Baldy removed his mirrored sunglasses and stared down into the center of the circle. His eyes glowed with blackness, his pupils fully vamped out, unaffected by the glowing crosses. His fangs snapped down with a sharp click. He bent forward and unfolded a square of dark cloth I hadn't noted before. From it, he lifted a new athame, this one solid silver, gleaming coldly in the white light. He looked at Little Evan.

I had wanted to see the opening steps to the ceremony, and now I knew. The gem was the key. But the intensity of the ward was growing fast. The circle was setting, and it was going to be powerful. Wc had to stop this now.

Beast lunged into my eyes and brain. Power shot into my blood. Saying softly, into the mike, "Go, go, go, go, go," I rushed forward. Time broke into sharp-edged segments, distinct yet interconnected. Movement from the semicircle of human fighters, each face forming a rictus of screaming purpose. Weapons up. Firing high over the hostages. The concussions thrummed against my eardrums.

I dove through the trees Beast-fast, flowing around trunks. As I moved I found Angelina's eyes open, and on me. *She's awake.*

Baldy raised his eyes in surprise and dawning anger. Two bright splotches of red appeared on his chest. Renee turned, nearly dropping the gem. Handed it safely to Rafael. Rafe glanced at his anamchara. Both of them looked to Baldy, who lifted his arms.

A branch tore my face, just missing my eye, across my cheek. Noted but unfelt.

A white light burst from the circle of white shells, rising like a mist. Red sparks danced in the mist, buzzing. Alive ...

My legs pumped. Beast-fast. Covering the distance in a heartbeat. The weapon fire was hitting the vamps. They were vamped out and bleeding but not dropping, even with silvershot.

Angelina's hands lifted. *They were free*. The little girl moved her fingers.

Hicklin burst from the dark. Screaming. Fell across the circle, through the white light. The red motes zipped, faster than thought, and fell onto him. His scream changed from rage to agony as he toppled. Into the pentagram. Baldy bent in a single smooth motion. And sliced Hicklin's throat. Blood spurted. Gushed over the silver blade. Angelina's eyes were on me. Holding me. Baldy whirled, faster than I could follow.

In an overlapped sequence, he cut downward to Little Evan.

Derek burst through the white light. Mouth open in a scream.

Caught the downward blade on his own.

Sparks flew. A belated clang rang out, metal to metal.

Angie's fingers moved, her eyes on mine. Something black gathered in her hands. Living darkness. Roiling and coiling.

I fell across the white light. Brilliant white flashed into the sky at my passage. The red motes raced to me, stung against my skin, hot, burning. Then darted away. Erupting into the night. The silver crosses on the trees blazed with furious light. More shots erupted, staccato and arrhythmic.

The vamps screamed in agony, shrill and piercing, the sound a death keen, nothing a human throat can make. My ears rang with the pain.

The vamps I passed reached for me. Slow as congealed blood. I whirled. Blocked one. Sliced diagonally upward at the other. Cut into his eyes. Blinding Tristan. The block sent the blow from Rafael to the side without damage. My leg stamped behind his knee. His own speed knocked him sideways. I blinded him too with a quick slashing strike. Beast-fast.

They raised their heads, adding their death keens to the piercing wail. Their blood fell slowly. Onto the pentagram. White light shot into the sky.

Baldy shouted, "No!" his face to the heavens. There were gunshot wounds on his bare chest and his slacks.

Derek whirled, arms out to either side. Took out Adrianna with a punching motion. A stake to the heart. Another marine staked Rafael. He fell, lifeless, as a third marine took off his head.

A heartbeat later, two more marines staked Adrianna. But I saw her face first. Lifeless. The mind-joined, ripped apart by death.

I pivoted on one toe. To Baldy. Somehow he had the bloody gem in his hand. He was leaning in. He touched it to me. Into the cut made by the branch. Into my blood. The gem was icy on my cheek. Colder than the deeps of space. Colder than a night in hell. It ripped all my warmth from me. As if I could see it happen, the warmth that was life moved to the gem in a single heartbeat.

The pain it left seared every nerve. Spasmed every muscle. I grunted. Stumbled. Baldy stood over me. And he shouted a word of power. A spell wrapped into a single syllable of might. A *wyrd*.

As I fell, the marines screamed. Heinous screams, as if tortured. Instantly, they started beating their own flesh. Cutting away at their limbs. Cutting at the dancing red motes of power that spiraled down and burrowed into them. Each man assailed by the motes. More flew up from the ground. Down from the sky. Stinging. Burrowing. Attacking.

I landed. Facing Angie. Frozen. Unable to breathe. The spell had frozen my will and my autonomic nervous system.

She smiled. Her mouth moved, but my ears were buzzing with the concussion of gunfire, vamp screams, and white noise and her words were lost. She reached toward Baldy, her fingers throwing, the blackness in her hands set free. I could see it move out, through the air. A shaped, pointed spear of power. Before it hit him, Baldy repeated the wyrd.

My heart . . . stopped. The world began to dim at the edges of my vision. I couldn't move. Beast couldn't move. The might of our twined souls was stilled. My hands opened. Dropped my knives. The black light hit Baldy.

Angie reached for me. Touched the river stone rune of power on my neck. I felt the ward rise around us. Around the marines and the blinded and dead vampires. But the red motes still attacked. Not me. Not the children. Not the

vamps. Only the humans. I was thankful I couldn't hear the
screaming, my ears deafened by the carnage.

Kits, Beast cried out, fighting the binding. Fighting the
death that claimed me. *Kits!*

Angelina moved her hands again. This time to touch my
face. The dark power that was hers to call shot into me. Like
black lightning. Like dark life. My body shuddered. An epi-
leptic spasm clenched down on me. Shattered through my
brain. My heart beat, a single, hard, painful compression.
And then another. I sucked in a breath. Dark power flowed
through me. My eyes opened and I saw Angie Baby.

She giggled. "Go, Aunt Jane."

I took in the tableau of death even as I reached for the
velvet bag and the sliver of the Blood Cross. The vamp children had been freed. Had fallen on the soldiers. Drinking
hard and frenziedly. Only Derek was still upright, a knife
in each hand, one cutting at Tristan, the other slicing at the
throat of Renee, cutting off their heads. But Derek was dying. Bleeding from too many sites to count. The red motes
were embedded in his skin. Eating at his life.

The velvet bag opened. Fell to the ground. I held the
sliver of wood. It was hot in my hand. Burning hot. But I
held on.

Baldy stood outside Angie's ward, legs braced wide at the
north point of the pentagram. His arms out and up at the
heavens, his mouth open as he spoke another wyrd. The silver and obsidian athames were in his hands pointing high.

The bloody gem was around his neck. Resting, canted,
over his heart. I rolled to my feet in a single kip. Screaming
my rage. From the arc of the kip, I lunged through the ward.
Right hand out. Small silver of wood pointed forward. I
saw the thin splinter pierce his skin. Just above the gem.
In the V of the gold chain. It slid between his ribs. Pricking
deep.

"A sliver of the Blood Cross," I whispered. "For your
sins."

His eyes widened. Mouth opened. Horror slithered
across his face and nested in his eyes. His blood gushed out
of the wound. Over the gem. His blood linking the sliver of
the Blood Cross and the gem and my hand over his heart.

Red light blasted out. Over me. Over the clearing. It crashed through me like a tsunami and I staggered. Ripped through the light of the circle ward. Smashed against the power of the pentagram and rolled over Angie's ward, mating with it. The white light swayed, almost an audible sensation as it absorbed the red. Both seemed to grow, as if they were greater than the sum of their own energies. It was a tide. A river. An ocean. It bathed everything in bloody, brilliant light. It rolled over my head. Cleansing. It was like going to water, if water were made of blinding crimson light. It tore through me.

I pulled the sliver of the vamp's greatest weapon from his flesh. An instant later, a bloody flame licked up from the wound. Spread over his torso in a flash. My skin went hot and I smelled my own hair burning. I rolled back fast. Smoke curled up from my hand, and I knew my fingers were burned. But I couldn't feel the pain. Not yet.

The maker of the young rogues flamed. The heat was enormous inside the circle of red power.

I reared back and kicked out. My foot landed in the middle of Baldy's chest. Flame kissed my boot. I kipped to my feet again and rammed Baldy with Beast-strength. The burning witch/vamp fell back, through the red light. Onto the forest floor. I whirled. There were no more vamps standing. They all were down. The heat of the burning vamp was intense, and I covered my eyes against the glare.

The soldiers were all down too, screaming and moaning. Cutting their own flesh. Even Derek, who was grunting with the motion of his knife as it flayed a length of his skin away, the muscles of his arm exposed and bleeding onto the earth. His fingers raked into the exposed muscle, fingernails digging at a mote of red light. He was chewing the tissue of his mouth, his bloody teeth working at a mote buried in his lower lip.

I looked at the sliver of wood. It was the Blood Cross. The true cross? I didn't know. But even if it wasn't part of the true cross, it was a powerful relic. I wiped it clean and pricked Derek. He screamed again, and the red motes burst from his skin and up into the night. Buzzing like bees, they rose in the air. Derek's spine jerked in a whiplash of agony. He eyes cleared. "Son of a—"

I turned and pricked each of the others, even Hicklin, who had died so quickly. The red motes left their skin, formed small clouds, and rose. Joining into a hive of angry red light in the sky above us. It didn't look like a safe place to leave them. I held the wooden sliver up at them. Nothing happened.

Angie sat up from the ground, bracing herself with one arm. "Aunt Jane, try the necklace. The one the mean man was using."

They'd all been pretty mean to my way of thinking, but I stepped to Baldy's smoking remains. In the center of his scorched rib cage, the bones curled up around it like protective hands, was the necklace, untouched by the heat, still bright red with blood. I wasn't about to touch it. I pulled a silver-bladed vamp-killer and reached through the ribs with the point. Lifted it from among Baldy's smoking vertebrae by the gold chain. It was a lot heavier than it looked.

I stood there, surrounded by gasping, bleeding men, all but one still alive, holding a vamp-killer, a powerful amulet draped across its blade. And I started laughing. I couldn't help it. The motes in the angry cloud above me paused. I could have sworn they could hear my laughter and were responding to it. They formed a long, ropy shape, and spiraled down. Right toward the bloody gem hanging on the knife blade. They coalesced into a cloud around the now-scarlet gem. And melted inside it.

Their passage made the gem swing and pulse as if it were alive. And for all I knew, it was.

In my other hand, the sliver of wood glowed with a white light.

And in Angelina's hands danced a black light of might.

CHAPTER 24

Hot to trot?

We tramped out of the forest, a short line of blood-soaked humans and I. Angelina riding my back like a horsey ride, her heels kicking my hipbones. Little Evan, still asleep, was nestled in Derek's arms. Bliss was limp in a fireman's carry held by one of the soldiers whose name I hadn't learned yet. Hicklin was carried by the rest of his mates.

Faces unmoved, the soldiers had dispatched the ravening teenaged vamps and beheaded the rest. I hadn't let Angelina watch, which had made her pout. The vamp heads were in a pile in the center of the pentagram, gathered for the bounty they would bring Derek and his crew, all but Baldy's, Bettina's, and Adrianna's. Baldy was mine, confirmation of my completed contract, and my proof for payment. Bettina was still bound, too hungry to be released without a proper blood supply, preferably several of her own servants. Adrianna still had her head, though stakes pierced in her heart where she lay, faceup to the moon. I hoped that Leo might be able get something from her about the plot. Who knew what resided in a dead brain, that could be retrieved by a master of the city?

The bloody gem and the sliver of the Blood Cross were secreted in my pockets, though it gave me the willies to have the gem anywhere near me. It was still bloody scarlet and glowed, warm to the touch.

"It's Mama!" Angie screamed in my ear, her whole body quivering.

I flinched slightly, my eardrums still sensitive from the death keens of the vamps and the gunfire. "Yeah. And your daddy and Aunt Evangelina."

Molly and Evan ran to me, Molly taking Angelina, Big Evan cradling his son. They fell together on the grass, in the dark, and I could see their magics blending into a protective and healing ward. Evangelina took over, directing the soldiers where to drop their burdens. She had them place Bliss in the back of a rental car and gave each of the human men a healing amulet. But her attention was for the witch, her face hard and set, and the power she pumped into the drained girl was visible in the night air.

I stood there, my arms empty, having no idea what to do or how to do it, the relics burning holes in my pockets and my mind.

From up the road, a heavy black Hummer moved toward us, followed by two unmarked cars. Leo was here and he'd brought Jodi and her crew. Maybe Leo had been summoned by Derek. Maybe by the amount of power we'd unleashed. Maybe by the death of so many vamps at one time. Either way, my shoulders tightened. As usual, I wasn't up to a battle with Leo. Wasn't sure I ever would be.

As the armored vehicle and its tails slowed to a stop, the soldiers fanned out, hands empty, waiting. Moving with that snakelike vamp grace, Leo stepped from the passenger side of the high truck and to the ground. He was in a business suit, and the wind caught the jacket, blowing it open, revealing the silk lining, shining in the full moon. His eyes were human, and more sane than I'd seen recently. The breeze caught his black hair and tumbled it back from his face.

Bruiser emerged from the driver's side, finding me instantly in the night. His eyes were dark, intent, as they looked me up and down and came to rest on my face, on my right cheek, where the gem had touched me. I was pretty sure I would have a scar even after I shifted again. It was hurting with a cold pain, like frostbite but with a blood-pounding thump. Bruiser wore slacks and a dress shirt, sleeves rolled up to reveal his forearms, a gun under one arm, and as the wind blew at his clothes, I spotted another holstered at his ankle. Two vamp-killers were sheathed on his thighs. He'd come to do battle. A little late.

Leo stopped at Derek and his men and they gathered in a small circle, voices low. I didn't bother to try to listen in. Bruiser came to me, stopping just inside my personal space, a bit too close so soon after a battle. His eyes still held mine. The silence between us had weight and texture, as if words were being said that I couldn't hear. His fingers came up and touched my right cheek, gently brushing, tracing down to my jaw, circling a wound that was a lot bigger than I'd expected.

To his side, I saw Jodi, Rick, and Sloan emerge from the unmarked van. I didn't watch to see where they went, my attention on Bruiser. He smelled of dry herbs, cracked pepper, and papyrus, of Leo and vamp blood. Faintly, of aftershave, spicy and spiky. His fingers were warm on my cold skin. I had no idea what to say. Bruiser said it for me. "I wanted to be here."

I understood. Wanted to be here. Couldn't. He was Leo's. I managed a twisted smile, holding in the spurt of disappointment. "You had to do what Leo wanted. Follow orders."

"Yes." His hand cupped my face, his palm warm and dry.

I wanted to lay my injured cheek in his hand and weep. Wanted to rub my pelt over him, scent-marking him. But I wouldn't do either. I closed my eyes on the need that thundered through me, sudden and violent and demanding. It was the full moon. Only the full moon. Nothing else. "You had to follow Leo," I repeated, not able to prevent the loneliness echoing in my words.

"For now, Jane Yellowrock. But not forever."

My heart leaped, and I raised my head. Beast, close to the surface, peered out through my eyes. "You're his bloodservant. That's forever."

"Not always. There are sometimes . . . options. With conditions. If you're interested."

I found a real smile. I had no clue what he was talking about, but Beast was happy to have him near.

"Jane?" Rick's voice. At my shoulder. Close.

I stepped back and found the cop in the dark. He was armed and wearing a dark blue Windbreaker, the word PO-LICE in bold white letters. I had to make an official report to both Leo and the cops. Might as well start now.

"I'm okay." I took a steadying breath and blew out. "But we have one human dead, from vamp and witch wounds. Hicklin. I don't know his full name." It was suddenly awful that I didn't know the first name of the man who had died tonight. I swallowed back tears. "We broke up a cere-mony intended to bring sanity to rogue vamps. To the long-chained. But it required the death of two witch children, which I wasn't gonna let happen. It was also, somehow, part of a plot to kill Leo and take over the city."

Bruiser flinched slightly. If I hadn't been watching for it, I'd have missed it. Protective instincts bred into him by sips of vamp blood. And maybe by love. Who knew?

"Bettina, the blood-master of Clan Rousseau, is bound and starving back at the site, next to a staked anamchara, part of a cross-clan plan to challenge and defeat Leo and return to the Naturaleza. Leo might be able to do some-thing with her memories. She still has her head. I'll give you a full report later. For now we have seven vamps dead, all involved with the creation of the young rogues, all sanc-tioned under my contract with the council. Two witch chil-dren and one witch adult saved. If we can keep her alive."

"Where?" Bruiser asked. I pointed at the rental and Bruiser went quickly to Leo, drawing the vamp away, to-ward Evangelina and Bliss.

That left me with Rick. The pretty boy. The Player. The Joe who had been undercover and now was back with the cops. I looked at him. He didn't have the smooth, effort-less movements of George Dumas, nor the charisma. But he smelled human, of cheap aftershave, of Leo's expensive coffee and pastries, of gun oil and ammo and faintly of horses. I smiled. He gave me back a half smile. "You with him? With Dumas?"

"I don't think so. He belongs to Leo. I'm not one to share, especially with a vamp."

"I have horses, four dogs, a barn cat or three, parents who live nearby, and too many sisters to make my life pleas-ant. No wife, no girlfriend, no vamp master."

I felt a warmth start in my belly and move up and out. "You offering yourself?" I hooked my thumbs into my leather pockets and dropped my weight on one hip. "For what?"

"For . . ." He stopped, his mouth quirking up, revealing the crooked tooth on his lower jaw. "For whatever you might want. We could start out with wild monkey sex and see what develops."

The heat shot through me, hard and fast, like gunning a bike motor and hitting the road with a growl of tire on asphalt. "I need a shower. And I have a houseful of houseguests."

Rick let his smile spread. "I have a shower. And a hot tub out back under the stars. Course I live in a single-wide trailer. It may not be up to your standards."

"Don't let the fancy house fool you. It's Katie's. My usual digs consist of an efficiency rental under the eaves of Old Lady Pierson's house. I have a shower but no hot tub, and if I did, Old Lady Pierson would want to join us."

"Hot to trot?"

"Nosy."

"My place it is, then. I can take you to your bike. You can follow me home?"

"Oh yeah."

He didn't touch me. Just turned and led the way, flipping a nonchalant wave to Jodi on the way by. I walked in his wake and sat in the passenger seat of the unmarked. He climbed in the driver side and started the engine. And pulled slowly past the other vehicles lining the road.

Leo sat in the rental, the window down, blood on his lips. I was pretty sure it was Bliss's blood. He took a breath that looked odd, not quite needed, not quite human when his chest moved, but he didn't notice me. He was healing her the way vamps healed, with sips of blood and a slow laving of tongue.

Bruiser stood on the sidewalk, staring at the car, catching my gaze. Holding it. No question in his eyes, no accusation. Just an uncomfortable patience and a quiet strength. But I'd made my choice. I didn't want a blood-servant, no matter how powerful and sensual and . . . No. Not a blood-servant. I wanted a human. I wanted this human. And mostly, I didn't want to share. I was pretty sure he read all that in my eyes. His gaze followed us as we moved out of sight, his mouth lifting at the corner, his expression plain in the side mirror.

By the time the night was over, I was tired and happy and satisfied, taking up more than my share of Rick's bed in exhausted contentment. I wasn't going home just yet. I figured it was best to give the Trueblood family time to reconnect alone anyway. According to Bruiser, who called on my cell just after sunrise to fill me in, Leo's reaction to what he learned at the battle site didn't result in a vamp bloodbath, but it was close. And the council—the ones still healthy after Leo finished punishing his rivals—was in pretty big disarray, not that I cared. The Blood Master of the City was intent on forcing certain new policies down their throats and they were going to have to give in, including bringing the witch/vamp cold war out of the past and to the bargaining table. They didn't have a choice. Killing children—even witch children—was worthy of death sentence in the Vampira Carta. And Leo was fulfilling the law with a new purge. This time there would be no forgiveness.

I listened to Bruiser's spiel while hanging head and shoulders off the bed, my legs twined with Rick's, his fingers tracing lazy circles on the back of my thigh.

"You're likely in danger for a while. The remaining renegades that Leo's chasing down have sworn blood vengeance on you." He sounded worried. "I want you to take care."

I laughed sourly. "I did the job the council hired me for, stopped a vamp war in the process, *and* brought the witches into the vamp's archaic treaty process. All in one night. Far as I can see, it's all good. You tell them I expect payment ASAP. In full." Taking a page from the locals, I disconnected.

"That your other boyfriend?" Rick asked.

Shock zinged through me and I rolled back on the bed, on top of him, slinging my hair out of the way. "*Other* boyfriend?"

"If you want to call me that."

"I'll think about it. But if had a boyfriend, there'd be only the one."

"Hmmm," Rick murmured. The vibration of his deliberation rumbled like a big purr. "Wonder if he knows that?"

EPILOGUE

When I left New Orleans for a stint in the mountains, a chance to clear my head and let Beast run and hunt, the vamp world was vastly different.

In a matter of days, the vamp hierarchy had been realigned, with some vamp clan leaderships decimated and their members absorbed by others in a purge that had to set records. The vamp-war-that-might-have-been never made the papers, but I talked with Bruiser and Troll often enough to keep up with the gossip. And I stayed out of Leo's hair. He was a bit too bloodthirsty for me to call on him right now.

When the depths of the rebellion had come to light, Leo killed some of his own scions who had signed on to the wrong side, and then he took over the vamp council, appointing his loyal scions as new clan masters in rival clans. I'd heard that he had forced the blood sharing that cemented their—and his—positions. By all accounts, the bloodbath I'd been expecting had happened in the end but it hadn't quite been war and was over now.

I spent the days between the last battle and my trip north getting to know my new boyfriend, sitting in his hot tub, and riding his horses. Eating a lot of steak. Meeting his family, for pity's sake. And having a lot of . . . well . . . Beast was happy. When I wasn't with Rick, I was getting ready to say good-bye to Molly and Angelina. It was a bittersweet parting, because I knew it would be a while before my life would be back to normal, back living in the mountains. And because a rift had opened between Big Evan and me. He wasn't a forgiving man, and the fact that my lifestyle had placed his children in life-threatening danger was a hard one to pardon. I was having a pretty hard time forgiving it myself, so I wasn't holding it against him.

I hadn't had to report in person to the vamp council, which was a relief, but I did have to write a full report for the ones left alive after the city's blood-master took his vengeance on the rebels. An amended report went to the police, as informational as my contract with the vamp council allowed, which meant a lot was left out. However, since I was sleeping with a cop, NOPD got a lot of info from an "unnamed source" and no one complained.

The cure for vamp insanity had indeed been worth going to war over. If the Rousseaus had succeeded—and it looked as though they had been close—my world would never have been the same. Baldy, Tristan, Renee, Rafael, and Adrianna had been five fingers of a huge fist. Together, they would have pounded Leo. One of them would have taken over as master of the city. Every vamp in the world would have done homage to Leo's successor. The other four would have had their choice of cities anywhere in the world. So, Rafael had wooed Adrianna away from her master and mind-joined with her, kidnapped Bettina, and made ready to challenge Leo.

I shipped the fifteen paintings detailing the vamp/witch dark magic back to Asheville to Evangelina. I figured she'd burn them, which made a lot of sense to me, but then, Evangelina was big on history and stuff like that, so maybe she would just put them someplace safe.

Settling with Derek was easy—I just deposited his checks. We didn't have a lovey-dovey relationship.

My own payment and a hefty bonus supplied by the new vamp council went a long way to giving me peace of mind. I made a donation to Hicklin's family by dropping a wad of cash in a donation box near the closed casket. I learned his name at the funeral. Corporal Leon Alphonse Hicklin had been home on leave between stints in Afghanistan and was killed trying to stop a robbery, according to the police reports. He was buried with full honors.

The witch children's missing persons reports stored in the woo-woo room at NOPD were finally getting a conclusion. Jodi and Evangelina told the witch covens what had happened to so many of their young over the years. I wasn't in on the meeting and didn't want to be. It was outside my contract and *way* outside my comfort zone. Jodi and she were going to try to heal some wounds between NOPD and the witch covens. It was a long time coming.

One afternoon, after a crazy long day of settling accounts and attending a funeral, I received a letter from Leo, hand-delivered by Bruiser. This one was also sealed with wax and Leo's blood.

Bruiser stood on my front porch, his heart in his eyes, and waited as I opened the seal. Avoiding his gaze, I read part of it aloud to Molly, who blocked the doorway behind me. "Leo officially 'rescinds the death threat against the Rogue Hunter, Jane Yellowrock. She is hereby offered permanent employment with the Council of Mithrans of New Orleans.' " I squinted at Bruiser, outlined against the sunlight. "Sorta like a retainer?"

"Yes." He smiled. "Much like a retainer, for services yet to be rendered."

"Huh. How 'bout that?" I turned and pushed past Molly, shutting the door in Bruiser's face. I could hear him chuckling through the door.

I hadn't decided what to do about the job offer yet, but it was good money. Real good money.

A bit over a week after the Battle, on a Friday, Rick and I left New Orleans for a long weekend, our gear strapped to our bikes and no particular destination in mind, except mountain roads and one certain trip along the Tail of the Dragon, the winding, twisty road that draws bikers to its curves as girly mags draw men to their pages. It's a lusty ride and Rick had never taken it.

I wanted him to see my home, in the hopes that . . . Well, some hopes had to be kept undercover for now, but I hoped someday he might meet Beast. And want to stay around for both of us.

ABOUT THE AUTHOR

Faith Hunter was born in Louisiana and raised all over the South. She fell in love with reading in fifth grade, and best loved science fiction, fantasy, and gothic mystery. She decided to become a writer in high school, when a teacher told her she had talent. Now she writes full-time, works in a laboratory full-time (for the benefits), tries to keep house, and is a workaholic with a passion for travel, jewelry making, kayaking, writing, and writers. She and her husband love to RV, and travel to whitewater rivers all over the Southeast. For more, including a list of her books, see www.faithhunter.net.